WESTWARD
the
DREAM

WESTWARD the DREAM

RIBBONS WEST

BOOK ONE

JUDITH PELLA
TRACIE PETERSON

BETHANY HOUSE PUBLISHERS

Minneapolis, Minnesota

Westward the Dream
Copyright © 1998
Judith Pella and Tracie Peterson

Cover design by John Hamilton Design
Cover photography: Getty Images/Germany
Costumier: Theresa Blake/Rossetti, UK

Scripture quotations are taken from the King James Version of the Bible.

Published by Bethany House Publishers
11400 Hampshire Avenue South
Bloomington, Minnesota 55438

Bethany House Publishers is a division of
Baker Publishing Group, Grand Rapids, Michigan.

Printed in the United States of America

ISBN 978-0-7642-2071-5

The Library of Congress has cataloged the original edition as follows:

Pella, Judith.
    Westward the dream / by Judith Pella, Tracie Peterson.
        p.   cm. — (Ribbons west ; 1)
    ISBN 0–7642–2071–3
    I. Peterson, Tracie. II. Title. III. Series: Pella, Judith. Ribbons west ; 1.
PS3566.E415 W385   1999
813'.54—dc21

                                            99–6614
                                              CIP

To
Bud and Casey

With love
for sharing your son
and for all of the other
wonderful things you do.

—Tracie

JUDITH PELLA has been writing for the inspirational market for more than twenty years and is the author of more than thirty novels, most in the historical fiction genre. Her recent novel *Mark of the Cross* and her extraordinary four-book DAUGHTERS OF FORTUNE series showcase her skills as a historian as well as a storyteller. Her degrees in teaching and nursing lend depth to her tales, which spin a variety of settings. Pella and her husband make their home in Oregon.

Visit Judith's Web site: *www.judithpella.com.*

TRACIE PETERSON is the author of over eighty novels, both historical and contemporary. Her avid research resonates in her stories, as seen in her bestselling HEIRS OF MONTANA and ALASKAN QUEST series. Trace and her family make their home in Montana.

Visit Tracie's Web site: *www.traciepeterson.com.*

Visit Tracie's blog: *www.writespassage.blogspot.com.*

CONTENTS

PART · ONE

APRIL-JUNE 1862

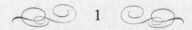

1

With a sheer will and determination to match any man in the rapidly growing audience, Jordana Baldwin studied the four-story brick edifice of New York City's Deighton School for Young Women and planned her strategy.

"You don't have to do this, Jordana," her best friend, Meg Vanderbilt, whispered. "Leave off with this nonsense and let's go back to our room."

Jordana grinned and tied her long brown curls back with a dark navy ribbon. "No! I said I'd do this and I will."

"But—" Meg tried to protest, but Jordana would have none of it.

"I can do this," Jordana insisted.

"My money's on Jordana," one of the young men gathered behind the girls called out. The crowd of observers from the neighboring boys' school was growing rapidly.

"You have no money," another chided, forcing the first to produce proof of his financial stability.

"I received a post from Mother this morning. She's always good to send me fortification."

"Then pay me back the money you owe me from last week and I can place a bet as well," a redheaded boy clamored.

Jordana took a deep breath and tried to ignore the revelry and ruckus. If she didn't hurry, they would all be found out, and then no one would fulfill the dare that Clarence Hooper had so thoughtfully issued only moments ago in the garden.

At sixteen, Jordana had no doubt in her abilities when it came to such physical demands. She just worried about how to get the thing done without causing herself any true embarrassment. Scaling buildings was a rage that had accompanied the technology to erect higher multiple-story structures. However, such a feat was usually left to the fearless males of their generation. Jordana thought this pure poppy-cock. She had lived in the mountains of Virginia for a good portion of her life and could climb rock-faced walls with the best of the men in her family. Of course, back home she had donned her brother's trousers to do such a thing. Here she had no choice but to hike her skirts between her legs in a most unladylike fashion and throw off the constricting jacket that completed the Deighton School uniform.

Carefully considering the best foot and handholds to be had on the brick structure, Jordana hurriedly pulled at the buttons of the navy wool jacket and tossed it to Meg.

"I think she's going to do it," Clarence Hooper announced in awe.

"No, she'll play around until the headmistress comes and puts a stop to this," another boy countered.

Jordana gave him a sharp look of irritation, then kicked off her shoes. "I have no plan to wait around for Mistress Deighton to show her prune face," Jordana declared. "But neither have I any plan to fail at this challenge. I know what I'm doing and I don't see you offering to join me, Struther Harris, so unless you are volunteering to accompany me up the wall, kindly shut your mouth."

The other young men laughed heartily at this and jabbed Struther in the ribs. They had come from the adjoining Deighton School for Young Men, where Mistress Deighton's brother, the most austere Reverend Obadiah Deighton, taught men of exceptional intelligence.

Meg leaned forward, a look of panic in her eyes. "Please, Jordana, don't do this. It isn't safe or becoming."

"Bah!" Jordana replied and reached down to pull the back edge of her skirt through her legs. At this particular school, girls were not allowed to lengthen their skirts to the floor until after their sixteenth birthday. Having just turned sixteen, Jordana found her longer skirts a terrible nuisance. Personally she had cherished the extra two inches she'd grown in the last year because it caused her own skirts to go from the prescribed six inches above the tops of her shoes to eight inches. She liked the freedom of shortened skirts. At least she did not yet have to wear those hideous hoops women had so stupidly adopted as an important mark of fashion, and she was still able to get away with failing to cinch herself into a corset.

However, by pulling her skirts up, she was exposing a clear view of stocking-clad, shapely legs, and it was this, rather than her threat to Struther Harris, that caused the male viewers to go silent.

Jordana ignored their stares and turned back to the wall. Her gloves would also have to go, she decided. There would be no other way to get a good grip on the bricks.

"Hurry, the band has stopped playing in the parkway. That only leaves prayers and hymns before the classes break up for the weekend!" Clarence declared.

"Oh, all right," Jordana replied, tossing her gloves to Meg. "Never have I seen more impatience from a group that has no intention of participating." She reached out and felt the texture of the building and smiled. This would be better than she'd originally figured. The wall was easy to grab hold of; the porous brick and poorly set mortar allowed good handholds for the young girl to stick her fingers around. It wouldn't be as nice as a rock face, where natural formations provided occasional ledges and resting shelves, but it would work.

She whispered a prayer, knowing that God had kept her safe in all other times of her life. She had no reason to believe He would fail her now. It never even entered her mind that He might frown upon her activities and punish her with less than success in order to teach her a lesson. In her mind, God simply didn't work in that manner.

Reaching high above her head, Jordana secured her grip on the brick, then found footholds where her toes seemed to mimic her fingers and grasp the very bricks set before her.

She was off!

The crowd behind her cheered as she made her way cautiously and thoughtfully up the side of the building. Jordana's thoughts were fixed on finding the next handhold, but she was also completely aware of her audience, and that gave her the momentum to press upward. She liked the attention—liked that she was impressing the young men of her social circle and scaring the girls witless. It entertained her far more than anything else she'd managed to accomplish in her years at Deighton.

Stretching her right hand upward, Jordana angled herself to the left. A nice gathering of lilac bushes ran parallel to the building, and Jordana figured if she slipped, they might at least break her fall. Probably not by much, she mused, trying hard not to think about the outcome of such a fall.

She passed the tops of the first-floor windows. Only three more stories to go. The cheers below were evidence of her captive audience, but other than this, Jordana had to force such thoughts from her mind. It was imperative that she focus on what she was doing.

Reaching out for a protruding piece of mortar, Jordana felt the piece crumble in her hands. Her grip now lost, she fought to throw her body weight to the side where her hold was more sure. For a moment, however, she very nearly dangled away from the building, causing everyone below to utter a collective gasp. Jordana felt her fingernails tear away as she tightened her hold on the brick. I can do this, she told herself over and over.

The one thing she had learned as a child was to never look down when climbing. Her brother Brenton, though rather awkward when it came to the outdoors, had used logic and reasoning to get himself out of many a tight spot and had passed such to her.

"Press toward the goal," he had said. *"Even the Bible speaks to the havoc created by looking back."*

With that in mind, Jordana found a new strength to continue. She maneuvered herself upward, seeking each handhold with a dedicated eye, pressing toward the goal of the ornate roof cornice. The cornice gave her some worry as it jutted out from the house and formed the base to the mansard-styled roof. Once she passed this obstacle, the remaining story would be a simple matter of easing up the concave slope to take hold of the roof cresting at the top. Then she would have met the challenge and shown them all that she was made of different stuff than most girls her age.

It seemed to Jordana she was always trying to prove something to someone. She took great pride in having been accepted to the Deighton School for Young Women in New York City. The school had a reputation of taking only the most intelligent young people and held the interest of surrounding colleges and universities as they eyed Deighton pupils as potential students for their hallowed halls. Jordana intended to go to a university once her two years were completed here at Deighton. She had wanted to go directly to college after completing her secondary studies at thirteen, but her father, ever the cautious one in the family, feared that exposure to a university might be a bit much at her tender age.

The top of the second-floor window offered her a brief bit of ledge to pause and catch her breath. Once again, she reminded herself to keep looking upward. Only after passing the third-floor windows and approaching the extended cornice did Jordana wonder quite seriously how she was going to get back down. Always when they'd climbed in the rocky hillsides of her Virginia home, they'd taken a bit of rope with them. It made for quick escapes down the mountainside and remained intact for future climbs. But this was different. Now she knew she had a most important decision to make.

"I'll simply stand for a moment on the top of the roof," she grunted the words as she sought to master the cornice. "Then I'll slip back

JUDITH PELLA / TRACIE PETERSON

inside one of the fourth-floor windows." Of course, it would help if one of the windows were open.

Without looking down, Jordana pulled her body up and around the cornice, where the concave of the roof afforded her a nice place to rest.

"Meg! If you can hear me," she called down as loudly as possible, forcing herself not to seek Meg's face for acknowledgment, "go open the window just above me."

A faraway voice called back in reassurance, and Jordana breathed a sigh of relief. Her journey was nearly over, and an exuberant feeling had begun to course through her body.

Easing herself upright, Jordana used the ledge above the window and the fish-scale shingles to master the fourth floor. And then, before she knew it, she was atop the roof looking down on the world below her.

The crowd had grown considerably, and Jordana's only sinking feeling of the moment came in the knowledge that no doubt her head-mistress was already aware of the stunt. "There will be a reckoning for this foolishness," Jordana could already hear Mistress Deighton say.

Trusting that Meg had had enough time to get the window open, Jordana eased over the cresting rail and started back down the roof. Without warning she lost her footing and slid a good two feet before she caught the side of the window and halted her fall. Breathing heavily and feeling her heart pound in her chest, Jordana maneuvered herself aright and felt for the opening of the window.

Good old Meg, Jordana thought. The window was open, and not only that, but protective hands were reaching to pull her inside.

"Meggie, I did it!" she declared as she practically fell into the room.

"I'll say you did." The voice was not that of Margaret Vanderbilt, however, but rather that of her brother Brenton Baldwin.

"Brenton!" she exclaimed and wrapped her arms around his neck in a loving embrace. "Did you watch me? Did you see? Wasn't it grand!"

Brenton had no chance to reply, for Mistress Deighton's booming voice of condemnation rang clear. "Miss Baldwin, you will conduct yourself in a *proper* manner to my office. Immediately!"

Jordana met the woman's piercing expression. Mistress Deighton's hair, pulled back into a tight, orderly bun, seemed to have taken on a few more strands of gray since morning. Could Jordana's stunt have actually caused the woman a fright? It didn't seem likely, for Jordana was almost certain that nothing scared the woman.

"Yes, ma'am," she muttered and reached her hand out to take hold of Brenton. "May my brother come along?" she dared to ask.

"Absolutely," the woman replied. "What I have to say will be important to him, especially since he's acting as guardian for you while your parents are in Europe."

Jordana flashed a smile to the obviously nervous Brenton. Poor goose, she thought. He really doesn't like things to be out of order.

He came to stand beside her, shaking his head and pushing up his gold-rimmed glasses. He looked so lean and even a bit pale, Jordana thought, immediately worrying that he'd not been eating right or taking care of himself.

With Mistress Deighton already halfway down to the third floor, Jordana paused and asked after Brenton's health. "Are you quite all right? You look to have been sick."

Brenton rolled his eyes. "I came here to take you to supper and instead find you dangling near death on the side of this building, and you wonder that I look sick?"

Jordana dropped her hold and put her hands on her waist. "Well, you do!" she protested.

Brenton sighed. "Why did you ever do something so foolish?"

"They dared me," Jordana replied as if it settled the matter.

"You ninny," he said, then reached out to pull her into a protective embrace. "You could have fallen and broken your neck. And then what would I tell Mother and Father?"

"Miss Baldwin!" Mistress Deighton's voice rang out from the floor below.

17

"Come on," Jordana said with a grin. "We can talk about this later. Old Pruney calls."

———

"Upon the death of our dear mother, my dear brother and I instituted this school for exceptionally intelligent children. With her fortune we were assured of creating a school of quality and educational benefit," Mistress Deighton droned on nearly half an hour later. Her office, a cramped, dimly lit room on the north side, seemed foreboding enough without the woman's haughty stare and evident anger.

"We must not . . . nay, we will not permit such vulgar displays of behavior," she said, bringing her right fist into the palm of her left hand. "Your sister, Mr. Baldwin, has continually managed to show an attitude of disobedience. She challenges the rules—"

"Only when they make no sense," Jordana interjected.

The woman gave her a withering stare. "She institutes disruption and encourages others to join her in her antics."

"I only suggest entertainments to amuse ourselves."

"Silence!" the older woman demanded. She appeared to steady herself for a moment before continuing. "And not only does she challenge the rules, but she puts her life and the lives of those around her in danger."

"That's not true!" Jordana declared, jumping to her feet. "I was the only one in danger out there, and it wasn't that much danger to begin with. I'm quite used to climbing." Brenton reached out to take hold of her arm, but Jordana shrugged him aside. "Accuse me if you will, but do not exaggerate in order to malign me to my brother."

"I demanded your silence. Not only have you nearly earned yourself an expulsion in this matter, but because you refuse to discipline your tongue, you will also be required to take kitchen duties for the next month."

Enraged, Jordana leaned toward the headmistress. "Well, you

can't expel me and have me work in the kitchen at the same time. What's it to be?"

"Jordana!" Brenton exclaimed.

Just then a knock sounded on the door, and while Mistress Deighton went to see who it was, Brenton pulled Jordana back into her seat.

"Please be quiet about this," he told her. "Let the woman have her say and let us be gone for the evening."

"But I didn't put anyone else in danger," Jordana protested. "And it isn't fair—"

Brenton put his finger to her lips. "Shhh. It doesn't matter." He glanced beyond her and pointed. "She's coming back."

The woman came back to her desk, her face ashen. The fire was gone from her eyes, and her tight-lipped expression had taken on a look of stunned confusion.

"Are you all right, ma'am?" Brenton questioned, quickly coming to his feet.

"It would seem this debate must wait for another day." Mistress Deighton's lips trembled as she spoke. "There has been a major battle in the war at a place called Shiloh. There have been many casualties."

Brenton and Jordana looked at the woman as if she weren't serious. Though the Civil War had been going on for a year, there had been hardly any major conflicts since the previous summer. Many had been lulled into thinking the war would fade away.

Jordana spoke first. "How can this be?"

The older woman waved them off. "Go now. We will discuss your punishment later."

Jordana reached out to take hold of her brother's hand, but Brenton, ever full of compassion, would not be moved. "Might I bring you a glass of water or call someone to sit with you, Mistress Deighton?"

The headmistress looked up and then shook her head. "No. Just take your leave."

Brenton nodded and followed Jordana from the room. Outside the door, one of the school's teachers stood waiting.

"Mistress Smythe," Jordana said and curtsied in acknowledgment.

"Miss Baldwin. Mr. Baldwin," the teacher responded.

"Mistress Deighton seems quite disturbed," Brenton said, turning to the teacher.

"Yes, her youngest brother was at Shiloh. She has been notified that he was wounded. She has no idea how seriously."

Jordana felt instant pangs of conscience. "Poor Mistress," she murmured.

"I'll take care of her," the teacher promised.

Brenton ushered Jordana out of the building, neither one saying a word until they'd reached the front walk.

"Brenton," Jordana finally said, looking to her older brother for wisdom on the matter, "we all thought the war would be over soon. It's been so long since anything has happened."

Brenton shook his head slowly in disbelief. "It would seem we have been mistaken."

2

After a volatile evening of discussing war and Jordana's foolish behavior, a very exhausted Brenton returned to his boardinghouse. The world had turned upside down and put him on his ear. Or so it appeared. Nothing seemed right.

"Good evening, Mr. Baldwin," his landlady, Mrs. Clairmont, said with a warm smile. "And did you have a good supper with your sister?"

Brenton smiled tolerantly. Mrs. Clairmont was by far the nosiest woman he had ever known. Without a doubt her next question would be concerning where they had chosen to take their dinner and whether they saw anyone of real importance while out on the town. But rather than await her barrage of questions, Brenton spoke first.

"Have you heard the news?"

Mrs. Clairmont pursed her lips and considered this a moment. "If you mean about the battle just fought, I did. I heard those traitorous Rebels attacked General Grant's troops in their sleep."

Brenton nodded. "There were heavy casualties on both sides."

"I am thankful now I had no sons," Mrs. Clairmont commented. She seemed very content that Brenton had bothered to make conversation with her. "But in your opinion, Mr. Baldwin, must it mean the war will not end as soon as expected?"

"My opinion is hardly worth the salt on your table," he replied.

"I'm only eighteen and certainly nowhere near my majority. People tend to ignore my opinion."

She tutted his words. "Now, you are well beyond your years in intelligence and consideration. Your mother raised a fine son, and your father should be proud to call you a man."

"My parents are among the few who consider me an adult," Brenton countered and added, "and, of course, I have your good opinion."

The woman nodded. "That you do. So sit with me a moment and tell me of this war. You are from the South, so perhaps you know better the Confederate intent in this matter."

Brenton laughed and followed her into the deserted front parlor. "We are alone this evening?"

"Well, it is nearly nine o'clock. Most everyone has taken themselves to bed."

"I should also be going," Brenton said, looking at his pocket watch as if for emphasis.

"Surely you can spare a few minutes with an old woman," Mrs. Clairmont replied.

For as long as Brenton had lived in this quiet brownstone building, the widowed Mrs. Clairmont had seemed anything but old. She fussed over everyone as any good mother would do, but she exhibited boundless energy, constantly cleaning her house from top to bottom, and could often be found making many repairs herself when necessary. She ran a quiet Christian house, as she put it, and required that all her boarders attend church with her on Sunday. If a person was not inclined to agree with this requirement, they simply did not rent a room. Brenton thought her a quirky woman with nosy interests and bossy habits. But frankly, he liked her well enough.

Giving her mousy brown hair a pat, Mrs. Clairmont took a seat in her favorite high-backed chauffeuse after pulling it close to the blazing hearth. The chair, designed to sit very low to the floor, made the woman appear almost childlike. Brenton thought her a most peculiar woman indeed.

"Sit. Sit," she ordered, motioning to a straight-backed chair with a horsehair cushion.

Brenton did as she directed, then gave a weak smile. What should he say in regard to the war that he hadn't already discussed with his sister? The entire matter was like a nightmare from his childhood. Since the beginning of the war he had been able to remain aloof because of his age, but since he'd turned eighteen a few months ago, the matter had pressed upon him.

"So the South is unhappy with us here in the North," Mrs. Clairmont began. "I say good riddance to them. Let them secede and take their troubles with them."

Brenton sighed. "Although I hail from Baltimore originally and grew up most of my years in Virginia," he began, "I am not in agreement with the decision on the part of the southern states to pull apart and form their own country. I believe we will find ourselves considerably weakened should this situation not be resolved and the Union restored."

"I say, if they don't want to be a part of this wonderful country, let them go."

"But of course," Brenton replied, "what seems the most obvious answer is not always the most productive, nor the most advantageous."

The older woman considered this for a moment. Again she pursed her lips as she was wont to do when contemplating a matter of extreme importance. "I cannot abide slavery," she finally stated.

"Neither can I," Brenton replied. "My mother was raised with slaves but as an adult would have no part in owning them."

"That's good. I don't know that I could hold with having a boarder who harbored slavery as an acceptable condition. Even as much as I cherish your company, Mr. Baldwin."

"Thank you, ma'am," Brenton said, giving the woman a courteous nod. "I believe, sadly enough, you will find this country torn apart over more than the issue of slavery. I believe this war is more one of testing the strength we have as a nation. It will deal with the states and their rights, the issues of slavery, immigration, importation and exploration, as well as settling of the vast country we call America."

"My, but you are a brilliant young man," Mrs. Clairmont said, clapping her hands together.

"I am merely well-read," Brenton countered. "I keep informed of events through the newspapers, but also my father and mother are good to send me letters detailing their thoughts on the matter."

"Does your father see a lengthy war?"

"I believe my father thought cooler heads would rule the day. He likened America's troubles to a rebellious child with growing pains. Coming of age is never easy, he told me, not for people, nor for countries. Still, he imagined there would be nothing more than a few skirmishes and the South would come to its senses. He would never have ventured abroad had he not been of that opinion. However, it was difficult for him to refuse in any case, as he was offered good money to render his expertise and aid to the Russian government."

"And what would your father be doing to aid them?"

Brenton smiled. "He is helping them build a railroad, of course. The railroad is his second love—his first being my mother. At any rate, their absence is the reason I have been left in charge of my sister Jordana. She is attending a wonderful school here in the city."

"Yes, you mentioned that she attends Deighton. Good people," she murmured.

"Yes, but my sister tries their patience, I'm afraid."

"Ah, but this is youth. Young women are not as reserved as they were in my day."

"I suppose that is true," Brenton agreed.

At the sound of the clock chimes, he took out his pocket watch. "I really must retire," he told her, sounding as though the thought disappointed him.

"Before you go," Mrs. Clairmont said, getting to her feet, "I must give you this parcel." She went to an artistically carved cabinet and opened one of the beveled-glass doors. "It came by post."

Brenton followed her to the cabinet. Smiling, he took the package. "My humble thanks, ma'am."

"Perhaps it will be good news from home," she said, eyeing the package enviously. "It's from Baltimore."

"Yes," Brenton nodded. "Our solicitor is good to forward our mail."

She looked for a moment as though she might expect him to open it there and then, but Brenton merely bowed and bid her good evening. Without waiting for her reply, he hurried from the parlor and bounded up the stairs, taking the steps two at a time.

His room was on the second floor, a lucky strike for him as, given his line of business, there was often a great deal of equipment to carry up and down the stairs. He had come to New York to apprentice with a renowned photographer, and even after a year of grueling training, Brenton loved it. On occasion, he would bring his camera and other materials home with him from the shop. This was usually only in the event that he had some assignment to perform in keeping with his training. The camera and tripod, glass negatives, and chemicals were heavy and delicate, and transporting them for more than the utmost necessity was offset by the idea that something might end up broken or, worse yet, cause an explosion. And given the fact that he'd not yet paid back his father for the loan that had enabled him to purchase top-of-the-line equipment, Brenton was determined to keep the items safe and whole.

In the hall outside his room a lamp gave off a pale amber light. Yawning, unable to suppress his exhaustion, he dug around in his pocket for the key to his room. Shifting the package from one hand to the other, Brenton fished out the key and made his way inside.

If not for the parcel, Brenton might not have lighted a lamp. He much preferred the idea of collapsing on the bed for a long, deep sleep. The day had been a trying one, first with multiple orders for studio photographs, then arriving at Jordana's school to find her hanging from the third-story ledge, and finally the dinner and discussion of their future regarding an honest-to-goodness war. Of course, Mrs. Clairmont's desire for companionship hadn't helped his state of exhaustion. But now the parcel demanded his attention, and Brenton quickly realized that retiring for the night must be put off for just a while longer.

He lit his lamp, then took the package to the small corner desk and opened it. Inside were letters from his family's solicitor, Mr. Marcum, his uncle York, Able Stewart—a good friend in Baltimore—and a belated birthday gift for Jordana from their aunt Virginia.

Ever the business minded, Brenton took up the solicitor's letter first. Inside he read of the upkeep and expenses of the family house in Baltimore, and of bank drafts issued to provide funds for himself and Jordana. Furthermore, the solicitor had it on the best authority that the city and surrounding areas continued to be in a state of great unrest, and it was his advice that Brenton and Jordana refrain from planning any visits home or to his mother's family in Virginia.

Frowning, Brenton realized the situation would only get worse. The war was rapidly taking on a more personal nature. His uncle's letter confirmed much of what Mr. Marcum's missive had stated. It was York's opinion and suggestion that Brenton and Jordana remain as far away from Virginia and Washington City as possible. Uncle York was seriously considering vacating Oakbridge for the duration. There was bound to be trouble, York declared, and only sheer good fortune and Washington connections had kept Oakbridge safe thus far. How foolish they had been to believe the war was winding down. Brenton thought of the ashen-faced headmistress of Deighton. There was certain to be a reckoning after the Battle of Shiloh. On the way home tonight, Brenton had already heard heated discussions on the street. The fevered pitch at the beginning of the war seemed to be growing again.

As he picked up the letter from his friend, another letter fell onto the table. It had apparently been stuck to the back side of Able's envelope. Looking it over, Brenton realized the post had come from Ireland and was addressed to his mother and father. Knowing his brother-in-law Kiernan's family hailed from this poverty-ridden country, Brenton quickly opened the letter, praying that no one had died or fallen ill.

> *Mr. and Mrs. Baldwin,*
>
> *We humbly beg your forgiveness in being so bold as to put our problems at your door. Our youngest sister, Caitlan O'Connor, is in need of your hospitality in America. She has suffered cruelly at the hands of a nearby landlord and has felt the need to depart her home. She will arrive in New York aboard the ship Water Willow in the month of May. We humbly ask for your assistance in getting her to our brother Kiernan in California.*
>
> *Ever Your Servant,*
> *Bridgett O'Connor Kildare*

Brenton ran a hand through his hair. This news was startling and most definitely a cause for worry. He pulled his glasses off in order to rub his tired eyes. What was he to do? With his parents away, the responsibility for the matter rested squarely upon him. He had written them shortly after the start of the war last April with assurances for them not to worry or rush home. He and Jordana were safely in New York and the war was far away. It had seemed a simple matter then to take responsibility. But suddenly things were growing extremely complicated.

Too tired to deal with the remaining letters, Brenton saved the rest for the morning and quickly disrobed. He blew out the lamp flame and crawled into the cool, crisp sheets of his narrow bed. It was only after settling here that Brenton realized how angry he felt.

"It isn't fair," he whispered in the stillness of the night.

His entire world had centered around his love of photography, and now a nation at war would no doubt make the pursuit of his own dreams an impossibility. Now that he was eighteen his family might well expect him to take up arms. It was something he had put off considering since his birthday in November because he'd still had his apprenticeship to fulfill, a commitment he had felt honor bound to complete. He would finish that in a matter of two months. He had to face the war squarely now. The dilemma would be in deciding to which side he should state his allegiance. He had family in the Confederate state of Virginia. Most of his relatives hailed from just outside of Falls Church and Washington City. No doubt some of them would take up arms against the Federal troops.

Of course, he had no love of slavery. In fact, he despised it. No man should own another. But the whole issue seemed a world away, a matter that never really required his attention. He had often listened to his parents talk of national politics and the many issues threatening the sovereignty of the country, but until now none of it had touched him personally. Now he wondered how he could avoid it and how he could protect those entrusted to his care.

His thoughts returned to the letter from Ireland. Kiernan O'Connor had married Brenton's older sister, Victoria, some seven years back. Deciding to seek their fortunes in the rich goldfields of California, the two had taken off for the West a year later without giving much consideration to the effect it would have on the family. Of course, Kiernan's plan had been noble. He had hoped to gather enough money on his own to bring his extensive Irish family to America.

Brenton thought highly of his brother-in-law and the sacrifice he was making for his loved ones. The man had no formal education and was only able to read because Victoria had taught him. That his wealthy sister had married a poor Irishman had never caused Brenton reason for grief. However, the attitude of his uncle and aunts toward their union was another matter entirely. And now Kiernan's youngest sister would be arriving, and he had no idea to whom he could turn for help. Even if a war was not a factor in their lives, Brenton knew his very prejudiced family would think twice about offering shelter to Caitlan O'Connor. If his mother and father were here it would be simple enough, but there was likely no chance of their early return.

With a sigh, Brenton tried to pray. "Lord," he whispered, an undeniable restlessness in his soul, "I don't know what to do. I am torn by my loyalties and obligations. I am overwhelmed by my uncertainties and disgusted at my own selfishness. That I should worry about my desires and dreams of photography while a nation stands torn apart is unthinkable. Forgive me for such a sinful nature and show me what I am to do about this matter and also about the issue of Caitlan O'Connor."

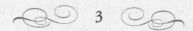

3

Victoria O'Connor pushed back an errant strand of dark chestnut hair and sighed. Mindful of her surroundings, she refused to focus on the side pork sizzling in the pan, refused also to remember they had eaten little but this and potatoes for over a year. She desired nothing more than a change of diet, a hot bath, and an honest-to-goodness bed to sleep in. Instead, she had a grubby, smelly tent in a California mining camp with no bath but that which could be had from a dishpan, and for sleeping, a pallet on the hard dirt floor.

This was far from the life she had dreamed for herself when she had married her dear Irishman. Kiernan! Even thinking of him caused her heart to beat faster. She loved him more than she loved anything else in life. The evidence of that was in the fact that she'd left a life of luxury in Baltimore to come with him halfway across the world to California.

She'd met Kiernan when her family had lived in Greigsville, Virginia. Her father was overseeing the building of a tunnel for the railroad, and Kiernan had been one of the Irish laborers working on the line. He had seemed different from other men. He was serious and responsible and totally committed to his family. He had told her on more than one occasion that family loyalty was everything to him. Blood stood by blood and to deny that was to deny yourself.

Unfortunately, problems with his older brother had caused a deep, unhealed rift between them. His brother had died in an explosion at the tunnel, and Kiernan had never quite recovered from his grief. In spite of his brother's shunning him, Kiernan had loved Red O'Connor with all his heart. He'd looked up to the man as a father image when his own da had died. But now Red was gone and Kiernan was the man of the family. An extensive Irish family of siblings and their children—all of whom lived in Ireland.

But more than this, Kiernan was her husband of nearly seven years. Though the years had been filled with peril and struggle, she had never once lost her deep, abiding love for him. Even now. Even in the midst of this mudhole of a mining district, Victoria felt confident their love could survive any tribulation the world could deliver.

Hot grease popped up to hit her in the face. She quickly wiped it away and chased back the same loose strand of hair. How hard it was not to remember the privileged life she'd led in Greigsville and then Baltimore. She had been born in Baltimore, and when her parents saw it necessary to return to that city, she had grieved only for fear of losing Kiernan. But Kiernan had followed them, and soon after, they had married in a quiet ceremony in 1855. Before coming west, they had even lived at her parents' new house. There they had enjoyed all the luxury life could afford them. Both had stylish new clothes, and they went out nearly every night to one event or another.

Victoria quickly saw how that life wearied Kiernan because he felt unsuited for it, and thus she had suggested they spend more quiet evenings at home planning their trip to California. They both longed for the adventure of going west and making their own fortune—together.

Shaking her head, Victoria forced her thoughts back to the present as she went to the overturned packing crate that doubled as a table and sat down to slice up some potatoes. Her love for Kiernan might never change, but her love for this place certainly had. When they'd first arrived by boat in San Francisco, Victoria had thought it a wondrous place. And even after Kiernan had packed them upriver

JUDITH PELLA / TRACIE PETERSON

to Sacramento, then Placerville, then north to half a dozen other settlements whose names she could no longer remember, Victoria had continued to love the country. She marveled at the beauty of the mountains and the crystal clear waters of the lakes and streams. She had told Kiernan then, and had honestly felt it to be the truth, that she was completely happy to spend her life in this place.

But the newness of the beauty wore off. Kiernan's desire to pan and mine for gold had sent them to one mining town after another, and Victoria's heart had begun to change on the matter. Suddenly, the beauty was scarred by ugly mining equipment and filthy, vulgar men. There were few women in the camps, except those who could not be considered respectable by a genteel, well-brought-up female such as herself.

Wives were rare, as well, and if they existed they were usually overworked and haggard in appearance and certainly never had time for socializing. They died young from bearing too many children or from sheer exhaustion, and they left men behind whose gold fever would soon either take their own lives or render them completely mad.

Victoria feared the lifestyle they'd chosen, but she knew Kiernan's commitment to earning back the fortune he'd lost her. A fortune her birth father had left her upon his death. Her adoptive parents, James and Carolina, had carefully watched over the fortune in order to see to it that Victoria need never live a life such as she was enduring now. But a financial crisis in 1857 had nearly wiped out her entire fortune. Kiernan blamed himself, as he had taken her money away from the investments back east and had brought it west with them to California. Unfortunately, no one had told him that gold was the standard used in California and that paper money and coins were considered suspect at all times. He was lucky to invest it at sixty cents on the dollar, and when banks started failing in the East, the results spread west in an alarming manner. The entire country's economy came to a halt nearly overnight, and the newly formed stock exchanges of New York suffered greatly.

Some blamed it on the end of the Crimean War. It was said that while the war was going on, the United States was making a strong profit via sales of wheat and other food goods to Russia. Cotton had made the southern states rich, and the invention of the sewing machine saw to it that cloth made from this lucrative plant could be fashioned into usable goods nearly as quickly as raw materials could be processed. But the unrest in the South, because of threats of secession, caused the market to slacken as the northern states became suspicious of their southern brothers. And when the European market pulled away in a similar manner, southern sales dropped drastically.

But whatever the reason for the economic disruption, Kiernan blamed himself for removing Victoria from the safety of her family and from the knowledgeable and sound investments her father and mother had procured for her over the years. Victoria could still remember when her parents had written to ask of their financial welfare. Had they survived the crash? Had they suffered much loss? Victoria had lied to them. Lied as boldly as any lie she had ever told.

It shamed her greatly to remember, but she justified it in that she had saved her husband from disgrace. After all, she was a world apart from the social life of Baltimore. No one here in the mining camps would remember that she once belonged to the powerful, wealthy Baldwin family. No one here would question her husband's lack of genius when it came to money.

She sighed again. It hurt to think of how badly Kiernan had wanted to impress her and her parents. He wanted to prove that he could take Victoria to another part of the country and still succeed without the aid of the wealth left to her by her father. Victoria knew it was a sore subject with the man. She had tried more than once to reason that he had no way of knowing anything about the Russians and the Crimean War and whether it would go on forever or end to wreck the economy of the United States.

Kiernan had been inconsolable. He'd gone to the panned-out

riverbeds and searched for a way to make it up to his wife. He didn't return until nearly a week later. And he didn't return with much gold.

Victoria tried not to remember the defeat in his eyes, but it was impossible to forget. Impossible, mostly, because he still wore that haunted look. Everything had changed after that. Well, most everything. Her love for him hadn't changed, but Kiernan's open manner of speaking with her—of sharing his thoughts and dreams—had definitely taken a different turn.

She cut up the boiled potatoes and stirred them into the pork fat. They popped and hissed and turned a golden brown as the grease greedily accepted her offering. Pork and potatoes—at least it was something hot and filling.

The worst part of her life, Victoria thought, was her homesickness. She had never thought herself all that devoted to a place or style of life. Nor had she worried overly much about being parted from her brothers and sisters—Brenton, Jordana, Nicholas, and Amelia. Little Amelia, some sixteen years Victoria's junior, had been a cute and affectionate baby, but she only made Victoria long for a child of her own. When she'd married Kiernan, Amelia was not quite two years old. Victoria had cried to leave them and make a new life west with her husband, but it wasn't a sorrow that had stayed with her for long. The adventure of being married and considered a grown-up woman in her own right had quickly captured Victoria's attention. The adventure of taking a journey by ship to California had left her with little time to think of anything but her seasick stomach and her longing to be on dry land once again.

But now, after a four-year absence and no hope of returning home for a visit, Victoria felt the longing build up inside until it threatened to choke out her happiness with Kiernan. Perhaps if she had children of her own . . .

This, too, was a subject she'd just as soon not dwell on. Because in seven years of marriage, she had been unable to conceive a child. Kiernan's child. At first they had both been relieved to know that she would not produce a child immediately upon their arrival to California. They had seen the blessing in her barrenness as they traipsed around that first year, trying desperately to find some place that hadn't been played out. A place where gold could still be had if a man was willing to work hard enough. But then the second and third year had come upon them and now the seventh, and still no child had been given to them. Victoria hadn't so much as even miscarried, and this caused her more fear than if she'd lost a dozen children.

Her womb was barren, or so it appeared. Barren wombs did not miscarry. Barren wombs carried no life at all.

She felt a tear streak down her face and quickly glanced around to make certain Kiernan had not crept into the tent unannounced. She could scarcely speak of the matter with him, for she knew he longed for children just as she did. To speak the words out loud might give them more validity and finality than they already appeared to have. And being barren was something Victoria was desperate not to accept.

" 'Oh, the sun shines bright on an Irishman's land' " came the distant sound of Kiernan's voice raised in a melancholy song. " 'And beats down such heat that he can hardly stand.' "

" 'And burns his back and blinds his eyes,' " Victoria whispered, straightening her apron. " 'And cares not for his mournful cries.' "

It was one of the many verses to the ballad he sang when life had dealt with him harshly. He probably never realized it, but it always let Victoria know what kind of mood he was in. She could take a moment to prepare her heart and mind for the man of the house—or in this case, the tent. And she could pray that God would somehow give them a restful night of peace and healing before Kiernan had to go back out and face the world once again.

"And where might be the wife of the house?" he called in his lilting brogue.

Victoria smiled. He tried so hard to be cheerful for her sake.

"I'm fixing the husband his food," she called back.

Kiernan pulled back on the opening of the tent and doffed his cap. "Ah, a veritable feast. I smell lamb chops and sweet potatoes like your good mother used to make."

"I see the sun has rendered you senseless," Victoria teased.

"What sun?" Kiernan countered. "Ya know, this place either freezes a body or burns him out. A wee bit o' sun wouldn't hurt my feelings. Instead, the good Lord sends me a late spring snow, and it's left me chilled to the bone."

Victoria nodded. "Well, draw the flap tight so we can warm you up. I've not felt the chill since I started your supper, but once I join you at the table, I'm sure to know it at my back."

Kiernan nodded and tied down the flaps. Then, without warning, he turned and pulled Victoria into his arms and swung her around in a circle. "You're a sight, Victoria O'Connor."

She grinned. "Oh, go on with ya, now," she said, mocking his Irish brogue.

"Hmmm." He let her feet touch the ground again and held her tight. "You smell like lilacs."

"You *have* been in the sun too long," she laughed. "I smell like lye soap and pork fat."

"No, I smell springtime in your hair," he replied.

Victoria loved him for his teasing. Though clearly defeated and discouraged, he proved himself a grand actor, and the fact that he longed for her to be happy was enough reason to give him his desire. Sometimes he tried so hard.

"I love you, Mr. O'Connor," she said, reaching up to take hold of his face. She pulled him down to meet her lips. "I've missed you today. Almost considered taking up mining myself just to be near you."

Kiernan kissed her long and hard before pulling away to eye her seriously. "If I thought you'd be a help, I'd drag you along. Truth is, the mine's played out, and we're gonna have to consider goin' elsewhere."

"Move? Again?" Victoria tried to keep the disappointment from her voice.

"Not far and not for minin'. I've been told about a job in Dutch

Flat. A man there needs help with some surveyin', and he's lookin' for someone with experience. I figured what with the trainin' I've had with your father, I could be his man."

"And if you're not?"

"Sure, and why would I not be the right man for the job?" he replied lightly, though his green eyes watched her closely.

Victoria shrugged and walked back to their makeshift stove. "I didn't say you weren't, but moving on the hope that some man will hire you seems a bit risky."

"No more so than diggin' in the dirt for your dreams—only to find it's your grave you've been diggin'. I'm weary to the bone, Victoria. We've scarcely enough to put food on the table, and what little I've been able to send to me family in Ireland can't begin to bring 'em all here." He sighed and sat down on a rough split-log bench. "We live like animals. I could make us beautiful furniture, maybe even build us a house, if I had me a job I could count on for pay."

Victoria nodded. "I've never faulted the idea of working for regular pay." She brought the pan of pork and potatoes and sat it atop the crate. "But this job seems awfully risky. You heard from a man, who heard from someone else, no doubt, that a man somewhere wants help. It isn't like you to go on rumor and speculation."

Kiernan laughed. "I came to California on little more."

Victoria had to laugh at this. "I suppose you're right." She retrieved their two tin plates and a pot of weak coffee. "But why not make a real move? Why don't we go back to Sacramento? You yourself heard talk of the railroad they want to build. You know the railroad, Kiernan. You could easily secure a job. A good job—one that wouldn't be nearly as backbreaking and hopeless as mining."

Kiernan laughed. "Now, are ya tellin' me that railroadin' isn't backbreakin' work?"

"No, I didn't mean it that way, but the checks were regular," she countered. She brought cups and forks and joined him on the crude bench.

"The Baltimore and Ohio Railroad issued regular checks—at least, they did in the end. But I'm not seein' the B&O mark on anything out this way."

Victoria chuckled and poured the coffee. "Give Mother and Father a chance when they get back from Russia. They'll see to it that their beloved B&O Railroad makes it west. After all, I'm here. What better reason will they need?"

Kiernan frowned at this. "Aye, what better reason?"

4

Jordana pulled her cape tighter around her shoulders. She hated the ferry ride from school to Staten Island, where Margaret Vanderbilt lived. Meggie had invited her home for the weekend, and because G.W. Vanderbilt, Meggie's young uncle, would also be there, Jordana couldn't resist the invitation. George Washington Vanderbilt, now in his twenties and commissioned as a lieutenant in the Union army, was a handsome, broad-shouldered man who treated Jordana as a woman of intelligence, even if she was only sixteen. He had been gone to war nearly since its inception, leaving them at the mercy of the army and postal services for communications. Now he was home on furlough, having succumbed to some illness during the Battle of Shiloh. It would be wonderful to see him again. He never failed to discuss issues of the day with her, accepting that she had the ability to reason and consider matters just as well as any of his male counterparts.

Still, enduring the chilly harbor ride for the sake of being accepted as an adult left Jordana questioning her own sanity. Turning to Meg, she forced her teeth not to chatter and smiled. "I'll be glad when the weather decides to stay warm."

"Oh, it's just a little storm," Meg replied, looking heavenward. "Mother calls it winter's last hurrah. It'll pass before you know it, and then we'll be longing for some shady place to cool our brows."

"You're certainly waxing poetic today," Jordana teased.

"I'm glad to be going home," Meg replied. "I hate Deighton and long only to return home for good."

"What about me?" Jordana questioned. "Who would keep me entertained at school if you were gone?"

Meg tossed back her hood and laughed, her brown ringlets dancing about her shoulders. "*You* are the entertainment at Deighton School. No one could come close to equaling your antics. When you were scaling the building, I thought old Pruney would faint."

"She did appear a bit pale," Jordana agreed. "I can only thank the southern states' rebellion for saving me from expulsion. Poor Brenton made me promise to be good until the end of this session. I don't think he's cut out for my kind of adventure."

"Few people are." Meg strained to see the shore. "Oh look, G.W.'s come to pick us up."

Jordana grinned and suddenly she didn't feel quite so cold. "I feared he'd be too sick. I hope he has plenty of new stories for us about West Point and his travels. I simply love hearing his tales."

"I think he simply loves you."

Jordana frowned. "I certainly hope you are wrong, Margaret Vanderbilt."

Meg looked at her in surprise. "You don't want him to love you?"

"I do not want him to love me. We're good friends, and that is how I want it to remain. I have too much to do with my life to consider settling down to be any man's wife. I want to learn what I can and travel. If I married G.W. he might treat me respectfully, but it wouldn't be long until he expected me to resign myself to keeping his house and bearing his children."

"You don't want a husband and children?" Meggie asked in disbelief. For all her spirited nature, Meg wasn't quite as given over to unconventional thought as her dear friend appeared to be.

"I want them both—someday," Jordana replied, waving to G.W. as the ferry approached the dock. "I just don't want them now. This war has people acting positively daffy, if you ask me. Three of our young ladies have returned to their homes in the South, two have left to marry while their beaus are on furlough, and the rest seem anxious to do likewise."

"Don't you worry that another major conflict will take the lives of our young men?"

"Of course I do. My own brother is now old enough to fight," Jordana said, frowning at the idea of Brenton going to war. She would have to do whatever was in her power to convince him that their mother and father would never approve of him joining up. President Lincoln had already called for seventy-five thousand state militia troops, and the last thing she wanted to see was Brenton obeying some patriotic conscience and following them into war.

The ferry docked and Meggie was the first to greet G.W. "I see Papa sent you to bring us home. How are you?" She reached out to embrace him and kiss his cheek.

Jordana watched their reunion, shocked at the amount of weight G.W. had lost. He was dreadfully pale and appeared as though he might even collapse. He released Meg, then opened his arms to Jordana. But her mind was on Meg's words of G.W.'s love, and she quickly waved him off. "Be gone with you," she said, rolling her eyes. "You aren't my uncle."

"Indeed I am not," he said, grinning mischievously. "And glad I am of that fact."

G.W. stood at least six feet tall and had once maintained the physique of an athlete. Of all the sons of Commodore Cornelius Vanderbilt, G.W. alone was the one considered the hope for the family line. The commodore found Margaret's father, Billy, to be a blatherskite and a sucker, two of the older man's favorite terms. But in spite of the commodore's having exiled Billy to remain on Staten Island while he himself lived in luxury on Washington Place in the heart of New York City, Billy had made a good showing on the farm. He had turned the ground into productive land and had, in fact, increased his holdings many times over. For all his father's lack of interest and confidence in his son, Billy seemed to do quite well at moving his family forward. Billy's younger brother, and the commodore's namesake, Cornelius, or Corneel as he was more often called, had been the commodore's second hope, but this had been quickly dashed when it was learned that the boy had epilepsy—something the commodore blamed himself for in light of having married his cousin. Not only had this been a conflict, but as Corneel grew older, he also spent more and more of his father's money and had no interest whatsoever in making more of his own.

Therefore, G.W. was the hope of the Vanderbilt patriarch. He was dashing and spirited, bold and brazen, and above all else, healthy, at least until the war had rendered him otherwise. But most important, he was willing to do his father's bidding. None of these things mattered to Jordana, however. She simply thought G.W. a wonderful conversationalist and loyal friend.

"You look more beautiful than ever," G.W. told her, then turned to cough fiercely into a handkerchief.

"Are you all right?" Jordana and Meg questioned in unison.

He tried to hide his weakness. "I'm fit as a fiddle, and don't ever think otherwise." Then before either girl could reply, he swept Jordana into his arms and deposited her in the open carriage. The action so took Jordana by surprise that she could only stare openmouthed at the man while he reached back to do the same with Meg.

"Don't you dare hoist me up there like a sack of grain," Meg told him. "There is no reason for you to be handling either one of us. You're sick and need to regain your health. Father would never hear the end of it from Grandfather if you somehow set your recovery back while on a visit to us."

"I can hardly injure myself by assisting a lady into a carriage." Then, helping Meg into the carriage in a more genteel fashion, he added, "I'll have you know, I'm well remembered for my strength. I made a name for myself at the Point last year when I lifted nine hundred pounds."

"Surely you jest! No one could lift that much weight," Jordana said before Meg could answer.

G.W. smiled. "Well, I certainly did. It's all a part of the record books now. Aren't you proud of me?"

"I scaled a four-story brick building," Jordana countered. "Are you proud of me?"

G.W. laughed and turned to Meg. "Did she indeed?"

"Upon my honor," Meg replied. "She nearly caused me to faint dead away."

G.W. looked back at Jordana and studied her for a moment. Self-conscious of his scrutiny, Jordana said nothing. She didn't want to encourage him to think anymore along the lines of what Meg had suggested he already felt.

"I am impressed," G.W. replied, reaching into his uniform to pull out a piece of newspaper. "But I already had it on the best authority."

Jordana took the paper and gasped. No one had told her that the newspaper had written a story on her escapades. "Look here, Meg. It doesn't list me by name, but it says I showed uncharacteristic bravery for a woman."

"Yes, and read on," G.W. said as he climbed up to take the reins to the carriage. "It also says you showed less than proper judgment. I suppose it was necessary to point that out in case you were given over to having swelled pride on the matter. Probably a good thing everyone refused to release your name to the reporter. If your folks caught wind of this, you would probably be on your way to Europe even as we speak."

Jordana ignored his teasing and refused to say another thing until they arrived at the Vanderbilt farm. She liked the coolness of the tree-lined drive and the scent of flowers on the air. The island was like another world compared to the busyness of the city. She smiled to think of G.W.'s assumption that it had been her antics that the newspaperman had written about. Having known each other only a couple of years, and even at that, years when G.W. had been mostly confined to the West Point grounds or Civil War battlefields, Jordana thought they were rather well-acquainted.

But this illusion met with an unceremonious ending when G.W. pulled up in front of the Vanderbilt house and spoke to his niece.

"Meg, you run along. I desire to speak to our guest for a few moments," G.W. said as a liveryman stepped forward to help them from the carriage. He turned over the reins to yet another stablehand before directing his attention to Jordana. "You will take a short walk with me, won't you?"

Jordana handed him back his newsprint. "Are you sure it wouldn't be yet another example of me exercising less than proper judgment?"

G.W. laughed. "Well, what if it is? At least a city full of people won't observe you doing the deed." He quickly took hold of her arm. "Please, walk with me."

"Are you quite sure you are up to it? You do look to have been quite ill."

"I suffered a bout of pneumonia and other complications, but I'll regain my strength. Your company will cheer me on to do so even more quickly."

His eyes implored her and Jordana nodded. "Very well." For all her fears of what he now might say, Jordana cherished their friendship.

"I'll tell Mother you had no choice," Meg called after them. "She understands G.W.'s rudeness and therefore will excuse your tardiness in bidding her good afternoon."

"Yes, tell her that G.W. was a complete ill-mannered oaf about the entire matter," Jordana replied. "She'll no doubt believe every word."

"You are ever the tease, Jordana," G.W. said, pulling her closer.

Jordana maneuvered her arm from his grasp and stepped away from him. "What is it you needed to say to me that couldn't be said in front of the family?"

G.W. grew serious. "I have a great deal to say. We've been friends for just about two years; is that not true?"

"Yes," admitted Jordana. "Good friends."

"Exactly. And because of this, I feel certain you will want to hear what I have to say."

"Very well."

Jordana tried not to show her apprehension. She concentrated on the newly greened landscape. So much of it still bore winter's mark, but here and there daffodils and crocuses were raising their colorful heads to the sun.

Please God, she prayed, *don't let G.W. make a scene with me about the war and his ardent love for me. I just want to go on being his friend.*

" . . . so it isn't easy for me to say this."

"What?" Jordana replied quickly. She hadn't been listening, and now she was caught red-handed.

"I thought you were going to hear me out," G.W. said, sounding hurt.

He began coughing again, and Jordana instantly felt guilty. "The landscape captured my attention for a moment. I promise it won't happen again," she replied, silently wishing she'd gone with Meg into the house. She worried fervently that she was somehow causing G.W. more harm than good.

"Jordana, I consider you a fine figure of a woman," G.W. began. "You make me laugh. You are intelligent and help me to think matters through, yet you have a gentleness to your nature that few women could claim."

"I think you're nice, too, G.W.," she countered, hoping to keep things light.

"You know full well there's more to this than that."

Jordana looked up at him and shook her head. "No, I don't. And, furthermore, I don't want there to be more to it."

G.W. looked puzzled for a moment. "Jordana, I'm twenty-three years old, and once I regain my health, I'll be leaving again to join the war. Being so ill has caused me to rethink my plans. I would like to know that I have someone waiting for my return. Someone who will miss me. Desire my return," he whispered, taking her hands in his.

Jordana felt the warmth of his touch even through her kid gloves. "Of course we'll desire your return, and Meg and I will continue to write to you."

G.W. shook his head. "I want you to marry me, Jordana. Marry me before I leave again for the battlefield."

"What!" she exclaimed louder than she'd intended. "G.W., I'm sixteen years old."

"That doesn't matter. A lot of women marry at your age. Some even younger."

"Yes, and a lot more marry when they are older," Jordana said, trying to pull away. "Let us use them as our example."

"No," G.W. replied, tightening his grip. "Hear me out, please."

Jordana stilled. "All right, but I won't like it and neither will you."

"But why?" He sounded very much like a little child being refused dessert.

"Because I have no intention of marrying you or anyone else for a good long time," Jordana answered. "I like my freedom. I cherish the idea of traveling west on my own. Of attending college and learning new things. I watched my mother with the same desires, and she gave them up to marry and have a family. I've listened to her regrets of never being allowed to attend college. I don't want that to happen to me."

"But you'll be my wife. We'll have more than enough money. We can travel to our hearts' delight. And you can pick up books and experiences wherever you go. I'm not suggesting we end your life, merely that we join both our lives together."

"It wouldn't work, G.W.," Jordana replied, trying to find a way to make light of the situation. "I'm not the kind of woman for you. You have too many responsibilities as the son of the commodore. Do you really think anyone would think as much of you if you marry the woman who scaled the walls of Deighton School?"

"Stop it!" G.W. replied. "I'm not making sport here, and I won't brook it from you."

"But don't you see?" Jordana replied, her hood falling back as G.W. reached out to touch her cheek. "I'm looking for adventure and sport. I do not desire to be your wife. We have something wonderful together. A friendship of grand proportion. Would you put an end to that?"

"Certainly not. I do not propose that we end our friendship, rather that we magnify it with an even deeper intimacy."

He stroked her cheek with his thumb, and Jordana knew that while she cared deeply for him, could probably allow herself to love him, she wasn't ready to give up her freedom.

"I love you, Jordana. I have loved you almost from the first moment we met. You are so unlike other young women. You have a zest for living and an adventurous heart. You do nothing by halves, but surround and engulf everything you touch. You have touched me that way, and I want to go on knowing that touch . . . and more—" His arms closed around her and he kissed her long and passionately on the mouth.

Jordana tried to give herself over to the kiss. Perhaps there was something in what G.W. said. Perhaps she was fooling herself, and it was only her fear of love that caused her to pull away. But while his kiss was pleasant enough, she found no real enthusiasm for it or his touch. When he pulled back, she looked away, and this time he dropped his hold.

Without waiting for him to say something, Jordana began walking down the path. She knew he would follow—knew, too, that the issue was anything but resolved. For several moments neither one said anything, and then Jordana knew she would have to be firm in her resolve.

"I cannot marry you, G.W. I care greatly for you, but I'm not in love with you or anyone. I cherish our friendship, and I do not relish its loss."

"There's no need for you to lose it," he said firmly.

Jordana turned to him. Hopeful, she asked, "Then you understand?"

"I understand that you are afraid of marriage. Perhaps you feel I would be some monster like my father, but I'm not that way. I will give you anything you ask for. If you want a palatial home, I'll have it built. If you want your own island, I'll find it and buy it. Don't you see?" he asked, his voice filled with desperation. "I love you. I want to give you the world."

"But I don't want the world," Jordana replied, "not at that price."

G.W.'s jaw tightened, and Jordana could see the slightest ticking play on his right cheek. Now he was angry.

"I didn't want to hurt your feelings, and I certainly don't desire that you be mad at me," Jordana began.

"Don't!" G.W. interjected. "Don't even say these things. Either you accept my proposal of marriage and agree to be my wife before I return to the war, or you want nothing of me."

"What?" Jordana was stunned. Here she had feared the loss of his friendship through marriage, and now he was making it clear that she would lose it without agreeing to marry him.

"I mean it," he said, his voice firmly resigned. "You either stop this nonsense and agree to marry me, or I'll have nothing further to do with you."

Never one to be backed against a wall, Jordana balled her hands into fists. "Agh! I can't talk to you like this. You make no sense." She turned to go, but he grabbed her and turned her back around.

"You can't dismiss me. I may be sick, but I'm not that milksop brother of yours."

"How dare you insult my brother!"

"He gives you too much freedom and allows you to run him like a horse at the track. I'm a man of considerably more strength."

"Yes, we all know. You can lift nine hundred pounds. It's in the record book," Jordana replied sarcastically. "So hold me here forcibly. Pick me up and carry me away, sick though you may be. But you won't get me to agree to marriage just because you're running off to play toy soldiers with your friends." She knew that was the wrong thing to say, but her own anger was getting the best of her. Mother had once said that anger in and of itself isn't a sin; it's what you do with that anger that causes the iniquity. Now she knew she'd crossed the line. She had only intended to speak harshly in order to hurt G.W. as he had hurt her. Calming, she forced herself to back away from that ugly place. "Forgive me, G.W.," she whispered, "but I cannot marry you."

She hurried up the path, but not fast enough.

"If you leave me like this, don't ever expect to hear from me again. I'll go to my grave hating you for what you've done this day."

Jordana bit her lip to keep from answering. She couldn't reply. Not in the heat of her anger. Not in the rush of emotions that threatened to engulf her.

5

"I don't know what we're supposed to do about the matter of Kiernan's sister," Brenton said once Jordana had read the letter telling of Caitlan's arrival. They were seated on a bench in the Deighton garden on a fine spring day.

"We must find her a place to stay, at least until the semester is over and we return to Baltimore."

"That's another thing," Brenton replied. "We aren't returning to Baltimore. Our solicitor has increased our stipend, and we are to remain in New York."

"Truly?" Jordana replied, her enthusiasm obvious. "What fun. But why?"

"There is still much civil unrest in Baltimore. Most of the town itself sympathizes with the South, despite the fact that Maryland is devoted to the North—at least on paper."

"So we are to stay here in order to avoid finding ourselves in the middle of a war? Is that it?"

Brenton nodded. "Apparently so. Uncle York has sent me a second missive, and his feelings are the same as the solicitor's."

"Well, since Caitlan is arriving within a few days, I suggest we secure a place for her to stay. Maybe you could find something that would either be appropriate for all three of us, or close enough to you that she and I could live alone."

"Indeed!" Brenton declared and got up to pace along the garden path. "As if I would allow you to live in a city such as this by yourselves."

"Don't be such a goose about things," Jordana declared. "I'm sixteen years old and hardly a child anymore."

"My point exactly. And Caitlan, as far as I can remember from Kiernan's discussions about his brothers and sisters, is very nearly my own age. Two young women living unprotected in New York is completely unacceptable. Mr. Marcum even suggested a governess could be hired—"

"A governess! What does our solicitor know of the matter? Has he forgotten we've managed quite successfully up here on our own?"

"I'm certain he hasn't," Brenton replied, clasping his hands behind his back. "But I'm sure he has also reasoned that during our time here in New York, you have been under the care of Headmistress Deighton, and I have been under the direction of my employer. The spring session at Deighton will soon come to an end, and Mother and Father will expect that we would return to Baltimore and then on to Oakbridge to stay with Uncle York." He began pacing again. "No one figured for us to have to stay here in New York."

"Well, no one figured on the war to get worse either. But don't you see?" Jordana said, getting to her feet. "This will work rather nicely. Caitlan will arrive and need a place to live until we can figure a way to get her to California to be reunited with her brother. We are to remain up here instead of returning home, and with the money allotted us we can easily find a place. Why don't you talk to your landlady and see if she might not have additional rooms for us?"

Brenton paused again and nodded. "That's a capital idea! I think there is an empty room."

"That way we will have a matronly figure looking over us, and Caitlan will have a place to stay when she first arrives. We will all be together, and there won't be any need to upset your routine. Perhaps your employer will even allow you to stay on and work through the summer."

Brenton frowned. "He's considering going south to photograph battlefields and warfare. Apparently he has a friend who intends to lecture on the vile repercussions of war and wants as many graphic pictures as he can get his hands on. Even now he's trying to deduce where the next battles might take place."

"How gruesome," Jordana said, coming to where Brenton stood. She looped her arm through his and pulled him along with her down the path. "You mustn't allow him to take you along. I won't have you killed on some battlefield."

"Jordana, there's so much here that confuses me. I have an allegiance to this country and an obligation to support the president."

"You are barely eighteen. And you have a responsibility to your family. I heard that men who are the sole support of their families don't have to go to war."

"I'm hardly the sole support. And I can no longer hide behind my age. Did you know many younger than I are joining? They are lying about their ages," Brenton replied. "In fact, I heard only yesterday that the more enthusiastic are putting the number eighteen in their shoe so that when asked if they are 'over' eighteen, they don't have to lie."

Jordana laughed. "It's ingenious, I'll give you that. But I won't allow you to go."

Brenton shook his head, and Jordana thought he suddenly looked far older than his years. "What is it?" she asked softly.

Brenton pulled away from her and looked around to make certain they were alone. Seeing no one near enough to overhear him, he replied, "I don't want to go. I want to continue my photography and go west. You know, I have always dreamed of this. I want to share the nation with the world through pictures, but I cannot ignore the feelings inside me. Feelings that suggest I am a coward to think the way I do."

"So you will enlist to prove to yourself that you aren't a coward?

What sense is there in that? Either you know yourself to be a coward or not. This action won't change matters either way."

Brenton looked down at the ground. "I knew you wouldn't understand. You aren't a man."

"What has that to do with it?"

"Plenty," Brenton replied, then added sulkily, "I'm sorry I brought it up. It's just that if I should have to follow my conscience and return to Maryland to sign up with the militia, I'll need to arrange for your safety. And now I'll have Caitlan to worry about as well."

"You aren't going and that's final," Jordana countered angrily. "I won't have you run off and desert me."

"It wouldn't be desertion. I'd see you safely to—"

"To where? Oakbridge, in the heart of southern support? Baltimore—which by your own admission is a city in conflict? Perhaps you would see me living with Aunt Virginia in Greigsville. Be reasonable, Brenton. All of our family is either in the thick of it or out of the country. There is no place to send me away to. You must stay and take care of me."

He looked at her sympathetically. "It is possible to keep you at Deighton. I've already checked into the matter."

"Brenton Baldwin, how could you even think such a thing!"

"If it meant your well-being, I would bear your wrath and do it."

"I would run away," Jordana declared, hands on hips.

Brenton offered her a weak smile. "Well, it isn't something that has to be decided this day. I still have time before my apprenticeship is over. Perhaps you could stay at the boardinghouse, and Mrs. Clairmont would look after both you and Caitlan."

Jordana instantly forgave his indiscretion. "That would be more reasonable, but I still won't allow you to go." She took hold of him again. "It's always possible that because of the war we could take advantage of the situation and deal with Caitlan's problem ourselves."

"And how do you figure that?"

"Well, we could take her west to Kiernan. She wouldn't have to travel alone, and we wouldn't be anywhere near the fighting. It would fulfill our family's suggestion that we stay out of harm's way, and it would solve Caitlan's problem as well."

"You and me?" Brenton questioned. "You're suggesting that we arrange to take Caitlan from New York to California? It costs money, you know."

"Yes, but you've already said we would have a healthy stipend. And I know you've saved money from both of our accounts. Surely we would have enough to purchase tickets for as far west as the train goes, and then we could travel with one of those bands of settlers who are moving west. Or we could go by ship."

Brenton shook his head. "I hardly think it would work. We would be completely out of our element."

"Don't be so negative. You consider throwing yourself into a war where people are bound to be killed, but you hesitate to participate in the trip of your dreams? Think of what you could accomplish on the way."

"I can't run away from my obligations," Brenton replied softly. "I can't just sweep this issue aside because it makes you uncomfortable. I haven't decided what I will do, but it isn't a decision that I will allow my sixteen-year-old sister to make for me." Jordana pouted and he added, "No matter how intelligent she is." He smiled at her and continued. "Come now, let us have a good evening together."

Jordana realized there was little more she could say to convince him. "Would you at least think about the idea?"

Brenton sighed. "All right. I'll at least consider it."

She gave him a generous smile. "Wonderful. Let's go to supper. I'm positively famished." Brenton nodded, but Jordana could see the heaviness in his expression. This struggle of conscience would not be easily resolved.

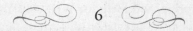

6

"It isn't much to look at," Kiernan told Victoria as they surveyed Dutch Flat.

"Looks like most of the other mining towns we've lived in or around," Victoria replied.

He stopped and looked at his young wife. She had once worn beautiful party clothes and known a life much easier than this one. Her hands, now callused and scarred from heavy work, were once smooth and soft. He hated knowing that he had taken her from that life. That he alone had been responsible for bringing her west and losing her fortune. He had only been able to see the possibility of being his own man, of earning enough to bring his family from Ireland to America, and of supporting the woman he loved without using her inheritance to see them through.

He felt a deep, abiding sorrow that she suffered for his choices. He knew what it was to live his life in a tent. He knew what it was to go hungry. But she didn't, and she shouldn't have had to know. He had taken her away from security and plunged her into the heart of all that threatened to destroy them. They were barely eating and had only the tent to keep them out of the elements, but of late the snows and rains had left them both chilled to the bone and sickly.

She tried not to complain, and for this Kiernan was grateful. His own conscience defeated him on a daily basis; there was no need for her to add her condemnation.

"Where are we supposed to find this man?" Victoria questioned, breaking into Kiernan's thoughts.

"He's the town druggist. I'd imagine we should try over there." He pointed to a false-front building that had crude writing to announce "Medicines, Doctoring, and Help for What Ails You."

Victoria pulled her shawl tight around her wool coat. "I suppose you're right. Maybe they'll have a fire."

Kiernan urged their pack mule forward, praying that he hadn't once again led them astray. Victoria seemed to sense his mood and reached over to pat his arm.

"Don't worry," she said. "There seems to be plenty going on in this town. If this man can't use your help, you're bound to find something else just as useful."

"I hope so."

They tied the mule to a crude hitching post, then entered the building and waited a moment while their eyes adjusted to the poorly lighted room. Every imaginable space in the room was taken up with some article. Jars lined the wall behind the counter and were marked with both legible and illegible wording. The counter itself was piled high with a variety of goods, including items of clothing and unmarked bottles of amber liquid, while mining equipment and tools hung on the walls.

"You lookin' for something in particular?" a rough voice called out. From behind a curtained doorway, a good-sized man emerged.

"I'd be lookin' for a gentleman by the name of Strong. I was told he could use help surveyin'."

"I'm Daniel Strong," the man replied. "Folks round here generally call me 'Doc,' seeing as how I doctor their injuries and prescribe their medicine."

Kiernan extended his hand. "I'm Kiernan O'Connor and this is me wife, Victoria."

"Irish?" Strong questioned.

"Aye, I am. She's not," Kiernan replied evenly, though his eyes narrowed slightly. "Is that a problem?"

The man continued to eye them for a moment. "Not at all. Is it a problem for you that I'm not?"

Kiernan relaxed and smiled. "I wouldn't be here if it was."

Strong laughed. "You both look half froze to the bone. Whereabouts you come in from?"

"We hiked over from Tahoe City. My mule's outside with our goods."

"And you came looking for surveyin' work? You have any experience?"

"Aye, that I do," Kiernan replied. "Me wife's father helped survey for the Baltimore and Ohio Railroad. He trained me. I've put down rail, blasted tunnels, and mucked out canals. I know a bit about railroads and heard tell ya were thinkin' to put one through to the East."

Doc Strong smiled. "That we are. Why don't you and the missus come on in the back with me. I've got someone I want you to meet."

Kiernan looked at Victoria and gave her a weak smile. At least it wasn't a rejection. Not yet. He would tell the man about his abilities and pray for God's hand in the matter. There had to be some manner of decent work for a man such as himself who wasn't afraid of hard work.

"Ted, this young man wants to help us with our railroad," Doc announced as they entered a small back room.

A rough-looking table had been set with mugs of coffee and a tray of sweet rolls. Kiernan thought nothing in the world had ever looked better. His stomach growled loudly, but he tried to ignore his own hunger and drew Victoria closer. A man and woman sat on the opposite side of the table, and as the man rose to his feet, he smiled and extended his hand.

"I'm Theodore Judah, but most folks just call me Ted. This is my wife, Anna."

The woman smiled and turned to look at Victoria. "Child, you

57

look so cold. Come sit here by the stove and get warm. Doc, let's have some hot coffee for these children."

Kiernan liked her immediately, even if she implied that they were children. He returned her smile. "Thank you." He watched the woman, though a complete stranger, instinctively mother Victoria, and he felt for the first time in a long while that all would be well.

"It seems fate has brought this young man to our doorstep," Doc said, plunking down two more mismatched mugs. Anna reached out to pour the coffee while he continued. "Mr. O'Connor here has experience in railroading."

"Is that so?" Ted replied.

Kiernan nodded but said nothing. Instead, he studied the man across the table. He appeared to be in his mid-thirties. Not much older than Kiernan himself. He had brown hair and dark, active eyes that seemed not to miss anything in his surroundings. His thick, full beard and moustache hid away the serious slant of his mouth, but his expression showed great interest, and this encouraged Kiernan.

"I worked on the Baltimore and Ohio back east," Kiernan finally said. Anna handed him a steaming cup and did likewise with Victoria. Kiernan thought nothing had ever smelled or looked so good. The coffee was strong and black, unlike the watered-down variety he and Victoria had been sharing.

"We were just about to partake of some further refreshment," Anna told them. "Would you care to join us?" She didn't wait for their affirmation, but rather acting the part of hostess for the group, she put a sticky bun on the table beside each person. "We don't stand on formalities around here," she said with a smile. "Doc's lucky to have enough cups to go around. I shan't dream of bothering him for plates."

"Good thing, too," Doc said with a laugh.

"We were just planning to take a trip out to the Donner Pass. We've surveyed much of the area in hopes of building a railroad," Ted told him. "Why don't you join us? It will give us a chance to get to know each other better and see if we like the idea of working together."

"I have to work at something," Kiernan told the men. "I don't have much left in reserve." It was a matter of pride to admit this, but Kiernan felt it the right thing to do.

"Well, I can't pay you much to start," Ted Judah said thoughtfully. "That is, if we decide on hiring you."

Doc chimed in about this time. "You can sweep out the store and help me keep it in order while we're working to figure this out. I can't pay much, either, but it'll keep you fed."

"It's generous, you are," Kiernan replied.

"Nonsense," Doc said, chuckling. "Ted is keeping me far too busy. I can't keep a decent eye on the store. So while we wait for the weather to warm a bit, you can stay here."

"We have a tent," Kiernan offered.

"Good. I'll show you where you can pitch it."

Kiernan felt a sense of relief wash over him as he sunk his teeth into the bun. The caramelized sugar melted in his mouth, and he thought that nothing had ever tasted as good as this sweet roll did just now. At least they would have a place to stay and food to keep them from hunger. He looked over at Victoria and saw the hopefulness in her eyes.

He had seen the same look in his mother's eyes. But that had been before their da had died and the famine had swept Ireland. It was before the landlords had risen up in an oppression far worse than any they had ever known—throwing people off the land, burning their cottages down around them. His mother had tried to remain hopeful even as her family suffered from starvation and the loss of all they had known. She had turned to her faith for strength and had remained true to it until her death—a very young death. Seeing Victoria's expression so similarly mirror his mother's gave Kiernan a sick feeling in the pit of his stomach. What if the same fate awaited her?

"So your father is James Baldwin. Is that right?" Judah was asking Victoria.

"Yes, he is," she said, her smile sincere. "He's abroad at present.

Mother wrote and said they had been asked to help with the Russian railroad."

"No doubt an even more ambitious project than our own," Ted Judah replied.

"If anyone is able to help accomplish the matter, it will be James Baldwin," Kiernan replied. "I hold me father-in-law in high regard. He looks forward to the day when a railroad will tie this country together."

"No more so than my mother," Victoria chimed in.

Anna laughed at this. "Of course, a mother would look forward to having a quicker route to her child."

"Aye," Kiernan added, "not to mention the woman has her own passion for the rails."

"A transcontinental route is absolutely necessary if we are to see this nation settled properly. We cannot expect citizens in the East to give their money and lives for states in the West when they can't even reach them without spending weeks, even months, en route."

They continued discussing the issue of a transcontinental railroad until Victoria yawned and Anna decided they could both use a rest away from the men.

"Doc, we shall borrow your guest bed," Anna said with a voice that betrayed her own exhaustion. "Come, Victoria. We shall have a nap."

Victoria looked to Kiernan before joining the woman. He could only nod his approval. God knew she needed more than a brief nap on a borrowed bed, but at least it was something.

Watching Anna Judah put an arm around his wife, Kiernan felt blessed that God had sent another woman into their lives. Sometimes Victoria seemed so isolated. So alone. He was certain she believed him to be ignorant of the fact, and it appeared they were both content to continue keeping their unhappiness from each other. Sometimes he thought to bring up the point that they were allowing some things to be put aside without solutions or discussions. But physical demands left him exhausted, and his own mental anguish over his lack of success left him with little desire to discuss emotional matters. Surely if the matter needed tending to, Victoria would bring it up. She was a strong woman, and he knew her to voice concern when need necessitated it. If her loneliness was too great, she would most likely approach him on the matter. Wouldn't she?

"I'll probably head east in another month or so," Ted was saying as Kiernan refocused on the conversation.

"East?" Kiernan questioned.

"Yes," Ted said, refilling his mug with coffee. "I have to convince the politicians of the eastern states that a transcontinental railroad is imperative to the growth and development of this nation."

A thought came to Kiernan's mind. "And does your wife travel with you?"

"Most times," Judah admitted. "I hate to be long parted from her. We only have each other. God never saw fit to bless us with offspring."

Kiernan nodded. It was an issue he knew for himself. Often he had hoped to hear Victoria tell him that they were to have a child. But seeing the reality of their life, Kiernan was just as glad that they remained childless.

"I've given some thought to sendin' me wife home to see her family," Kiernan said, hoping he didn't sound too pretentious. He'd just told these men of his poverty, and to mention the expense of a trip seemed ludicrous. But perhaps this was God's direction.

"Her family is in and around Washington, is that correct?" Doc asked.

"Aye. Her folks are abroad, but her uncle is keepin' the family plantation in Virginia."

"With the war on, heaven only knows what the situation would be like there."

"Aye, the war," Kiernan said. "We hear so little about it, especially in the isolated mining camps. To be sure, I thought it might even be over."

"I'm afraid not," Doc answered. "A good friend just joined me from a journey on the Central Overland Stage. He said a major battle

JUDITH PELLA / TRACIE PETERSON

was fought in Shiloh in Tennessee, and the Union forces will also soon move against Richmond."

"He's right," Ted confirmed. "I will most likely leave Anna here if I journey to Washington. We have no way of knowing exactly what's taking place back east, but I certainly wouldn't want to expose my dear Anna to the ugliness of warfare."

Kiernan shook his head. "For sure I wouldn't be puttin' my Victoria in that kind of harm." He felt both a sense of relief and of frustration. Frustration, because he knew he was failing miserably at being a good husband. Relief, because he didn't know how in the world he could ever live without Victoria by his side.

7

Caitlan O'Connor pulled her ragged bundle of belongings closer to her breast. The crowds on the docks were impossible, and pickpockets and confidence men seemed to abound at every corner. She knew their kind. Knew them well. Many of her best friends in Ireland had resorted to such behavior in order to stay alive. Even the church leaders had taken to turning a blind eye when the thieving and conniving had to do with feeding hungry children and keeping fuel in the homes of the elderly.

After enduring weeks below deck in steerage and then the frustrating confrontations at Castle Garden, the immigration examination station, Caitlan relished the feel of the sun on her face and the wind in her hair. She hardly minded that she was a stranger amidst a sea of people. No one here knew her, nor did they expect anything of her. She had filled out her paper work as best she could, explaining that she was to become her brother's financial responsibility. She had allowed them to poke and prod her past what she considered decent and necessary for establishing her medical condition, and she had allowed them to rummage through her meager belongings to verify the contents she'd listed on her immigration papers.

When the man had marked her papers and passed her through, Caitlan felt like dancing a jig. She was free. Free from the worries that had haunted her in Ireland. Free of the frustration and misery that had been her fate.

Everyone back home had spoken of America as a magical kingdom of wealth and grandeur. Stories were told of how gold could be had for the taking—how the very streets ran rich with milk and honey. Staring down at the filth and garbage strewn about New York's docks, Caitlan could only grin at such misguided thinking.

"And for sure it smells more like spoilt milk and putrid honey," she murmured aloud.

"Are ya lookin' for work, honey?" a heavyset man asked, pressing his body close to hers. He reached out to give her backside a pat, but Caitlan was too quick for him, sidestepping the lewd gesture.

"I'd not be lookin' to work with you were me mum laid out and her wee babes starvin'."

"Yar an uppity piece, ain't ya?"

Caitlan threw him a look that she hoped would appear menacing. "I'm sure yar wife doesn't like ya to be late to home. I know me kin over there would be particularly offended if he knew what ya were thinkin' just now." She nodded toward a burly man who leaned casually against the dock railing. She knew the man to be a fellow traveler and had little doubt that should she ask for his assistance, he would come to her aid.

Looking back to see what the fat man's response would be, she found him gone. Smiling to herself, she searched the crowds again for some sign of those who had come to meet her. She actually had no idea whom to expect. No idea whatsoever. Maybe no one would come. Maybe the letter had never arrived to announce her journey to America. And even if it had arrived, maybe no one would care.

She started to feel a tightening in the pit of her stomach. Even if someone had been sent to retrieve her, how would they ever find her? Kiernan had as much idea of what she looked like as she did him. They were strangers, though brother and sister. If anyone did come, would they know the process of immigration? Did they know about the place called Castle Garden?

"Caitlan O'Connor!" a voice called loudly.

She jerked her head toward the sound, then elbowed her way forward through the crowd, struggling to ease by a woman and her five children—four of whom were crying.

"Caitlan O'Connor!"

"Here!" she cried out, still unable to find the source. What if she couldn't be heard above the din?

"Where?"

"Over here!" she called back and waved one arm in the air while clutching her things with the other.

Finally she saw him. He stood precariously balanced atop a roped pyramid of barrels. He took her breath away. He looked so serious— almost worried as he searched the crowd. Who was he?

His tan suit of cotton broadcloth was obviously tailored to fit his lean, trim frame. Both the cut and style revealed the expense of the piece, reminding Caitlan once again that she had come from one world and was about to be plunged into yet another. She had heard tales of her sister-in-law's rich family and how her brother had married into money. They used to sit around and imagine what it might be like to have great wealth. Kiernan had written, telling them of a pillared mansion in Baltimore, carriages with fine leather upholstery, and clothes so rich and wondrous that one gown would keep a peasant family in Ireland fed for half a year. They had marveled, dreamed, tried to imagine what it might be like—but always it was an ocean away.

"Caitlan O'Connor, where are you?" he called, cupping his hand to his mouth.

And a lovely mouth it was, she decided, still watching him silently. He looked terribly young, though—maybe as young as her own seventeen years. His gold wire-rimmed glasses made him appear studious and intelligent, but the way he swayed and practically danced to keep his balance made it clear that he was out of his element when it came to physical activities. He seemed gangly and awkward, but it somehow endeared him all the more to Caitlan.

"Caitlan O'Connor!" he called again.

"Here!" she finally answered, taking pity on him.

He looked down at her, an expression of surprise on his face. "Truly?"

Caitlan laughed self-consciously. "Aye, I'm Caitlan." She was suddenly aware of her shabby, travel-worn appearance. Her curly copper-colored hair was hopelessly tangled, and she was certain her skin must be smudged with the ship's filth. Her dress was too short, for she'd had a growth spurt before leaving home and could not afford new clothes to fit her healthy and rounded five-foot-six frame. She ran a hand uselessly over the wrinkled garment.

The man jumped down from the barrels, losing his balance and nearly tumbling right into Caitlan's arms. But he caught a post, and by the time he took hold of her arm, he had, much to Caitlan's disappointment, steadied himself. "I didn't think we'd ever find you. It was all I could do to keep Jordana from climbing to the rooftops to catch sight of you."

"Who's Jordana?" she asked rather breathlessly.

"My sister. I'm Brenton Baldwin," he replied, easily maneuvering through the remaining people separating them. "We've a carriage just over there."

" 'Tis yar sister Victoria who'd be married to me brother?" Caitlan questioned.

The young man stopped in his tracks and smiled. "That's right. I should have better introduced myself, but I hated to keep you standing out there on the docks."

Caitlan laughed softly. "I'm sure I'd be no worse for it."

Brenton smiled and gave her a gentle nudge. "Come on. Jordana is anxious to meet you."

"For sure?" Caitlan found it hard to believe that anyone would be anxious to meet her. Much less a family of such quality and refinement.

He led her to a bright blue open carriage, which had been richly upholstered in black leather. A driver sat waiting, while a young girl dressed in a blue serge afternoon dress waved cheerily from the carriage seat.

"Caitlan! I'm Jordana!" the enthusiastic girl exclaimed. "Come sit beside me."

"I smell of cattle and all manner of foul things," Caitlan replied. "Best I sit opposite, or at least downwind. Perhaps I should ride with the driver."

"Nonsense!" Jordana laughed and shook her head. "I've no doubt smelled worse. Now, come sit beside me."

Caitlan was taken aback. This delicately refined young woman was actually welcoming her. She was nothing like the uppity women and prosperous landowners' daughters who sneered down their noses at the workingwomen in their presence. Gathering up her skirt, Caitlan allowed Brenton to help her into the carriage. She hesitated only a moment before joining Jordana. Sitting gingerly on the edge of the seat, she tried to act natural about the entire matter.

"So what do you think of America?" Jordana asked. "Isn't it big and loud and wonderful!"

Caitlan laughed. "Aye, that it is."

"Mother and Father took us abroad once when we were younger, and I thought America surely the loudest of all the countries I had visited," Jordana said, her eyes twinkling as though it were somehow a great joke to be shared.

Brenton joined them and closed the door to the carriage. "We'll take you to the boardinghouse and get you settled in. Then, if you like, we can go for a walk and see a bit of the city and perhaps get something to eat."

"I'd just as soon have a bath," Caitlan replied.

"Of course," Jordana said, sounding as though Brenton should understand this to be the natural order of things.

"Where do ya live?" Caitlan looked around with wonder as the carriage moved through the busy docks streets.

"Well," Brenton replied hesitantly, "Jordana is currently finishing a semester in a school for young women. I'm staying at a boardinghouse several blocks up Broadway. I've managed to secure a room for you there, and when the semester is over, Jordana will join us."

"Ya had to purchase a place for me?"

Brenton smiled. "We needed a place for Jordana to stay when school finishes for the summer. You see, because of the war we are unable to return to our family's home in Baltimore. Thus, it just seemed natural to go ahead and rent the room early on and put you there as well."

"I can't be havin' ya spending yar hard-earned money on me," Caitlan said, tightening her hold on her meager possessions. She frowned. "I don't suppose any of us thought much past gettin' me here. I have some money but—"

"Don't give it a second thought," Brenton replied. "It just so happened my landlady, Mrs. Clairmont, had an open room. You'll be just two doors down from me and quite safe."

"Me safety isn't a-worryin' me. I can't be havin' ya pay me way."

Jordana turned to offer her a smile. "We have a regular stipend from our parents. It's not a problem. Brenton works with his photography, and I have very few needs after paying tuition and board. Believe me, the money isn't a problem."

Caitlan shook her head. How could she explain to someone who had never had to do without what it was to take charity from strangers? How could she explain the pain it caused her just to know that she'd forced her family to use up the savings Kiernan had sent them in order to buy passage and bribe enough officials to get her out of Ireland in quick order?

"I don't take charity," she replied softly. "I'll have to work."

"Nonsense!" Jordana countered. "I'm looking forward to us being together." She reached out and touched Caitlan's hand. "I want us to be great friends."

The younger girl's obvious sincerity instantly disarmed Caitlan.

"Jordana always gets her own way." Brenton leaned forward slightly and gave her a coy look. "You might as well give up."

"I've a bit o' Irish stubbornness meself," Caitlan said, grinning. She liked these Baldwins. They were unconcerned with her ragged appearance and filthy condition. They were openly welcoming and kind, and she hated feeling contrary.

"This isn't a time to worry about such matters," Jordana said, squeezing Caitlan's hand. "We can discuss all of this after you've had a chance to bathe and eat and sleep in a real bed. I'm staying the weekend with you at the boardinghouse, so don't be worried about the cost of the room."

"What about your school?" Caitlan asked.

"I hate it there," Jordana admitted, scrunching up her face. "It's so very boring. Anyway, the semester is nearly over, and on weekends I can receive permission to take leave of the school. Brenton obtained that permission, and now I'm to stay with him at Mrs. Clairmont's boardinghouse. So you see, it isn't charity at all."

Caitlan looked first at Brenton and then back to Jordana. "I suppose there's little choice. However, I'll be needin' a job."

"What kind of job?" Jordana asked, as though the idea were some sort of game.

"I suppose housekeepin'," Caitlan replied. "That's really all I'm good for. I can sew and wash clothes, as well, but 'tis not me favorite job."

"You needn't work as a housemaid," Jordana replied. "Why don't you just allow us—"

"I won't be takin' charity," Caitlan said in a serious tone, as firmly as she could without being rude. "I already owe me passage here to Kiernan. I can't be owin' you as well."

Jordana appeared almost offended. "No one said you would be owing us anything."

"And that's just how I'd like to be keepin' it," Caitlan replied. She realized she had pushed a bit hard and smiled. "I do want us to be good friends," she added, "but if I'm to be on me own, I must earn me keep."

"We know several families who might be interested in hiring you on," Brenton said, seeming to understand better than his sister. "There are many fine families in New York, and if you are capable of doing a good job, you shouldn't have any trouble earning your way. However, what shall we do about getting you to California?"

" 'Tis a worry, to be sure," Caitlan said, relaxing against the plush cushioning of the carriage. "I can't be goin' to me brother like this. I'll have to earn enough money to pay him back and then some. Is it a far piece to go?"

"Jordana has an idea, but we've not given it much consideration," Brenton admitted. "She thinks we should escort you to California. Her thought is in keeping with a dream I have to photograph the countryside between here and there."

Caitlan smiled, trying to imagine the dreams of this handsome young man. He smiled in return and her heart beat faster. What a gentle spirit he seemed to have. Even in the short time she'd shared his company, he'd worked to put her at ease and to keep her pride from becoming an issue between them.

"And how would this work?" Caitlan finally questioned.

Brenton shrugged and laughed. "We've never taken it any further than the initial idea. If you think it might work for you, although it wouldn't get you there in any record time, we could probably find a way to work our way west."

"A possibility, to be sure," Caitlan said, nodding thoughtfully. "I would be happy to consider it. I'm supposin' I'm in no great hurry."

"I'll speak to my friend Margaret Vanderbilt," Jordana suddenly interjected. "It seems her grandfather Cornelius Vanderbilt, one of the richest men in New York, is always hiring someone. They have a huge house on Washington Place, and they are forever needing new help. I'll put in a good word for you with Meg and see what is to be done. She doesn't think very highly of her grandfather, as he treats her father poorly, but she knows much about the family dealings."

Caitlan felt hopeful that everything would work out. "I'm beholden to ya both. The fates were good to send me here."

"The fates?" Brenton questioned. "You mean God, don't you?"

Caitlan's sharp intake of breath couldn't be disguised. "I don't suppose I do," she replied softly. "I'm more familiar with fate and luck and ill omens than I am of religious nonsense. Forgive me if that offends."

Brenton stared at her for a moment, his blue eyes never looking away, even though his discomfort was obvious. "Perhaps, in time, you will come to feel differently."

Caitlan gave him a weak smile. "Perhaps," she said aloud, then sighed and thought . . . but it isn't likely.

———

Later that night Caitlan and Jordana lay awake in the double bed at Mrs. Clairmont's boardinghouse. A single candle burned on the nightstand beside Caitlan, throwing muted golden light across the room.

They should have gone right to sleep. Jordana knew Caitlan was exhausted. But instead, they found themselves having a great deal to discuss. They had hit it off instantly, finding their lack of concern with social etiquette and cultural divisions to be a marvelous cause for joining together. Caitlan was fascinated with the stories Jordana told of her privileged childhood, but to Jordana it was just everyday life. It didn't seem that special.

"I've always had plenty," Jordana admitted, "but it never seemed important."

"It would have been important if it weren't there," Caitlan countered.

Jordana leaned up on her elbow and said thoughtfully, "I suppose you're right. I never gave it much consideration. Victoria has talked of when we first moved with Mother and Father to Greigsville. It was a tiny mining town, and there wasn't much in the way of housing or supplies. She said it was horrible, but by the time I had memory of the place, we had fixed up our house and it was quite comfortable. Then we moved to Baltimore to a very lovely house."

"Ours was a tiny place," Caitlan said softly. "I lived with me sister and her husband. She didn't need the extra mouth to feed, but our mum had died and I was still quite small."

"Did you go hungry often?"

"Aye, more often than I'd like to remember."

Jordana frowned. "I'm sorry about that. I can't imagine having to worry about such things. You won't have to worry about that here. Not if I have anything to say about it."

Caitlan laughed softly. "Ya can't be going around savin' the world, Jordana. I'm a grown woman, and takin' care of meself is what I've always had to do."

"Yes, but we're friends now," Jordana said emphatically. "Promise me—you won't let your pride keep you from coming to me if there's something I can help with. I know you're proud; I am too. But I don't want to see you suffer because of it. If I can help you, I will. Not because of obligation, and not because you're kin, but because we're friends."

Caitlan wiped a tear from her cheek. "I don't believe I've ever heard anything so lovely. Ya hardly know me. How can ya just be givin' of yarself like that?"

Jordana shrugged and eased back against the pillow. "With you, it just seems right."

"Aye," Caitlan admitted. "That it does." She fell silent for several minutes before adding, "I promise to come to you as a friend—should the need arise."

Jordana knew it had cost her much to say the words. "And in turn," she told Caitlan, "I will also come to you as a friend—should the need arise."

It seemed a strange moment and place for such a commitment. Two strangers from vastly different worlds had somehow found each other in a most unusual manner. In her heart of hearts, Jordana knew she'd just made a dear friend. She felt certain that Caitlan would continue to be an important person in her life, and with that thought warming her heart, Jordana drifted into an easy sleep.

8

Jordana didn't know whether to be happy or sad that the Vanderbilts had so easily taken Caitlan on as their newest upstairs maid. Caitlan was ecstatic, and because of that, Jordana tried to be happy for her new friend, although it meant she might not see her for a while. Perhaps when G.W. stopped being so angry, he would allow Jordana to come visit at his father's house. His physical recovery also seemed to be slow in coming, and Meg had mentioned that he'd even grown weaker since their last visit. Jordana felt extremely guilty over her reaction to G.W's marriage proposal, but she knew that once he had given it some careful thought, he'd understand her reasoning and they'd be the best of friends again.

While Jordana was wishing for more time with Caitlan, the Irish lass had been excited at the prospect of getting right to work. Her code of ethics only seemed to endear her more to Jordana. She liked Caitlan O'Connor. Liked her a great deal. There wasn't a pretentious bone in her body, and her open honesty was refreshing.

"We can be visitin' on Fridays," Caitlan had told her before departing for the Vanderbilt house four days earlier. " 'Tis me day off and I can be comin' here to the boardin' house to talk to ya."

Jordana knew it would have to be enough. And since today was Friday, the idea seemed at least bearable. The spring term was completed, and since she wouldn't be staying on for the summer, Jordana felt the pressures of her life lifting from her shoulders. Deighton was a good school and she had learned a great deal, but she resented the regimentation and rules that haunted every hallowed hall of the establishment.

There were rules for how to wear your uniform and for how to wear your hair. The standard navy ribbon was acceptable as ornamentation for one's hair, but nothing else was allowed—unless, of course, you were going outdoors, in which case the standard navy bonnet was allowed. No variance on the uniform was ever acceptable. Jordana remembered the time when Meg had returned from a weekend stay at home and had brought with her a lovely broach. The pin had been a birthday gift, but when she wore it on the Deighton uniform, the headmistress quickly saw to its removal.

"Contrast in uniformity diminishes the effects of discipline," Mistress Deighton had said.

It was sheer boredom to Jordana's way of thinking.

But it was behind her now. She would think about the university in the near future, but for now she could look forward to a wonderful few months living close to Brenton at the boardinghouse. She cherished her time with Brenton. He was an adorable and considerate older brother, and she had never known a time when they hadn't been close. Now the added treat of having Caitlan around on Fridays made the entire matter even more delightful. What fun they would have together!

Slipping a last item into her valise, Jordana hurried downstairs to Deighton's formal parlor and awaited Brenton's arrival. He would come for her as he had on several other occasions when his landlady had been willing to have Jordana as a weekend guest and the headmistress could be charmed into consenting. Lately, Mistress Deighton had been of a particularly good nature, given that her brother's wounds at the Battle of Shiloh had not been serious.

How excited Jordana was to have the weekend amusements extend for the entire summer. They would take in parks and museums, art galleries and concerts. The pleasure that she most anticipated, however, was the conversations she would have with her brother. Brenton treated her as an equal, and he very seldom laughed at her ideas. In fact, quite often Brenton sought her out for advice, declaring that even at sixteen Jordana was more capable of sound reasoning than many folks their senior.

"I see you're ready and waiting," Brenton announced as he strode determinedly into the room.

"I didn't see you arrive," Jordana said, surprised to find him here already. She was perched in the window seat overlooking the street, certain she would have seen him come up the lane.

"I know. I came early so that I might talk to Mistress Deighton," Brenton replied, looking away as he spoke.

Jordana found his attitude a puzzle. She handed him her valise and asked, "Why would you want to talk to her?"

Brenton pressed the small of her back with his hand. "I'll tell you on the way to the boardinghouse."

"I have more luggage in my room."

"I'll send someone for it later," he answered vaguely.

Jordana saw the tightening of his jaw and knew instantly that something was afoot. Brenton never acted this secretive unless the news was unpleasant. He led them to an awaiting carriage. He helped her up onto the seat, then joined her and waved to the driver.

"Brenton, I want to know this instant what this is about," Jordana said seriously. She knew her brother well enough to know that these actions did not bode well. "Is something wrong with Mother or Father? G.W.?"

"No," Brenton replied, looking beyond her at the passing street scene.

Flowering gardens were in full bloom, while dogwood and redbud trees along the lane snowed down petals to carpet their way. It all seemed so peaceful, so serene, but Jordana wasn't fooled. She refused to be lured into the beauty of it all.

"Brenton!"

He looked back at her and nodded ever so slightly. "I know you aren't going to like what I have to say."

"That much is evident," she replied sarcastically. "Suppose you just have your say, and then I can tell you what I think on the matter."

"Look," he said, leaning forward as if to ease her mind, "you know I only have your best interests in mind."

"Stop bandying words and tell me what this is about," Jordana demanded.

"I've arranged for you to stay on at Deighton for the summer."

"What!" If the carriage had not been moving, Jordana would have jumped to her feet. "What in the world is this all about? You know how I feel about that place."

"I'm leaving New York, and I can't have you staying alone at the boardinghouse."

"What do you mean you're leaving? Where do you plan to go?"

Brenton looked away, then reached up and took off his glasses. Rubbing them gently with a handkerchief, he spoke. "You know about President Lincoln calling for seventy-five thousand state volunteers."

She nodded.

"And I believe you know, too, about the attack on the Sixth Massachusetts Militia upon their arrival in Baltimore."

"Yes, we discussed it in school. It caused President Lincoln to declare martial law and suspend the writ of habeas corpus between Philadelphia and Washington, allowing arrests and imprisonments to be made without having to file charges. So what? How does that have anything to do with me?" She watched him replace his handkerchief in his pocket and put his glasses back on. He was playing this too calmly. Something of major import was about to happen, and instinctively, Jordana knew it would change their lives. Maybe forever.

"It has a great deal to do with us. That area includes our home in Baltimore and our family property. It includes the Baltimore and Ohio Railroad, which you know is vitally important to our family's financial affairs. Not to mention how important that line is to Mother and Father for sentimental reasons. Suspending the writ has meant that men are arrested for little more than being in the right place at the wrong time. The world, as we know it, has gone haywire and innocent people are suffering—a state of affairs that has not improved in the last year. Perhaps it has even worsened."

"I know all of this. What I don't understand is why that means I have to stay in school for the summer. I've finished my requirements here, and we were going to make plans for my fall attendance to the univeristy."

"I'm going to enlist," Brenton suddenly declared.

Jordana hardly heard him. The words were there—floating around inside her head—but they made no sense. She glanced past him to see unfamiliar buildings and parkways. He had obviously arranged for the driver to take a longer way back to the boardinghouse while he explained his decision. She looked over at him and found him biting his lip. He so wanted to be strong and reliable, yet Jordana so often bullied him into letting her have her own way that she could tell even now this was a concern of his.

"Please explain," she said simply, fearful that if she said anything more she'd be guilty of hurting his feelings.

"I believe it's my duty to enlist. It's only for ninety days."

"But you aren't yet finished with your apprenticeship," Jordana replied flatly.

"I will be soon enough," Brenton replied.

Jordana nodded but said nothing. Already she was feeling sickened by the thought of Brenton risking his life in this war over states' rights. As much as she might try to make their collective decisions, he was her pillar of strength and reliability.

"Jordana, listen to me. I have to do this. I have to at least try. I'll return to Baltimore and see to the affairs of our property and the welfare of our friends. If it makes you feel better, I'll even go to Oakbridge and have a talk with Uncle York."

"He won't support your signing up for a northern militia," Jordana replied. "He's clearly in favor of defending the institution of slavery and the fight for southern independence."

"I know that, but I still value his wisdom," Brenton insisted.

Despite her brother's obvious effort to be firm with her, Jordana could hear the uncertainty in his voice and knew he was conflicted over this.

"And even if he doesn't support me," Brenton continued, "I can still let him know my worries and concerns on the matter."

"I'd like to know them myself." Her voice was soft, almost child-like. She prayed her fears weren't evident.

Brenton leaned back in the seat. "I feel it's the right thing to do. I'm not sure if this is what God is calling me to do, but it seems so." He paused for a moment, then shook his head slowly from side to side. "Jordana, you know I don't want anything to interfere with my plans for going west, but I don't feel I have a choice in this. To run away would make me a coward."

"You aren't a coward," she replied, trying hard to understand his masculine pride. "No one should desire this war, and no one should want to go and fight in it."

"But duty is something I can't ignore. I think Father would understand, even if Mother protested."

They had arrived at the boardinghouse, and as the driver slowed, Jordana fought to keep her emotions under control. "Why can't I come with you? I mean, I could stay in Baltimore as easily as in New York. We'd have the household staff to look after me and—"

"No," Brenton stated emphatically. "Baltimore's a volatile city. I don't want you in harm's way."

"Neither do I want you there," she replied, reaching for the carriage door as soon as the driver brought the team to a halt. "But that doesn't seem to matter."

"Jordana!" Brenton called after her, but Jordana jumped from the carriage and hurried toward the boardinghouse, afraid that if she didn't focus on something other than Brenton for even a moment or two, she would break into tears.

"Ah, Miss Baldwin, your friend is waiting for you in the front sitting room," Mrs. Clairmont announced as Jordana practically flew through the front doors.

"Caitlan?" Jordana replied. "She's here already?"

Mrs. Clairmont nodded as Jordana hurried from the foyer. Jordana heard Brenton thank her for seeing to Caitlan's comfort, and knew she had been unforgivably rude to the woman.

"Caitlan!" Jordana declared, spying the girl standing beside the heavily draped window.

"What do ya think?" Caitlan gave a twirl of her black maid's uniform. Her copper curls had been arranged in a neat bun, accenting her concise appearance.

"Are you in mourning?" Jordana teased, letting herself momentarily forget Brenton's announcement.

"Aye. I'm mournin' my freedom," Caitlan replied with a grin. "This is me uniform. Sad as it may seem, I've never before had such fine clothes."

Jordana nodded. "I've seen them before. I've gone with my friend Meg to visit her grandparents. The commodore does nothing by halves. He expects all of his house staff to look their best." She pulled off her gloves and reached up to untie her uniform bonnet. "I didn't expect you until this evening."

"I know. I didn't expect to be let go so early. I'm allowed to leave after my morning chores are done." She paused and smiled. "Hello, Mr. Baldwin."

Jordana ignored Brenton's entrance into the room. She was still upset to know that he would make such major decisions about their lives without consulting her first. She wanted him to understand how much he had offended her. To imagine that he would assign her to Deighton while he went off to the battlefield was unacceptable.

"Now, I thought we agreed you'd call me Brenton," he said softly.

"Aye, we did. I forgot," Caitlan replied.

They took seats and waited until Mrs. Clairmont had gone about her business before Jordana asked Caitlan how she liked working for the Vanderbilts.

" 'Tis a grand house, to be sure," Caitlan said appreciatively, "but I've already made trouble for meself. The housekeeper in charge doesn't much like me. I'm supposin' it's because I have a temper." She smiled at this and a giggle escaped Jordana's lips.

"Surely not!" Jordana teased, deciding she could deal with Brenton later. She longed for news of G.W. and waited patiently for a chance to interject his name into the conversation.

"Aye, 'tis true enough," Caitlan continued. "She's jealous of me popularity with the old commodore, but frankly, 'tis not a position I want to be in. The man has no shame."

At this, Brenton grew concerned. "Has he accosted you?"

Caitlan laughed. "Not outright, mind ya, but I can see mischief in his eyes. Apparently he favors red-headed women."

"Would you like me to speak to him about this matter?" Brenton questioned. "I mean, it's completely uncalled for, and I wouldn't feel right about letting you go back without some assurance of protection."

"Oh, I can take care of meself," Caitlan replied. "He's an old man with fast hands, that's all. At least he's a better sort than me employer in Ireland."

"What happened there?" Jordana asked, watching as a dark cloud seemed to cast itself over Caitlan's face.

"His son took a fancy to me. Wanted me to be a bit more friendly than I was of a mind to be. He threatened me. Said I was good for nothin' more than warmin' a man's bed and told me he'd see me family ruined if I refused to give meself over to his boy."

Jordana gasped at this and Brenton grew noticeably uneasy. They were neither one used to such open discussion of intimate matters.

"I'm sorry," Caitlan said, instantly realizing her mistake. "Me mouth gets me into trouble aplenty. I shouldn't have said that."

"It isn't that," Brenton replied before Jordana could speak. "It's just unthinkable that such behavior would go unpunished."

"I tried to handle it meself," Caitlan said thoughtfully. "I just didn't expect to be treated so brutally. The old man encouraged his son to have his fun, and it finally got to be too much for me comfort. 'Tis why me family had to get me to America in short order."

"I had no idea," Jordana replied. "But now that I do, I can't imagine letting you continue in the same situation with the Vanderbilts. It's no wonder they have to constantly hire new maids."

"I should go and speak to him," Brenton interjected.

"Yes, you should let Brenton at least talk to him. After all, my brother won't be around here much longer," Jordana said, unable to keep the disapproval from her tone.

"Yar leavin'?" Caitlan glanced quickly at Brenton with unmistakable regret in her tone.

Brenton looked first to Jordana and then to Caitlan. His expression was one of pleading, but Jordana refused to allow him any comfort in the matter. She simply crossed her arms and cocked her head slightly to the right.

Finally Brenton spoke. "Yes. I'm returning to our hometown of Baltimore, where I plan to enlist in the militia. Our country is at war, and I feel it is my duty."

"I don't know much about that kind of duty," Caitlan replied, "but I've had a gutful of warrin' ways. Me country is always in some state of war. The landlords fight the tenants. The government fights the church, and the church in turn fights with God." Her voice betrayed the bitterness in her heart. " 'Tis not a noble thing, these wars. And in a war such as yars, no one can win."

Jordana could tell that Brenton was moved by Caitlan's words. She wondered if they might make a difference in his plans. She prayed they would. Prayed that somehow God would help her beloved brother see reason before it was too late.

"It may seem that way," Brenton replied, "but there are right and wrong issues in this matter. There are things that must be dealt with and issues that can't be ignored. I have a duty to those needs."

Caitlan nodded. "Aye, duty is a strict mistress."

Jordana watched the exchange between the two, wondering if there wasn't something she was missing. Brenton's prideful nature seemed to be determining his future, while Caitlan's past seemed to be determining hers. That only left one question. What would determine the future for Jordana?

"So tell me of G.W. Has he regained his strength?" Jordana finally asked.

"No, and in some ways the family says he seems worse. The doctors aren't at all sure what's wrong."

"I suppose I'm to blame," Jordana replied weakly.

"How can you say that?" Brenton questioned.

"Ya can hardly be to blame for the young master's illness."

"He's probably dying of a broken heart," Jordana said with a sigh. "I refused his offer of marriage, and now you tell me he's sicker than he was. What am I supposed to think?"

"Ya've no business to be thinkin' that way," Caitlan said, patting Jordana's hand. "Men are a tough lot. He'll soon be right as rain. Ya can't be grieving yarself for havin' answered him honestly."

"Maybe you're right," Jordana said softly, but inside she wasn't at all convinced.

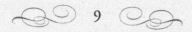

9

It had been agreed upon that Jordana wouldn't come to the Vanderbilt house to socialize with Caitlan. And with G.W. refusing her notes and cards, Jordana was hard-pressed to find an acceptable reason to go calling.

She thought the issue of denying knowledge of Caitlan was poppycock. They all worried that the crossing of such an obvious line of division between the upper crust of New York's most influential people and the lowliest of Irish housemaids might cause more conflict than anyone was willing to allow. Everyone but Jordana thought it far better to pretend the distance existed than to toy with the rules of society.

But Jordana worried when Caitlan failed to show up one Friday in late June. By Saturday morning Jordana decided that whether Brenton agreed to the matter or not, she would take a carriage to the Vanderbilts and check up on Caitlan. She was relieved when she came to Brenton's room only to find him hopelessly overwhelmed with his work.

Struggling to adjust the legs of a tripod that seemed to have lost all hope of control, Jordana stared at her brother silently for several moments before speaking.

"What will you do with your things while you're off playing soldier?" she asked petulantly.

Brenton looked up and frowned. "I don't believe you've ever been quite this angry at me." He put the tripod aside and straightened. "But if you must know, I've already arranged it with Mrs. Clairmont. She's going to keep all of my things here, safe and sound."

"I see." Sighing, Jordana leaned against the door. "I'm not really angry. I'm more hurt. You have always discussed things with me first. Now you saddle me with more months at Deighton, and because you are my guardian under Uncle York's guidance, I have no say."

Brenton came to her and put his hands on her shoulders. "I did what I thought was right. For both of us." He gave her the barest hint of a smile. "Won't you at least try to understand that?"

"I do understand. I'm just afraid of what might happen."

He nodded. "I am too. But I'm also afraid of what might happen if I don't go."

Jordana said nothing. She didn't want to spend the day arguing over what he'd decided. She'd hoped to make him see reason, but time was quickly slipping away from her because Brenton only had a short time left to fulfill his commitment to his present job. With every passing moment, she realized Brenton was determined. There would be no changing his mind this time.

"I'm going shopping," she suddenly said. "There are a few things I need. Do you want to come along?"

"No, I can't. But don't go out alone. I'll speak to Mrs. Clairmont and see if her gardener, Mr. Revere, can take you in her carriage."

"Thank you. That would be very nice."

And so, within a matter of twenty minutes, Jordana was smartly seated in the rather worn Clairmont carriage, heading up Broadway to Washington Place. She'd not bothered to explain to her brother her intentions to see Caitlan. She had simply decided to take matters into her own hands, much as he had done in deciding their future. Perhaps in doing so, she could even resolve her problem with G.W.

"If you'll wait here in the sun-room, Miss Baldwin, I'll send Miss O'Connor to you. I do hope this isn't a matter of concern for our household," the Vanderbilt housekeeper boldly stated.

"No, I assure you it isn't," Jordana answered, refusing to tell the woman why it was she had need of visiting with a lowly chambermaid.

Jordana saw the woman's expression and knew she wasn't pleased to have failed at getting the information. The woman reluctantly left Jordana to retrieve Caitlan, but before Jordana could even sit down, a gruff voice called out in greeting.

"Miss Baldwin, I can't rightly account for the last time I saw you in this house."

Jordana looked up to find the white-haired commodore himself staring at her from across the room. His cheek bulged from an obvious plug of tobacco, and his appearance, as usual, was rather unkempt. "I heard Lizzy say you had come, but I figured her to be wrong."

"Yes, sir, it has been some time." Jordana fidgeted with the ends of her purse strings.

"Well, take a seat and tell me why in the—that is, why you refused to marry G.W. Poor boy is wastin' away upstairs and tells me you won't have him for a husband."

The commodore, well known for his lack of social refinement, not only talked crudely and swore often but also harbored no illusions of propriety. He simply pushed toward the goal he'd set for himself, which in this case was to receive some answers in the matter of his son's love life.

Jordana was unshaken. She knew many a man on Wall Street would rather cut out their tongues than offend this giant of their industry. But Cornelius Vanderbilt hardly seemed a threat to her.

"That, I would have to say, is strictly between G.W. and myself," she replied. "I would very much like to see him."

The old man eyed her seriously for a moment. The look would have wilted a less worthy opponent, but Jordana held her own. "My son is a good catch. Are you addlebrained or dim-witted?" he questioned, ignoring her comment.

"Neither, I assure you, sir. I simply do not wish to marry." She moved closer to where he stood leisurely watching her.

"G.W. always told me you were smart. Refusing to marry into a family with a fortune the size of mine doesn't sound like a smart thing to me." He glanced around him, then spied the spittoon and unleashed a stream of tobacco juice that narrowly missed Jordana's skirt.

"Mr. Vanderbilt," began Jordana, "I am fully in control of my faculties, if that is what concerns you. If you must know, I refused your son, first of all, because I do not desire to marry anyone at this time in my life. Secondly, I refused, because while I cherish my friendship with G.W., I do not believe myself to be in love with him." She gave him a tight-lipped smile. "Does that answer your question?"

"I suppose it does, but it's still addlebrained," the commodore said, spitting again and this time staining the floor of the solarium. " 'Course, I saw what they wrote about you in the paper a while back. Wouldn't have known about you climbin' up that buildin' if it weren't for G.W. tellin' me all about it. I figured it to be scandalous behavior, but G.W. seemed actually quite proud. That was before you met him at Billy's farm."

"Yes, I remember he had the article with him."

"Seems to me that such spunk and bravery is to be admired. You are obviously unafraid of a challenge. So I have to think you must have somethin' of a brain in that pretty l'le head."

Jordana felt her ire building. This old man might well own half of New York, but she wasn't about to be pushed around or insulted by him. "Mr. Vanderbilt, I have already told you more than I had intended. I have come here to see Miss O'Connor, not to discuss my shortcomings. I'd also like to see your son."

The commodore shook his head. "G.W.'s left strict instructions to refuse you. I can't say I understand it, but as sick as the boy is, it hardly seems fitting to go against his wishes."

Just then Caitlan appeared in the doorway. She seemed confused to find the commodore in his frumpy old-fashioned frock coat confronting Jordana.

"Miss Baldwin," Caitlan stated as Jordana opened her mouth to speak. "I didn't expect ya today."

"What is this all about?" the commodore demanded.

"I came to see Caitlan O'Connor," Jordana replied.

"Aye," Caitlan interjected quickly. "I'm to be makin' some dresses for her in me spare time."

Jordana looked at Caitlan and shook her head, but the look on the older girl's face gave evidence to her desire that Jordana say nothing to contradict her statement.

"I expected to meet with you yesterday," Jordana finally said.

"Aye, and sorry I am for not havin' kept our appointment." Caitlan then turned to Mr. Vanderbilt. "Friday is me day off, but what with losin' three maids this week, I couldn't be takin' the time away."

"Yes, well, I can see this ain't no real concern of mine. Miss Baldwin, it was good to see you again. I will tell G.W. that you stopped by," the commodore said. Then after spitting again, this time hitting his target, he made his way off to another part of the house.

"Come on, I'll walk ya out," Caitlan said in a whisper, grabbing Jordana's arm.

"What in the world was that all about?" Jordana questioned. "I was worried sick when you didn't show up yesterday. And now you're treating me like a stranger."

"Ya can't be showin' yourself here as me friend. The likes of the Vanderbilts won't be understandin' such a thing. 'Tis shockin' enough to have ya scalin' buildin's and rejectin' their son's proposal. No sense in further puttin' them off."

"Oh, I couldn't care less," Jordana said as Caitlan led her outside to where old Mr. Revere waited in the carriage. "I was worried about you. After all you said about the commodore, I feared something horrible had happened."

"Oh, to be sure it has," Caitlan said, trying to keep her distance. "The old man sent three girls a-runnin'. One on Monday, another on Wednesday, and the last one on Thursday. The housekeeper told me I had to stay and make up the work until she could hire some more help. She hates me enough, so I didn't want to cause her any more reason to pick on me."

"I don't understand why she hates you," Jordana said, moving toward the carriage, with Caitlan nodding intently, as though receiving instructions.

"I show her up. I work harder than she does, and I know shortcuts to cleanin' things better. Then, too, the old man seemed more favorable toward her until my arrival. It didn't seem to matter that he chased off three maids in one week because of his bloomin' escapades, but when it comes to me, well, that's a different matter."

"I wish you'd just give this up and let us take care of you," Jordana replied. "It wouldn't have to be forever. There's no shame in taking honest help when it's required, especially from family."

"Aye, but it isn't required. I'm quite capable. The housekeeper may hate the Irish, but she doesn't scare me, and neither does the old man."

Jordana climbed into the carriage and leaned over the edge. "I miss you, don't you know? I hardly see Meg now that it's summer, and I was hoping we would have a nice day together. Besides, I was hoping you could tell me about G.W."

"I know, but, Jordana, ya can't be comin' here again like this. There be lines between us and our two worlds that can never be seen as acceptable to each other. The Vanderbilts might think less of ya if ya were to say ya were here as me friend. And I might even lose me job."

"I hadn't thought of it that way," Jordana said softly. "I know this job is important to you."

"Aye, it is. Until I can earn enough money to get to me brother—"

"Oh, that reminds me," Jordana said, reaching into her purse to take out a letter. "I had word from Victoria. It's several weeks old, but look here." She scanned the letter and pointed a gloved finger at the page. "They were making plans to move. She wasn't sure where they would be in the days to come but said we'd best wait to hear from her again before writing another letter." Jordana paused long enough to fold the letter up and return it to her purse. "She says they are doing well—that Kiernan is healthy and happy. She promises to write again as soon as they're settled. I thought you might like to know."

Caitlan beamed her a smile. "Aye, that's good news indeed."

"I've been thinking more about us getting you to California. The more I think about it, the more positive I am that it could work. If we can only convince Brenton to put off this nonsense of joining the militia." Jordana leaned closer before continuing. "And that is where you come in. He cares for you, Caitlan. He considers you as much his responsibility as he does me. If you were to say to him how important it was to you that he take you to California, well, I'm thinking he would agree to it."

"But I'm not in any hurry. Kiernan doesn't even know I'm here. I've been doing some thinkin', and I figure to make me own way and pay him back the money he sent us."

"But that could take years," Jordana argued.

"Most likely it'll take months. I'm very frugal. But at least I won't be goin' to him with me hand empty. I can't do that."

"But this could save Brenton's life. He doesn't know what he's doing," Jordana continued to protest. "I just believe if we give him a chance to see the truth of the situation, he'll see for himself how foolish his ideas are."

"I wouldn't call them foolish," Caitlan replied. "He's a good man, yar brother. He must be all torn up inside to see what's happenin' to his kin and to his home. Men seem to take it especially hard, given their upbringin' to protect what's theirs and hold their families together."

Jordana straightened up and looked at Caitlan in stunned silence. "I suppose I never saw it that way. He's a good man, but he's so young, and he's always been sheltered from life. He's not at all the kind who would make it very well living as a soldier. He couldn't hurt a flea."

Caitlan nodded. "I'm sure yar right. After all, who would know him better? Just don't be afraid to let him make his own way. Ya won't be here alone. I know where the school is. Brenton drew me a nice manageable map for gettin' around. Somehow, we'll see each other and we'll be the good friends we promised to be."

"I'm sure you're right," Jordana said with a sigh. "I just want to keep him safe, even if I know that's God's job."

"It's Brenton's job, Jordana. Leave it to him."

10

"This is a beautiful view," Victoria admitted to Anna Judah. The older woman had convinced her husband to bring Victoria and Kiernan along on this final expedition to Donner Pass before the Judahs returned to Sacramento.

"I fell in love with this country when I first set eyes on it." Anna's eyes glowed as they scanned the horizon. "It has a rugged, unspoiled nature, in spite of the mining communities that surround it. I like to imagine that I could live out my days here in perfect contentment. But I do miss my family back east."

Victoria nodded and looked away to keep Anna from seeing the tears in her eyes. How could she be so easily moved to tears by such a simple statement?

"It isn't easy to be a woman in the West," Anna continued. "There is an isolation out here that threatens to eat you alive. And when your husband is gone, you sometimes question the sanity of allowing yourself to be left alone for weeks on end while he seeks his dreams.

"It's even worse for those women whose husbands die, and that is a common fate out here. Widows are faced with so few choices. Most remarry immediately; others less fortunate end up in nightmarish situations. Frankly, I think we females need to band together and form some sort of social club to look after one another. Our husbands can't always be there for us, and as this transcontinental railroad becomes a reality—and knowing my Ted, it won't be long before it is—more and more men will be sent out on the lines away from their loved ones."

Victoria didn't know how to reply. She hadn't thought about what might happen if Kiernan hired on with the railroad. Anna didn't give her long to consider an answer, however, as she continued to speak on the matter.

"Women seem more inclined to pine away for the things they've left behind. It wears on them, and it wears on the men they love. Some women are never able to deal with the isolation, and it ruins their lives and their marriages." She took a deep breath and exhaled slowly. "I suppose I've even had my moments. I've thought about telling Ted how hard it is when he goes away, but I know it would only cause him to worry."

"I've tried to adapt," Victoria finally said. "I don't always like it, but I deal with it. I do miss talking to my mother and seeing my friends, but I love my husband and do not wish to be separated from him any more than I have to be."

"I feel the same way, which is why I often travel with Ted. I've learned to pack on a moment's notice, and I know just how little we can take with us and still be comfortable."

Victoria smiled. "I don't suppose I've learned the knack of that. It seems we are always at a loss for something. I tried to encourage Kiernan to settle in a bigger city where we wouldn't have to worry about such things, but he doesn't know yet what God would have him do."

Anna laid a comforting hand on Victoria's shoulder. "Sometimes we have to set out, expecting God's direction as we go. Seems to me an awful lot of folks miss the truly important opportunities of life because they hesitate. Fear holds some back, but many are lost for their inability to make up their minds."

"Kiernan is good at making up his mind, but unfortunately he's made some poor choices, and those continue to haunt him," Victoria admitted.

"Everyone makes poor choices."

"Yes, but his poor choices cause him to question his value as a man."

"Men are always like that. Women make a bad decision, and they face the consequences with emotional outbursts and broken hearts. Men, however, see it as a question of their virility and ability. My Ted is no different than your Kiernan. He hasn't always done the right thing, and sometimes even when he has, it has cost him dearly. But he holds on to his dreams, and your husband must do the same. After all, the dreaming is free."

Victoria shook her head at the woman who couldn't be more than ten years her senior. "No, the dreaming comes at a price. And we've paid dearly."

Anna smiled sympathetically. "The actions of trying to bring about the dream might well cost you, but keeping the thing alive in your heart is not only free—it often pays you. The dividends are encouragement, hope, even endurance."

Victoria looked out across the vast expanse of granite gorges and white-rapid rivers. Sometimes she felt as though her life was a series of maneuvers to get from one canyon across another. Would it never be easy?

"I suppose you're right. I just desire so much more."

"But perhaps once my husband talks to yours, you'll have your desire fulfilled."

"What do you mean?" Victoria asked, turning to Anna.

"Ted wants you both to come to Sacramento. We live there, as you know. It would be such a pleasure to have you there with me. You could live nearby, and we could be great friends and share our dreams. Maybe even set up that social club for women. It is just as well I probably won't travel east. That would give me plenty of time to get you established and introduced in town."

Victoria's heart quickened. "That would be glorious." She could very nearly picture it in her mind.

"I can tell it would make you very happy," Anna said softly. "But even if it doesn't work out, I know we will remain good friends. I have greatly enjoyed your company. I know the years between our ages aren't all that many, but never having children of my own, I suppose I tend to mother other women's children."

The reminder of children caused Victoria to instantly close her heart. She wasn't yet ready to give over this part of herself to Anna. The pain was too intense, and in spite of the fact that she'd heard it said that Anna and Ted suffered the same fate, Victoria couldn't bring herself to discuss the matter.

The light was already fading in the west, and with the absence of the sun's warmth, the air had turned chilly. Victoria rubbed her arms. "It's getting colder. I suppose I should go back to our camp and build up the fire. The men will be back from their surveying and expect to eat something hot."

"I suppose you're right," Anna replied with a nod. "Let me gather up my sketching materials, and we'll make our way back together."

Victoria waited while Anna picked up her pencils and sketch pad. Ted Judah had put his wife to work sketching out the countryside. He believed her sketches would speak for themselves and convince investors and legislators alike that the transcontinental railroad would have every possibility of making it through the Sierra Nevadas. It was with Anna's prints and the men's surveys that Ted hoped to inspire the president and Congress to offer aid in seeing the transcontinental line accomplished.

Back at their campsite, Anna reached out to stop Victoria. "Please don't be afraid to come to me if you should need to talk. I sense there is a great deal troubling you, but I won't pry."

Victoria smiled and pushed her chestnut braid back over her shoulder. The older woman's face was softened with concern and sincerity, and Victoria longed to know her better. "Thank you for being so considerate. You remind me a lot of my mother, except she would have happily pried to learn the truth."

Anna laughed. "I'm sure I would like her very much."

Victoria nodded. "Yes. I'm sure you would both be great friends."

Later that night, Victoria snuggled against Kiernan in the shelter of their tent. She knew nowhere else in the world where she could find such comfort and happiness.

"Did ya have a good day?" Kiernan asked her softly and placed a light kiss upon her forehead.

"Anna and I climbed up the mountain a ways, and she made some very lovely sketches. I've never seen country quite so beautiful, unless of course it was in Virginia."

"Ya miss it a lot, don't ya?"

Victoria stiffened. "I wouldn't be happy there without you." She prayed he wouldn't start talking about sending her home to be with her uncle or aunt until her parents returned from across the sea.

"Aye, and I wouldn't be happy without ya here. Still, I know ya miss yar family. I know ya wish for a family of yar own."

The last thing Victoria wished to discuss was their lack of children. Now the issue had come up twice in one day, and the guilt she felt inside was steadily eating at her. She didn't know why God had refused to give her a child, but the issue haunted her and made her life miserable. She had often thought that at least with a child, she might not be so lonely. But still no baby came.

"Victoria?" Kiernan called her name softly.

"Hmmm," she said, trying to sound nearly asleep.

"I hope ya know how much I love ya. Yar all the world to me."

"I love you too," she replied and fell silent.

He kissed her again on the forehead and said nothing more. For this, Victoria was grateful. Her heart condemned her for turning away from Kiernan and shutting him out. She knew the issue of children was one they would have to discuss, but she feared that once the details were laid out on the table, there would be no taking them back. She would have to face that she had failed as a wife, and Kiernan would love her less because she could not give him a son.

She was certain of this. More certain of this than of his promises to love her forever. A tear slid down her cheek, but she refused to wipe it away. Any movement would let Kiernan know she was still awake, and because his breathing had not yet fallen into its deep rhythmic pattern, Victoria remained still. She could not bear to disappoint him, and yet as each month passed by, she was more and more certain she would never be able to give him a child.

What will happen then? she wondered silently. Will he leave me? Will he close his heart away from me? She forced herself to calm. It wouldn't be good for either of them if she began to cry in earnest.

Oh God, she prayed, please help me. I feel so inadequate—so hopeless. Is it too much to ask that you might give Kiernan the son he desires? That you might give me the child I long for?

She thought of Hannah in the Bible. She, too, had prayed for a child, and God had given her Samuel. She had pledged that child to God. Perhaps, Victoria thought, this is what I'm doing wrong. I haven't offered my child to God.

I would do that, she said, her eyes trying to focus in the pitch-black darkness of her tent. I would give him back to you, Lord. I would raise him to love you—to serve you. Couldn't Hannah's prayer be mine?

Kiernan began to snore and Victoria sighed in relief. He only did this when he slept on his back with her in his arms. Easing away from him, Victoria knew he would automatically reach out for her and roll toward her. He did this, and in turn the snoring ceased. Victoria found comfort in the fact that he was so certain she would be there. He put his arm across her waist and sighed.

The action caused Victoria to choke up again. Would the day come when he stopped reaching out? If she couldn't give him a child, would he no longer care whether she was there or not? The questions had no answers, and they pierced her heart with a sorrow she could not put into words. Her only hope was that God would hear her prayer.

No, she thought, remembering her mother's words from long ago. *"God is your hope."* With or without giving her a child to love, God would still be her hope. She had to remember that. She had to cling to that one thought.

97

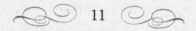

11

"Now, don't cry," Brenton said, sounding impatient. "I'll be back before you know it."

Jordana shook her head. "You don't understand. You're leaving me here all alone."

"You have Caitlan," Brenton encouraged.

"Aye. I'll not let ya get lonely," Caitlan assured, looping her arm through Jordana's.

Jordana glanced into her new friend's green eyes and found nothing but sympathy and assurance. Somehow, even though they'd known each other barely a month, Jordana felt confident of Caitlan's sincerity. She was a woman of her word.

"When do you suppose you'll be able to write to me?" Jordana tried hard to control her emotions.

"I'll write just as soon as I can. I'll go first to Baltimore and check out the situation there and speak with our solicitor, then I'll drop you a line before going to see Uncle York. It shouldn't take more than a week or so."

Jordana looked at him and thought he seemed so much younger than his eighteen years. His features were more refined than rugged, and she knew his constitution was not one that would lend itself to great feats of athletics. How in the world would he ever survive being in a battle? He could scarcely shoot straight. Why, she was a better marksman than he was!

"You know this is madness," she said, deciding one final time to try to dissuade him from going. "You can't shoot straight to save your life, and on the battlefield it may well cost you your life."

"Jordana"—Caitlan gently squeezed her arm—"ya don't want to send him off like this. Brenton can decide these matters for himself. He must be trustworthy, else yar folks wouldn't have left him in charge."

Jordana wasn't pleased with the rebuke, even if it was spoken in a kind manner. Still, she reminded herself that Caitlan was only trying to help. Perhaps she saw something in Brenton that Jordana failed to see. Cocking her head ever so slightly, Jordana reconsidered her brother for a moment. Could it be that he was truly as capable as Caitlan believed him to be? Always before, Jordana had figured them to be reliant upon each other; now Caitlan was showing her a side of Brenton she'd not yet considered. The side that allowed Brenton to be strong and independent—totally independent.

Frowning, Jordana decided to keep the matter to herself. She adored Brenton and knew he loved her as well. He was always doing sweet things for her, always considering her needs. Well, most of the time. He'd certainly not considered her feelings when he arranged for her to stay at Deighton. But if that was the way he wanted it, then so be it. She'd have time enough to make her own way, and if Brenton never returned, that was exactly what she'd be doing.

"I'll pray for you," she finally said. Leaving Caitlan's side, she threw herself into Brenton's arms. "Please don't get yourself killed."

Brenton grinned. "I don't intend to."

"I'm sure no one intends to, but people die just the same," Jordana replied, then realized how macabre she sounded. Forcing every protesting particle of her being into submission, Jordana smiled. "But knowing you, you'd be too stubborn to die."

"That's the spirit," Brenton said, but Jordana knew he, too, was trying hard to sound brave for her. "You must both pray and keep each other encouraged."

"We will, won't we?" Jordana replied, pulling back from Brenton to see Caitlan's expression.

"I'll do me best to keep yar sister happy and out of trouble," Caitlan replied.

"But no prayers?" Brenton asked softly.

Jordana knew Caitlan's heart on the matter of God. They had spoken often of the deep wounds inflicted by the religious warfare of her homeland.

Caitlan blushed and turned her gaze upward to the cloudy skies overhead. "If God is up there—He's not listenin' to me." She looked back at Brenton and smiled. "I don't believe in prayin'. No sense givin' ya bad luck by pretendin' I do."

"I don't believe in luck—bad or good," Brenton replied.

They seemed almost at an impasse. Brenton stood quietly studying Caitlan, while she met his gaze with what looked to Jordana to be an expression of pain. Jordana couldn't begin to understand how Caitlan's misery and bitter past had led her to discredit the power of prayer. She wanted to question her more on the matter but knew that now wasn't the time.

Looking back at Brenton, Jordana expected to find him making a stance for supporting his beliefs. Instead, his face held a look of tender concern, and it was evident he had no desire to add to Caitlan's pain by debating the issue.

Deighton's chimes rang from the bell tower and combined with several others from all directions in the city to announce midday.

"You'll have to hurry if you're going to catch your train," Jordana finally said.

Brenton nodded and turned from Caitlan. "Please promise me you'll stay out of trouble while I'm gone."

Jordana smiled impishly. "Would you not go if I refused to promise?"

Brenton laughed and shook his head. "No, but I would go with an easier mind if you would just do this last thing for me."

"Don't say it like that!" Jordana declared and reached out to hug him tightly. "It isn't the last thing I'll do for you. I will behave, I promise. But in turn, you must promise to come back to me quickly. Mother and Father would never have wanted you to leave me here in New York by myself."

"But you won't be by yourself," Brenton reminded her. "You'll have the school and Meg Vanderbilt and Caitlan. I know you'll be in good hands, and you'll hardly even notice I'm gone."

Jordana shook her head, tears spilling onto Brenton's coat. "I'll notice," she said, her voice barely a whisper. "I'll notice."

12

Baltimore shuddered under unreasonable chaos. An attitude of suspicion emanated from every corner of the city. Doors that had once stood open in welcome were now closed and barred. Brenton found it appalling that his hometown should suddenly seem so foreign. He had always loved Baltimore—more than any other city. Perhaps it was its stately grace and charm or the peacefulness of its citizens. But peace was far from evident now, and the sight of armed soldiers marching in menacing order appeared completely out of place.

Baltimore was, in many ways, a city under siege. A cannon atop Federal Hill was directed not at the south, from where the enemy was known to be, but rather toward the city, where the enemy was hidden and could do more harm. Trains were stopped by Federal troops well before reaching the city limits and their contents searched and sometimes even seized. Questions were asked and answers demanded by blue-clad troops who seemed nervous and edgy in their new line of work.

Brenton had argued to be let back into the city. The guards were reluctant to allow anyone in, but especially those who admitted to having been away for long periods of time. It didn't matter to the man in charge that Brenton had lived in Baltimore prior to his departure and had family holdings in the city. Nor did it matter that Brenton had made his residence well to the north in New York City. The man saw Brenton as a potential threat and that was all.

Luckily for Brenton, his good friend Able Stewart was one of the new soldiers to stand guard at the depot. Able had vouched for Brenton, pledging on his honor that Brenton would not take up arms against the Federal troops. The guard had grudgingly allowed Brenton admission into the city, but now that he was here, Brenton longed only to return to New York and forget that he had ever seen such sights.

Anxious to understand what was happening, Brenton made his way first to Andrew Marcum's office. The solicitor stared in surprise for several moments before instructing Brenton to take a seat.

"I had no idea you were coming."

"I know," Brenton said apologetically. "I should have sent a telegram, but I was afraid if I did, you might urge me to remain in New York."

"For certain, I would have," Marcum replied. "Why did you come to Baltimore?"

"I've come to enlist." Brenton took a seat on a hard red leather chair and waited for the barrage of protest that was bound to come.

"Enlist? Your mother and father would never agree to such a notion. Why would you wish to trade your freedom and safety in New York to come here and enlist? The matter is serious, no doubt, but there are men in better positions to see to it. I can see no sense in including you in the fracas."

"It's a matter of honor, sir. I feel it is my duty to support the land I love. I desire to protect Baltimore and the railroad. I believe my parents would appreciate this effort on their behalf."

"But which side will you choose?" Marcum questioned. "Baltimore is greatly divided. Nay, in fact is far more southern in its sympathies. Will you join the Confederacy and support slavery and states' rights to secession?"

"Of course not. I don't believe in the institution any more than you do," Brenton countered. "But the railroad is in danger of being destroyed. People and property will be completely wiped out unless we afford them protection. There's already been a great deal of destruction at Harper's Ferry. I can't stand by idly and do nothing."

Marcum, a man in his late fifties with graying hair and a thick beard, rubbed at his whiskered chin. "It is my sad opinion that we will be hard-pressed to protect the great Baltimore and Ohio. The track runs throughout hostile territory now. You must know this."

"Of course."

Marcum shrugged. "The southern states consider the B&O to be theirs by rights of the land it runs on. Of course, President Lincoln refuses to see it that way. There has been great destruction along the line—fires, explosions, rails torn apart. Protecting the railroad now consists of arresting anyone who looks even remotely suspicious. Why, two days ago I myself saw Union soldiers hauling in an old man and his wife for questioning, all because they were walking to Baltimore via the cleared and easy pathway of the tracks."

"That's outrageous and completely uncalled for. What about our rights? Lincoln suspends habeas corpus and throws innocent people into jail, and all because they were walking down the tracks?"

"The railroads have been nationalized for use by the troops," Marcum replied. "Troops must move freely in order to be successful. This is the first war in America to have such mobility. The railroad may well change everything, and whichever side controls the railroad will probably be the victor."

Brenton's temper got the best of him, and he slammed his fist down on Marcum's desk. "I can't abide this war! We are supposedly fighting for men's rights and freedom, yet I see nothing but freedom repealed."

"In many ways you're right. Businesses have been closed and citizens arrested for nothing more than showing themselves to support the southern cause. As Maryland stands, so must Baltimore, but she will do so only by being held there at gunpoint."

Shaking his head, Brenton closed his eyes and tried to reason the situation in his mind. "Everything has changed."

"It's worse in Virginia. I had a friend come through not long ago, and he was heartbroken at the sight of it. The Union has removed many Confederate families surrounding Washington. Some have been arrested; some simply fled for their lives as the soldiers marched through. Robert Lee's house at Arlington has been confiscated for its superb view of Washington. It's a necessary vantage point according to the Union."

Brenton opened his eyes and stared at Marcum. "How awful! I've been there. I've enjoyed parties upon their lawns. My grandfather Adams is a good friend of the Lees—my father and mother as well." Brenton hesitated before asking the question most on his mind. "What of Oakbridge?"

"Your grandfather's ties to the government and the fact that he freed his slaves has kept it safe thus far, as you know. But now that your uncle has joined the Confederate army—"

"When did this happen?" exclaimed Brenton. "I have heard nothing."

"I recently received a letter from him, in which he also included a letter for you that I was preparing to send to you in New York."

Brenton felt sickened. He would easily side with the Union on matters of slavery and obedience to the law of the country. He would proudly stand with the North and remain faithful to the ideas of a unified nation and liberty for all mankind. But his own family was now at risk. And what of his grandfather's plantation? The ancestral home was now under the care of the eldest Adams son, York. York Adams was, in fact, to act as advisor and guardian to Brenton and Jordana in the absence of their parents. But now that he had joined up with the Confederacy and was no doubt an officer, it was very possible that Oakbridge had been taken over by Federal troops.

With this thought, a hundred questions came to mind. Where would York's family have gone? Uncle York and Aunt Lucy and all of their children lived there. Would they have made it to safety?

"Perhaps I've worried you unduly," Marcum continued. "I can't say that anything has happened to your family."

"Neither can you say that it has not," Brenton countered. "This is complete insanity. How can I take up arms against the South—against many members of my own family? Yet how can I sit idly by while others decide the fate of this nation?" He pulled off his glasses and, placing them on Marcum's desk, leaned forward and rubbed his eyes. "This affair will not be settled easily."

"Without a doubt, you are correct on that matter," Marcum replied. "If the citizens of this city are any indication of the nation as a whole, we will see much bloodshed before we see peace. The riots at the beginning of the war were enough to open my eyes to the seriousness of the situation. To see those in Baltimore who support the South appear with their Confederate flags and clubs, then to watch them attack the Union soldiers and even innocent citizens who happened to be in the way—well, let me tell you, it was a sight I'd just as soon never see again."

Brenton couldn't even bring himself to look up. He simply shook his head and sighed. "I came here with the purpose of enlisting, and now I am hopelessly torn. I pray God will give me some direction, but no matter the answer—it will come at the cost of someone's blood."

"My suggestion is that you go to the house and sleep on it," said Marcum.

Brenton sat up and nodded. "Perhaps." In his mind he was already plotting a trip to Oakbridge to see Uncle York for himself, and if he wasn't there, to attempt to find him. Knowing this would haunt him until he saw it through, Brenton took up his glasses and looked at Marcum. "You should know that my sister Jordana is staying at Deighton for the summer. No matter what happens to me, continue to send her portion of support, as well as mine. She may need the extra money in the maddening days to come. There is also the matter of our brother-in-law's sister Caitlan O'Connor. She is working presently for the Cornelius Vanderbilt house because she refused to take what she calls charity, but who is to say how long this will last? I don't want to worry that either of them are struggling for funds while I'm away from New York."

Marcum nodded and went to his desk to note Brenton's instructions. "I will increase the stipend accordingly. I'm certain your parents would heartily approve of your care of Miss O'Connor."

"I'm certain they would as well." Brenton slowly got to his feet and secured his glasses in place. "If something should happen to me . . ."

He didn't know how to continue the thought. He wanted to make sure that Jordana had everything she needed, and he wanted all of his family to know how much he loved them—that he was willing to die for them.

"If you would care to write a letter," Mr. Marcum suggested, "you could leave it in my care on the chance that the unthinkable should happen."

Brenton considered this for a moment. "Yes. I believe that would be a sound and reasonable thing. I'll bring something by tomorrow."

Brenton struggled with his conscience for over a week before giving up the fight. He would go to Oakbridge and talk to his uncle York, if he was still there. He knew the man to be pro-slavery, but he also knew him to be a loving husband and father who cared greatly for the welfare of his family. Brenton hoped they would still be in residence—and safe from the onslaught of war. If not, then he prayed there would be a way to find them.

Going to the railroad station had proved fruitless. Brenton could in no way secure passage to Washington.

"You should understand, son, all rail travel will be strongly devoted to the military's use. We're moving troops to Washington right now, and I haven't got a spare seat among the lot of them. And what with the renegade activities around the track areas—well, I'm not exactly sure I'd want to ride a train just now," the ticket agent told Brenton that humid summer morning. "It's getting mighty dangerous, and President Lincoln has ordered extra guards along the rails to Washington."

"I have to get to my uncle's home. It's near Falls Church."

The man shook his head. "I wouldn't try it if I were you. They're arresting just about anything out of uniform and shooting anyone wearing colors that don't match their own. I'd stay put."

"Thanks for the help," Brenton replied and turned away to walk back home.

If I can't get there by rail, Brenton reasoned, then I'll simply have to go by horse or on foot. He made his way to the Baldwin house to make his plans. There would be no escaping the city by means of the regular roads, so Brenton figured on finding another way out through the forested edges and back roads. One way or another he had to reach Oakbridge. He decided to seek out Able Stewart's help and see what his friend might suggest.

Days later, the plans were in place and Brenton needed only to wait for the opportune moment. Able had alerted him as to Federal troop movement, as well as sharing what little he knew of Confederate movements. There was no sense in getting caught by either side because either group might be inclined to shoot first and ask questions later. Then, too, in spite of Brenton's support for the Union, his travel to a Virginia plantation would no doubt make him suspect in the minds of the northern soldiers. Just as true, the Confederacy would never accept him because of his inability to support their views. Tempers were hot now, needing little to ignite them. The war was new and men were driven to the cause—whatever that cause might be. Both sides would probably just as soon kill him as have to contend with him.

Brenton stretched out on his bed and tried not to think about the possibility of his own death. He knew his soul to be firmly secured in salvation, but that didn't make him long for heaven as he'd once heard an elderly lady in their church congregation convey. He didn't want to die. He had too much to live for—there was still so much he wanted to do.

He felt a twinge of loneliness, while at the same moment finding himself grateful that his parents had had the good sense to close the estate down in their absence. He relished the silence of the house—the stillness that seemed to engulf him like a mother's arms. This place held good memories for him. Happy times and family. The house represented all that was good and right in his world, and now it welcomed him back. It seemed to have just been waiting for his appearance, as if asleep and unconcerned with the affairs going on around it. But it couldn't stay that way forever.

Startling awake, Brenton realized by the darkness that he'd slept for some time. Yawning, he got up, stretched, and realized his moment of truth had come. Hurriedly gathering his things, he made his way to the stable. The balmy warmth of the night seemed to beckon him into his nocturnal escapades, and Brenton almost began to enjoy himself. He'd never gone on an adventure of such proportions, and the thought of doing something extraordinary and noble appealed to him. Perhaps he would find a way to bring peace to both sides. After all, he had connections to important men in both camps of the war.

The thought fueled his senses. Perhaps that was why God had led him here in the first place. It might be he was on a mission of much greater importance than he had realized. He opened the stable door as quietly as possible and went to the stall where he'd left the borrowed horse he intended to ride.

Brenton quickly saddled the bay and led him from the stable under the shroud of a moonless night. He worked his way down back alleys and side streets until he reached the edge of the city. Now the navigation would become more difficult. He had to remember Able's instructions to the smallest detail because if the war didn't claim him as a victim, then nature might well do the job. There were boglands and ravines, gorges and woodlands so thick a man could lose his way completely. Brenton had to be sure of his moves.

After riding for over two hours, however, Brenton started to relax. He'd seen no sign of anyone, and Able's suggestions were proving a true course. He started to whistle, then caught himself and chuckled softly. It would certainly do no good to announce his presence. He realized more than ever how unskilled he was in secret missions and such.

Father, guide me into your plan. Show me what it is I'm to do next, Brenton silently prayed.

The words were still echoing in his head when he heard the unmistakable sound of a horse's whinny. Startling, Brenton reined back too hard on his mount, causing the horse to protest in like manner. Realizing he'd just exposed himself, Brenton eased back on the reins and sat perfectly still. But it wasn't still enough.

"Look here," a deep male voice called out. "I think we've caught us a spy."

Brenton felt his blood run cold. Weren't spies usually hanged—or shot on sight?

"I'm not a spy!" he declared quickly, hoping the man would listen to reason.

"And I say you are," a big, beefy man replied, coming out of the shadows to take hold of Brenton's reins. "Luke—John—Davis, get over here and help me. We've got us a spy!"

"No, you don't understand," Brenton said, trying hard to remain calm. His heart was in his throat and his hands had gone clammy, but noting the man was garbed in a gray uniform he decided to take a risk. "I'm trying to get to my grandfather's house near Falls Church. It's called Oakbridge. Perhaps you've heard of it."

But no one was listening to him. The burly man held the horse while someone from behind knocked Brenton from the saddle.

"Get up," one of the men ordered. "We'll go back to camp and let the cap decide what to do with ya."

Brenton got to his feet quickly and tried again to explain. "You don't understand—"

"I understand that you're gonna get the butt of my gun if you don't shut up. Now move out," the big man told him.

Brenton did as he was told but found his legs were like rubber.

Fear gripped his heart as never before. He thought of the times he'd allowed Jordana to talk him into stupid adventures. Rock climbing, sledding off the side of a train tunnel, and a half dozen other senseless dares. But never before had he been as frightened as he was just now.

I thought I was on a mission for you, God, he silently implored. *I thought I was doing the right thing.*

They marched through the heavy underbrush for nearly half an hour, and just when Brenton started to tire a bit, the trees opened up onto a small camp. They must feel secure here, Brenton reasoned, because a small fire burned in the center of the camp. Around it, several gray-clad soldiers talked in low whispers.

"Caught me a spy," the big man announced. "Figured you boys would like to help hang him."

All eyes turned to Brenton. The stares were filled with anger, resentment—even hatred.

"I'm not a spy. My name is Brenton Baldwin. I was making my way to my grandfather's plantation. It's called Oakbridge. Maybe you've heard of it."

"I've heard of it all right," a voice called out from behind him. "I know it well."

13

From out of the shadows stepped a tall blond-headed man. He secured a high-crowned forage cap atop his head and finished buttoning the double-breasted gray frock coat that completed his uniform. For a moment, recognition failed Brenton, but as the man drew closer to the fire, the details of his face became clearer.

"Nathan!" Brenton exclaimed.

"You know this spy, Captain?" one of the men questioned.

Nathan Cabot laughed. "I suppose I do. This is my cousin Brenton Baldwin. It's just as he said."

The big man grumbled, looking quite disappointed that there wouldn't be a hanging after all.

"What in the world were you thinking, stalking about on a night like this?" Nathan questioned. "Don't you know there's a war going on around here?"

Brenton looked at the gathering of Confederate soldiers and exhaled rather loudly. "I was going to see Uncle York. I wanted to make sure they were all right. Someone in Baltimore told me the Union troops had thrown Robert Lee's family from the property and now occupied Arlington House."

"It's true enough," Nathan replied. "Most likely true for Oakbridge as well." He looked around him at the loafing men. "Who's on picket duty?"

"We were, Cap," the burly man replied. "That's how we caught us this here man."

"Well, I suggest you men get back to your post until you're relieved," Nathan ordered. The men glanced at one another before giving Nathan a brief salute. Disappointment registered on their faces. Nathan seemed to understand. "Oh, and, men, you did a good job here."

The men grinned, patted each other on the back and, after handing Brenton the reins to his horse, disappeared into the woods.

"Would you like some coffee?" Nathan asked, eyeing Brenton as if trying to size him up and figure out what he was all about.

"That sounds good." Brenton hadn't seen Nathan in at least two years, but they had always gotten along. Nathan's father had disappeared after serving a prison term for attempting to kill Brenton and Nathan's grandfather. There were always ominous whisperings between his mother and Nathan's regarding the man. Aunt Virginia, Nathan's mother, had moved with her little family into the Baldwin house in Greigsville just as the Baldwins returned to Baltimore. There had been several weeks, however, when they all lived together, and while Brenton didn't think much of Nathan's conniving twin sisters, he liked Nathan well enough. The man was quiet and thoughtful, and to Brenton, he made an amicable companion.

Nathan returned with a tin cup for each of them. "Just tie your horse over there." He motioned to a small tree.

Brenton did as he suggested, not wanting to do anything that might be misinterpreted as hostile. He realized there would be no discussing the war without Nathan easily knowing which side he was on. But in truth, Brenton surmised that Nathan already knew which side he'd be on—if, in fact, he must pick just one side.

Moving away from the tents and the other men, Nathan found a dried log and straddled it before handing the cup of coffee to Brenton. "So tell me what this midnight ride is all about."

Brenton took the cup and sipped it. "It's just like I said. I wanted to see Uncle York. I wanted to know if everyone was all right."

"I thought you were up north—New York, right?"

"I was. Jordana still is. I forced her to take a summer term at school. She's not too happy with me," Brenton replied, taking a place on the log. "I figured it would be better for her to stay there while I came down here to check things out."

"I agree. I talked Mother into taking the girls farther south. Uncle York and his family are also gone. I didn't want to make it common knowledge in front of everyone."

"I understand," Brenton said, eyeing Nathan intently. He was little more than a year older than Brenton, but he stood taller and broader, and in many ways made Brenton feel much younger. Perhaps it was the uniform. Perhaps it was the way he'd taken charge when the men had brought Brenton into camp.

"So everyone is safe?" Brenton finally asked.

Nathan nodded. "As safe as they can be. I barely convinced Mother to move before a company of Union soldiers moved in to secure the tunnel area."

Brenton remembered the Baltimore and Ohio tunnel near their home. His father had helped to supervise the building of it, and Kiernan's brother had died in an explosion while trying to break through from one side to the other.

"There are troops all over Baltimore," Brenton said absentmindedly, then instantly regretted having revealed this bit of information. He couldn't quite convince himself that Nathan was the enemy. He fell silent and sipped his coffee, wondering how they could possibly have a conversation without betraying one loyalty or another.

"I know what you're thinking," Nathan said after several moments. "We are in an awkward position here. I know you can't possibly be considering signing on with the Confederacy. I know your opinion on slavery—it just so happens I share that opinion."

"Then how—I mean, why—"

"Why did I join up with the South?" Nathan interjected. "I suppose because I don't like the idea of the Federal government telling the states what they can and can't do. I'm all for being a united nation, but I can't abide that people sitting in one location can possibly understand the needs of folks sitting in another."

"But that's why we have congressmen to represent us," Brenton countered.

"Yes, but it isn't the same. You know it isn't. Do you imagine that folks up New York way understand the difficulties of a southern planter? Do you imagine that we can comprehend the needs of those living west of the Mississippi? Sure, you send a fellow or two to speak out for the cause dearest to your heart, but then ten other fellows who are more closely associated and understand the needs of each other's areas overrule the one or two whose needs are very different. Majority rules. I think the states should make their own decisions, and the government in Washington should stay out of it."

"I can agree with that to a point," Brenton replied. "But we have to have some rules that govern us as a whole."

They fell silent once again. They weren't so very different in their opinions, Brenton thought. He wondered just how divided the nation truly was, or if a few hotheaded men had made a war out of misunderstandings.

"Are you planning to enlist?"

Brenton was startled by the question. "Does it matter?"

"You know it does."

"I suppose I am," Brenton said sadly. He wondered how to explain the situation. "I imagine the choice was easy for you, but for me it wasn't. I'm not a coward—I'd die in a minute if it meant saving the lives of those I love. But sitting there in New York, listening to the excitement—many people are almost celebrating going to war—I was torn. I wanted to show myself as honorable and noble, but the dichotomy of which side I belonged to haunted me. It still does." He stared dismally into his tin cup. "I love my family—all of my family.

That includes Uncle York with his beliefs, and you with yours. To take up arms against them is unthinkable. But I also love my country. I listen to people like my brother-in-law and his sister as they talk about Ireland and the oppression they've come from, and I realize what a blessing it is to be a part of this nation. How can I stand by and watch it be torn in two—and do nothing?"

"I know," Nathan replied, taking his hat off and toying with it in his hands. "I thought becoming a man would give me a sense of power and control, but now life seems just as unreasonable and unpredictable as childhood ever was."

Brenton felt compassion for his cousin. After all, he himself was as confused by the issues of this war. Then a thought came to him. "Would you really have killed me? I mean, if your men had brought in a total stranger—would you have put him to death as a spy?"

Nathan's hands stopped moving and his head bowed slightly. "Two nights back, we found ourselves near the rail line to Washington. A Union patrol spotted us, and before we could all slip into the woods and find cover, they shot two of my men. One was just a kid. He died in my arms—slow and painfully. They knew I was out there watching, and they called to me and taunted me—promising to kill us all. I'd never seen men so angry. With that one simple act the war became very personal. It forever changed me." He swung his leg over the log and got to his feet. Looking down at Brenton, his expression half hidden in the shadows, he added, "Had you been a stranger, I would have handed my men the rope."

He walked away, leaving Brenton there to consider his words. He was alive only because of Nathan Cabot's mercy. He reached his hand up to his throat, feeling a terrible constriction there. He had nearly lost his life this night. It made the war even more real.

Brenton lost track of how long he continued to sit on the log. He watched the comings and goings of the soldiers in the small camp and silently wondered what he should do. There was no sense going on to Oakbridge. Who could tell where his uncle might be assigned? But neither did there seem to be much sense in returning to Baltimore. He was quickly losing his heart for enlisting.

He thought of Jordana and how she might have grieved if he'd been killed, and then he thought of the men Nathan had mentioned and wondered if they, too, had sisters. Who would have gone to them to tell the story of what had happened? Would they believe their brothers to be heroes for the cause? It all seemed so pointless. Brenton felt disillusioned and frustrated.

"What am I supposed to do now, Lord?" he whispered, glancing heavenward to the starry night skies. Without the moon, the stars shone bright and seemed so clear that Brenton could imagine reaching up to touch them. He wished he could photograph the sight and keep it with him always—crisp, clean, glorious. But even if such a thing were possible, he knew the photograph would never equal the awesome wonder of the real thing. Maybe he appreciated it more because his life had just been spared. It seemed strange to even consider such a thing—he would be dead by now had it not been for one man's intercession. And God's.

"Brenton!" Nathan called as he emerged from what appeared to be the main tent.

Brenton got to his feet and grabbed up the empty coffee mug. He walked slowly toward Nathan, whose features now held a more severe expression.

"The major wants to see you," he said simply and pulled back the flap to his tent.

Brenton entered, his heart thudding. Had Nathan's orders been overturned? Were they now going to reverse the matter and hang him anyway?

A small, unassuming figure sat at a crude table. He eyed Brenton for a moment, then gave a laugh. "You look just like your grandmother."

Brenton was taken aback for a moment. "I beg your pardon?" It was a comment he was used to hearing, but this time it was most unexpected.

"I knew your grandparents, Edith and Leland Baldwin. Captain Cabot was just telling me about you, and I knew I would have to speak with you myself. The name is Van Dyke. Major Van Dyke."

"I'm glad to make your acquaintance, sir," Brenton said, holding out his hand nervously.

The major shook it, then glanced down at the paper on the table. "I understand you've not yet enlisted on either side for this war."

"That's correct, sir."

"Are you still of a mind to enlist with the Union?" questioned the major, his small beady eyes narrowing as he watched Brenton.

"To be quite honest," Brenton said, deciding that total honesty was the only thing he could give the man, "I'm hard-pressed to know what to do."

The man nodded. "Captain Cabot was just telling me of your dilemma."

Brenton felt his knees begin to shake and prayed for strength to endure whatever might come.

"Mr. Baldwin, I am going to consider you a prisoner of war," the major said after a lengthy pause.

"But I already told Nathan—"

"Hear me out," the major interjected, picking up a piece of paper from the table. "As a prisoner of war, your fate is in my hands. I am offering you a parole—on one condition."

Brenton tried to force himself to breathe normally. "What condition is that, sir?"

"You must sign this agreement. It simply states you will not bear arms against the Confederacy at this time—or anytime in the future." A slow smile crept across the man's face. "I believe it will relieve you of this entire complicated matter. It's an honorable way out, because believe me, if you do not sign, I'll be forced to send you south with the men who are camped just beyond this ridge. You may not know it, but there are over three hundred men out there, and I don't think they'd treat you quite as kindly as your cousin has—or for that matter, as I have. There's fighting going on all over Virginia, and these men are itching for a fight. To many of them this is just a big adventure."

Brenton looked at the man and realized what was happening. By signing, he would pledge his good name and honor to uphold the conditions of the arrangement. No one could question his bravery or his politics then. He would have signed a gentleman's agreement, and as a gentleman he would be expected—although reluctantly by some—to uphold it.

"I'll sign it," Brenton said, reaching out to take the paper. Gone were all illusions of becoming some great mediator for God and man.

"I thought you might," the major replied. He handed him a pen. As Brenton signed a copy for each party, the major added, "Captain Cabot will escort you to safety. I wish you the very best."

Brenton handed him the paper, keeping the additional copy for himself. "I wish the best for all of us. I pray this war might be resolved before any more men die."

The major's expression grew solemn. "It is my prayer as well."

———

Back in Baltimore, Brenton tried hard not to think of the regretful look on Nathan's face as he had turned to rejoin his regiment. There was something in his expression that made Brenton believe he would just as soon have joined him on the journey back to Baltimore and north.

Brenton said nothing of his escapades to Andrew Marcum. He picked up a letter from his mother and father and advised his solicitor that he was returning to New York. The man seemed pleased with this news.

The letter, in his mother's handwriting, could not have been more timely. How he missed his parents' guidance. His mother had always kept herself aware of the most current world affairs and now was no different. Her comments on the war made Brenton more sure than ever that he had done the right thing in signing the paper. His mother was understandably worried over a war in America. Especially a war that hit so close to the heart of issues within their own family.

> *It is hard enough to be away from you and your sister, but knowing there is a threat to your well-being causes me great worry. I have prayed and asked God to strengthen you as you face this crisis. Your father and I are unable to leave at this point. Amelia has taken ill, and though she is out of danger now, she must have an extensive time of recuperation before we can even think of traveling. But please know that you are never far from our prayers. York and Virginia will no doubt ally themselves to the cause of the South, but it is my desire that you refrain from engaging in this conflict. Should York be unavailable to you, remember Mr. Marcum is highly regarded by your father and me. He will help you make the best decisions. Nick and Amelia send their love, as does your father. I love you both so very much. Please remain safe.*

There was a postscript added by their father, confirming his approval of their mother's message. He added that the war would most likely be resolved soon, but regardless, he was counting on Brenton to oversee Jordana's welfare.

Brenton refolded the letter and felt a confidence in returning to New York. His only sorrow came in having felt certain that God was leading him to great things. Now it seemed he would spend the war hidden away in a photography studio in New York, useful only to his sister and Caitlan.

Caitlan. The name made him reflect on all he'd just come through. He'd thought of her briefly when certain he was facing his death. The feelings in that thought had been of regret. Regret that he'd not had a chance to know her better. That he'd not found a way to help her see God as good and loving—or really caring what happened to His children.

Perhaps now he would have a chance to speak with her about her anger toward God. Maybe going back to New York would settle a bigger, more spiritual war.

PART · TWO

JULY-DECEMBER 1862

14

Jordana was awakened by a strange tapping sound. At first she thought she'd only dreamed the noise, but as it became more persistent, she opened her eyes and sat up in bed. Meg was back on Staten Island for the summer, and her bed was very obviously empty. So where was the noise coming from?

Tap. Tap. Tap.

There it was again! Jordana got up from the bed and went to the window. Pulling back the drapes, she nearly screamed aloud at the sight of Caitlan O'Connor hanging on to the ledge.

Opening the window quickly, Jordana took a firm grip on Caitlan's arm. "What are you doing?" she hissed in a frantic whisper.

"Breakin' me neck if ya don't pull me in!" Caitlan's voice quavered fearfully.

Jordana could see that she'd climbed up the narrow trellis that barely came to the bottom of the second-story windows. She anchored her feet against the wall and pulled with all of her strength while Caitlan got a good tight hold on the windowsill and began to hoist herself upward.

"I'm glad ya showed me yar room last time. I might not have known where to find ya," Caitlan said just as Jordana fell backward, with Caitlan plunging hard onto the wood floor right beside her.

"Are you all right?" Jordana was still unable to think clearly.

"Aye. I am now," Caitlan said, easing into a sitting position. "Sorry to give ya such a fright, but I'm in trouble and ya were the only one I could turn to."

Jordana sat up. "You're in trouble? Why?"

"The housekeeper thinks me a thief and threatened to call the police. 'Tis the commodore hisself who could be explainin' it all, but I'm doubtin' he will."

Jordana was completely confused. "Wait a minute. Back up. Why did the housekeeper accuse you of being a thief?"

"Because the commodore lost his watch, and she found it under me bed. For sure she thinks I stole it, but the truth is the old man came to me room and we had a bit of a wrestlin' match."

Jordana's mouth dropped open in shock. "That old man is incorrigible."

"I had to leave," Caitlan said, and her voice sounded sad. "I couldn't explain why the watch was there without havin' the commodore agree with me story."

"But surely he would have," Jordana replied. "After all, everyone already knows how he is with the ladies. Why, he even told Meg that he keeps you there because he likes your spirit. He thought your cheekiness was refreshing compared to those other cowering ninnies."

"My 'cheekiness'! Why, the nerve of the man after the way he behaved!"

"Well, I think he meant it as a compliment." Jordana jumped up from the floor and gave Caitlan a hand up. When they had plopped more comfortably onto the bed, Jordana added, "So what happened?"

"I managed to slip away; then when the watch was found I tried to talk to him. I asked him to clear me name, but he knew all along where they'd find the watch, and he figured it'd give him leverage with me. He offered to keep me out of trouble if I'd be a bit more friendly with him."

"You don't mean—"

"Don't even say it," Caitlan replied, putting her finger to Jordana's lips. "It's foreign ya are to such things. I wouldn't ask ya to help me, but yar the only one who can."

"Besides, you made me a promise," Jordana said, taking hold of Caitlan's hand. "We're friends, and friends look out for each other. I'll hide you here until morning, and then we'll decide what is to be done."

"Are ya sure?"

"Positive," Jordana replied. "Come on. You can sleep the rest of the night in Meg's bed. Things will look better in the morning."

But in the morning, Jordana had no better idea of what to do for Caitlan than she had had in the middle of the night. Dressing for morning devotions, Jordana bit her lip and pondered the problem with grave concern.

A loud knocking on the door startled both girls. Jordana and Caitlan exchanged looks of sheer panic before Jordana motioned Caitlan to get under the bed.

Opening the door, Jordana beamed an innocent smile at one of her classmates. "Good morning, Sylvia."

"Good morning, Jordana. Mistress Deighton has sent me to collect you. She says you are to come straightaway to her office."

Jordana felt the blood drain from her head. Somehow, the headmistress must have found out about Caitlan. No doubt she would severely punish Jordana for her indiscretion. Maybe even expel her.

"I'll be right there," Jordana said, swallowing hard. She closed the door and whispered to her stowaway, "I don't know if Mistress Deighton knows about you or not, but stay here and keep out of sight. I'll be back as soon as I can." She finished tying back her hair and hurried downstairs.

Bolstering her courage, Jordana lifted her hand to the headmistress's door and knocked. The door opened, but instead of finding Mistress Deighton, Jordana was astonished by the sight of her brother.

"Brenton!" she cried and ran across the room to throw herself into her brother's arms. "Oh, Brenton, you are a godsend. I was so worried about you, and you only wrote the one time, and I thought I might never see you again."

Brenton laughed at her enthusiasm and set her away from him. "That might well have been true, but everything has changed. I'll save that story for later. For now, you'll be happy to know I've come back for good. I had a letter from Mother and Father, and they want us to stay as far from the war as possible. I knew you'd want to read it, so I brought it with me."

Jordana took the letter and tucked it into her pocket. "Brenton, you can't know how pleased that makes me! And the timing of your return couldn't be more perfect. I have a rather pressing problem to solve," she said, suddenly remembering Caitlan.

"Oh? I thought you were going to stay out of trouble while I was gone."

"I did," she said with a coy grin. "But this isn't really my problem. Well, it is, but . . ." She glanced around the room and pulled Brenton to the window. "Caitlan's hiding in my room upstairs."

"What!"

She put her hand to his mouth. "Shh. The headmistress will hear you." She glanced around the room. "By the way, where is she?"

"She went to get your records."

"Why?"

"I told her we'd changed our minds about your being here this summer."

Jordana stared at him in wonder. "Truly? You're going to let me out of here?"

"Don't make it sound like I've locked you in a prison."

"Well, that's how it feels," Jordana replied but quickly moved on. "Look, Caitlan's in trouble. I'll explain it all later, but for now we have to make a plan. We need to get her out of New York, so I thought maybe we could all go to Baltimore and—"

"No, we can't go there," Brenton replied.

"Why not?"

"You wouldn't believe what's going on there just now. I think we'd be much better off to stick it out here."

"But Caitlan is being accused of stealing from the Vanderbilts. She didn't do it, of course," Jordana added quickly at the look of shock on Brenton's face. "The old commodore was being too fresh with her, and apparently his watch came off and rolled under her bed."

"What was the commodore doing in her bedroom?"

"You *know* what he was doing," Jordana countered, continuing to glance around suspiciously. "Anyway, the housekeeper threatened to turn her over to the police, and the commodore will only help if Caitlan is more cooperative with him—the scoundrel! So she ran away, and now we have to help her get out of New York."

"I see what you mean," Brenton said thoughtfully.

"Since we can't go back to Baltimore, maybe we should go to Oakbridge," Jordana suggested.

Brenton shook his head sadly. "That wouldn't work either. No one is there, except the Union army. Many of the homes around the Potomac have been confiscated for the army's use. Uncle York has joined the Confederate army, and his family has gone—I don't know where. Probably to stay with relatives in the deep South. So have Aunt Virginia and the girls. I saw Nathan—in fact, he saved my life."

"What!"

"I'll explain it all to you later. Look, I'm not sure what we can do at present. Perhaps Mrs. Clairmont has space at the boardinghouse, though I gave up my own room when I left. I've gotten us rooms in a hotel temporarily. Caitlan could stay in your room until we figure out what to do and find more permanent lodgings."

"Do we have money?" Jordana asked.

"Some. Why?"

"Why don't we take her to Kiernan? I mean, it's summer and you are pulling me from school. You want to go west and photograph the country, and Caitlan must get out of New York and away from the commodore."

"We don't have that much money at our disposal."

"Then why don't we at least go as far as we can?"

"It wouldn't be reasonable. Mother and Father would never approve of it."

"They are very obviously not here," Jordana countered. "Caitlan needs us, Brenton. We can't let her down."

"I don't intend to let her down. What about Meg? Maybe we could take Caitlan to their farm. The commodore would never dream of going there, and Caitlan would be safe until we could figure out what to do. In fact, if I know Meg's father, he'd probably be open to hearing the whole story and still offer his protection."

"Yes," Jordana nodded. "Yes, I didn't think of that." It was such a logical solution that Jordana realized more than ever how much she needed her brother. However, she was just a little disappointed that the adventure of a desperate flight from the city had been nixed. Trying to be more practical, she added, "Meg has extended an open invitation to me. I'll send a message to her right away and let her know what has happened."

"Then the matter seems under control for the moment at least," Brenton said with a smile. "It's so good to see you again. I feel like I've been gone for years instead of just weeks."

Jordana chuckled joyfully. "Mother always said we were more like inseparable twins."

Brenton laughed, then sobered rather suddenly. "You know, we still have the matter of sneaking Caitlan out of your room. How do you propose we accomplish that?"

Jordana shrugged. "She could go back out the way she came in, but I think she'd probably protest. I know—why don't you keep the headmistress busy, and I'll get her downstairs and outside? I'll tell her to meet us in the garden by the big fountain. There's plenty of places to hide out there, and I'm sure she'll be just fine until we can get to her."

"All right. You go along, then, and I'll keep the warden busy," he teased with a smile that lit up his eyes.

"What fun we shall have now that you're home!" Jordana exclaimed. "Without you, I might have perished from boredom."

Brenton shook his head. "Never. You make excitement wherever you go. Father always said you were a one-woman circus, and now I know why."

Jordana smiled smugly and tilted her chin in the air. God had answered her prayers and suddenly everything seemed perfect. Her life was her own again and Brenton was back. Nothing bad could happen to them now.

15

"I think it's terribly rude to make Caitlan pose as my maid," Jordana protested to Brenton as she clung to the rail of the Staten Island ferry.

"I don't like it any better than you, but to do otherwise would arouse suspicion," Brenton replied.

"He's right," Meg affirmed. "My father will love hiding Caitlan out from my grandfather, but he will never accept her as an equal. No insult intended, Caitlan," she added with an apologetic glance at the extra traveling companion.

"None taken," Caitlan said, then turned to Jordana. "Don't be frettin' about this, Jordana. Ya'll see. 'Tis the best way we can be dealin' with the matter."

Jordana frowned and Brenton watched her walk away from the group as if needing time to think it all through.

"Meg, would you be so kind as to keep Caitlan company while I talk to my sister?"

"Of course," Meg said, smiling sweetly.

Brenton nodded, gave a curt bow, and hurried off to join Jordana.

"I hate the ferry ride," Jordana said without turning around to acknowledge Brenton's presence.

"I know you do."

"It's just so frustrating to have to stand about waiting."

"It's better than swimming," Brenton offered.

"Marginally."

"Please don't fret over Caitlan. We aren't trying to demean her. It's just that some folks refuse to see things as we do. Mamma taught us to be kind to all people—to not judge them by the way they talked or the color of their skin. But you have to know that our family was the exception. Remember how the different factions of Irish even fought amongst themselves?"

Jordana nodded. "I remember. Kiernan said it was because they held different beliefs and interests, and some just fought for the sake of fighting."

"Right. Folks here in America are no different."

"It doesn't mean we play along with it," Jordana protested.

"No, I suppose it doesn't. However, this is a bad situation. We need to get Caitlan away from the false accusations. That's what matters now."

The ferry docked and Brenton took hold of Jordana's arm. "Come on. It'll just be us playing parts. Caitlan understands."

Jordana turned and gazed toward the shore. "It's not only that."

"What, then?"

"I guess coming back here also forces me to think about G.W. Nothing seems fair or right, and G.W. figures into that as much as Caitlan. He hates me, Brenton. I asked Caitlan about him, but she couldn't tell me anything. Apparently the commodore has whisked him away to some sanatorium to recover. They believe he has tuberculosis. He refused all my letters," she said in a rather distant voice.

"Your rejection wounded him deeply, but he'll get over it."

Jordana gazed up to meet Brenton's eyes. "But I didn't reject him. Why must a man think that a rejection of marriage is always a rejection of the man himself?"

"Because generally it is," Brenton replied softly.

"The loss of his friendship has left a hole in my heart. First he went away and then you . . ." Her words trailed off as she reached her gloved hand over to hold tightly to Brenton. "Please don't leave me again. I couldn't bear it."

Brenton smiled. "We'll both go our way one day, and it will be good and right. But until then, I'll take good care of you."

"I shall never go away from you," Jordana protested.

Brenton touched her nose with the tip of his finger. "You are such a goose. One day you will find the perfect man, and you will marry and settle down to a happy life."

"Not for a good long time," Jordana replied. "I have no desire to marry anyone."

"What if I find a wonderful woman to marry—?"

"And then you won't need me anymore. We won't have our wonderful talks, and you'll move far away with her and raise a family and take your pictures." She looked as though she might go into a full pout. "And I shall pretend to be ever so happy for you both, but inside I shall know that I've lost my best friend."

"Let us not put the cart before the horse," Brenton teased. "I haven't taken a wife yet."

They rejoined Meg and Caitlan and said very little until they arrived at the Vanderbilt farm. Billy Vanderbilt, Meg's father, greeted them and, after hearing the entire story of Caitlan's plight, laughed heartily, though sympathetically, and declared he might well have a solution.

"But I don't understand," Billy Vanderbilt interjected. "Why are you so devoted to a servant girl? I mean, I thoroughly enjoy thwarting Father's efforts to force the poor child into reprehensible behavior, but I hardly understand your part. Why should you be responsible for getting her to her brother in the West, and why should you have to go along with her?"

His question was directed to Brenton, but before Brenton could answer, Jordana jumped up from her seat, nearly spilling a freshly served cup of tea.

"Because her brother is married to our sister!" Everyone gasped in surprise at this declaration, but Jordana appeared unconcerned. "No one wants to be truthful about the matter for fear it might leave a bad taste in your mouth, but frankly, Mr. Vanderbilt, lying leaves a bad taste in mine. Caitlan is very nearly family, and I won't have her relegated to the scullery so that upper society might refrain from discomfort." She crossed her arms defiantly across her chest and stood her ground.

Brenton and Meg stared dumfounded for several seconds before Billy began to roar with laughter. "Well said! This makes much more sense now. Why didn't you tell me the truth in the first place?"

Jordana took her seat and stared smugly at Brenton, who immediately felt he should be the spokesman for the matter. "We simply weren't thinking clearly, Mr. Vanderbilt. Our concerns have overwhelmed us, and all I can do is beg your pardon."

"I pardon your lies, for although uncalled for, they were given for the best of intentions. However, I do not pardon my father's snobbery, nor his lascivious behavior. My father would do well to remember his own humble roots."

"Beggin' yar pardon, sir, but I found yar father's servants to be far more difficult than hisself. So ya see, there are levels to be maintained no matter yar station," Caitlan said shyly.

Billy nodded. "Well, I think you are all admirable for your pursuits. I'm also quite eager to discuss a little business idea with you, Mr. Baldwin. You say you intend to take photographs of the American wilderness. Is this something you believe yourself to be talented at?"

Brenton felt his cheeks grow hot. "My former employer said I am. All I truly know is that I love doing it."

Billy considered this for a moment. "Ladies, if you'll excuse us, I believe I might be able to provide young Mr. Baldwin with a solution."

The girls looked at each other, then at Billy. They were obviously curious about what the men would discuss, and they were hesitant to be shooed away. They were three headstrong young women, yet they also knew when they had reached their limit, so in unison they rose and exited the room with the briefest of glances over their shoulders.

Had the moment not been so intriguing to Brenton, he might have laughed out loud at the little train of maidens as they seemed to puff from the room.

"You want to go west and photograph the countryside," Billy said when he and Brenton were alone. He went to a secretary and opened a drawer, and pulling out a thick stack of bound papers, he held them aloft. "I have here the beginnings of a major investment scheme. My father believes me to be a simpleton and a dimwit, but in truth, he is the one whose vision is shortsighted. He feels comfortable with his New York empire. He has his railroad and his millions, and he believes the world trembles at his every word.

"But I, on the other hand, see the potential of expanding this country. Sad though it may seem, this war might well be the best thing in the world for the growth of this nation."

"How can you say that?" Brenton could not hide his distaste at such a statement, especially after what he had experienced in the last month.

"It's a simple matter of economics. No," Billy said, pausing to reconsider, "it is more than that. The war, however long it lasts, will end, and then people will seek to heal their wounds. This country will not be divided for long. It's no different than an argumentative man and his wife. They are bound to each other, and a separation is more costly than staying together. When the war ends, people will desire to get on with their lives. Moving west will appeal to their sense of adventure and their need to focus on something less destructive."

"But without sounding callous, because I am hardly without feeling when it comes to this war," Brenton began, "where do I fit into your scheme?"

Billy chuckled and brought the papers with him. "Mr. Baldwin, the potential is there to set the investment in place prior to the war's ending. If you were to go west, under my financing, and take photographs on my behalf, even act as my land agent, I would have these to offer my potential investors. They would have a chance to survey the West and see the possibilities for themselves."

"To what end?"

Billy pushed aside delicate china cups and saucers and plopped the papers down on the artfully carved table. "To the end that I could convince them that their world is much larger than they think, and in doing so, allow them to participate in the westward dream."

"So I would photograph the country, and you would convince men to invest their money and futures in the great American wilderness."

"If your pictures speak half the volume I see in your eyes, they should do just that. You would also become my eyes and ears west of the Mississippi. By relaying information to me from the West, and by my own ingenuity and supply of information in the East, I can assign you monies to purchase land for me with the hopes that such purchases will prove advantageous."

Brenton smiled. "And you would be willing to back my trip—to help me get Caitlan to California in the process?"

Billy nodded. He smiled and leaned forward. "In fact, she may stay here until the arrangements are made for your journey. My wife can always use another hand with the household. Mr. Baldwin, I believe we can work together on this and benefit both dreams. What say you?"

"I say this may well be the answer to prayer I've been seeking," Brenton said with a smile. "And I know it will meet with Jordana's approval."

"Then I propose a toast," Billy said, raising his glass. "To dreams."

Brenton lifted his own iced lemonade and touched it to Mr. Vanderbilt's. "To dreams."

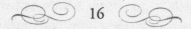

16

"Surprise!" the colorfully dressed partygoers shouted.

Brenton, rather flustered, looked first at his sister and then at Billy Vanderbilt. Both grinned and seemed to thoroughly enjoy his embarrassment.

"Happy birthday, Brenton," Meg Vanderbilt said as she moved closer and offered him a small package. "We've been waiting for you."

Brenton had noticed of late that the girl was growing sweet on him, but he had never seen her as anything but his sister's little friend. Nevertheless, he took the gift and gave her a most chivalrous bow. "Thank you, Miss Vanderbilt."

"Oh, don't go being so stuffy," Jordana said, grabbing hold of his arm to propel him across the room. "We've created an entire birthday supper for you, Brenton. Caitlan even made the cake."

"Where is Caitlan?" Brenton asked, looking around the room. The twenty-five or so people gathered there in Billy Vanderbilt's parlor were fashionable and elegant in their afternoon clothes, and all seemed to be having a wonderful time. Caitlan, however, was nowhere to be seen.

"I'm not sure," Jordana replied with a frown. "Meg lent her a gown, and I was certain she would be here. I don't know what's become of her. I'm afraid I didn't pay much attention."

At that moment a huge cake was carried into the room, and the revelers began to applaud. Brenton felt his cheeks grow hot. He hated anyone making such a fuss over him. But despite his embarrassment, he was touched that the Vanderbilts would rally their friends to act in the absence of Brenton's own loved ones.

Nineteen years had passed since Brenton's arrival in the world, but such affairs and celebrations had never come easy to him. He hated fanfare when he was the focus of it. He would have much preferred being the photographer at someone else's party. It wasn't that he minded being made to feel special, but to become the center of a event was more than he had ever desired. He was glad that only girls had large coming-out parties. Men—at least the men in his family—simply drifted into adulthood rather unannounced.

"Come now and cut the cake for us," Billy said in his fatherly way. It was clear to Brenton that in many ways Billy had simply adopted both him and Jordana into the family. Billy leaned forward and added, "You're about to rob me of the best maid this house ever had. The least you can do is enjoy my party for you."

Forcing a smile, Brenton nodded. "Very well," he said, taking up the knife Jordana held out to him. "But I warn you. I do this very poorly."

"Perhaps you should have trained to become a surgeon instead of a photographer," Jordana teased.

"No," Meg replied, shaking her head. "They would have forced him to join in the war."

Jordana gave her brother a quick look. Though Brenton's avoidance of the army was completely honorable, he still occasionally found himself in situations where others refused to understand, and it caused him distress, as Jordana well knew. She gave a light laugh. "That's true, Meg. We must be grateful for small favors."

Brenton knew she was trying to protect him and was grateful for it. He kept up the light banter as he put the knife to the cake. "So my photography work is a small favor in your eyes, is that it?" He smiled at Jordana, knowing she would realize his teasing was a way to move the subject past the morbid dwellings of the war. It might have worked, too, except that Billy was completely unaware of the exchange between brother and sister.

"As I was telling my colleagues," Billy said, "this war has done a great deal to boost the economy here in the North. After that ridiculous bank scandal a few years ago, this was just the kick in the pants we needed to get things up and running again."

Brenton saw Jordana pale slightly at the comment, but before she could open her mouth to speak, Meg reached out to her father.

"Please, Papa, let's not talk of war today. It's all so sad, especially with G.W. having suffered so miserably from it." She obviously regretted having mentioned the subject in the first place.

But, unfortunately, the poor girl had unwittingly opened another tender subject. The comment about G.W. caused Jordana to wince, and though she tried to turn away from him, Brenton reached out to pat her arm reassuringly.

"G.W. will no doubt recover from his ailments to go forth again into adventure," Billy assured them. "I have a recent letter if anyone would like to read it. He sounds in good spirits, although he grows quite bored with doctors and their treatments. He does try to keep up with the war. He's lost a great many friends already, and it worries him greatly knowing there is no real end in sight. He says the men try to stay positive, but they're discouraged by the entire matter. With the exception of Antietam, the last four major battles have been Confederate victories."

"No doubt it is hard on the Union men to see victories like the Second Battle of Bull Run go to the Confederates," one of Billy's investors said rather stoically. "The Union felt certain they would have victory there and make up for the first battle."

"We've made up for it in other ways," someone else added.

Billy laughed. "If only President Lincoln can settle on a commander. I heard tell that Lincoln once sent a post to McClellan asking that if he wasn't going to use his army, could Lincoln maybe borrow them for a spell?" This brought uproarious laughter from the men in the room, encouraging Vanderbilt. "Then the president got Pope but wasn't happy with him and begged McClellan to come back. Now I hear tell he's gone and fired McClellan again."

As talk of the war droned on, Brenton noted the tension building in Jordana. She was no doubt thinking about G.W. She felt totally responsible for his lack of recovery. He'd questioned Meg, and even Billy, about finding a way to get G.W. to at least take Jordana's letters, but it was all to no avail. It seemed G.W. was nursing his wounded pride. Having been a handsome, well-muscled man, G.W.'s ego had been completely deflated by Jordana's rejection and his own sickness.

"I've heard there is much concern over whether Britain will join in the ruckus," someone said, bringing Brenton's attention back to the conversation at hand.

"That's all we need. The British have been nothing but a thorn in our sides," one of Billy's cronies contended.

"I heard tell they might send troops into Canada," another man added.

"I heard the same," Billy replied. "I say let them. Perhaps it will refocus our own people, and then we can leave off with this war against ourselves."

"I suggest we leave off with this conversation, Mr. Vanderbilt," Billy's wife said, coming gracefully to her husband's side. "You men would talk of nothing but war and profit if we women allowed it. I suggest we eat cake and allow Brenton to open his gifts; then you may all retire to the drawing room and discuss war until your hair turns gray."

"That won't be hard for me," Billy said, laughing. "I've already a sprinkling of the matter."

"Better than our friend Witherspoon here," one of the men laughed. "He suffers from more than a sprinkling." Again laughter filled the air, and Brenton felt a deep gratitude for Mrs. Vanderbilt's intercession.

A half hour later, Brenton found himself the center of conversation in the smoke-filled Vanderbilt study. Billy puffed on a fat cigar, as did many of his associates, but Brenton remained absorbed by a map of the United States and her territories.

"I believe the interest in a transcontinental railroad will drive men west," a thick-chested man said after blowing a long puff of smoke into the already saturated air. "I believe this scheme of yours holds great merit, Billy."

"I wouldn't risk the capital if it didn't," Vanderbilt replied. "Young Baldwin here has impressed me as an honorable and capable young man. He has shown me proof of his work as a photographer, and I must say I'm notably impressed. He has assured me he will not only act as our eyes by photographing our interests, but he will be our voice as well. He will make purchases of prime real estate on our behalf. In return, we will bankroll this expedition and see to it that he is able to fulfill his own dream of putting together a book of western regional photography. Not to mention getting his brother-in-law's sister to California."

Brenton listened to their discussion of his future, all the while forcing himself to appear completely engaged in the map before him. Things were finally coming together. It had taken Billy much longer than anticipated to raise interest in his plan. Throughout the summer and early fall, Brenton had despaired that their plans might be for naught, but now as the month of November opened, he knew an overwhelming apprehension as things were finally taking form. Perhaps because he realized that once they left New York, he alone would be responsible for Jordana and Caitlan. Perhaps because he felt inadequate to do the job.

He looked up to see that the men had completely forgotten him in their enthusiasm for the conversation. He watched them for a moment. They had no concerns except for how to expand their purses to accommodate the new influx of wealth to come. He admired Billy Vanderbilt and thus tried to ignore the rumors that Vanderbilt was often like his father, the commodore, in business dealings. Usually he was completely above board on all matters, yet at other times there were issues that remained questionable. Brenton could only pray this wasn't one of those times.

But given the war and Caitlan and his own parents' absence from the country, Brenton felt he needed Vanderbilt in order to accomplish what was to be done. He would simply distance himself from the details. That way he wouldn't be responsible for any underhanded dealings. At least, this was how he comforted himself.

————————

Brenton wandered over to a window in the study and noticed a familiar figure strolling in the now-dormant garden below. Caitlan O'Connor seemed as forlorn as the dried and withered plants. Yet to Brenton she was also as radiant as the oaks and maples with their brilliant amber and orange and red leaves. The wind blew her gray woolen cloak open, revealing the green satin gown Meg had loaned her. She looked as refined as any of the ladies in the house with her copper curls artfully amassed atop her head. The green fabric must make her eyes seem like perfect emeralds. His thoughts had often strayed to her that day, worried about her absence from the party. He wondered what she might be thinking out there all alone on that chilly autumn day. Then he decided he didn't have to wonder at all. Perhaps she would welcome company.

Vanderbilt's cronies hardly noticed when Brenton made his exit from the study. On his way outside, he noted the ladies were still in the drawing room involved in their own conversations. The party would manage quite well without its guest of honor.

A gust of wind caught him as he stepped outside, and he regretted not stopping for his overcoat, but he had feared being seen by the ladies and pulled into their company. He forgot all about the chill air when he reached the garden and Caitlan glanced up at him, an immediate smile on her lovely face. Her countenance seemed to reflect the golden hue of the trees above.

"Do you mind some company?" he asked as he joined her.

"Not a bit. But is yar party over so soon?"

"They are having a grand time without me." He grinned. "I've never been completely at ease as the center of attention."

"I be feelin' the same way."

"But I thought all Irish liked a raucous time."

"That would be like saying all Americans are industrious," she countered. "And we both know 'tis not so."

"And is that why you didn't come to my party, Caitlan?"

She glanced up at him; then her gaze skittered away. "Would ya be walkin' with me, Brenton?"

Brenton held out his arm, and she hesitated only a moment before linking hers with his. He tried to think it was merely a gentlemanly gesture, yet he couldn't ignore the thrill that coursed through him at her touch and her closeness.

"So, Caitlan," he said to get his mind off what he was feeling, "you didn't answer my question."

"And ya know exactly why I did not come," she answered shortly. "It was yarself who convinced Jordana when I first came here of the masquerade of me bein' her maid."

"But I realized soon after that it was a foolish idea. You are family, Caitlan, and I don't know how it is in Ireland, but at least in the Baldwin family we respect and accept one another equally."

She lifted grateful but sad eyes to him. "And for sure, yar the rare one, Brenton. Ya know well enough most people don't feel that way. The Vanderbilts might have accepted me for your sake, but the fact would never change that I did not belong as a guest at their party. Ya can dress me up all ya like, and I'd still not be fittin' company for the likes of them. And it makes it even worse that I work for them. How do you think the other servants would be feelin' havin' to serve me, their equal?"

"Well, I missed you."

She smiled at him, and he saw that she needed no green material to highlight her eyes. Even with the gray cloak pulled over her dress, her eyes were as green as the isle where she was born.

"I wanted to be there . . . for ya." She sighed and looked away. "I'm hopin' ya understand."

"I do," Brenton answered with sincere intensity. "I see that it is hard to place yourself into a position where you feel less than qualified to perform. It's rather like this whole idea of going to California."

Her gaze returned to his. "And why would ya be seein' it that way?"

Brenton shrugged, initially hesitant to share his inadequacies with this dear girl. Yet he sensed that she more than anyone would understand, and, for reasons he couldn't quite explain, he wanted her to know his whole heart. "My parents entrusted a huge responsibility upon me by placing Jordana in my care, so now I feel I may jeopardize that trust by taking you two west. I feel I am not worthy of the task—not only for Jordana's and your care, but also for the work with which Mr. Vanderbilt is entrusting me."

"Ya'll do a good job." Caitlan's green eyes penetrated his worried soul. "Ya always do."

"Jordana says I'm a ninny for my worry."

"Yar no ninny, Brenton," Caitlan protested, the emphasis of her words touching his heart. "Yar an honorable man. There aren't many like ya in the world, and those we find should be cherished—that is, I mean . . ." She ended in a fluster.

He felt his cheeks grow hot and prayed she didn't look at him just then. "I suppose I must just step out in faith." Caitlan's gaze wandered to the played-out flower beds.

They were silent for some time. Brenton grew so lost in thought he did not notice that Caitlan had looked back to study him, until her soft Irish brogue caused him to turn his head and meet her eyes.

"Yar a good man, Brenton. I believe in ya. I know ya won't fail us."

Her confidence in his ability caused his heart to swell with pride.

She treated him as no other woman did. Even Meg Vanderbilt, in all her girlish adoration, was no more than an awestruck little sister. Not so Caitlan. She treated him like a man. She made him feel alive, special, powerful. If she had asked him to sprout wings and fly, he felt he would be able to do so on nothing more than her desire. She believed him capable of anything—and with her near, he could almost believe it himself.

———

It was after dark when Brenton and Jordana bid their farewells to the Vanderbilts.

"Mr. and Mrs. Vanderbilt." Brenton gave each a bow. "Thank you so much for the birthday party. You have truly helped fill the void left by my parents' absence. I am honored and quite content. I look forward to embarking on our business venture, but I shall miss the company of such valued friends."

"We shall keep in close touch." Billy slapped Brenton on the back. "Come, I'll see you to your carriage."

As a servant was helping Jordana into her burgundy wool cloak, she turned toward her host. She had struggled the entire evening over the matter of G.W. and knew she could not leave without somehow easing her pain. "Mr. Vanderbilt, would you please answer a question?"

"But of course, Jordana," Billy replied. "What is it?"

Jordana finished up her buttons as though gathering her courage with each closure. She looked up to meet Vanderbilt's curious expression and bit her lower lip.

"I never meant to hurt your brother. You must believe that. I care very much for G.W., and I long only that he would allow our friendship to continue. I wonder if you might approach him on my behalf. Might you appeal to him as one brother to another, pleading my cause?" Each word was an agony for Jordana. She took friendship seriously and maintained only a few friends whom she could call intimates. G.W. had been one of those, and now he was gone—not only physically but emotionally as well. The fact tore at her heart.

"Jordana, I will speak to that pigheaded fool and do what I can to rebuild your bridges." He placed a fatherly arm around Jordana's shoulders. "G.W. can be ten kinds of idiot when it comes to getting his own way. No doubt he thinks if he makes you suffer long enough, you'll capitulate to his proposal. But I say stand your ground and follow your heart. Perhaps once this war is over, and you've had time to grow up and experience your own adventures with Brenton, you'll be more inclined to consider G.W.'s request. And by that time his health should be restored and he'll see things more reasonably."

"Perhaps so," Jordana conceded. "But for now, I miss his friendship and hate that he's angry with me. I've never known such a burden before."

Billy chuckled. "I've had many a man angry at me, and my skin is pretty thick, but I wouldn't wish such toughness upon you even if it would lighten your present load." He gave her shoulders an affectionate squeeze. "You are like a daughter to me, which I don't mind telling you is both good and bad. Good, because I hold great affection and concern for you. Bad, because after all these years of fatherhood, my daughters remain great mysteries to me."

Jordana smiled. "My father says that women are always a mystery to men. And my mother assures me that it will always be so."

At this, both Vanderbilt and Brenton laughed.

17

"I think with a little more rest, she'll be just fine," Anna Judah told a worried Kiernan. "Victoria's young. A little pneumonia is a frightful thing, but Doc did a good job in getting her on the way to recovery. And you were right to leave your surveying work in the mountains in order to seek my help in caring for her."

She arranged the covers and touched the back of her hand to the younger woman's forehead. Victoria slept on in complete oblivion, while Kiernan felt useless and totally miserable. He had failed Victoria and their dream, and now, in spite of his finding steady work, they were still practically penniless and dependent upon the care of their friends.

"Now, Kiernan, don't you worry about a thing. Ted told me he was sending you out to talk with Charles Crocker about a job at his dry-goods store. That will tide you over until you can return to the mountains. I think you'll like it there, and I know you'll love it here in Sacramento. Just give it a chance."

Kiernan shrugged, his gaze still fixed on Victoria's exhausted form. She looked like a little girl snuggled there under the covers. Her rich chestnut hair splayed across the pillow, framing her pale face. She'd lost weight she could ill afford and looked as if she could scarcely bear the assault of the sickness. Sighing heavily, he stepped out of the room, leaving her to the care of Anna Judah.

The kindness of Anna and Ted had been overwhelming. It couldn't have come at a more perfect time, and because they were already well acquainted, sharing a working relationship and friendship in Dutch Flat, Kiernan didn't feel quite so misplaced in accepting their charity.

But in spite of this, Kiernan could not put aside his feelings of failure. He had taken Victoria from the family she loved—from the city of her birth—and dragged her halfway across the world. Or it might as well be. There was still nothing short of a lengthy, dangerous trip to reunite them with the eastern coast of the country. And given their financial status, it would take a miracle to ever secure enough money to make their way east.

Kiernan walked to the end of the hall, gazed out the window that filled the little reading nook, and plopped down on the cushioned bench seat. The cranny seemed like something Victoria would enjoy. A little place to curl up with a good book or a basket of sewing and escape the noise and rush of the world.

Putting his head in his hands, Kiernan tried to pray. He prayed for strength and wisdom in order to know what to do next. He prayed for guidance and the ability to endure whatever came his way. He prayed, too, for the health and recovery of his young wife. But no matter his words, his prayers seemed to go no higher than the ceiling before bouncing back unanswered. It was like undeliverable mail. Posts written in haste and scribbled off to the last known address, only to be returned because the occupant had moved to another location.

Had God moved to another location?

Kiernan smiled at his own contemplation. God hadn't moved at all—but perhaps Kiernan had. He didn't want it to be so. He had nearly lost his faith as a boy in Ireland seeing the hopeless plight of his family. Such had indeed happened to his brother Red and other family members. But upon arrival in America, Kiernan realized that facing life alone in a new land without faith was an even worse plight. As he relied more upon God, he gained a hope and strength that his tough, burly brother lacked. He knew he must now cling to his faith, even though, and especailly because, things seemed so dark.

"Kiernan?" Anna Judah called softly.

He looked up and forced a smile. "Sorry, I felt like I should go. Doesn't seem to be anythin' I can do."

Anna smiled sweetly and reached out to take hold of Kiernan's arm. He got to his feet and allowed her to lead him downstairs. "You have a great deal to do. There is much you must and should be responsible for. Don't feel bad that you are unable to be nursemaid as well."

Kiernan nodded and let her guide him to a chair in her dining room. "Now, we will have lunch and then you will go and speak with Ted's friend Mr. Crocker. While you are gone, I shall send my maid out to inquire about housing for you and Victoria. I thought I heard about a little apartment not three blocks from here."

Kiernan sighed. It took every bit of his nerve to admit they were broke. " 'Twould do me little good, even if such a place were available. I've used most of our money just to get us here. For sure we couldn't hike out with Victoria so sick, so we took the stage and it drained our funds. I barely have enough to give ya for Victoria's care."

"Nonsense," Anna said firmly. "You owe me nothing, and you and Victoria will stay on with Ted and me until you're back on your feet. Kiernan," she paused and reached out to take hold of his hand in a motherly fashion, "don't let your pride defeat you. There will be plenty of other chances to prove your manhood. To my way of thinking, it takes a stronger man to admit his need for help than one who allows his family to suffer for his pride."

"Aye," Kiernan replied with a sigh. Anna was a fine woman, but she thought and reasoned as any female would. It was impossible for her to understand the dynamics of his situation. He had taken a wife, and it was his responsibility to support and keep her. His da had never needed to seek another man for help—not while he'd lived. Of course, his mother had needed a great deal of help after his father's death, but that had been different. He and his older brother, Red, had been quite proud, and once they were able to take on the full responsibility of their mother and younger siblings, Kiernan had felt a purpose to his life that he'd never known before. People needed him. People he loved and cared about. Their well-being was dependent upon his ability to provide and do his part. Selflessly he had labored and toiled, always thinking of them and their need.

Coming to this great land had been an extension of that task. He had desired nothing more than to earn enough money to bring his remaining family to America. He mourned that his mother had succumbed to her fragile health and broken heart, but he had sisters and brothers, and they deserved a chance in this golden land of opportunity. The only problem was, Kiernan hadn't seemed able to hang on to that opportunity for himself.

"Ah, here's Li Xian with our soup," Anna said, breaking into his thoughts.

Kiernan looked up into the black eyes of the Chinese maid. She was a tiny woman, barely matching his height while he was seated in a chair. Anna had told them that Li Xian was only sixteen years old but had been rescued out of a life of slavery in San Francisco and brought here by kindly missionaries.

The girl refused to look Kiernan in the eye; instead, she placed the soup in front of him and put another bowl at the place of her mistress.

"Thank ya," Kiernan murmured, knowing the girl would say nothing in response. She gave a tiny bow and hurried back to the kitchen before anything more could be said.

"She's so quiet," Kiernan said as Anna took her seat.

"Yes. She's very shy. It's the way of most women in her society. They are taught to remain silent."

Kiernan grinned. "I can't imagine Victoria assumin' that role."

Anna laughed. "Nor can I. Your wife is quite a woman. I have come to love her company, and I shall miss her when I go east with Ted."

"And when will ya go?"

"Not for a time. Ted thinks maybe next summer or even later. Hopefully by then the war will be over."

Kiernan nodded. "I know Victoria will miss ya greatly. Maybe the war will indeed end before then, and maybe I'll strike it rich in the meantime and she can accompany ya in order to visit her parents." He paused and shook his head in defeat. "Of course, maybe the Sierra Nevadas will simply part like the Red Sea and let yar husband lay the railroad through without any need to blast."

Anna smiled. "Have faith, Kiernan. This is but a minor setback. Things will get better. You'll see."

———

Kiernan's meeting with Charles Crocker seemed to reaffirm Anna's suggestion. Crocker, a tall, heavyset man of forty, was one of the board of directors for the newly formed Central Pacific. He had a lighthearted, almost comical disposition—quick with a joke or some other witty quip, and a personable nature that drew both men and women to frequent his store.

"If Ted says you're worthy of my attention, then I trust that's true," Crocker said, securing a white canvas apron to cover his clothing. "Why don't you tell me about yourself?"

"There doesn't seem much ta tell," Kiernan said, his brogue getting the best of him. Whenever he was nervous or filled with emotion, the telltale sign of his Irish heritage would ring loud and clear in his words. It wasn't that he tried purposefully to deceive anyone into believing him anything but Irish, but he had tried to talk with less of an accent since first stepping foot in America. It seemed appropriate somehow that he make himself as much an American as possible. After all, Ireland had turned her back on him long ago, and America had welcomed him with open arms. Somehow, his allegiance had made a transfer in the process.

"I came here durin' the famine," he told Crocker. "Me brother Red and I worked for the Chesapeake and Ohio Canal Company for a spell. Then we went to work for the B&O. They were good to us there, and for certain I'd work for them again."

Crocker seemed to perk up at this. "Yes, Ted told me you had railroad experience. Tell me all about it. What did you do for the B&O?"

Kiernan shrugged. "Whatever I was told." He grinned, beginning to feel relaxed by Crocker's easygoing nature. "I laid track, blasted mountains, surveyed on the line with me father-in-law—only, he wasn't me father-in-law then."

"So you met your wife through the railroad."

"Aye," Kiernan replied with pride. "And she's quite a woman. Followed me out here, she did, and I don't reckon I could have asked for a better mate."

Crocker nodded. "I heard tell she was sick."

"She is, but Mrs. Judah is carin' for her. She believes Victoria will be feelin' quite herself before long."

"That's good news. If you need anything at all, you just have Anna send Li Xian on over to get it."

Kiernan didn't know what to say. The man offered him help as though Kiernan could repay the kindness. Boldly, he took his chances. "And would that be meanin' yar offerin' me the job?"

Crocker laughed. "It's always been yours, Kiernan. Once Ted told me about you, I figured you were a man I'd want to keep close at hand. We'll be able to use you once the Central Pacific actually breaks ground. Would you mind going back into railroad work?"

Kiernan thought about it only long enough to remember the image of his exhausted wife so tiny and frail in Anna Judah's guest bed. "I'd go back in a minute."

18

Victoria thrived under Anna Judah's care. She found the woman to be amazingly like her own mother and realized with an aching in her heart just how much she missed her mother's company. It had been so very long since she'd seen any of her family, and even the letters she had come to count on as links to the home she'd left behind were no more in coming. The war had made a mess of things back east, and mail and information were always at a risk of confiscation by the enemy—whoever the enemy might be. In addition to that, Kiernan's and her frequent moving made it difficult, if not impossible, for mail to catch up with them.

Anna's ministerings were welcome in light of this loss. Victoria found her concern to be touching and her company to be the closest thing she could have to home.

"You look simply lovely," Anna told her as Victoria entered the sitting room. "I think that rose color looks much better with your dark features than it ever looked on me."

"You were very kind to have it made over for me," Victoria said, absentmindedly smoothing down the lace-edged collar. "Kiernan said it's his favorite of all the dresses you so graciously gave me."

Anna laughed. "They needed a home, so there was nothing gracious about it. Now come and tell me how you are feeling today. Every day your color looks better and better. Are you quite yourself again?"

"Very nearly so," Victoria replied, taking a seat on the small sofa opposite Anna's chair. "I didn't know a person could be so sick." It had been a month since she had fallen ill in the mountains. And though she still felt weak, she was determined to regain her strength.

"We get a lot of sick folk in the area. Maybe one day you can help me out. I do charity work with the Chinese immigrants. They seem particularly susceptible to our sicknesses. Probably because they've never had to deal with them in their own country."

"I'd like to help you," Victoria replied.

"Then perhaps when you are completely well," Anna continued, "I shall introduce you to the ladies of the local aid society. But for now, we shall simply enjoy each other's company and get you well."

Victoria nodded and thought how very fortunate they were to have made the acquaintance of Anna and Ted Judah. If they'd never gone to Dutch Flat, she might never have known the kindly woman. And that, Victoria decided, would have been a tremendous loss.

Just then Kiernan arrived home, unusually early according to the routine he'd established at Crocker's store. With him came a man Victoria was only now coming to know. Mark Hopkins, another member of the group of men who were quickly becoming known as the "big four" because of their influential involvement with the Central Pacific, was also a co-owner of a local hardware store. His partner, Collis Huntington, was even now in Washington with Ted Judah, and many others who represented the eastern railroad interest, to discuss a transcontinental railroad. The trip had come as a surprise to the Judahs, who hadn't anticipated Ted's return east so soon after his earlier summer journey. Victoria felt guilty that Anna had remained behind to continue overseeing her recovery, but Anna easily dismissed any of Victoria's worries.

"Ted can focus all his energy and attention on his Pacific Railroad bill without worrying about me," Anna had told Victoria. "With the passage of this bill last July, the transcontinental railroad can now become reality. But only if the men involved keep the dream alive."

"Mr. Hopkins, how nice of you to drop by," Anna said, getting to her feet.

"Please don't feel you must rise on my account, madam," Hopkins said, giving her a bow.

A much more serious fellow than any of the other men Victoria had met in connection with the railroad, Hopkins was nevertheless a complete gentleman.

Kiernan left his side and made his way to Victoria and, leaning down, whispered, "And how are ya feelin', me darlin'?"

"Much better," Victoria assured him. "Stronger every day."

"Ya were sleeping so peaceful-like this mornin', I couldn't go wakin' ya up to ask how ya were doin'." He took a seat beside her and waited for Hopkins to join them.

"I had word from Mr. Huntington, and in turn he sent word from your husband," Hopkins told Anna.

"How marvelous. How is the state of affairs in Washington these days?" she questioned, as though she were not in the least bit excited at the prospect of hearing news about her husband.

Victoria knew Anna had been pining away in Ted's absence. In spite of Anna's many assurances that the rest would do her good, Victoria and Kiernan were not convinced by her act. Victoria felt that had she not taken ill, Anna would have found a way, in spite of the war, to convince her husband to let her accompany him to Washington. She and Ted were very close—her love for him quite apparent. With Ted gone, Anna seemed to have lost an important part of herself. Most likely it was this reason that had put Kiernan's mind at ease over accepting charity by living at the Judah home. Victoria surmised this on more than one occasion when her husband had spoken of Anna's needs and felt that at least in this way he was serving an honorable purpose while working to put together enough money for them to start over.

"The state of affairs in Washington remains as always," Hopkins said, his thin, bearded face seeming to take on an even more dour expression. "Too many men playing a game of politics, while the rest of the company sits in wait for some form of assistance. The war is accelerating and thus demanding more attention from the government."

"And my husband?" Anna said.

Hopkins nodded. "He is well. Mr. Huntington and he seem to be at odds quite often, but there is certainly no news in that."

"No, I imagine not," Anna replied with a bit of a laugh. She looked at Victoria and smiled. "Ted and Collis do not always see eye to eye on matters of the Central Pacific."

"Begging your pardon, Mrs. Judah, but your husband seldom sees eye to eye with anyone on the Central Pacific's board," Hopkins interjected.

Anna turned her smile to the man. "Of course, there are times when my husband seems unreasonable, but you must admit, his background more than qualifies him for his opinions. After all, he was responsible for engineering the great Niagara Gorge Railroad in New York, a feat most said could not be accomplished. He was also the man to engineer the twenty-two-mile-long Sacramento Valley line, this state's very first railroad."

"I do not doubt your husband's qualifications," Hopkins replied. "Rather, I question his direction and vision for this line."

At this, Anna again turned to explain to Victoria, who thought the entire matter somewhat confusing. "The board would like to see a freight line established as the Central Pacific continues to develop and survey its railroad. You remember the Donner Pass area, don't you?" Victoria nodded, and Anna continued. "They would bring freight in over the mountains to earn them money while building the CP. My Ted fears that attention will focus solely on profits from this freight road and a local railroad, and that the board will soon forget the dream of a transcontinental line. Is that not so, Mr. Hopkins?"

"Indeed it is true. But your husband need not fear. Just because our pacing is slow and our interests diversified, he needn't believe us to have tabled the matter of this new railroad. The project is one involving multimillions of dollars. It is too big a project to undertake without some formal backing of the United States government."

"But with the government so focused on war," Kiernan interjected, "are ya supposin' they'll have time to worry about a railroad?"

Hopkins shrugged. "That's why we have representatives there even now to help remind Congress and the president of our needs. This railroad cannot build itself on the backs of private citizens. We need the help of the Federal government. Between Judah's perseverance and Huntington's diplomacy and ingenuity, we are bound to see action before they return to California."

"But will the politicians understand the need as they do?" Kiernan asked.

"Let us pray they will," Hopkins replied. "There is already worry among many that if California is not assured of an end to her isolationism, she will find herself seized by the southern sympathizers of this region and declared a seceded state. There is further concern that if the North continues to irritate the British, we will find ourselves facing an even bigger opponent. Huntington says there is fear that the British navy positioned off the coast of California will attack San Francisco. Then surely the whole of California, Oregon, and Washington Territory will fall into their control."

"And for sure we can't be lettin' that happen," Kiernan declared.

Victoria watched her husband in silence. She felt proud that he could hold his own in such a conversation. She knew him to be an intelligent and driven man when the need presented itself. She'd seen that drive when she'd taught him to read so many years ago. She saw it return when she'd grown gravely ill and he'd feared for her life.

She loved him more than she could find words to admit, and she admired his desire to better himself and his family. Now if she could only help him find a way past the guilt and blame he'd heaped upon himself in regard to her illness and their living arrangements.

"I understand," Anna was saying, "that our own representative

Aaron Sargent has become our biggest proponent for the Central Pacific. On more than one occasion he has demanded the immediate construction of the transcontinental line so that another generation of Californians does not grow up separated from the eastern states by the vast western wilderness."

"This is true," Hopkins replied. "However, many are of the mind that we should get this Civil War behind us first—to pay off all expenditures incurred from these hostilities before even considering a transcontinental line."

"Why, that would mean years, maybe even as many as twenty or thirty, before we would see some kind of work proceed toward a unifying railroad," Anna protested.

"Exactly so, madam," Hopkins agreed.

"Well, that certainly is something," Anna replied, easing back in her chair. She allowed the silence to fill the room for several moments, almost as if in deference to her husband, before changing the subject. "Would you like to stay for tea, Mr. Hopkins?"

He shook his head and stood. "No, I'm expected home. Mr. O'Connor was making his way here and was good enough to allow me to accompany him. I only thought to bring you news of your husband. He is well and working hard to come back to California."

Anna got to her feet, and as she did so, Kiernan and Victoria stood as well. "I appreciate your kindness, Mr. Hopkins," she said, extending her hand. "Please do come again."

Hopkins touched her hand lightly, then bid them all good day. It was only after Anna left to walk him to the door that Victoria felt she could ask her husband the reason for his early arrival home.

"Are you unwell?" she questioned.

"And why would ya be askin' that?" Kiernan questioned. "Am I lookin' green?"

Victoria laughed. "No, silly. It's just that you're never home this early. I found it a shock to see you walk through the door."

"And so ya want an explanation," he said, his tone teasing. "Well, then first ya must be givin' me a kiss o' welcome."

Victoria felt overwhelmed with happiness. Kiernan was acting much the same as he had when they'd first married. He seemed light-hearted and jovial—something she'd greatly missed since their arrival in California. She looked through the open archway of the sitting room, torn between flying into her husband's arms and maintaining proper decorum. "But Anna will be coming back."

Kiernan crossed his arms and raised his chin slightly into the air. "Then ya will not be hearin' a word from me lips."

Victoria glanced back again to the open arch. "Oh, very well." She came to Kiernan and melted against him as his arms opened wide. "But just one kiss."

He lowered his lips to hers, and the passion ignited a spark that Victoria had long missed. She had been sick for so long that romance and intimacy had been quietly and most unceremoniously pushed aside. Now, however, she knew the aching, the longing for her husband's touch. She remembered the warmth of his breath against her neck and the shivers it sent down her spine when his fingers would play in her hair.

She heard herself moan softly as Kiernan ended the kiss, and opening her eyes, she met his gaze. His green eyes seemed filled with laughter, and his expression suggested a teasing remark was not far behind. She thought to still such a comment by leaning toward him for another kiss, but he only chuckled.

"Ya said there'd be only one kiss."

She rolled her eyes and shook her head. "Perhaps my senses left me in the wake of my illness."

He laughed and pulled her down to sit beside him on the sofa. "I have news for ya."

Victoria smiled and snuggled against him. "I figured as much. So what is it?"

"We're movin'."

Victoria felt a wave of mixed emotions. Moving? This late in the year? What was he suggesting? Would he tell her how he'd heard about another big gold strike upriver? Or maybe suggest the idea of trekking over to the Colorado territories, where gold was thought to be plentiful?

"And don't ya want to know where we're movin' to?" he asked softly.

"In truth," she admitted, "I'm afraid to ask."

He laughed and tilted her face up to meet his. "Mr. Crocker found us an apartment not far from the store. It's only two rooms, but he says it's a decent place to live, and we'd not be fearin' for our lives or worryin' for our souls."

"An apartment? Here in Sacramento?"

"Aye, and why do ya sound so surprised?" Kiernan questioned. "Did ya think I'd let us go on livin' with the Judahs forever?"

"Why, no, I thought—" She refused to finish. It might make Kiernan feel terrible to know exactly what she had feared he was saying.

But he knew.

"Ya thought I was goin' to move us off to distant parts again, didn't ya, now?"

She drew a deep breath and contemplated whether to be honest with him. He was only now acting like his old self. She didn't want to lose that, yet she didn't want to lie to him either. "I just didn't know what you had planned for us. I was hoping we could stay close to Anna and Ted."

"Yar a terrible liar," Kiernan said, his thumb gently rubbing her jaw. "I know what yar afraid of, and I'm makin' ya a promise here and now. They want me for the railroad, and I'm of a mind to help them out. So at least for a good long while, we'll be stayin' right here in Sacramento. That is, if it meets with yar approval."

She smiled and reached up to take hold of his hand, kissing his fingers lightly. "Thank you, Kiernan. I can't express what it means to me. Anna and Ted have been so good to us, and I've so enjoyed their company."

"Aye, and for sure I know ya have. Ya deserve to have it better, but 'tis all I can give ya right now."

Victoria heard the emotion in his voice and turned more fully in his arms. "It's enough, my love. It's enough."

PART · THREE

JANUARY-FEBRUARY 1863

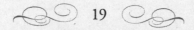

19

"What a wonderful hotel!" Jordana declared, bouncing in an unlady-like fashion upon the end of the double bed. "I can't believe we have found such a fine hotel here in Chicago. The porters were so attentive. Did you see the way they simply whisked our possessions up here and wouldn't let us lift a hand to help? Don't you just love it!"

Brenton shook his head. "I wish I knew what Billy was thinking by sending us to Chicago."

"The railroad commissioners are meeting here, silly," Jordana reminded him.

"I know that much," Brenton admitted. "But Billy doesn't want any of them to know we're at all connected to him. He and his investors want no attention, and I can't help but wonder why."

"Powerful men are always seekin' their fortunes in secrecy," Caitlan said, carefully lifting her suitcase from the floor to the broad window ledge.

"I know." Brenton's voice reflected his worry. What must Caitlan and Jordana think of him? "I'm afraid I won't be of much use to you two. Billy has arranged for me to assume my photography duties. I'm to take pictures of the gatherings, appeal to the commissioners' sense of importance, and listen to whatever talk they offer."

"And what talk will they offer?" Jordana jumped up and retrieved the case that had been placed by the door.

Brenton shrugged. "As I understand it, they are to settle the issue of the location for starting the Union Pacific Railroad. Billy's instructions were quite clear. I am to learn all I can regarding the actual starting point for the railroad. I suppose he will want to buy more land there than in some of the other places we've considered."

"Boring places, if you ask me," Jordana replied. "Such quiet, sleepy little towns. People must perish from boredom out here in the West."

"They aren't perishing from boredom in Minnesota," Brenton replied. "I read not long ago that the Sioux Indians have been on some sort of uprising. It's rumored that hundreds of people were killed in September, and more are surely to perish this winter."

"How awful," Caitlan murmured.

Jordana stared in surprise. "Truthfully?"

"Would I jest about such a grave issue?" Brenton snapped. "You pride yourself on being an intelligent woman. Why don't you entertain yourself with learning what's going on around you?" He immediately wished he'd said nothing. He hadn't meant to get angry at her. It wasn't Jordana's fault, after all. Here they were hundreds of miles from home, and the only news of the land surrounding them and farther west was bad. The war continued to rage long after many had predicted its end. He carried with him not only worry for his family and friends endangered by the conflict but also the nearer anxiety for the journey on which he had brought Jordana and Caitlan. They had been able to come thus far by train, but from here on out their travel would become far more primitive. He constantly questioned his wisdom.

In addition to this, he had found communication lines with their solicitor nearly shut down due to the war, not to mention other natural factors. And in the midst of this worry, Billy had forwarded word that G.W. was not recovering from his illness.

Brenton had said nothing to Jordana. He knew she had been deeply wounded when, shortly before they departed New York, Billy had told her that in spite of his trying to reason with G.W. concerning her need for freedom, his brother refused to reinstate correspondence with Jordana. He told Jordana that G.W. had ceased to be the man she'd once known. Brenton thought from Billy's point of view this knowledge would somehow make it easier for Jordana, but instead it only pierced her heart more deeply. How could he possibly tell her that G.W. was continuing to fail? Surely in time, he would recover. They had only to find the proper doctor and cure, and perhaps with so much time to think, G.W. might even come to terms with his feelings and send Jordana a letter. There was no sense in worrying her until Brenton knew more about the situation and G.W.'s condition. Still, he hated not telling her. Seeing her there so trusting of him, so confident in their mission, Brenton felt a weight of guilt in keeping this secret.

Brenton decided he had to leave before he revealed more of his own fears than he already had. He had to escape the girls' searching expressions, looking so to him for wisdom and direction. "Look, my room is next door—it adjoins your own," Brenton finally said. "I'm going to prepare a few things for the meeting. Why don't you girls have a bit of a rest?"

He walked briskly to the adjoining door and slipped the key into the lock. "See here, it's unlocked now and I will leave it thus. Close it for your own privacy, but know that should you need me, you have only to call for me."

He didn't wait for their response, even though he knew his abruptness might betray his anxiety. He prayed they would believe he was simply wrapped up in issues of railroads and terminus sites. Brenton figured the less they knew about the war and their family and friends, the easier the separation from home would be.

He pulled the door shut behind him and glanced around his room. The porter had stacked all of his photography equipment in a neat pile at the end of the bed. Brenton hoped everything remained in proper working order. If he had learned one thing, it was that life as a photographer had been much easier when the equipment was mostly confined to a photography studio.

Slipping out of his brown frock coat, Brenton loosened his tie and detached his collar. He would have to see about having it washed and starched, along with the cuffs. Vanderbilt would expect him to look his best, but there was no sense in going overboard with too many frivolous expenditures. He could brush the dust from the coat himself and give his own boots a bit of a shine. He knew Caitlan could manage the washing—probably the starching, as well, if given a chance to find the necessary tools for the job—but he didn't like to impose that kind of work upon her. He wanted her to feel equal to him and Jordana. He wanted her to know that he saw her as a woman to be cared for and protected—just as he did his sister. Of course, his thoughts about Caitlan were anything but those of a brother for a sister. She had grown more lovely in his eyes as each day passed, but he said nothing to her. He couldn't even consider speaking to her of his feelings, especially in light of the fact that they'd been upon the road for Billy Vanderbilt for only a month and were scarcely a third of the way through their journey to reunite Caitlan with her brother. It would appear improper, not to mention awkward, to travel as they have been if he made such declarations. But her position regarding God also caused him to hestate, for this was an important issue to him.

When Brenton's last attempt to contact the solicitor via telegraph had proved fruitless, he had apologized to the girls for their predicament. He had no idea where Victoria and Kiernan lived, given that the last letter the solicitor had managed to forward to him had spoken of another move. That letter was nearly six months old, and it seemed foolish to try to locate them based on nothing more certain than this.

Caitlan had actually laughed off the entire affair. She reminded Brenton that she didn't even know Kiernan, and that her escape to America, and secondly, from New York, had been the true driving force behind her travels. Two weeks earlier when they had made a brief stop in Pittsburgh, Brenton had shown Caitlan a telegram from Billy in which he had explained how his father had never intended to have Caitlan arrested. The commodore had found it most amusing that the housekeeper had planned to use the watch incident to rid herself of her main competition for the old commodore's affections, namely Caitlan. Caitlan had been less than amused but was relieved to know there was no wanted poster bearing her likeness in New York City.

The stuffy air in the hotel room seemed to stifle creative thinking, and ridding himself of his waistcoat, Brenton opened a window and stuck his head out into the cold night air. He needed to think—to formulate a plan.

Vanderbilt wanted as much information as Brenton could absorb. Brenton found it fairly obvious that Billy's team of associates could position themselves in the key cities being considered as a starting point for the Union Pacific, and could thus buy up a good deal of the valuable property even before the railroad began laying track. What Brenton didn't fully understand was why Billy wanted it all hush-hush.

Perhaps Billy feared that if the commodore caught wind of his schemes he would do what he could to thwart Billy's efforts. It wouldn't be the first time something like that had happened. Billy had told him of a time when the commodore had purposely advised Billy to take a certain action with his railroad stock—but Billy, knowing his father's competitive and sometimes mean nature, did exactly the opposite of what his father had suggested. The end result was that Billy made thousands of dollars instead of losing his shirt, and the commodore had amusingly told his friends that there might be hope for the old beetlehead, after all.

Brenton couldn't imagine such attitudes and actions between father and son. His own father had always been good to guide Brenton. He could trust his father to have only his best interests at heart when attempting to offer suggestions or direction in affairs related to becoming a man. How Brenton wished he were here now to guide him. Of course, had James Baldwin been in residence when Jordana had talked Brenton into this scheme, they might not be in this Chicago hotel seeking secrets like the good spies they had become.

Spies.

The word reminded Brenton of his run-in with Nathan Cabot back in Virginia. It seemed like a hundred years ago. He wondered how Nathan was faring. Wondered, too, about the rest of the family—family he'd not seen in years—family he might not ever see again.

The Civil War was almost like a distant nightmare now. The paper wrote of it and people fussed about it, but even before their arrival in Chicago, nothing had seemed very real about the conflict. People spoke of battles and of loved ones who'd gone off to join in the affair, but to Brenton they seemed not to fully understand the impact of the situation. Some were almost jubilant to have some link to the ruckus. Didn't they realize how deadly war could be?

"Father, I wish you were here with me," Brenton said sadly. Below him the streetlights flickered hypnotically and carriages moved, sometimes three abreast, as people hurried from one place to another.

"You would tell me what to do and how to go about making confidants of strangers." He smiled to himself. "Or you'd berate me for ever allowing Jordana to set us upon this course."

He shook his head. It wasn't fair to blame this on Jordana. She might have pushed for the adventure, but she wasn't totally selfish in her desires. He knew that if no one else in the world cared about his dreams, Jordana would support them to the death. She loved him and he knew this. They had grown up to appreciate each other, to solicit each other's advice, and to comfort each other in their losses.

No, he wouldn't blame Jordana. Not wholly. She had the adventurous spirit that he lacked. He had the vision and the dream but often found himself void of the nerve. Jordana quickly filled that void with her own enthusiasm and encouragement. She sometimes made him feel as though she looked down on him as a younger brother, instead of an older one, but she never meant it to be cruel. She had merely assumed a role he had allowed her to play. How could he fault her for that?

Yawning, he put down the window and stretched. Tomorrow he would face the challenge of ferreting out information for Billy Vanderbilt, but tonight he longed only for the comforts of home. He pulled off his boots and lay back on the soft bed. He really should check out the equipment and make certain that nothing was broken.

He yawned again. Chicago would no doubt have easy access to anything he needed, should anything be damaged. And since Billy Vanderbilt was picking up the tab . . .

His mind drifted into hazy sleep, while the weight of the world and all his assumed responsibilities pinned him to the bed. Adventure was an exhausting companion.

20

"Frankly, I'm glad Brenton has something with which to occupy his time," Jordana told Caitlan as they dressed for the day. "He seems to feel responsible to look over my shoulder at every turn, and that's hardly the adventure I've been seeking."

"He just cares about keepin' ya safe," Caitlan replied, helping Jordana do up the buttons of her gown.

"That may be," Jordana said, barely waiting for the final button to be secured before hurrying across the room to the dressing table. She picked up her hairbrush and tried to work the tangles out of her hair. "But Brenton needn't worry for me. I'm not as addlepated as he might think."

"I doubt he thinks ya to be addlepated," Caitlan countered. "He's a level-headed man, yar brother."

Jordana tied a ribbon in her hair and took up her bonnet from the table. "He is a good man. I've never said otherwise. I just wish he wouldn't be so serious. He needs to enjoy life. Come on, let's go find our way about town."

"I thought Brenton preferred that we stay here," Caitlan reminded Jordana. "Besides, I'm thinkin' it might be too cold."

Jordana frowned. "You may stay behind if that's your desire, but

I'm going exploring. Brenton says I've been remiss in studying what's happening around me. I shall seek to remedy that this morning."

"Jordana, I want to say somethin' first."

Jordana looked at the worried expression on Caitlan's face and stopped short of opening the door. "What is it?"

Caitlan crossed the room and took hold of Jordana's hand. "I think of ya like a sister, and so I'm givin' ya advice like one. But just as me sisters didn't always care to listen to what the baby of the family had to say, ya might well ignore me too."

"Of course I won't ignore you. What is it?"

"Ya aren't a little girl anymore. Yar a woman, full grown, and men look at ya as such. Ya don't see the changes the way I do, but just in the last few months yar figure has done some remarkable things."

Jordana laughed. "I know I'm filling out a bit here and there."

"Not just a bit, deary," Caitlan laughed. "I seriously doubt ya could scale a wall again, even if yar life depended on it. Just look at ya. Remember the work we've had to do on yar gowns. And tightness across yar bodice ain't the only change. Ya walk like a woman now, yar hips naturally swayin'. Men look at ya in a different way. I've watched the change."

"I think you're overly worried about nothing. I'm not a looker, not in the sense of being any great beauty. My figure may be filling out, and I might no longer resemble the boyish child I once was, but that doesn't mean my spirit for adventure has changed. I won't be cooped up here just because the bodice of my dress has grown tighter."

Caitlan shrugged. "I didn't think it would do any good to speak to ya on the matter." She retrieved her own bonnet and cloak and opened the door for Jordana. "So I guess I'll just have to be comin' along with ya."

Jordana grinned, securing her coat. "We shall have great fun."

———

Jordana made her way from the Tremont Hotel as though she were a woman with a real purpose and destination. She wanted to explore Chicago before Brenton could appear to tell her the idea was out of the question. Not that she'd necessarily let that keep her from enjoying her day outdoors, but she did like to heed his advice whenever she could. She felt it probably bolstered his confidence and ability to lead them. He seemed such a ridiculous worrier, but Jordana knew he honestly cared about her well-being. If only he wouldn't try to fill their father's shoes and fuss over her about everything, from money to her missing out on school.

"Life is a school," she had told him. And to her, it was the best of all possible classrooms. She had always been far ahead of her friends in school. Her time at the Deighton School was more college preparation than finishing and polishing of feminine charms, so her education couldn't truly be found lacking.

"Just listen to the noise," Jordana told Caitlan as they stepped onto the city streets. "It's like New York all over again. I love the city!" She tied the ribbons of her bonnet and waited while Caitlan did the same. It was a frosty winter day, but there was enough of a cloud cover to keep the cold from being unbearable, and for a change there was little wind.

"It stinks," Caitlan murmured.

"It probably smells far worse in the summer when the lake isn't frozen."

"Then I'm glad we didn't come then. I've never cared for the smell of rotting fish and wet canvas," Caitlan replied. "And I heard tell when the cattle are brought into the stockyards for shipping on the trains, the whole city smells of dung."

Jordana snickered. "But I'll bet you will love the land out west. It stretches out in vast prairies and deserts, or so I've read. Just imagine all that fresh air. Don't you simply love the adventure of it all? The exploration—seeing things for the first time?" Jordana glanced around excitedly at the surrounding buildings. "What a wonderful life we have. Just think how different it could be."

"I know very well how different it could be."

Jordana stopped and looked at Caitlan for a moment. Yes, she did know a bit more about life than Jordana did. Jordana figured that because of her growing closeness with Caitlan, the Irish girl would automatically identify with Jordana's lifestyle. But this simply wasn't the case. Caitlan never appeared overly at ease, and no matter where they traveled or how, Caitlan always assumed the role of maid to their little entourage no matter how strenuously Jordana and Brenton protested. Perhaps old habits were hard to shed.

"You know, sometimes I forget your background," Jordana finally said.

Caitlan nodded slowly, a faraway look in her eyes. "But I can't."

Jordana wished she could better understand her friend. Sometimes it appeared as if they knew each other quite intimately. Then at other times, Jordana didn't think she knew Caitlan at all. Caitlan seemed to be good at keeping her feelings and thoughts buried deep inside. Feelings for everything except Brenton. Jordana smiled. Maybe that was the very key she needed to get Caitlan to open up and share her heart.

Pressing on, Jordana hailed a cab and grinned when Caitlan seemed surprised at her boldness. "Come along," Jordana insisted. "I have money for our outing, and I intend that we should have a great and glorious time." Reluctantly Caitlan joined her as Jordana instructed the driver. "We should like to see something of the city." She pressed money into the palm of his gloved hand and waited for him to acknowledge it. "Take us wherever this will allow and tell us everything you can about the sights."

The man grinned. "I'd be happy to, miss."

The carriage driver took them up the precisely ordered streets, which were icy now and banked with shoveled snow. Some neighborhoods were fashionable with lovely carriages in the road and well-dressed people gracing the walkways. Others were less impressive with great swells of garbage in the gutters and animals rooting around for their meals. The river was unimpressive, as were the stockyards with their lingering stench, making both Jordana and Caitlan cover their noses with a handkerchief.

"Have ya had enough of adventure?" Caitlan teased.

"So sometimes adventure smells less than favorable," Jordana replied, laughing. "I'm still not sorry we came out." Looking up the street, Jordana could see that a crowd had gathered to line the avenue.

"What's going on up there?" she questioned the driver.

"I'm not sure, miss."

"Drive closer. I want to have a look."

"Jordana, are you certain this is a good idea?"

Jordana tucked her handkerchief back into her sleeve and cocked her head. "Caitlan, you may go back to the hotel if you wish, but I'm getting out to see what the fuss is all about. Perhaps they are having a parade. Wouldn't that be fun?"

"I'm doubtin' there would be a parade on a cold day like this," Caitlan replied.

The carriage driver pulled as close to the growing crowd as he dared. Jordana thanked him for his kindness and jumped down unassisted. Turning to look back up at Caitlan, she read the anxiety registered on the older girl's face. "Come on, we'll be fine!"

Caitlan stepped down from the carriage and shook her head. "I'm not thinkin' this is a good idea, Jordana. There are a great many dangers in a crowd like this. Too much can happen when ya get men riled up for any reason."

"Oh, don't be such a goose," Jordana protested. She reached out and pulled Caitlan along with her. It was hard to imagine why the girl insisted on being such a ninny when it came to a simple parade. After all, Caitlan had crossed the entire Atlantic by herself. Why should a little crowd and parade unnerve her?

Jordana pushed her way through the mostly male throng, slipping once or twice on the icy sidewalk. Several women were pressed close to the sides of men who were obviously their protectors in this mob. Their expressions were the first clue to Jordana that something other than a pleasantry might be at hand.

Still, she was determined to see whatever was going on, and so she elbowed her way through like a common ruffian. It was in the midst of pressing for a place near the front that Jordana accidentally stepped on the booted foot of one man. She looked up and smiled sweetly, batting her eyes apologetically, and met the stern countenance of the injured party. The man's entire demeanor changed as she continued to smile.

"I'm so sorry," she offered.

"Why, little lady, you'll get swallowed up in this crowd. Let me make you a way."

Jordana loved the feeling of power from his reaction. Maybe there was something to those womanly wiles her mother had often spoken of. She grabbed hold of Caitlan's hand, noticing the disapproval in her expression, as the broad-shouldered man edged out other onlookers and helped Jordana to the front of the line.

"Thank you, sir. You are most kind."

He beamed her a smile just as an armed Union soldier came forward to move them all back. "Step back and clear the streets. We're marching over a thousand prisoners through here, and you'll be trampled in the process."

Jordana looked to Caitlan and then to the soldier in front of her. He reminded her a bit of G.W. Only G.W. was an officer, and this man clearly appeared to be no different from many of the other soldiers who were even now being dispersed among the crowds.

"Sir, what prisoners are you talking of?" Jordana asked him, again smiling and batting her eyes.

The man scowled at her and spit on the ground. "Reb prisoners. There's an exchange going on, and these men are being shipped out. Now, get back like I told you or I'll let them Johnny Rebs run you right over."

Jordana was disappointed that her womanly appeal had not worked in this case, but she was undaunted. At least until he reached out to push her back. Caitlan came to intercede, calling the man several names before admonishing him about his manners.

"Have ya no better sense than to be manhandlin' a lady?"

"A lady wouldn't be standing here with the likes of this mob," the soldier countered. "If you're her nursemaid, then I suggest you get her out of here."

"Now, wait just a minute—" It was the man who'd helped get them to the front, and he wasn't at all happy with the soldier. "This lady has just as much right to see the enemy marched out in defeat as anyone else. You apologize to her."

The man leveled his rifle at the crowd. "This is the only other word you'll get from me on the matter. I said move back and I mean it. This enemy isn't marching to defeat. They're marching back to their homes and will no doubt be back in the war within forty-eight hours. At least one of them will probably attempt to kill one of us before the trip is over, and I don't need the distraction of *ladies* . . . or gentlemen for that matter."

"We shouldn't be exchangin' prisoners for any reason," one of the nearby observers offered. "Should've just put a bullet through their heads and been done with it."

No one replied to this. In fact, the crowd around Jordana became rather quiet and, surprisingly enough, seemed to move back a pace from the street. It was almost as though the reality of the matter had finally sunk in.

Jordana suddenly realized that Caitlan's grip had become quite painful. "Caitlan, you're hurting me."

"Oh!" Caitlan replied, putting her hand to her mouth. "And for sure I'd almost forgotten what I was doin'. I'm sorry."

They could hear drums beating out a cadence, and both turned to see the gray-clad soldiers being herded through the icy Chicago streets. Some men seemed scarcely able to stand, much less keep step with their comrades. Jordana hadn't known what to expect, but what she saw there was more disturbing than she had imagined it would be.

The men were ragged, their uniforms torn and dirty—sometimes not even complete. They must have been freezing in their threadbare coats and shoes with large holes. They blended together in a hodgepodge of colors ranging from gray to tannish brown to a butternut. Different-styled hats and coats were apparent, and very seldom did more than two or three men appear to be dressed alike, but they all shared the same weary expression.

Worse still, some of the men had been gravely wounded. Many slipped along on crutches, often missing a leg or foot, the flap of their pants leg blowing awkwardly to and fro. As they drew closer, Jordana witnessed the evidence of other wounds. One man wore a patch over his left eye, and his right sleeve had been pinned up because there was no longer an arm to fill it.

"You Johnny Rebs should've died in the field," a man nearby was yelling. Others joined in.

"My brother's dead because of the likes of you. I hope you die slow like he did. I hope you know the pain and suffering you've caused!" someone else called out.

"The Union forever!" the man standing next to Caitlan yelled. This drew a rousing chorus of voices who chanted the same.

Jordana grimaced at the hatred. The crowd seemed to cheer each curse and suggestion of death.

The soldiers were now directly in front of where she stood. Row after row, somber faced and silent, they marched by, hardly seeming to notice the crowd that jeered and called out names. Someone threw a tomato at one soldier. He glanced down at the splattering of red, then looked up at the gathering of people. Jordana met his stare and saw the emptiness in his eyes. His devastated expression took her breath.

The Union guard, who only moments earlier had threatened her, now stepped forward to nudge the idle soldier with the bayonet affixed to the end of his rifle. The southerner remained stoic, glancing only at the guard for a moment before wiping the tomato pulp from his coat. This done, he resumed his place with his comrades and hobbled off toward the transport that would take them home.

Jordana felt ill and longed only to get away from the scene. She backed up against Caitlan and turned to her. "Come on," she said simply.

Caitlan nodded, immediately understanding.

They slipped from the crowd, believing themselves to be unnoticed, but the man who'd so kindly helped them to the front now followed after them in protective concern.

"Are you all right?" he questioned Jordana.

"I had hoped we were there to see something wonderful," Jordana replied. "Instead, I'm ashamed to have even been a part of that crowd."

The man nodded. "I have a carriage. Allow me to take you wherever you need to go."

"I hardly think that would be appropriate, Jordana," Caitlan whispered. "Ya don't even know the man."

But Jordana felt weak in the knees, and she longed for nothing more than the privacy of her hotel room in order to think through the events of the past few moments. And the cab they had taken there was now gone. "I'm Jordana Baldwin," she said, extending her hand. "And this is Caitlan O'Connor."

"George Pullman," the man replied, tipping his hat. "Say, you wouldn't be related to those railroading Baldwins, now, would you?"

Jordana nodded and gave him a weak smile. "Yes, as a matter of fact, I am. My father is James Baldwin. He has involved himself heavily with the building of the Baltimore and Ohio Railroad, and there are other Baldwins, distant relatives of his, who are also fond of the rail works."

"I know of them all. You see, I have great plans to affix my name alongside theirs."

"In what way?" Jordana forced her mind to focus on this man's words, trying hard to forget the nightmare behind her.

"I have plans to create a glorious sleeping car. It will be the finest you have ever seen. A hotel on rails. I only need to raise about twenty thousand dollars to put it all together."

Jordana studied the man carefully. He appeared to be more a common laborer than a businessman. "And that is what you are doing here in Chicago?"

"Oh, not just now," he admitted. "I was here in the fall to help mud-jack the city. And I have stayed on to see what might come of the various railroad commissioners meetings."

"How interesting." Then Jordana shivered as a gust of wind blew over them.

"Come," he said with a smile. "Let's get out of this cold. We can visit as I take you home. My buggy is right here."

Jordana looked briefly at Caitlan, who appeared to be totally against the idea. "Very well, Mr. Pullman. Since you are a railroad man, I shall put my trust in you."

He laughed. "Well, I sincerely hope to be a railroad man."

She let him hand her up into the carriage, then watched as he did the same with Caitlan before joining them himself. It was a tight fit, but Pullman did not seem to mind.

"Now where to?" he asked, picking up the reins.

"The Tremont Hotel," Jordana replied.

"Ah, are your people here for the railroad commissioners convention?"

"No, not really," Jordana said, trying to remember what Brenton had told her to say if questioned about their presence. "We're on our way to California."

"Well, you have a long trip ahead of you. Maybe you could wait until the Pacific Railroad is put into place," he said, smiling. "That's why the commissioners are here. They started with a meeting in September and have been arguing ever since. They're deciding all manner of issues related to the transcontinental railroad."

"Do tell," Jordana said, glancing at the man briefly. "Perhaps you will have your sleeper cars in place when the railroad is completed."

"That would be my dream," he admitted. "But for now I've received some satisfaction in seeing the city of Chicago made healthier."

"And how have you done that?" Jordana asked.

"We've raised the elevation of the city by some six feet, bringing the houses and businesses up away from the water. Doctors believe there are dangerous fumes coming from the river and lake. By raising the elevation we hope to give folks better air to breathe."

"We smelled some of those dangerous fumes today," Jordana replied. "But I daresay you will need more than six feet to clear that stench, which I understand is worse when the lake is thawed."

"Aye, that's to be sure," Caitlan finally joined in, appearing to relax a bit now that she was bound to the situation.

Before long Pullman reached the Tremont. He halted the horses at the curb and jumped down. "Let me help you," he said kindly as Caitlan began to dismount. She allowed his help, as did Jordana.

"Thank you so very much, Mr. Pullman," Jordana said. "I hope we shall see more of you and your sleeper car in the future."

He tipped his hat and smiled. "I pray it might be so, Miss Baldwin. It was very nice to meet you. Give my best to your folks." With that, he jumped up into the buggy and was gone.

"A very nice man, don't you think?" Jordana commented as she began walking toward the hotel.

"Yar too trustin'," Caitlan chided. "Yar brother will have yar hide for such a spectacle."

"He doesn't have to know," Jordana replied with a wink. "I won't tell—if you don't."

21

To the best of Brenton's knowledge, the sole purpose of the Chicago railroad gathering was to continue creating a foundation for the Union Pacific Railroad and Telegraph Company. Congress had passed the Railroad Act last year, and Lincoln had signed it into law with the most generous of details put into writing. From there, one hundred and fifty-eight commissioners from twenty-five states and territories were somehow to transform the dream from paper to reality. They would meet along with five additional men, appointed by the secretary of the interior to represent the government's interests.

Brenton had studied the basic details of the act and understood most of it. Congress had decreed that work on the transcontinental railroad would begin simultaneously from both a western and eastern site. The Central Pacific Railroad Company, apparently headquartered in Sacramento, California, would have permission to run track east from Sacramento to as far as the company could manage. Of course, they would have to contend with the granite barrier of the Sierra Nevadas from the very start.

The Union Pacific was to create a main line and central branch that maintained a close proximity to the forty-first parallel. However, to everyone's amazement, the railroad terminus was not to be fixed at the Missouri River, as most had assumed it would be, but rather somewhere around the one hundredth western meridian, which placed it some two hundred fifty miles west of Omaha.

"You look deep in thought, Mr. Baldwin."

Brenton glanced up from his notes to find a man whom he'd met earlier at breakfast. "Mr. Madison, correct?"

"That's right."

Brenton considered the man for a moment. He was tall and lean but younger than most of the other men in the crowded lobby. Perhaps it was his youth that had drawn him to seek Brenton's company; after all, neither one seemed overly suited for the argumentative business of the day.

"My father is tied up with the commissioners," Madison told him.

"Ah, so you're here with your father?" Brenton inquired.

"Yes. He's quite delighted by this railroad expansion business. How about you?"

"I'm a photographer. I'm recording some of these events for posterity."

"How fascinating. But I see no equipment."

Brenton put away his paper and pencil and smiled. "I'm still arranging for some of the settings. These things must have a very definite order."

Madison nodded. "So what do you discern of this affair? Quite a bit of madness, don't you think?"

"I suppose so. I am curious about one piece of information I learned," Brenton said, deciding to just come right out with some of his questions. Surely Madison wouldn't concern himself with why Brenton cared about the details of the railroad.

"And what would that be?" Madison replied, chest puffing out a bit as he threw his shoulders back, obviously pleased to be treated as an equal.

Brenton nearly smiled at the sight of the man, who was so easily made to feel important. "I wondered about this issue of putting the

Union Pacific eastern terminus in the middle of the one hundredth meridian. What is that all about?"

Madison nodded as if he had anticipated Brenton's question. "The problem is the rivalry of Missouri River towns. Kansas City, Sioux City, Omaha, Council Bluffs, St. Joseph, Atchison, Leavenworth. All of these were in fierce competition to become the starting point for the main stem of the UP. So Congress stipulated that they could all build branch lines to the UP. Some will be direct branches; others will be spurs into those branches. But in order to avoid another war, one which would have rivaled the current one, I might add, they have decided that the president will appoint the starting point for a central branch to join the main line. This branch will be set somewhere upon the Missouri River in or around Iowa. All in all, the establishment will allow for the eastern railroads already in place to be easily aligned with this transcontinental railroad."

"I see," Brenton replied, hoping he could remember all the details for his notes. No doubt the cities with branch lines would be of just as much interest to Billy Vanderbilt as the main line's starting terminus.

"I believe what they will find, however, is that the central branch appointed by Lincoln will take precedence over the others. This is supposed to be fair because of the central location and the fact that much of the Nebraska prairie has been surveyed for the purpose of building this railroad, but there are already shouts of foul from those visionaries who believe it will change the course of their town's history."

"But serious building surely can't take place until the war is behind us," Brenton commented.

"My father says the war won't be a deterrent. Determined men will accomplish their will."

"I suppose so," Brenton replied.

"Baldwin, isn't it?" a short, stocky man inquired as he joined the two younger men.

"Yes, sir."

"I believe you're one of the photographers we have here on the premises," the man stated rather than asked.

"Yes."

"Well, then, I need to speak to you on the matter of taking some pictures."

Brenton excused himself from Madison. "It was good to talk with you again. I hope we get another chance before this is all settled and you've gone back home."

Madison gave him a slight bow and went off in the opposite direction while Brenton turned his attention to the portly man at his side.

"Have you ever seen such disorganization?" the man muttered. He waved his hands at the madness around them. "It was less trouble creating the world."

Brenton grinned. "Yes, but the one in charge knew what He was doing."

The man laughed at this and slapped Brenton's back. "I like a man with a sense of humor."

———

With his equipment in place and a full gathering of the commissioners arranged in a frosty outdoor courtyard, Brenton found himself one of three photographers vying for their attention. The air of anticipation was thick, and the men seemed well aware of the profound task before them. The course of a nation would be changed with the decisions made by these men. Brenton marveled at the thought.

For over a week he'd listened to the stories and conversations of the various commissioners. He heard talk of the land beyond Chicago and of the great Rocky Mountains. He listened intently to the conditions of the Railroad Act and how the government would lend money against the building of this great work of giants. Public lands would be given to the railroad companies for each mile actually built; timber, stone, and earth along the way would be open to the railroad's use. The only thing denied them on these lands was the mineral rights.

Brenton thought the offerings were quite generous. So, too, did Billy Vanderbilt, who was enthusiastic about the variety of properties that would likely be affected by the new transcontinental line. He was recruiting more investors as the days passed by, and enthusiasm for the project increased within the hearts of the eastern dreamers.

Brenton also found himself stirred to interest in a way that he'd not been before. As each new detail or complication was resolved, Brenton gained a better understanding of the plans put before them. He could imagine that his parents' joy at seeing the Baltimore and Ohio come to fruition was similar to what he was experiencing as he watched the transcontinental line take shape. He could very nearly put himself in their place, watching and wondering what the new railroad would mean to them and their families. A transcontinental line would allow travel from the East Coast to the West in a matter of days rather than weeks, or more often than not, months. And these men gathered in Chicago would be the ones to see it through.

Brenton studied the commissioners with an artistic eye, but he also tried to see them with an infinitely broader perspective. These were men like Vanderbilt—men like his own father, James Baldwin. They were people who accomplished great deeds and lived life to its fullest. These were men who were unafraid to take chances, or if they were afraid, they buried their fear inside and refused to give in to its destructive power.

He admired their drive—their confidence. Silently he wished he shared more of their characteristics. What made the difference between him and them?

Shaking his head, Brenton rechecked his equipment. The collodion process he would use for this photograph was one that required a great deal of preparation. First he had to secure a nearby room in which to work at preparing the glass plates. The room would be used again to process the photograph after the picture was actually taken.

The trouble with collodion photography was that the plate had to be wet with the solution when exposed to light and, subsequently, the subject matter. Brenton had worked long hours to learn the tricks of evenly distributing the collodion—a mixture of guncotton dissolved in ether and alcohol—but it was ever a challenge to keep the plate wet long enough to be sensitized, exposed, and developed.

He noted that the other photographers were using the simpler calotype process, the one Brenton had used for many of his traveling photographs. With that process, he could prepare the paper negatives ahead of time, expose them on location to whatever scene he chose, then develop them when he returned to his room or wherever else he had managed to set up shop. But because this was more a portrait photograph, Brenton wanted the cleanest image possible. Calotype photography was good, but collodion was better, needing less exposure time and resulting in crisper images. The only problem that worried Brenton was that the air might be too cold.

Seeing the men were ready, Brenton went into his darkroom and began his preparations. The calotypes would require more exposure time, so he felt confident that he could coat the glass plate and return to take the photograph with time to spare.

When he finished, Brenton knew he would have the best photograph of anyone in the group. He hurried his equipment back into the darkroom, where he bathed the glass negative in a carefully prepared solution. Developing the photograph required a bevy of chemicals, most of which were highly flammable, if not downright explosive. Pyro-acid, glacial acetic acid, alcohol, ether, and potassium cyanide were among the tools of Brenton's trade. It was imperative that he maintain his concentration and not lose track of a single element required for his duties. It might have seemed an oppressive task for some, but Brenton delighted in his work. When later he would hold the finished product in his hand, he couldn't imagine himself doing any other job in the world. This would be his legacy to the rapidly growing nation.

Two weeks later, with a package of photographs, including the one of the commissioners, safely off to William Vanderbilt, Brenton found himself wondering exactly what they would do from this point forward. Billy had indicated that he might be joining G.W. in Europe, where he had been sent to convalesce, and if he did so, what would Brenton, Jordana, and Caitlan do in the meantime? Then, too, Brenton realized he would have to speak to Jordana sooner or later about G.W. He had hoped he wouldn't have to tell her of his continued illness; he had figured he could wait until G.W. was on his feet and fully recovered. But from the sound of Billy's letters and telegrams, that didn't seem likely anymore. G.W. might well not recover at all, and to keep that information from Jordana was unthinkable.

"Lincoln frees slaves!" a newspaperboy called out. "Get your paper and read all about it!"

Brenton heard the boy and tried to imagine the impact of the statement. Maneuvering through the crowded street, Brenton handed the boy a coin and took a copy of the paper. He had nearly forgotten the emancipation was to become official that very month. It was a wonderful way to bring in a new year.

"The emancipation of southern slaves substantiates once and for all President Lincoln's desire to lead this nation into an establishment of free men."

Despite Brenton's support of the president's action, he wondered what it would mean to the war itself. Brenton shook his head. Surely Lincoln knew that by issuing an emancipation proclamation for the slaves, he was ensuring that the war would not be easily concluded. The southern states, whose very nature disallowed for so much as a consolidated uniform for their troops or a focused plan for their future, would never be dictated to by a man they already hated and perceived as the enemy. Lincoln could issue all the proclamations he liked, but it wouldn't change the hearts of the southern loyalists.

22

The balmy January day drew citizens from every walk into the glorious California sunshine. Sacramento was alive with activity, as any
capital city might be, but on this particular day the normal pace was
even more pronounced. Today they were celebrating the breaking of
ground for the Central Pacific Railroad, and all of heaven seemed to
be smiling upon their efforts.

It was perhaps a bit pretentious, and definitely premature, considering the sluggish progress of the actual building, but celebrating
the Central Pacific was a much-needed focal point for the masses.
Breaking ground on the railroad that would make its way east to
defeat the granite barrier of the Sierra Nevadas and join the Union
Pacific was something worthy of every citizen's attention. Most of the
revelers had come to California from other parts of the country, but
many of the children who joined in the celebration were native, the
first generation of Americans born in this isolated state. The railroad
was their future—their destiny—as it was every citizen's.

Kiernan and Victoria found the entire matter a strange reminder
of their lives in days gone by. Both had been on hand for the celebration of the opening of the Kingwood Tunnel in Virginia, and both
had shared in the revelry of the B&O reaching completion. Breaking

ground on a new railroad seemed to offer every bit as much enthusiasm as concluding one, and the memories were acute.

"They have no idea what they're up against," Kiernan said as he led Victoria past the swollen Sacramento River and farther up Front Street to where the speeches were about to be issued.

"No doubt that's true." Victoria lifted her skirts a little higher to avoid the worst of the muddy roadway. "But neither did my parents, nor you or any of the others who dreamed of a railroad reaching from Baltimore to the Ohio River."

Kiernan nodded. "Sometimes not knowing is more a mercy than a harm."

Glancing around, Kiernan spied crowds of women positioned on the second-floor balconies of many of the Front Street businesses. Some were clapping along in time with the patriotic marches of a local band. Others simply waved flags and cheered the passersby. He couldn't resist a smile. This day would certainly go down in the annals of the town's history.

Up ahead, near the American Exchange Hotel, a horse-drawn cart stood ready and waiting for the celebration. Draped in bunting and filled with dirt, the side was decorated with a banner that read "May the Bond Be Eternal."

Kiernan found a place for them to watch, just as Charlie Crocker, Ted Judah, Mark Hopkins, and California's governor, Leland Stanford, mounted the steps to the speakers' stand.

"Hey, Charlie!" a man called out, and several voices raised in cheer.

Charles Crocker was extremely personable, and it was probably for this reason that he had been chosen to introduce the governor and start the festivities. A large, robust man, he smiled and waved to his many friends, then raised his arms as a signal to still the crowd. They quieted as their beloved Charlie came forward to address them.

Kiernan knew very little of California's young governor. He listened with an attentive ear as Crocker spoke of Stanford's strong support for the Central Pacific Railroad. He praised the dark-haired man, whose six-foot height and commanding presence brought Kiernan an immediate sense that this was a man who knew how to take charge. Of course, Charlie himself was no slacker in that area. In fact, all of the men positioned on the speakers' platform were men of power and vision. It made Kiernan feel rather insignificant.

"I give you the governor of this fair state, the Honorable Leland Stanford."

The crowd cheered wildly as the bearded Stanford came to take his place at the podium.

"Fellow citizens," he began. "I congratulate you upon the commencement of this great work—" Cheers rose up to drown out his next words, and Kiernan could only guess at what was being said. He'd heard these types of speeches many times over, some with the building of the C&O Canal, others with the B&O Railroad. They were always pretty much the same. Words of encouragement, praise, and vision for the future.

Victoria pressed closer to him as the throngs of people moved into a tighter knot around the speakers' platform. He slipped his arm around her shoulders and drew her near. He felt a sense of pride just having her at his side, but even as this sensation washed over him, he knew the nagging reminder of having been less than the husband she deserved. They seldom shared anything more than a few words in passing or an occasional time of intimacy in the stillness of the night. Their lives were certainly nothing like they had been in the early days of their marriage, and it troubled Kiernan to believe that their previous joy was gone now.

When Stanford finished speaking, a minister came to the platform and began a lengthy prayer, requesting God's guidance and direction for the railroad board as they saw the project through to its goal. Kiernan found himself also praying for guidance and direction. He wanted very much to make Victoria proud to be his wife. He knew she acted distant at times, almost as if she harbored something down deep inside—something she didn't want him to see. He feared it was as simple as her shame of his inability to master what seemed to come easily to other men. Worse yet, he actually found himself afraid that she might regret their marriage. After all, what did she have to show for it?

Still, there were times when she was open and warm, easily reminding him of their early days of courtship and of why they'd fallen in love in the first place. Back then she had clearly admired him and looked to him with pride for the way he conducted himself.

Let her be happy, Lord, he prayed. It was really all he wanted at the moment. Oh, there were other issues—desires for the family he'd left in Ireland, desires for financial security and freedom from worry. But more than anything else, he desired that Victoria find happiness in life. He knew she longed for children, as did he, but he also knew that it was a mixed blessing they were yet unable to conceive. Now that he had agreed to take up employment on the Central Pacific, Kiernan often questioned if their life would be better. Dragging a wife from one mining town to another had been nothing but sheer stupidity on his part. Never mind that his intentions had been honorable. Now he would return to something he felt confident of—the railroad.

He wondered silently as the prayer at the podium continued if Victoria had any idea how the railroad would take up his time. Crocker was already talking about Kiernan and Ted making additional surveys in the mountains. Kiernan knew Victoria would expect to be allowed to come with them, but he wasn't going to let her. He didn't want to risk her getting sick again. After that, the true ground breaking would come to the forefront of their duties, and Kiernan would find himself consumed by long hours of backbreaking labor. It wearied him just thinking about it.

The prayer finally ended, and with it, the decorated cart was drawn forward by equally bedecked horses. Stanford took up a shovel and began tossing dirt into the muddy street below. This was the symbolic ground breaking that the entire city had waited for.

After that, various men made speeches. Senators and representatives addressed the group with compelling words that promised enthusiastic support, while the crowd seemed to eat up every word as though a choice morsel of a gourmet feast. In conclusion, Charlie brought the crowd once again to a momentous round of cheers before dismissing the group to go where they would, taking the memory of the day with them.

"Well, it wasn't much for actual progress," Kiernan said, swinging Victoria out of the way just as a hearty foursome, singing at the top of their lungs, pushed past.

"Kiernan!" a familiar voice called to him from across the muddy road.

Turning, Kiernan saw Ted Judah making his way to where he and Victoria stood.

"Come to the house. We need to talk," Ted declared.

Kiernan looked at Victoria, who gave a brief nod of assent.

They made their way to Ted's buggy and allowed him to drive them back to the Judahs' small house. Ted seemed overly quiet, a sharp contrast to the revelry of the day.

"Is something wrong?" Kiernan questioned.

"Not as far as the 'big four' are concerned." There was a definite edge to Judah's tone.

"But I was thinkin' that yarself was a part of that number."

Ted laughed, but it was bitter and harsh. "This entire project has been my dream from the start. I pressed for support. I've given my lifeblood to it, and they treat me like a poor relation."

"I'm sure I don't understand," Kiernan said as they came to a halt outside the Judah home.

Ted handed the reins over to his stableman, then motioned for Kiernan and Victoria to follow him into the house. "I'll explain it better once we've sat down to some of Anna's pound cake and coffee."

"Men can always think more clearly over such refreshment," Victoria teased as Kiernan lifted her from the buggy.

"Aye, that we can," Kiernan said, squeezing her hand.

Ted escorted them inside and Anna greeted them with great

enthusiasm. "I would have been there today, but Li wasn't feeling well, so I stayed here with her."

"I hope it's nothing serious," Victoria said, her voice grave.

"Oh no," Anna assured her. "At least, not too serious. Li's expecting a baby."

"But she's just a child herself," Victoria replied with a pained expression.

Kiernan wondered if the grief on her face was as much for her own childlessness as it was for Li's ill health. It must be hard for Victoria to hear of someone else's blessing.

"She married just last October, as you know. But come, we mustn't spend our time worrying over this," Anna said, drawing Victoria with her to the kitchen. "Victoria, would you mind helping me serve?"

Kiernan was grateful for the older woman's request. He knew the situation was hard on Victoria and could only pray that Anna would help draw her attention elsewhere.

Ted led the way to the front sitting room and motioned for Kiernan to take a chair. "I fear this railroad may well be nothing more than a dream. My comrades in this scheme seem only interested in luring the freight traffic away from the various teamsters in the area."

"So yar thinkin' they're only good for the ride so long as there's immediate money to be made?" Kiernan questioned.

"That's one way of putting it." Ted dropped into a chair and shook his head. "I'm afraid my colleagues may stop at simply seeing a short line put in rather than worrying about connecting to the East. Congress already sees the Central Pacific as a feat bordering on impossible. They gave us the provision that should we master the mountains we might be allowed to build eastward indefinitely—so long as the Union Pacific hasn't yet reached the western edge of the Nevada Territory. They are requiring us to complete fifty miles of road within the next two years and to build at least fifty additional miles per year thereafter. And while the Union Pacific must do twice that, I don't believe our board of directors truly appreciates the circumstances.

Collis Huntington has said we have drawn the elephant and must find a way to harness him."

"Then we'll be havin' to show them," Kiernan said, trying to lighten the mood of his friend. "I have yet to see an elephant," he continued, "but surely the beast can be managed in one way or another."

"I'm just afraid the management might come in the form of trading one beast off for another. With Crocker now set to employ men to build the line, I fear they'll ignore my suggestions altogether and seek another direction."

"But yar surveys are good, Ted. Congress themselves acknowledged yar help. Ya can't be givin' in to worry over this."

Just then the women returned with the refreshments. Victoria looked rather red-eyed, and Kiernan wondered if she'd been crying over the issue of Li's baby. How he wished he could make at least this issue in her life right, but again he was helpless.

"You might as well give up on telling Ted not to worry," Anna told Kiernan as she placed the tray of cake on a nearby serving table. Victoria did likewise with her tray of coffee and china.

"Well, I just can't see that it gains a fellow much ground," Kiernan replied. "A transcontinental railroad is mighty important to this state. I can't see them lettin' it go for the likes of a freight road."

Ted nodded. "I know that sounds reasonable, but you haven't been a part of their meetings. There are so many issues I can't see eye to eye with. Issues that may well make or break this railroad."

"Ted," Anna said, reaching out to touch his shoulder, "we're supposed to be celebrating. You are ruining our good nature with your doom and gloom. Come now, can't we at least pretend that all is well and that your railroad is off to a good start?"

Ted sighed. "I suppose you're right. I don't mean to cast dispersions." He smiled at Kiernan and Victoria and reached up to pat Anna's hand. "Every cloud has its brighter lining, right?"

Kiernan chuckled, but deep inside he knew only too well how fickle the railroad business could be. He understood his friend's concerns and he knew they were valid. The real problem wouldn't be in maintaining enthusiasm for the project; it would be in seeing that project continue to stay an elephant, instead of being redesigned into something far more easily managed.

23

Charles Crocker resigned his position with the Central Pacific board in order to sign a four hundred thousand dollar contract to construct the first eighteen miles of track. The choice was seen as a means of avoiding any future legal backfire, but the fact that his brother Edward took over the position made the move almost humorous. Nevertheless, Edward's background as an engineer and lawyer made him a tremendous asset to the board, as he was already handling all of the Central Pacific's legal affairs. Still, many perceived this as Charlie's way of keeping a hand in.

However, with his position resigned, Crocker was finally free to move ahead with the contract. He immediately set about the task of hiring supervisors and crews to get to the actual task of laying track and boasted that the Central Pacific would soon see real progress.

Kiernan was happy to find himself promoted from store clerk to crew boss. He felt a sense of awe and pride that Crocker would offer him such an important position. He had already convinced himself that even if Crocker offered him nothing more than the job of digger, Kiernan would take it. The pay would be better, and Kiernan could feel more confident about the duties. Working in the store had proved to be acceptable, even beneficial, but it wasn't at all what Kiernan desired for his future.

Because Crocker sublet the construction work to several local firms, there were many supervisors and bosses to answer to, and Crocker found himself quite preoccupied with the details of building the railroad. It didn't matter that he'd never had experience with such a responsibility—his charm and quick wit seemed to keep arguments and protests at bay, and because he was an intelligent man, Crocker was more than willing to learn. And with over two hundred men now employed to build a railroad, Crocker's education was a daily issue.

With this in mind, Kiernan didn't worry about sending a note to Charlie requesting he come to the track site. Kiernan had found a troublesome complication to their progress and figured it was best to get the details out in the open as soon as possible.

"You said it was important," Crocker said, dismounting his horse.

"Aye, and it is." Kiernan came forward to greet the man. "Ya can see here for yarself, we've hit a snag in our progress." Kiernan led him to where the men were even now trying to grade out a road. "The topsoil runs for a foot, sometimes two, then we hit what might as well be concrete. The stuff is as hard as granite."

Crocker stepped into the newly dug ditch and squatted down to see the matter for himself. "Is it like this all along the way?"

"Aye. I've already been talkin' to some of the other gangs. This is goin' to double the time needed to make the road."

"Double the cost, too, if I know anything about anything," Crocker said in complete frustration. He stood and dusted off the crusty bits of rock and sand. "This isn't how I envisioned it."

Kiernan waited for him to climb back out of the ditch before continuing with his concerns. "The weather is warmin' a bit, and the miners who've signed on to work are headin' back out to the mines. Nobody cares about seein' this through."

"Don't I know it," Charlie said, shaking his head. "Kiernan, we've got to figure out a way to get reliable workers in here. Men who will work for little pay and long hours and not be lured away by stories of gold. Otherwise, this railroad will be nothing but dreams on paper."

Kiernan fully appreciated his boss's concern. He knew Ted felt the same way. "At least yar makin' good progress in the river," Kiernan offered.

It was true that the great pile-driving hammers were sinking mammoth thirty-foot pilings into the riverbed at the rate of seven a day. Soon an impressive railroad bridge would span the American River, and this would surely bolster the spirits of those who considered the railroad an impossible feat.

"They want me to go to Donner Pass and oversee the construction there," Charlie said after a long silence. "I want you to come with me."

Kiernan knew his expression revealed his surprise. "Me? And why would ya be wantin' me?"

"You already know Doc Strong and you know the area. Ted told me you were a part of one of their surveying teams and that the territory would be very similar to what you've already worked on back east."

"Whoa now. For sure it ain't the same as back east. The mountains there were not to be compared with what we'd be up against at Donner Pass. As I recall, that area has a history of killin' people off by its very nature."

"It's a harsh land, but the railroad must be built through it. The board is sending me, and I'm asking you to come with me. I need you, O'Connor. You have experience and expertise in blasting and tunneling. Judah estimates we'll need eighteen tunnels before we ever make it from one side of the Sierras to the other. You are the one to help me see this accomplished." Then, almost as an afterthought, Crocker added, "I'll double your pay."

Even without this enticement, Kiernan realized the tremendous opportunity to prove himself. He felt a pride in the fact that Crocker had chosen him for the job. The only problem was that he would no doubt have to leave Victoria behind. He couldn't see dragging her back to Dutch Flat when she so loved Sacramento. To do so would be nothing short of heartless. Still, having his income doubled would be a benefit to both of them—maybe even to his family in Ireland.

"How long will ya need me there?"

Crocker shrugged. "There's just no telling. I feel certain, however, that the process will take a whole lot longer without you helping to see it through."

Kiernan drew a deep breath and exhaled rather loudly. "Give me some time to think on it," he said, knowing even as he did so that his decision was pretty much made for him. It was an offer too tempting to pass up.

Crocker smiled. "I know you'll see things my way."

———

"I'm so glad you've come for a visit," Victoria said as Anna Judah stepped into the small two-room apartment.

"I was busy all morning with errands and thought some time in quiet conversation with you would do me well," Anna explained.

"I can fix us some tea, if you like," Victoria offered. She glanced around at the shoddy furnishings and wished she had something better to offer her friend.

"No, don't bother. I can't stay long. Just come sit with me and share what news there is to tell."

Victoria followed Anna to the tiny threadbare sofa. "I haven't much news that you aren't already privy to."

Anna removed her bonnet and smiled. "Then we shall just talk of the day. What have you been busying yourself with?"

Victoria thought for a moment. "I went down to Charlie's store and helped with the counter for an hour this morning. Kiernan thought it would be all right, and Charlie needed the help. He's going to sell the place off, Kiernan said." She paused and considered whether or not to continue. "I wish I could invest in it. He's selling portions off to his clerks, and I would truly love to talk to him about buying in."

"Why don't you?" Anna asked. "It would be perfectly acceptable work for you. That is, if you want to work elsewhere. I'm sure your duties here are enough to keep you occupied."

Victoria looked away. How could she explain that the emptiness of the house only seemed to magnify her homesickness and the fact that she had no child to mother? "Sometimes this place is too empty. I do the things that are required of me, but while I see to those tasks, I have too much time in which to think."

Anna nodded sympathetically. "And sometimes that is more of a burden than too much work."

"It certainly can be."

Victoria knew Anna would understand, but she hated even speaking aloud the details of her longing.

"Are you still missing your family?" Anna finally asked.

Victoria nodded. "I think of them often. I worry about them, what with the war and all. It seems that we know so little about what's going on in the East. I read of familiar places—towns I know from childhood—suffering from the ravages of battle. I realize those places are forever changed by the cruelties of this war. I haven't heard from my mother or father in ever so long, and while I presume upon their safety in Russia, I still fear for them."

"Of course you do," Anna replied. "Who in your position would not?"

"Still, it seems silly. There is nothing to be gained by worry." Victoria smiled rather sheepishly and ducked her head down. "Of course, I've not yet been able to convince myself of the truth in that."

Anna reached out and patted Victoria's hand. "You mustn't fret. I'm sure they are fine."

Victoria looked up and met Anna's compassionate gaze. "I hope so."

"I shall change the subject as a means of proving my confidence in their well-being. I am, as you must know, more concerned with how you are. I've worried about you ever since you visited me and learned of Li's pregnancy."

Victoria felt the blood drain from her face. "It's just so hard," she murmured.

"I know."

Anna's compassion overwhelmed Victoria. Anna was the one person with whom she could plead her case and be assured of full understanding. Anna had never been able to give Ted a child, and she would understand the longing in Victoria's heart.

"Victoria, I know your heart. I've never stopped wanting a child of my own, but God has always had other plans for me. I can't say I like it, but I am resigned to it. At least for now."

"Well, I'm not!" Victoria burst out before she could stop herself. "I'm not resigned at all. I'm angry and worried, and I simply cannot find acceptance for this circumstance."

"I wasn't suggesting that resignation be acceptance," Anna continued. "You are young, and there are many chances yet for you and Kiernan to have a baby. I merely spoke for myself. Ted is a wonderful man. He has given me more than I could have ever asked. We have had a good life together, and I've learned that he is my portion in full. I find that in seeing this, my contentment is so much greater. I am only suggesting that you draw attention to what you have rather than what you don't have. God may one day make both of us mothers, but we must be prepared for the fact that He also might not."

"But I can't imagine never being a mother. I know Kiernan wants children, and I feel so inadequate because I can't provide him with the son he desires." Victoria felt her emotions giving way. Her eyes filled with tears. "I can't help but think it will one day come between us."

"It doesn't have to," Anna said earnestly. "Ted and I have discussed the matter at length. Perhaps you and Kiernan should do the same. It's important to talk about your fears. You should let Kiernan know how you feel and find out how he feels as well."

"But I know how he feels. I see it when he spies a mother with a baby in her arms. I know he's saddened as each month passes by and we are still without a child."

"Perhaps these are more your own feelings than his," Anna suggested. "After all, have you spoken with him on the matter?"

"No." Victoria stared with shame down at her hands. "I can't. I can't bear to know the truth—even though I'm already certain of it."

"Perhaps you should refrain from judging Kiernan's heart until you give him a chance to speak his opinion. I found with Ted that I often misunderstood his feelings about a family. He has always wanted children; that much is true. But he also enjoys the vagabond life we live. He would be hard-pressed to continue dragging from one end of the country to the other with a baby along."

"But he would probably be happy to settle down if there were a child," Victoria replied.

"And you think that of Kiernan, as well, don't you?"

Victoria nodded. "He's just so restless. I sometimes see him look at me as though he wants to say something, then he turns away and the moment is lost. I know I've driven him away by being less than what a good wife should be."

"Nonsense!" Anna declared. "Victoria, you have been a good helpmate to your husband. You have followed him willingly around the country, you have cooked and cleaned for him, you have borne his moods and his transgressions, you have been his lover and friend. No man could ask for more."

"Oh yes he could," Victoria replied. "He could ask for a child. Kiernan deserves a child."

"And you believe that just because you've been unable to bear him one, God is somehow remiss in His duties?"

Victoria shrugged. "I don't know what to think. I thought I had a strong faith in God. I thought I understood about trusting Him and living a good life, but now I just don't know. Now I'm confused and I wonder if my faith is even real."

"Faith is like a flower in the garden. It needs a certain amount of growing time to come to its fullest potential. You are simply in a time of growth. Don't let it defeat you. Instead, you must find a way to thrive—to see that faith is more than understanding your circumstances: it's enduring in spite of them. Believing that the circumstances aren't necessarily indicative of the final outcome."

Victoria dabbed at her eyes. "You don't think me to be a lost cause, do you, Anna?"

Anna laughed. "No more than I consider myself to be. These are but momentary trials. The bad comes with the good, but it will pass. You'll see. You must simply let go of your fears and trust God for the outcome. And," she paused to reach out and hug Victoria affectionately, "you must open your heart to Kiernan and tell him of your worries. Don't keep this wall of fear between you."

24

With the stunning news that Kiernan would soon be bound for Dutch Flat with Charlie Crocker, Victoria also received word of a celebration party. Collis Huntington, ever hard at work in Washington, had managed to persuade the president to set the transcontinental railroad at a five-foot gauge. This was exactly what the Central Pacific had hoped for, because track already laid by the Sacramento Valley Railroad, as well as track graded out for the CP, had a width of five feet. Very few had believed Huntington could pull it off, since many of the eastern railroads had settled on a four-foot, eight-and-a-half-inch gauge. If they set the gauge at five feet, many railroads would either have to change gauges in order to hook up with the Union Pacific, or they would have to hand over their freight at the places where one line ended and another began. Either way, it would mean a tremendous loss of revenue.

But Californians had confidence in Collis Huntington, and because their man had managed to secure the needed width and save California railroads from having to rethink their plans, they decided a party was in order.

Victoria, still moping because of Kiernan's news, felt a party would do little to help bolster her spirits. She had convinced herself that

Kiernan had actually sought this transfer to another location in order to be away from her.

"I'm not the wife he wants," she mourned aloud. Looking out from their second-floor apartment window, Victoria longed to share her fears with Anna. Her friend would understand and say the right thing to help Victoria see that all her fears were for naught. But Anna was busy making preparations to attend the celebration. She'd already brought Victoria another of her old gowns, insisting that Victoria and Kiernan attend the party that night. There had been no time to talk of Kiernan's leaving or Victoria's sorrow.

Instead, Victoria had done what was expected and had donned the hand-me-down. The gown, looking anything but old, had been made over for Victoria's slimmer frame. The dark apricot taffeta was the epitome of fashion with its huge bell-shaped skirt and off-the-shoulder bodice. Anna had even thought to lend her a hoop to wear beneath the shiny folds of the skirt. Victoria loved the way it fit and felt—loved, too, the way it reminded her of happier days long gone by.

Unfortunately, dwelling on those days only served to make her miserable. She had been so naïve, so young and carefree. How was it possible to have gone from that point to this one? It seemed she had lived life by extremes. She remembered when her father and mother had moved the family from Baltimore to Greigsville in order for her father to supervise the building of the Kingwood Tunnel. She had immediately hated the horrid little town—if a person could even apply that grandiose name to such an insignificant collection of tents and unpainted buildings.

But it was there she had met Kiernan. Suddenly, Greigsville hadn't seemed so bad. Kiernan had been exciting and handsome—everything a young girl's heart could desire. He talked of foreign lands, of noble causes, and of love.

Now he seldom talked of love. He seldom talked of anything.

Victoria turned from the window to continue dressing, desperate to put such thoughts from her mind, but she knew it was an impossible battle. Every day she grew more silent, and every day Kiernan grew more distant. Erected between them were issues that neither one wanted to deal with. It was easier to refortify the wall with painful thoughts than to tear the thing down by speaking honestly to each other.

Quite frankly, Victoria was scared to death by what Kiernan might say. If she brought up the issue of her fears—and her belief that he had distanced himself because of her inability to get pregnant—he just might confirm her beliefs. Then what? It was one thing to assume he felt that way. It would be entirely different to deal with the painful realization that she had been right all along. What if he wanted a divorce?

Once again she pushed aside these thoughts, forcing herself to concentrate on dressing her chestnut hair. Dark, haunted eyes stared back at her from the mirror of the tiny dressing table. So much was buried behind those eyes, she thought. So many dreams. So many nightmares.

She brushed her hair slowly, all the while contemplating her own reflection. Convinced that she had lost Kiernan, at least in spirit, she felt a desperation grow inside her. What could she do to win him back?

"My, but yar lookin' lovely tonight, Mrs. O'Connor." Kiernan paused at the bedroom door just to look at her.

Victoria finished securing her hair atop her head, then got to her feet. She wanted very much for this evening to be wonderful. "I might say the same for you, Mr. O'Connor." She considered his formal attire. He cut a dashing figure in his borrowed clothes. His auburn hair was combed back off his forehead, and his black double-breasted coat seemed to accentuate his broad shoulders and narrow waist.

Victoria smiled in spite of her morose mood. "I've not seen you like this in some time."

He came forward to where she stood. "Yar a true beauty, Victoria," he said, reaching out to take her in his arms. "But ya don't need fancy clothes for me to see that."

Victoria felt encouraged by his words. He seemed more like his old self. Happy, carefree, lighthearted. She could only pray it would last. But with his next words, Kiernan ruined her moment.

"I'm glad yar not still sulkin' about my goin' to Dutch Flat."

She stiffened in his arms and pulled away. "You didn't need to bring that up. We might have gone on having a pleasant evening without such talk."

Kiernan looked a bit forlorn at this comment and at her action. Victoria shook her head and went to retrieve her shawl.

"I wasn't tryin' to hurt ya with such talk. I only wanted to say I was happy ya had come to terms with it," Kiernan said as Victoria moved toward the door.

"I haven't come to terms with that or anything else," Victoria replied, stepping around Kiernan to go into the main living area of their two-room apartment.

Kiernan followed. "That's fairly obvious now. I suppose I was hopin' ya had."

His remark sounded caustic to Victoria, but she refused to argue with him. Stopping by the front door, she turned. "Are you ready to go?"

Kiernan eyed her intently for a moment. He looked as though he might say something more, then shook his head and opened the door for her. "I'm sure it wouldn't much matter whether I was ready or not."

Victoria held her emotions inside, refusing to give in to her frustration and anger. She wanted to have fun this evening, and arguing with Kiernan wasn't going to help.

They walked in silence to the hotel where the celebration was being held. Victoria hated that Kiernan was angry, but she feared what might pass between them if she apologized. She wished Anna could help her figure out a way to deal with Kiernan's decision to leave. Yet if she sought Anna's advice, she knew her friend might insist the younger couple talk openly about their feelings. Victoria was certain that wouldn't work. She and Kiernan would only argue about unimportant matters in order to keep from having to deal with the real issue.

Victoria frowned. A baby was the real issue. If she could only have a child, Kiernan wouldn't feel the need to run off.

They entered the hotel lobby and were instantly swept up into the spirit of revelry. It seemed this group of people looked for any reason to celebrate, and the issue of Collis Huntington's success was no less a reason to party than the ground breaking for the Central Pacific had been.

A group of men immediately moved in to talk to Kiernan. Victoria recognized them, smiled, and made polite conversation with each one before they dragged her husband toward the far side of the room. He didn't seem the least bit reluctant to go with them.

About this time a band struck up, and the center of the room cleared for the dancing to begin. Victoria wished Kiernan might leave his companions and come back to dance with her, but she knew it wouldn't happen. He was absorbed in his railroad work.

"I can't believe that the most beautiful woman in the room is standing idle" came a rich baritone voice from behind her.

Victoria turned around quickly and looked up to find a handsome dark-haired stranger. There was something slightly familiar about him, and it took Victoria only a moment to realize he reminded her of a painting she'd once seen of her real father, Blake St. John. Before Carolina and James Baldwin had adopted her, Blake St. John had been a sporadic presence in her life. She had no memory of him except for the stories told her by others, and only one likeness of him had ever been painted. Even that was now in safekeeping in her parents' house in Baltimore.

"I can see that I've startled you. Perhaps I should start over. I'm Christopher Thorndike. I own Thorndike Emporium and several other small businesses. And you are?" he questioned with just a hint of a smile.

"Victoria O'Connor," she replied. The way the man looked at her, as if she really were the most beautiful woman in the room, gave her gooseflesh. "*Mrs.* Kiernan O'Connor," she quickly added.

He bowed low, reached for her hand, and placed a kiss atop it. Victoria felt a tremor run up her arm. She swallowed hard and tried not to appear nervous.

"I wonder if you might do me the honor of a dance. There seems to be a rather pleasant waltz being played."

She felt helpless to refuse. He was powerful and dynamic, and without giving any thought to what she was doing, Victoria allowed him to lead her to the dance floor.

Before she knew it, they were caught up in first one dance and then another, and it wasn't long before an hour had passed. Victoria realized with no small amount of horror that not only had she danced her first dance with this man but all of the subsequent dances as well.

"I really should go speak to Mrs. Judah," she said, pulling away from Thorndike. "I fear I shall ruin my reputation if I dare another dance."

"But I've so enjoyed talking with you. It's been some time since I've been in the company of a lady. I'm so often gone on one trip or another. However, I assure you, had I realized the potential in Sacramento, I might have stayed home more."

Victoria frowned. Was he implying that she was a potential interest for him? "I need to find my husband," she murmured and fled in the direction of the refreshment table.

But Kiernan was nowhere to be found. Catching Anna in discussion with several other ladies, Victoria managed to wait until the other women had moved along before questioning her about Kiernan.

"Do you know where my husband might have taken himself off to?" Victoria asked nervously.

Anna laughed, giving no apparent concern to Victoria's behavior. "Where else would he be? The men have congregated in one of the back rooms to discuss railroad business. I swear, the lot of them are a waste of time when they have a project on their minds." She glanced across the room to take in the dancing couples. "Are you having fun?"

"I suppose I am," Victoria replied. "I've made the acquaintance of a Mr. Thorndike."

"Hmm," Anna said as if trying to recall the name. "I'm not sure I know him."

"He said he's often gone on business trips. He has even journeyed to the Orient, and his emporium deals in all manner of antiquities and treasures from China."

"Do say?"

"He also is very interested in the railroad. He's been asking me a lot of questions about the line and thinks he might want to invest in it."

"Perhaps we should direct him to the back room," Anna said. "Which man is he?"

Victoria didn't need to search for him. Her mind had never lost track of where he stood amidst the crowd. Even now as she looked up to make certain of his position, she caught his gaze—stern and brooding—fixed on her.

"There," she whispered, leaning closer to Anna. "The man standing by Mrs. Reems."

"Ah, a very pleasant-looking gentleman," Anna replied. "Yes, I do recall seeing you dance with him."

"I've danced only with him," Victoria said. "That was why I came over here. I thought I had better find Kiernan."

Anna laughed. "You sound worried. Has there been some problem?"

Victoria didn't quite know how to express what she was feeling. Christopher Thorndike made her feel most uncomfortable, but he'd not truly overstepped any proper bounds—except that he'd monopolized her dance time.

"There's no real problem. I suppose I'm just disappointed that Kiernan has deserted me without so much as a word."

Anna smiled. "Go and have fun. The men will wrap up their business and join us before you know it."

Victoria nodded and felt rather like a lamb being led to the slaughter. Thorndike disturbed her in a way she couldn't explain. Without

Anna or Kiernan at her side, she knew she'd be open game for this stranger.

Moving in the opposite direction of Thorndike, Victoria tried to rationalize her fears. She found the man attractive; that much she couldn't deny. And the fact that he talked to her and questioned her about her life and showed a definite interest in her answers made Victoria feel special.

Biting her lip, Victoria glanced up to see the dark stranger slip away into the crowd. She let out her breath, not even realizing she'd been holding it. Maybe it was nothing more than the man's similarity to Blake St. John. That part of her life was such an enigma. She had been born to one man and woman, then given over to another. Her mother had died shortly after her birth, and her father had hired a nanny to care for her. That nanny turned out to be the woman who would become her new mother. Carolina Adams had married Blake St. John for the sole purpose of giving Victoria a mother. St. John had died not long after this platonic arrangement, leaving Carolina and Victoria free to seek whatever life they chose. Carolina had then married James Baldwin, and it was James, not St. John, whom Victoria thought of when she spoke the word "father."

"I don't suppose you would care to dance again" came the sound of Thorndike's voice.

Turning rather abruptly, Victoria found the man standing directly behind her once again. He had an uncanny way of sneaking up on her.

"I believe we've danced enough," Victoria said, trying hard to keep her voice even.

"Perhaps some refreshments, then?" he questioned softly, seeming to sense her nervousness.

"Hmm," Victoria replied, quickly looking away to see if anyone else was disturbed by her encounter. No one else appeared to even notice her standing there with the tall, dark-haired man. "I suppose some punch would be nice."

"Then I shall be happy to bring you some," he said, bowing before her. As he lifted his head his eyes met hers. "I'll only be a moment."

Victoria felt silly as the butterflies played in her stomach. *Why am I acting like this? I'm a married woman and I'm acting like a schoolgirl.* She chewed at her lower lip and tried to think of some reason to tell Thorndike that she couldn't remain in his company. Such behavior might have caused a scandal in the East but was far less noticeable in the isolated West Coast society. A much more relaxed attitude existed here concerning the proper deportment of men and women.

She thought hard about why Christopher Thorndike caused her to feel so skittish. So far he'd only danced and talked with her. There was absolutely nothing wrong with the way they'd conducted themselves. Victoria took a deep breath and rationalized her behavior. *I've done nothing in this man's company that I would be ashamed to have Kiernan see. I'm just being silly and nervous because this man has taken time to pay attention to me.*

It was then that Victoria realized it was not only Thorndike's attention that was stirring her guilt but also her *enjoyment* of his attention. She liked that he asked her questions, then genuinely seemed to care about the answers.

"Here we are," he said, returning with her cup of punch.

"Thank you," Victoria barely whispered. Kiernan should have been the one to fetch her punch, not Thorndike. But Kiernan had taken himself away from her. Kiernan had made his choice for the evening, and it clearly wasn't Victoria. Her anger at this thought fueled her ability to overlook her feelings of guilt.

Sipping the cool, sweet liquid, Victoria decided to stop acting so silly. She smiled sweetly at Thorndike, having determined she was doing nothing wrong. She would talk and dance and enjoy her evening, and if Thorndike was the man to pay her attention throughout the process, then so be it.

"Might I talk you into another dance? I know you worry after your reputation, but I've already danced with two other women—both married, I might add—in the interim."

Victoria laughed and put her cup down on the nearest table. "I suppose one more dance wouldn't hurt."

Kiernan walked out of the smoky back room, determined to leave off with arguing points of interest on the Central Pacific. He thought their celebration premature and told them so. He could see no profitable way that Lincoln could stay with his decision to assign a five-foot gauge to the transcontinental railroad. And he told his companions just that. Of course, they didn't want to hear such nonsense. If Kiernan was right, it would require having to pull up miles and miles of track already in place. The cost would be oppressive.

Looking around for his wife, Kiernan was rather shocked when he spied a flash of apricot whirling by him. A woman wearing a gown similar to Victoria's laughed and danced in the arms of a lean, handsome man. It was only after giving the couple a second glance that Kiernan realized the woman was *his* wife. He watched as the stranger maneuvered her around the dance floor. The waltz allowed for him to have his hand around her waist, while the other hand held hers most possessively. Kiernan felt as though he'd just been dealt a blow as the man pulled Victoria closer to avoid running into another couple. The hooped framing underneath caused her skirt to flare out behind her as their bodies were pressed more closely together. She laughed and said something. The man leaned close to her ear, a hint of a grin on his face. He apparently replied—saying something uncalled for as far as Kiernan could think, because it made Victoria blush and pull back.

Without considering how it might look, Kiernan stalked across the dance floor to intercept the couple. Victoria stared at him in open surprise as he reached out and took her by the arm.

"It's time to go home," he said without bothering to introduce himself to the stranger. "Ya will excuse us," he told the man.

Barely keeping his temper, Kiernan could only pray that Victoria's shock would carry her in silence to the street. He had no desire to make a scene, especially after Victoria had made her own.

The cool night air hit him and immediately forced him to calm down. His behavior had been most foolish. No doubt, people back at the party were already talking about his ignorant actions. So his wife was dancing with someone else. So she blushed in the stranger's arms. It didn't mean he had a right to publicly embarrass her. He would have to apologize. He simply hadn't thought clearly. But as he stopped just inside their apartment building and turned to speak to Victoria, he could see the anger and hurt in her expression.

"How dare you!" she exclaimed, then pushed past him and rushed up the stairs.

He followed at a slower pace, and with each step he took, he felt a mixture of emotions. He no longer wanted to apologize. Instead, he was angry all over again.

He entered the apartment and could hear her throwing things around in their bedroom. Following the noise, he was surprised to see Victoria wrestling the combs from her hair and kicking her shoes off, all at the same time.

"You humiliated me in front of our friends!" she declared.

"Ya humiliated yarself," he retorted without thinking.

Turning, hands on hips, Victoria stared at him for a moment before shaking her head. "And how was it I did that?"

"Ya know full well. Ya were dancin' with the man as if he were yar husband."

"Well, my husband didn't see fit to be my companion this evening," Victoria responded in uncharacteristic snippiness. "Perhaps if you'd remained by my side, I wouldn't have needed to seek company with someone else."

"So ya sought out his company?" Kiernan countered, praying it wasn't true. He already felt guilty for the time he'd spent away from her at the party, but he wasn't about to admit it now.

"No, as a matter of fact, I didn't." Victoria's tone calmed slightly. "He came to me."

"I see. And did ya spend all evening with him?" Victoria's face flushed and Kiernan knew the answer even before she spoke it.

"Mr. Thorndike wanted to talk to me and so we talked. We danced several dances and he brought me punch. I'm sure that someone at the party will vouch for the fact that I did nothing out of line."

"I never said ya did," Kiernan said sarcastically. "But yar own face seems to suggest otherwise."

"What is that supposed to mean?"

"Just that yar all red in the face, even talkin' about him."

Victoria sat down on the chair at her dressing table and began to brush her long, dark hair. Normally, Kiernan would have loved to have watched the sight, but tonight he was confused and angry, and the scene did nothing but further irritate him.

"Ya've been all bottled up inside for so long that I haven't any idea what the problem is. Ya won't talk to me and ya won't listen to me. I'm asking ya what happened tonight and what that was all about, but yar clearly not of a mind to be honest with me. I sometimes doubt that yar ever honest with me."

Victoria dropped the brush on the table and turned. "You want my honesty. All right. You've distanced yourself from me since our arrival in California. Oh sure, there are moments when you seem more like your old self. When you appear to love me like you once did. But those times are so few that I scarcely dare to consider them as real."

She got to her feet and stepped toward him, her expression one of pain and misery. "I know you're upset over the loss of my fortune, but that was years ago, and it's not the real reason you've put a wall between us."

"Oh, and what would the real reason be?" he asked angrily. "Yar figurin' to know my mind on the matter. I suppose ya don't even need me here for this conversation."

Victoria shook her head. "You love me less because I can't give you a child. It's that simple." Her voice was barely audible, but the intensity of pain and longing in her words cut Kiernan to the heart.

He opened his mouth to speak—to deny it—but she raised her hand. "No," she whispered, "you don't need to say anything. I know the truth of it. It's very apparent that this is an issue. You married me hoping for a big family and a prosperous life, and now you have neither, and you are no longer content to be my husband."

Kiernan was stunned by her words, yet even as she spoke them, he had a nagging fear build within his heart. Could there be some truth in what she said? She deserved to know the truth, and yet at that moment he wasn't entirely clear on what that might be.

"I can't be talkin' to ya about this. Not now," he said, crossing the room. He slammed the door behind him as he exited the apartment, feeling an emptiness engulf him. Was it true? Had he distanced himself from her because she'd proved to be barren? Had he caused her this misery?

 25

It had been late in the night when Kiernan returned to the apartment. Victoria was already asleep when he slipped into their bed. Relieved that he did not have to face her just then, he simply turned out the lamp and closed his eyes in prayer.

When he awoke the next morning, Victoria was still sleeping soundly. Rather than wake her and have to deal with the issue of their fight before going off to a morning appointment with Crocker, Kiernan left her alone. There would be plenty of time to talk about the matter later, and frankly, Kiernan wasn't at all certain what that conversation might entail.

He'd come to the conclusion there was some truth in what she'd said. He still felt enormous guilt for taking her from her family and then losing her money. He supposed that perhaps their lack of children was some kind of divine punishment for his failures. Weren't children supposed to be a gift from God?

Perhaps the fault was not Victoria's at all, but rather his own. Perhaps he was facing the consequences of his actions. Either way, it troubled him more than he could say. He didn't like to think that he loved Victoria less than the day he'd first given his heart to her. They had both been practically children then, but the future seemed to be at their command. How different it was to grow up and know adulthood and the problems and fears that come with age.

When he reached Charlie Crocker's house, Kiernan was surprised to find Ted Judah arguing heatedly with the man.

"This is going to cost us plenty. I should have gone to Washington myself."

"And what would the problem be now?" Kiernan asked lightly, hoping to diffuse some of the tension.

"Lincoln has changed his mind. The five-foot gauge is out, and the four-foot, eight-and-a-half-inch gauge is in. Apparently Congress overruled Lincoln's decision. Their eastern constituents no doubt felt that by keeping the smaller gauge, it would be California that would bear the brunt of the expense in making compliance."

Kiernan nodded. "I was afraid that might well be the case."

"Well, there's the devil to pay for it," Crocker protested. "We'll have to tear up the track already in place and totally rework the road."

"Aye," Kiernan said with a nod. It seemed that instead of his job offering him some small amount of comfort, it would only add to his problems.

———

Evening twilight was already upon them when Victoria opened the door of her apartment to a Mexican boy. He smiled sweetly and told her in broken English that señor had sent him to say he would be very late in coming home that night.

"Did he say why?" Victoria questioned.

"I no speak English good," the boy said apologetically.

She tried again. "My husband, the man you talked to—"

The boy nodded.

"Did he say why he would be late coming home?" She talked slowly and tried to think of any other way to help the boy understand.

"He no tell me more," the boy replied with a shrug of his shoulders.

Victoria thanked the child and closed the apartment door in

dejection. She'd fallen asleep before Kiernan had returned the night before. Her own temper had gotten the best of her, and she'd said things she now regretted—things she fervently wished she could take back.

"If I hadn't already felt guilty for the evening," she murmured, "his words would have never bothered me." But it wasn't Kiernan's accusatory tone regarding her actions with Thorndike that hurt her most. It was the fact that he'd said nothing in reply—he'd not said a single word to dispel her fears when she'd spoken of him loving her less because of her barren womb.

The hard truth of the matter was more than she could bear. Tears came again to her eyes, and without any desire to think further on the matter, Victoria took herself back to bed. She'd already spent most of the day there moping. She might as well spend her evening there too.

She'd no sooner settled onto the bed, however, when another knock sounded at the door. With a sigh, she forced herself to her feet and went back into the main room of the house to answer the door. A deliveryman, dressed in a white coat and bearing a long, deep box, greeted her by tipping his hat.

"Yes?" Victoria questioned.

"I have a delivery of flowers for Mrs. O'Connor."

"I'm Mrs. O'Connor," Victoria replied, her heart beginning to feel hope at the sight of the gift.

The man handed her the box, then left without another word. Victoria held the box for several moments without doing anything but stare after the man. She'd never received hothouse flowers—well, at least not since marrying Kiernan and moving to California.

She closed the door and gently placed the box on the table. Opening the lid she found a glorious bouquet of assorted blossoms. The wonderful scent wafted up to greet her, and leaning down, Victoria buried her face against the blossoms and took a deep breath. Marvelous!

Her heart beat faster at the thought of Kiernan sending her flowers. Perhaps this was his way of apologizing. He couldn't be there with her for some reason, but he'd sent the boy to let her know of his lateness, and he'd sent the flowers by way of an apology.

Spying the card that accompanied the bouquet, Victoria picked it up and read "Christopher Thorndike." There was nothing more. No note to explain this unexpected gift—no word of greeting. Only the man's name. A name that didn't belong to her husband.

26

Exhaustion wracked every portion of Kiernan's body. Sweat had dried and caked itself with particles of dirt and sand, coating him from head to toe. It wasn't exactly the way he'd hoped to return home to Victoria, but because of the lateness of the hour, Kiernan hated to delay his trip.

"You could at least stop by my pump," Crocker offered. "Wouldn't take you more than a minute to get the worst of it off of you."

Kiernan nodded and followed the man to the back side of the house. Crocker even offered to pump the water while Kiernan very nearly immersed himself in the flow. Standing erect, his water-soaked body dripped great puddles around him while Crocker only laughed.

"You look like a drowned rat, but at least the stench is lessened. I'm going to do the same and then go soak in a hot bath. See you tomorrow."

"Aye, tomorrow," Kiernan said, his voice betraying his exhaustion. Wrapping himself in a blanket borrowed from Crocker to ward off the chill night, he turned toward home.

He worked his way through the dark streets, very nearly asleep on his feet, yet thoroughly aware that it was necessary to pay attention to his surroundings. Robbers and confidence men loved to haunt the streets at night, all in hopes of rolling a drunk for his last bit of money.

Kiernan steadied his step and forced himself to be alert. There was no sense in being mistaken for someone in his cups.

His apartment window, facing the street, was lit with a warm, cheery glow. Kiernan hoped that meant Victoria had waited up for him and that her anger had abated somewhat. He still didn't know exactly what to say to her. He had labored with the thought of her declaration, even during Crocker's arguments about how to best rework the track plans.

He hated to think of himself as a petty man—a man who would hold against his wife her inability to bear a child. That wasn't how he saw himself. He was proud, to be sure. He held a tremendous sense of family. But if he truly loved Victoria any less because of her child-lessness, then he must indeed be an ill-mannered, heartless monster.

He entered the apartment building and trudged slowly up the steps to his home. He couldn't shake the feeling of anxiety from his heart. What should he say to her? How could he reassure her, when he couldn't figure it out for himself? Of course, he would never consider divorcing her. He did love her. Loved her as he loved his own life. How could she imagine that he would put her away from him in disgrace?

He opened the door, took a deep breath, and called her name. "Victoria?" He closed the door softly and waited for her to reply.

She came from the bedroom, hair down and tousled as if she'd been asleep. Her face was drawn and pale and her expression one of shy, almost embarrassed contemplation.

"I kept some supper for you. Are you hungry?" she asked without looking directly at him.

"Aye. I'm starvin'." He suddenly realized his wet clothes were leaving a puddle at the door. "Let me change these clothes first."

She said nothing but went directly to the tiny stove and began pushing pots around as if with purpose.

Kiernan hurriedly changed and returned to the room just as she was portioning out a thick piece of pork. The plate already contained a generous helping of fried potatoes, and on the table she had placed a loaf of golden crusted bread and a bowl of butter. Kiernan smiled at the sight, and the aroma caused his stomach to growl loudly.

Victoria made no comment, but Kiernan laughed and took his seat at the table. "This will make a fine snack," he teased as he sometimes did when ravenous.

"I can fix something more if you'd like," Victoria replied, bringing the coffeepot and Kiernan's mug to the table.

"No, this looks fine," he said, realizing she wasn't going to go easily into a conversation with him.

He offered a silent prayer over the meal, then asked her, "So what did you do today?"

Victoria shrugged. "I helped at the store and then came back up here."

He dug into the potatoes and smiled. If there was one thing he could say about his wife, it was that she had a way with cooking. He never had reason to complain about any of her meals. Even when they'd been so very poor and isolated in the mining camps, Victoria had always managed to give him satisfaction when it came to their meals. He felt his heart warm toward her. Perhaps that was the way to put this issue of anger and children behind them. Focus on something pleasant—something good, something as close to perfect about the other person as possible.

"This tastes great," he told her, then took up the knife and began slicing away at the pork.

Victoria said nothing, but instead seemed to be in a worse state of mind now than when he'd left her the night before. Kiernan decided that perhaps the best thing to do would be to avoid talking about their argument. Surely it was better to move ahead than repeat their past mistakes.

"Why don't you come sit with me, and I'll tell you all about the Central Pacific's latest complication."

Victoria turned and looked at him for a moment. Her gaze never quite met his, but at least she gave the pretense of considering his words. She put down the dish towel she'd been holding and took a seat at the table.

Kiernan waited for her to make some comment or question about what the problem might be, and when she didn't, he forced himself to continue.

"Well, for sure ya know that money has been a problem for this line since the start. The government won't be issuin' the promised loan money until there are at least forty miles of CP track laid and functionin' like a proper railroad." He explained this in between bites of food, all while Victoria looked on in quiet indifference.

"Then there's the point of how much money the government will give us," Kiernan continued. "It seems there's to be a $16,000-a-mile subsidy for the flatlands, those lands between here and the Sierras. Then it jumps to $48,000 for actual mountain work in the Sierras or the Rockies. Then the government dropped the amount down to $32,000 a mile for the distance between the Sierras and the Rockies.

"Well, it seems the powers that be have it in their minds now to question where the Sierras actually start. And for sure they won't rest until it means more money for the CP." Kiernan paused long enough to take a drink of the rich black coffee. Smiling, he put the mug down. "Ah, and that hits the spot in a way a man can appreciate."

Still Victoria remained silent. At least she actually looked at him now, but the expression on her face was like someone meeting the dead. He'd seen his mother look at his da that way, and he didn't like the feeling he got from the memory.

He ate for a few moments in silence, then wondered about the wisdom of continuing. Perhaps he should say something about their argument. But what could he say? That he'd been smitten with jealousy to see his wife so happily intimate in the arms of another man? That he hated to admit that having a child was important to him, and therefore the lack of one was tearing apart the foundations of their marriage? Was that even true? He sighed and decided to stick with the safer subject of the railroad.

"So anyway, it seems our good governor remembered some such nonsense about the Rocky Mountains beginning at the point of the Mississippi River. Some geologist was thinkin' that because the land made a continual rise to the west from that point, that it only figured to be that the mountains themselves were beginning to take shape. Stanford decided to call in a geologist to help us, and the man is fairly certain that he can cut the distance down and have us set up for bigger money long before we would have had it."

"And this is a problem?" Victoria finally spoke.

Kiernan looked up to meet her searching eyes. "It is if we want to be honest. Crocker told me they were fixin' to say that no more than seven miles to the east where Arcade Creek crosses our planned track line is where the Sierras begin."

"But that's all flatland," Victoria replied.

"Aye, and for sure it's no mountain peak to be earning them $48,000," Kiernan replied, grateful that she was finally communicating with him. "The geologist said there is a definite change in the soil, which makes it a legitimate decision as far as our big four are concerned."

"But you said they wouldn't get the money until at least forty miles were in place," Victoria replied, her voice soft, almost childlike.

"That's true enough," Kiernan replied, "but Stanford is having better success raising funds from private sources, and those men are apparently more likely to continue giving so long as the government money is in sight."

"Hmm, I see." Victoria got up from the table and went to retrieve the cast-iron skillet that sat warming on the stove. "I have more potatoes if you want them."

Kiernan nodded and she scooped out the remaining contents of the pan before replacing the skillet on the side ledge of the stove.

"Then there's that whole issue of me going with Crocker to the Donner Pass." He waited, hoping she might at least offer him some real conversation on this issue. But instead, she simply looked at him as though he should already know how she felt on the matter.

"I'm thinkin' ya don't want me to go, but at the same time, I'm thinkin' ya want to be rid of me," he finally said.

Victoria's face contorted as if the words had caused her great pain. She got to her feet and began clearing the table of empty dishes. "I suppose you'll do whatever you please."

Kiernan had had enough. He slammed his fist on the table, causing the remaining plate to clatter. "Faith, woman! Ya would try the patience of Job with yar meager words and mournful stare."

Victoria froze in place, setting the dishes back on the table. "So now I'm the one with meager words? You might remember that you're the one who ran off and left me here to fret and worry."

"Ya were sleepin' when I came home last night, and it hardly seemed right to be wakin' ya up for an argument."

"And that's what it would have been? An argument?" Victoria asked tartly.

"Isn't that what we're havin' now?" Kiernan countered.

Victoria shook her head and moved to the sofa. This forced Kiernan to either get up from the table or continue the discussion with his back to her. Not relishing either, he finally got to his feet and followed her. And that was when he saw the bouquet of flowers.

"And where did those come from?" Kiernan demanded.

Victoria looked up as though she hadn't a clue what he was talking about. "What?"

"Those flowers," he replied, trying to moderate his inner anger and fear. He had a sneaking feeling that he already knew the answer, but he wanted to hear it from her own lips. After all, maybe he was wrong. Maybe Anna Judah had sent them to cheer her up.

"Oh," Victoria replied, glancing at the bouquet as though seeing them for the first time. "They were delivered earlier."

"I can be seein' that for meself. Who are they from?"

"Mr. Thorndike."

Kiernan felt the intensity of his anger build. "And why would the likes of Mr. Thorndike be sendin' me wife flowers?"

Victoria shrugged. "He didn't say. He simply signed his name to the card. I suppose they were his way of apologizing for whatever misconceived wrongs you believed him capable of."

"Then he would have been a-sendin' them to me," Kiernan replied sarcastically.

"Well, then," Victoria said rather haughtily, "maybe he felt sorry for me."

"And I'm supposin' ya'd like that just fine, now, wouldn't ya?" Kiernan hated that he'd let his emotions get the best of him, but he'd be hanged first before he'd let another man court his wife right under his nose. "I'm thinkin' Mr. Thorndike and I should have a little discussion."

"You have no right to go barging in on him," Victoria protested even as Kiernan went to pull on his boots.

"I have every right, bein's yar still me wife." He watched her flinch at his statement but refused to calm down and deal with the matter in a more civilized manner.

He was out the door and halfway down the steps when he heard her call after him to come back. This infuriated him even more. To imagine that she would be in defense of Thorndike's unforgivable actions was more than he wanted to contend with.

Slamming the front door and making his way down the street, it suddenly dawned on him that he had no idea where Thorndike lived. This sobered him in a way that nothing else could have. How ridiculous it seemed to be traipsing about the city, looking to pick a fight with a man, and having no idea where the man could even be found. He would have laughed at himself had the situation not been so serious.

This isn't about Thorndike, he finally allowed himself to realize. Thorndike should never have been an issue, but then perhaps if Kiernan would have been a better husband and listened to the needs of his wife, she wouldn't have been enticed by the dashing man's attention.

Turning, Kiernan forced his hands into his trouser pockets and made his way slowly back to the apartment. What was he to do?

He climbed the steps very reluctantly and, with each movement of his foot, wondered how he could possibly explain his heart to Victoria. It seemed logical to just spill out his thoughts, but women were queer creatures. Sometimes they reacted to the silliest things, while other issues of graver importance were cast aside in indifference. If he explained to her the fears and inadequacies he faced every day, would she understand? Or would she shrug them off and call him foolish for his thinking? He didn't think he could stand it if she found his thoughts to be senseless and foolish.

He came into the apartment and immediately spied her sitting on the sofa, tears streaming down her face. He drew a deep breath and tried to force his own emotions into order.

"I'm sorry," he said softly. "I know yar thinkin' me a big fool."

"No, not really," Victoria replied in a barely audible voice.

"I saw the flowers and it reminded me all over of how I'd failed ya at the dance. I should've been with ya and I'm sorry."

She looked up and nodded. "I'm sorry too."

But Kiernan noted something in her demeanor. A stiffness, an unyielding spirit that seemed to mask her pain. This wasn't over. He knew it without her having to say a word. The issue wasn't Thorndike, but for the present, Thorndike seemed to be all that either one was willing to deal with.

27

Victoria couldn't shake the depression that engulfed her in the week following her argument with Kiernan. She longed to put the matter behind her, but her heart kept reminding her that their fight had had very little to do with her indiscretions at the party. In fact, Kiernan had made it clear that she had done nothing wrong. This made her feel only marginally better, but still the guilt worked at her. She alone knew the thoughts that had been on her heart as Thorndike had shown her attention.

Determined to focus on something other than her misery, she set about to clean her house. She swept the floors and dusted their few pieces of furniture, but the fact that the apartment needed so little cleaning only magnified the emptiness of her life. She went into the bedroom and began rearranging dresser drawers. That done, she turned her attention to the trunk. Perhaps some of the summer clothing she had stored there needed mending. The hot season would be upon them in no time.

But rummaging through the trunk, Victoria found an item she had forgotten all about. It was a small quilt top she had started years ago on her journey from Baltimore to California. Her heart clenched as she remembered with what wonderful hopes she had begun the project. In honor of the home she was leaving, she had chosen to do a Baltimore Album quilt. Each appliqué block was to represent something special to her and Kiernan. A wreath of four-leaf clovers for Ireland, a basket of daisies—Victoria's favorite flowers—a circle of railroad track with little cars. That's as far as she had gotten. Actually, the train was not even half finished. Victoria had lost interest after that, or rather, she had lost heart for it. It was supposed to be for her baby. A baby that had never come. As they'd moved from one mining settlement to another, Victoria had packed and repacked the unfinished quilt to take it along with them.

It seemed silly to keep it, in light of the fact that Victoria now felt confident there would never be a baby to wrap it around. But it seemed even more foolish to keep the thing put away and idle in a trunk at the foot of her bed.

Smoothing the pieces out, Victoria smiled at her own perfect stitches. Her mother had marveled at the way she had taken to sewing, something Carolina had never really mastered. It had been their housekeeper Miriam who had taught Victoria. She had loved quilting from the start—the creativity, the skill, and the immense satisfaction with the finished results. It wasn't until that moment that Victoria began to realize just how long it had been since she'd done any real sewing. She'd mended Kiernan's shirts and pants, taken in or let out her own dresses and skirts, but mostly it was the kind of work that required no real skill. She had chided Anna for paying Li extra money to make over the hand-me-down gowns, when she herself could have performed the task for free. But Anna had reminded Victoria that the young girl needed all the money she could get. Li was yet another immigrant who hoped to bring her family to America, and money was as good as a ticket.

Victoria focused once more on the quilt top. Perhaps she should finish it off for Li. But even as the thought came to mind, Victoria knew she could never do that. This quilt was for *her* baby—not someone else's. Lovingly, she studied the pieces. The fabric had come from many of her own girlhood dresses. Most of the colors were pastel and dainty, most befitting of a young girl. Victoria had worried that perhaps it would be too feminine in the event a son was born to them instead of a daughter. That's when Kiernan had suggested the "train" block. After all, they both hoped to have a son as their firstborn. But now she'd gladly take a boy or a girl, and it seemed unimportant that the quilt might not be exactly perfect.

Tears came to her eyes. She drew the pieces to her heart as though drawing her infant there. Oh, God, she prayed, please send me a child. A baby of my own. That's all I ask.

A knock at the front door drew her attention away from her pleadings. She put the pieces aside and, sniffing back tears, tried her best to dry her eyes.

Opening the door, Victoria was surprised to find her landlord on the other side. "I have a couple of letters for you," the man announced, shoving the envelopes forward.

Victoria took the much-welcomed mail and smiled. "Thank you so much."

The man muttered something incoherent and shuffled down the hall to continue his deliveries. Victoria didn't mind that he wasn't the type to make small talk. She was too excited about the letters in her hands. Mail rarely came to them with all their moving around, and glancing down to read the script, she felt her heart skip a beat at the unmistakable handwriting of her mother.

Hurrying to the table, Victoria put the other letter down and opened her mother's missive with great delight. It had been over a year since she'd had any word from anyone back east.

Dearest Victoria,

Lest we seem remiss in our communications, I must apologize and tell you of our circumstances. We returned to America in February, only to find that Baltimore had become a city of great unrest. The war has escalated to a point that gave your father great fear for the safety of his children and thus has hastened our return home.

Our solicitor, Mr. Marcum, passed away some weeks ago, and in

his passing, a great deal was left undone. I suppose this war is to blame
for much of it, but in spite of this, there have come several issues to my
attention that I felt should be shared with you.

The most important is that Brenton and Jordana have taken it
upon their shoulders to leave New York and journey west with Kiernan's
sister Caitlan.

Victoria gasped. Kiernan's sister was in America! But when had
this happened and why hadn't anyone notified them? Victoria thought
of the letters she'd sent to the solicitor and realized quickly that the
man had probably been too ill to forward word of their ever-changing
location to Kiernan's family in Ireland. She quickly read on.

We haven't a fixed location on where Brenton and Jordana are at
the present. Apparently they are working on some photography project
of Brenton's, or so the correspondence he's forwarded would imply. Your
father is even now trying to get information regarding their precise
whereabouts. We've had no word of York or Virginia and feel rather
hard-pressed as we pray for our scattered family.

The rest of the letter was mostly news about their time abroad
and how much Carolina missed Victoria. She also expressed her worries about the war and concluded the letter by giving Victoria a new
address for them in New York City. It seemed that her mother and
father both felt New York would be safer than remaining in Baltimore
or Washington.

Victoria reread the letter twice before settling back to consider
the contents. Caitlan was somewhere in America, making her way to
California. In fact, her own brother and sister were accompanying
her. How wonderful it would be to see Brenton and Jordana again!
They had both been children when Victoria had headed west, and
now they would be grown.

Then a worrisome thought came to mind. How long had they
been making the journey? When had they started, and by what means
were they making their way west? The letter said nothing of this.

Her first reaction had been to give Kiernan the news of his sister's arrival in America, but with these thoughts spinning through her head, Victoria began to wonder if that would be foolish. He already had so much to worry about, and if she told him that Caitlan and Brenton and Jordana were somewhere en route to California—well, he might insist on going out to meet them. And even if he didn't, Victoria knew there would be no living with him until he knew they were safely in his care.

She folded the letter and put it in her pocket. Perhaps it would be better to say nothing. She picked up the other envelope and began to open it. The only writing on the outside was a feminine penning of her own name.

Victoria,
    Please meet me for lunch at the Tea Room on J street. Eleven-thirty.

Anna

What fun! Victoria thought. It was so like Anna to do something like this to boost her spirits. She glanced at the clock and was startled to see that it was already eleven o'clock. She would have to hurry to get ready in order to meet Anna on time.

She took Anna's invitation and the letter from her mother and tucked both inside the quilt pieces and put them back into the trunk. Kiernan would never think to go snooping there, so the news about Caitlan would be safe for a time. She wondered how she could possibly keep the issue from her husband until Caitlan's arrival, but then she thought of the fact that he would no doubt be joining Charlie Crocker up at Donner Pass for most of the spring and summer. That should give the trio more than enough time to make their way to California, she surmised.

Dressing in her favorite lavender afternoon dress, Victoria struggled to get the last few buttons done up. It was always nice to dress when Kiernan was present in order to have him help her, but she knew he wasn't due home until later that day and would have to make do herself.

Finally accomplishing the task, Victoria carefully styled her hair and pinned a net around the bulk of it. Feeling quite smart, she pulled on white gloves, again a discard of Anna Judah, and took up her small purse. She hadn't been treated to luncheon out since the last time Anna had gotten the idea for them to share the afternoon in fashionable splendor. No doubt they would walk to one of the parks and enjoy the fine spring day after dining on delicacies from the Tea Room.

Victoria hurried down the stairs, then forced herself to calm. There was no sense in making a spectacle of herself. She felt a surge of excitement, however. A day out, a wonderful letter from home—it was all enough to help spring her from her depressed state. She would simply forget about the concerns of the day and enjoy herself. There would be plenty of time to take up her miseries when the evening came.

The Tea Room had been designed as a fashionable gathering place for ladies of society. Victoria felt quite honored when the maitre d' appeared and led her to a small, secluded table. A fine Irish linen cloth graced the top, and at the center of this was a small bouquet of carnations and lilies of the valley. Victoria allowed the man to seat her and waited in awe for Anna to appear.

The establishment had several rooms, most with only a few tables per area in order to give the diners a feeling of privacy and leisure. Victoria immediately relaxed and remembered with fondness a place she and her mother had loved to frequent in Baltimore. They had gone shopping for her bridal trousseau and paused in the midst of their mounting purchases to enjoy lunch together. These were the memories Victoria faced with bittersweetness, for they both bolstered her soul and discouraged her heart all at the same time.

"I wasn't sure you would come."

The masculine voice caused Victoria to start. She looked up to find Christopher Thorndike standing over her table.

"What are you doing here?" she asked, forcing herself to sound unconcerned by his presence.

Thorndike grinned conspiratorially and took the seat opposite her at the small table. "I suppose some explanation is in order," he said, his dark eyes piercing her facade of control.

"I'm afraid you can't stay here," Victoria began. "I'm meeting a friend."

"Yes, I know. Anna Judah."

He said the words so matter-of-factly that Victoria instantly knew she was in trouble. "You sent the invitation."

"Yes, I did," he replied, leaning forward. "I inquired around and learned you and Mrs. Judah were friends. I knew you would not have come to meet me under any other circumstance."

"And Anna is not coming?" Victoria already knew the answer.

"No."

He seemed to challenge her with his expression. Victoria knew in that moment she should get up and leave. She realized, too, that Thorndike expected her to make one move or another—to either accept his scandalous behavior or snub him and leave, as was her right.

His expression softened. "Please don't be angry with me. I couldn't help myself."

Victoria felt her armor slip away. "No?" she said, her voice almost a squeak.

He reached across and caught hold of her gloved hand. "I so thoroughly enjoyed your company on the night of the party. You are so different from other women, and I knew I had to see you again. And here you are, more lovely than ever."

Victoria warmed under his scrutiny. There was something almost mesmerizing about the man, and Victoria found rational thought leave her. "I'm . . . I'm . . . not sure—"

"Not sure of what?" Thorndike interjected the question as though this were nothing more than a passing hello.

"I'm married," she finally managed to say.

He chuckled softly, causing the hair on the back of her neck to prickle. "Yes, I'm well aware of your Irish-tempered husband. Quite the bully, eh?"

Victoria shook her head, trying to force herself to look away. "He's not."

"He didn't seem to care at all what you wanted the night of the dance. Why, people at the party were appalled that he should so callously drag you from the room."

Victoria felt her face grow hot. Her breathing quickened, and for a moment she actually thought she might be sick. "I should go," she murmured.

"Nonsense. We are in a public establishment, and no one can fault you for having tea with a friend."

"But you are hardly a friend, Mr. Thorndike."

He frowned and looked almost hurt by this statement. "I thought us to be at least that."

Victoria fought against her emotions. She reminded herself of Kiernan's anger over the flowers, but as soon as this thought came to mind, she also remembered that he had apologized. He had told her there was nothing wrong in her behavior. It wasn't the same as saying that it had been acceptable for Thorndike to send the flowers, but it assuaged her guilt for the words she uttered next.

"I suppose we can be friendly acquaintances."

He tightened his hold, and only then did Victoria realize that he still held her hand. "Perhaps we can be infinitely more."

"No, that wouldn't be proper," Victoria replied, pulling her hand away from his. "Mr. Thorndike, my husband does not approve of your attention toward me."

"No doubt," the man replied and leaned back in his chair. "I show him up."

"What?"

"I make him see where he fails to meet your need."

Victoria knew Kiernan already felt inadequate. Perhaps that was the reason for his anger at Thorndike's actions. It wasn't that she had done anything improper—at least, not by western society. But Thorndike made Kiernan feel remiss in having spent the evening sequestered away with his railroad cronies. Victoria suddenly felt a weight of guilt removed from her shoulders. If Kiernan felt guilty for having left her to her own devices, then why should that be her problem?

"Victoria," Thorndike said her name softly—seductively—foregoing any pretense at formality. "I didn't come here to discuss your husband. I merely wanted to see you again. I enjoy talking with a woman of intelligence, and I find your interest in the railroad to be fascinating. Please agree to stay to lunch with me. I promise nothing improper will happen."

Victoria realized she was being foolish. They were in a public place, albeit a rather secluded one. But it wouldn't be long before other diners gathered in their little alcove.

"All right," she found herself replying. "Just this once."

He smiled, his dark eyes gleaming. "Just this once."

Nearly two hours later, Victoria was amazed to find that the time had slipped away so quickly. She was also surprised by the fact that no one else had come to join them in their room. The two other tables had remained conspicuously empty.

Thorndike had asked her a million questions. Furthermore, he'd openly and honestly listened to her answers. Victoria found herself confiding things in him that she would never have thought to share with another man. She told him of her homesickness, of longing to see Washington and Baltimore and her family. She shared her worries about the Civil War and how dreadful it was to think that she had family on both sides of the issue. Thorndike had been sympathetic and reassuring, explaining to her the details of several battles and how unlikely it would be that any of these would cause harm to her beloved cities or loved ones. She thought perhaps he had simplified things a bit too much, treating her as though she were too precious to be burdened with the truth. But she almost preferred that to knowing the details that frightened her so much. Kiernan, who rarely shared any conversation with her these days unless it pertained to the railroad, was always quite forthright with his opinions. He never seemed overly

JUDITH PELLA / TRACIE PETERSON

worried that his comments might cause her grief, whereas Thorndike seemed to care greatly.

She refrained from allowing him to escort her home, reminding him that to be seen together would imply something other than the truth. She left him standing by the table, a warm, deliciously pleasant smile upon his face and an intriguing gleam in his eye.

"Until we meet again," he whispered and kissed her hand.

Victoria shook her head. "That mustn't happen, Mr. Thorndike. For reasons of which we are both very much aware."

She exited the Tea Room and breathed deeply of the afternoon air. What had she done? She felt her breath come in quick gasps as she considered how her actions would be perceived by anyone who had witnessed her that day in the restaurant. Why did she have to feel so confused? How was it that this man could disarm all of her convictions with a single glance?

She picked up her pace and was determined to go see Anna. She had to have someone else's perspective on this, and Anna would be the only one to understand. But upon arriving at the Judah home, Victoria was met at the door by an obviously pregnant Li.

"Mistress gone. She be back plenty soon," the tiny almond-eyed girl told her.

"Please tell her I called," Victoria instructed, then turned quickly for home.

I don't understand my feelings, Victoria told herself. I don't know what to do. I love my husband, but everything seems so wrong. Christopher makes me feel cared about. He listens to me. He opens his heart and soul to me.

She pressed her hands to her forehead and tried to force out the disturbing thoughts.

"I love *you*, Kiernan," she whispered, grateful no one was nearby to hear her talking to herself. For some reason it did nothing to ease her sense of panic. Something was happening to her—something out of her control.

PART · FOUR

MARCH–DECEMBER 1863

28

Brenton struggled to harness the two draft horses to the wagon. He had no one to blame but himself for the fact that his life had so completely turned upside down. It had started with the collodion photograph he'd sent to Vanderbilt. Billy had been so impressed by the quality of the picture that he insisted Brenton make all the photographs from this process. Brenton had tried to explain that in order to travel and maintain a supply of collodion processing equipment and chemicals, he would have to purchase a wagon and additional supplies, but Billy didn't care. He simply ordered Brenton to buy whatever he needed and to draw on the draft of funds he would wire to one of the Kansas City banks.

Brenton knew he should be glad for the opportunity, but instead he worried about what all it involved. He now would have to care for horses and a wagon, not to mention keeping the proper supplies on hand. It also changed their lifestyle. Before, Billy had very graciously moved them from place to place aboard steam packers or trains, and always they had stayed in comfortable hotels or, at the least, proper boardinghouses. But now they would travel much slower, and Billy wanted detailed photographs of all the Missouri River towns.

In a discussion between Jordana and Caitlan, the decision had been made to purchase equipment that would allow the trio to remain on the road. The girls would help drive the wagon, but an additional horse would be purchased, and they would each alternate riding ahead of the slower team in order to check out the lay of the land and ensure that the path was clearly accessible to the wagon. Jordana thought it great fun to learn how to handle the larger geldings. The horses were thicker and more sturdy than the riding horses she had enjoyed as a girl. They were bigger, too, than the carriage horses she was used to seeing in and around the towns they visited. Caitlan, who'd had more experience than either Jordana or Brenton, easily showed them how to go about harnessing the team and hitching them to the wagon. She was undaunted by the size of the horses—undaunted, too, by the change in their travel plans.

Brenton admired her for her abilities. She never seemed to mind when he needed her help on one matter or another. In fact, she had taken quite an interest in his photography and was rapidly becoming an asset to him in that area as well.

The horse shifted, momentarily setting Brenton off balance as he tried to secure the lines. Putting his shoulder against the chestnut gelding, Brenton pushed with all his might until the animal was inclined to shift back in line with his partner.

Jordana laughed. "Sometimes it's hard to tell who's harnessing whom."

Brenton completed the task and pushed up his glasses with a grin. "Next time you can do the job."

"I'm getting pretty good at it," Jordana countered. "It might take me a while, but I'd get the job down."

"Yes, but by then the war would be over and the railroad built and Billy would have no need of us to be out here in the American wilderness."

"I'd hardly be callin' Kansas City a wilderness," Caitlan said, coming from behind the wagon. "Look, I've loaded the rest of those supplies. Will ya be needin' anything else stored back there?"

Brenton shook his head. "No, I think that's the last of it. Did you ladies get everything you need for the trip? Warm clothing? Blankets?"

"I have everything," Jordana replied.

"Aye, I'm thinkin' we're as ready to head out as we could possibly be," Caitlan answered.

"Well, then, I need to make my way to the bank," Brenton said, dusting off his pants and donning his jacket. "I need to get our traveling funds and see if Billy has left any additional instructions. I'll leave you ladies to stay with the wagon. I shouldn't be long." He mounted the saddle horse, then looked down at the two women who were his dearest friends in the world. "Now, you're absolutely sure I can't get you anything while I'm away?"

"No, we're fine. Just hurry back," Jordana replied for them both.

Brenton found his banking business to be without complications. There was, however, a letter from Billy Vanderbilt. Opening the missive while still inside the bank's lobby, Brenton was taken aback at the news.

G.W.'s health continues to fail. The commodore has asked me to join G.W. in Europe, as it is hoped that the curative powers of the French Riviera will soon see him right again. I suppose it couldn't have come at a worse time, given our project, but there should be enough money here to see you through for a time. Go ahead with our plans for photographing the area towns, and I will instruct Daniel Davidson to act in my stead. He will advise you on what property to purchase and will wire you funding if that becomes necessary. Continue sending the photographs in care of my home, and Davidson will make arrangements here to pick them up for the investors' consideration.

There were other details, comments on the war and the dangers that would no doubt complicate Brenton's life should they go farther south than Kansas City. Billy advised them to continue working north, taking care to avoid any conflict with border ruffians. Brenton knew this would be the real challenge of the trip. Border ruffians, bushwhackers, and jayhawkers from Missouri and Kansas were in a constant state of war with one another. It came as a kind of unofficial extension of the Civil War, with younger, meaner, less organized warriors who marauded the Kansas-Missouri border looking for trouble and profit.

Billy had concluded the letter by stating that it was uncertain if G.W. would recover, but it was his intention to see him through to the end. Brenton felt a burden of guilt for not having told Jordana of the situation. She would no doubt have wished to have tried one last time to send G.W. a letter, and now it might be too late. Brenton noted that Billy wouldn't be sailing from New York for three days. Perhaps Brenton could telegraph Billy a message from Jordana to G.W.

Hurrying back to the wagon, Brenton found Jordana and Caitlan laughing gaily over some matter. He hated to break into their happy moment but could think of no other way to allow Jordana to get word to G.W. except to do it immediately. Summoning up his courage, Brenton dismounted and tied the horse to the back of the wagon.

"Jordana," he began hesitantly. "We need to talk."

Caitlan seemed to sense his gravity first. "I'll go recheck the equipment," she offered, then slipped into the back of the wagon before anyone could protest.

Brenton studied his sister for a moment and wondered how best to break the news. She was nearly full grown, and as he studied her more closely than usual, the fact shocked his senses. She looked a great deal like their mother. Dark hair and brown eyes. She was spirited like their mother as well.

"So what has you looking so serious this time?" Jordana questioned with a smile.

"Come walk with me a ways." Brenton reached out to help her down from the wagon seat.

Jordana nodded, hiked up her serviceable wool skirt, and stepped down onto the wheel. From here, Brenton easily lifted her to the ground and slipped his arm around her shoulder.

"Something happened a while back, and I didn't tell you about it right away because I thought I would wait and see what came of it before worrying you."

Jordana stopped and looked up at him. "Is it Mother and Father?"

"No," Brenton replied softly. "G.W."

"G.W.? Is he . . . ?"

"Dead?" Brenton shook his head. "But he doesn't show signs of getting any better. Billy is off to tend to G.W. in Europe, and frankly . . . well . . . it doesn't look good."

"What?" Jordana said, shaking her head. "Are you saying that he *will* die?"

Brenton shrugged his shoulders and tried to think of some way to affirm her worry without just coming right out and saying it. "Billy says he hasn't responded to the doctor's treatments. They've spared no expense; obviously money wasn't a worry."

"He's dying. That's what you're trying to tell me, isn't it?" Jordana questioned, her voice rising slightly.

Brenton nodded. "I suppose it is."

Her face contorted as her brows knit together in worry. "Why didn't you tell me immediately?"

"I had hoped his sickness would be short-lived, and then I could just mention it in passing with the assurance that he was well and fine. But apparently that isn't going to happen."

Jordana looked down at the ground. "I can't believe this. You should have told me sooner."

"I'm sorry, Jordana. I was only trying to save you grief. I knew you'd feel bad, especially in light of his refusal to correspond with you. I just didn't want you worrying about something you couldn't do anything about."

Her head snapped up at this. "You should have told me!" she declared more angrily. "I deserved to know. He was more my friend than yours. You were wrong to keep it from me, Brenton."

Brenton swallowed hard, realizing that he'd hurt her more deeply than he'd ever intended. "I'm sorry."

"So am I," Jordana replied curtly. "Sorry you didn't trust me to be strong enough to handle the truth. G.W. said he'd go to his grave hating me. I guess you've played right into his plan."

She stormed off down the street, arms crossed to her breast as if trying to force her emotions to remain inside. Brenton thought to go after her, then decided it would be better to give her a few minutes to gather her composure. When she came back on her own accord, he would suggest sending Billy the telegram. He didn't care if it cost a fortune. He would encourage her to say whatever she wanted, no matter the length.

He came back to the wagon and sat down on the back gate. Jordana was just a girl in many ways, he reminded himself. She had just turned seventeen. How could he expect her to deal with any of this? He began to feel guilty all over again. Guilty for having allowed her to talk him into going west. Guilty for having put her life in danger. Guilty for having kept the news of G.W.'s increased sickness from her for so long.

"Are ya goin' to be tellin' me what this is all about?" Caitlan asked from behind him.

Brenton looked upward over his shoulder. "G.W. Vanderbilt is dying. I just had a letter from Mr. Vanderbilt, and it would seem that recovery will now take a miracle. Billy is even going to Europe to be with G.W. through to the end. The thing is, I've known for some time that he was slipping away and I chose not to tell Jordana. I kept hoping that G.W. would get well."

"I'm sorry, Brenton," Caitlan replied, kneeling down beside where he sat. She put her hand on his shoulder. "Ya only did what ya thought was best."

He reached up and touched her hand with his own. "Thank you for saying so. That was the plan, but now I fear I've hurt her more by keeping it from her."

A nagging headache seemed to spread out from somewhere behind his eyes, and Brenton let go of Caitlan's hand and pulled off his glasses. "I should have told her everything. The moment I knew about G.W.,

I should have told her." He rubbed his eyes, trying to isolate the pain and work away the tension. It refused to go.

"Brenton, ya know I don't share yar beliefs in God." Caitlan surprised him with this bold declaration since she usually avoided the subject. He stopped rubbing his eyes and looked over at her. "But maybe this is one of those times of trial ya always seem to be talkin' about. Maybe God is usin' this for yar good." She smiled. "I feel silly for even sayin' such a thing."

"Don't," Brenton replied. "I think you care more about those things than you let on. I think you're hurt from what you've seen and heard in your country, but I think you still have hope that God is really a God who cares and loves us."

"It's a lovely thought, Brenton," she replied, getting back to her feet. "But so, too, is the thought of pots of gold and fairies grantin' wishes. Ya can't convince me that one is more real than the other."

Brenton wanted to say something more, but Caitlan spied Jordana. "Ya should go to her," she gently urged.

Brenton looked up and saw Jordana walking slowly back toward the wagon. She had obviously been crying, and Brenton's heart nearly broke in two at the sight of her.

He went to her, opening his arms. Jordana quietly slipped into his embrace, and mindless of the traffic upon the streets and walkway, she began to cry again.

"He was a good friend," she murmured. "He made me laugh and he took me into his confidence. He trusted me and I betrayed him, and now I've caused him to—" She couldn't even say the word.

"You didn't cause G.W. to take sick, and your refusal to marry didn't worsen his condition. You simply weren't ready for what he had in mind. It didn't make you wrong and him right or even the other way around. It simply was the way things worked out."

"But now he'll die and that's it. There'll never be a chance to tell him my heart. He won't even read my letters."

"I thought of that," Brenton replied. "Billy sails in a few days.

There's still time to get a telegram to him. Why don't you put all of your feelings for G.W. into a message that Billy can take with him to Europe?"

Jordana sniffed and looked up at her brother. "Could we? Do you really think Billy would do that for me?"

"I'm sure he would. G.W. would have to listen, and maybe now, maybe facing the possibility of his own death, he'll put matters to rest."

"Do you suppose he might get well?" Jordana asked hopefully.

"Of course, anything's possible. With God, all things are possible."

"But that includes his death," Jordana replied.

"If that's God's plan, then, yes, I suppose so."

Controlling her emotions, Jordana squared her shoulders. "I must accept that possibility." She gave the tiniest hint of a smile. "Of course, G.W. is rather stubborn. God might well want him, but G.W. may not be inclined to go."

Brenton grinned. "It would be just like him to argue with God."

She nodded. "Take me to the telegraph office, please."

"On one condition," Brenton replied.

"What?"

"That you promise to forgive me. You don't have to do it right now, but I couldn't bear it if you held this against me. I know I should have told you sooner, and I'm sorry—more sorry than you'll ever know."

Jordana hugged him tightly, and he knew in that moment that she would never let anything come between them. "Of course I forgive you. I love you."

Brenton breathed a sigh of relief. The burden was gone. "I love you, too, little sister. I only pray I've done right by you." He glanced up to find Caitlan watching from the wagon. "I pray I've done right by both of you."

————

The next day, the trio was deep into the Missouri woodlands headed for St. Joseph. They'd been advised, due to skirmishes between border ruffians, to take a riverboat. But paying the freight on shipping the horses and wagon was outrageous, and since Brenton had just managed to have the wagon made to his specifications, he wasn't about to leave it behind. And because the wagon and horses had cost more than Brenton had planned on, he was trying hard to be frugal with their remaining funds. He assured the girls that God would see them through, but at times he appeared worried.

Caitlan was still amazed at the strength Brenton and Jordana took in their faith. Jordana had spoken on many occasions of how following God's Word had given her life order, but Caitlan found it difficult to believe. So far, all she had ever known in association with religious beliefs and God had been chaos and struggles.

Yet to Jordana and Brenton, God seemed not only real and trustworthy but orderly and consistent. This baffled Caitlan in light of the many times she'd struggled to understand God. In her homeland, men of faith had argued among themselves as to who was right and who was wrong. One faith condemned another in such a way that Caitlan grew weary of the protesting arguments and the physical fighting. And while it was true that most of the physical violence was more directed toward heavy-handed landlords and English bullying, there was a constant underlying hatred between those of one religious affiliation and those of another. It didn't make sense, and it didn't matter to the parties concerned that it didn't make sense.

Sitting beside Brenton as he drove the wagon down the chilly wooded trail, Caitlan pulled her shawl tighter and glanced overhead at the dimming light. It was the first of April and the trees were just now greening up and their leaves were a pale, almost silvery green that came with new growth. The countryside around them was coming alive with the warming of the season. But as the wind picked up a bit, Caitlan was quickly reminded that April would certainly not yet offer them summer warmth.

"Should we be findin' a place to camp?" she asked Brenton, keeping her gaze fixed on the sky.

"I suppose so," he replied, his tone rather breathless, weary, as if each word was an effort.

She looked at him and for the first time noticed that he looked pale. "Are ya ill, Brenton?"

"I think I might be," he replied without much ado. "My head's been hurting since yesterday, but I thought it was only my ordeal over Jordana and G.W."

"Here," Caitlan said, reaching out, "let me feel yar head." She touched him and found him to be burning hot. "Ya have a fever!" she declared. "Give me the reins and go inside to lie down. Jordana and I will find a place to stop for the night."

"No, I'm all right. Let's just keep moving. I'm sure I'll feel better."

Caitlan hated to argue with him, but she felt she couldn't let the situation go on. "Yar sick, Brenton. Now, let me help ya."

He reined back on the team and looked at her with a glassy-eyed stare that left little doubt in Caitlan's mind that the illness was serious enough to stop. "Please, Brenton," she said softly. "Don't be tryin' to impress me—ya do that all the time as it is."

He smiled in a crooked, lopsided way, then leaned back heavily against the wooden frame of the customized wagon. "All right. Take the reins, but I'm staying right here until we stop."

She nodded. "Jordana!" Caitlan called to Jordana who was riding ahead. "We should be findin' some place to camp."

"Looks like a clearing up ahead. I'll go check it out." She urged the horse forward while Caitlan kept the team moving at a steady pace.

"We should be stoppin' soon," she said to Brenton. He made no comment, and glancing over, Caitlan found that he'd already closed his eyes in sleep.

Worry consumed her. They should have stayed in Kansas City. Now they were well too far away to get back should Brenton require a doctor's attention, and St. Joseph was not anywhere near enough.

Jordana came back smiling. "There's a nice clearing up ahead with

a good place coming off the river where we can water the horses."
She noticed Brenton and laughed. "Have we already worn him out?"

Caitlan shook her head. "He's sick, Jordana. He's got a fever."

Jordana's smile faded. "Sick?" She let the wagon come up even
with her mount, then reached out to touch her brother. "Brenton?"

"Hmm?" he barely stirred.

She threw a worried look at Caitlan. "What shall we do?"

"We'll make camp and take care of him," Caitlan replied. What
else could they do?

29

Caitlan fussed over Brenton while Jordana gathered wood and water. Neither woman wanted to admit her fear, but Caitlan knew Jordana was every bit as worried as she was. This part of the woods wasn't a safe place for anyone, not during these border-war times. Caitlan remembered Jordana reading an article in the newspaper while they were still in Kansas City. It spoke of the animosity between renegade groups who used the war as an excuse for all manner of lawlessness. And the authorities seemed to have little or no control over these ruffians.

Because of this trouble, Brenton had insisted they purchase a rifle to take with them, figuring it was cheaper than traveling north by river, but it gave Caitlan little reassurance. If a group of ruffians overran them, there would be little time in which to go running for the rifle. And now, with Brenton ill, they were essentially two vulnerable women—regardless of how independent both girls liked to think of themselves.

Brenton stirred and Caitlan swabbed his head with a wet cloth. "Ya have no right to go getting' sick now, Mr. Baldwin," she chided, knowing full well he was beyond hearing her words. Somehow it made her feel better to just ramble in conversation to him.

"How's he doing?" Jordana laid another branch on the small fire.

They knew to be cautious about fires in this area, but both agreed they needed the fire to keep Brenton from chilling.

"He's the same. Sleepin' mostly." Caitlan glanced up to meet Jordana's worried expression. "I'm supposin' he could use some of those prayers yar so fond of."

Jordana grinned. "I'm supposin'," she began, mimicking Caitlan's brogue, "that ya could be offerin' up some of yar own."

Caitlan smiled. "I guess I had that comin'."

Jordana shook her head. "You shouldn't distance God, Caitlan. He really does understand." She paused and Caitlan was glad Jordana didn't choose to pursue the subject. She only added, "Look, I'd better see to the horses."

"And for certain do ya think ya can manage? They can be a fiercesome pair."

The younger woman laughed. "I'm as certain as I can get—under the circumstances." She tramped off to where the horses were awaiting their care.

Caitlan felt a twinge of guilt. She supposed she should leave Brenton and go help Jordana. After all, she was more experienced in the care of animals. In Ireland, her brother-in-law had two rather mean horses that plowed the fields and pulled the wagon. She remembered being nipped by one in particular on more than one occasion. The memory would have made her laugh, except she couldn't take her eyes from the pale face of the man she'd fallen in love with.

It hurt to see him like this—so vulnerable and weak. That was how the world usually saw him, but not Caitlan. To her, Brenton was a pillar of strength. Perhaps he tended to fight his own conscience too much, but he only did so because his heart was so full of caring for those he loved. Of course, there was the issue of God and the faith that Brenton held dear. Caitlan smiled. He seemed to know her heart better on the matter than she did herself. He had told her on more than one occasion that he didn't believe she'd given up on God, but rather had given up on herself and her people.

Perhaps he was right. At least, at the moment she truly wished it were so. She reached down and smoothed back a strand of his light brown hair. His chin and jaw bore signs of stubble, and Caitlan smiled as she ran her fingers along the lines of his face. She thought him very nearly perfect.

"I know ya can't hear me, but ya just better get well," she leaned down to whisper. "I've lost me heart to ya, Brenton Baldwin, and I won't have ya dying on me now." Mindless of his illness, she leaned closer and, without thought to being seen by Jordana, kissed Brenton lightly on the lips. "Ya have to get well, me love."

———

Brenton stirred in the night and, with a rush of fear, opened his eyes and tried to take in his surroundings. His head still ached, but he didn't feel quite so chilled. He wondered how long he had been ill. Glancing to his right he could see the outside of the wagon. In the shadowy light he made out a form underneath it and wondered if it was Jordana or Caitlan.

Struggling to raise his head, Brenton looked to his left and found their only source of light, a small campfire. He saw just beyond this another form that he could now definitely identify as Caitlan sleeping peacefully on the ground. He smiled and fell back against the ground. What pleasant dreams he'd had of her. Dreams of sweet words and kisses as soft as summer rains. He closed his eyes, hoping the dreams would return. She was quite a woman, he decided. Sleep began to overtake him once again, even as he heard Caitlan stir and throw more wood on the fire. She was all that a man could want in a wife.

———

The next morning found Brenton's fever gone and his appetite returning. His companions told him he'd been two full days in the delirium of fever. The day after that he was much improved, but because he was still in a rather weakened state, the girls decided it would be best to remain where they were for another day.

"Ya'll soon be on yar feet," Caitlan told him, "then we can press on to St. Joseph."

"I don't think we should even bother," Jordana surprised them by saying. "I mean, Billy Vanderbilt is out of the country for who knows how long. You have no way of knowing what the investors will want from you or how well they will keep to Mr. Vanderbilt's agreement. I say we head back to Kansas City and see about hooking up with a wagon train. I heard tell they leave out of there, or nearby, all the time. We could still get your pictures taken along the way, Brenton, and we'd get Caitlan to California in shorter order."

"Don't be changin' yar plans on my account," Caitlan protested. "Ya said yarself ya have no idea where to take me once we get to California. Better we wait until we hear from yar folks or that lawyer of yars."

"The last we heard, Mr. Marcum was ill. Who knows when we'll hear from him again?" Jordana protested.

"I don't like running out on Vanderbilt," Brenton said matter-of-factly.

"He's run out on you," Jordana countered.

"For a very good reason," Brenton replied.

"Well, this would be just as good a reason. Caitlan deserves our help. I think it's time we concentrated on getting to California."

Caitlan smiled. "Ya've helped me more than I had a right to. We've had a good time together, and I'll not be havin' ya change yar plans on account of me and that's final."

"To tell the truth," Jordana said more solemnly than usual, "I think we're in more danger here than we've ever been before. I mean, you know what the papers said."

Brenton nodded. This was perhaps the first thing she'd said that made a reasonable argument for leaving off with Vanderbilt's project and picking up with their own. "It is dangerous. I'd feel much better if we were farther north."

"Or in Kansas City," Jordana countered.

"I suppose she's right," Brenton said, looking at Caitlan. Something stirred inside him as he met her gaze. He remembered his feverish dreams of her, and it caused an involuntary grin to bend his lips. Covering this as best he could, he added, "Even Jordana deserves to be right some of the time. But I think we should push on for St. Joseph. It would get us farther north, and also it's where Vanderbilt will expect us in case he has any communication for me."

So it was decided that they would at least consider the possibility of ending their employment with Billy Vanderbilt. But they would wait until they reached St. Joseph before making the final decision. There would also be wagon trains departing from there should they opt for continuing immediately on to California.

"Are ya sure yar feelin' well enough to travel?" Caitlan asked Brenton as they ambled along toward the wagon.

"I'm much better," he said, pausing to look at her. "Thanks to you."

Caitlan blushed. "I cannot be takin' the credit. Jordana says that God of yars was the one to be doin' the healin'."

"Yes, I believe that's so," Brenton said, surprising her by reaching out to take hold of her hand. "I think you had something to do with it too. He used you to be His hands." He squeezed her fingers, then climbed up into the back of the wagon, trying hard to ignore the way she'd trembled at his touch. "I'm going to take a picture of that area over by the river before we leave. I think it will make a nice addition to my own collection."

"Ah . . . aye," Caitlan murmured.

Brenton smiled to himself as he went into the wagon and gathered his supplies together. She had feelings for him, of this he was certain. Now if only he could help her to see that God really loved her—then Brenton would feel free to prove that he loved her as well.

As Brenton packed his equipment, he noted with pleasure that everything was holding up nicely. Even with the rain a few days ago, all the contents of the specially designed wagon with its wood canopy had remained dry. Brenton had customized the wagon to suit his needs.

At the back was the tiniest of dark rooms where he could develop his photographs. All along one side were cabinets, built especially to house the precious chemicals for processing. On the other side a drop-down counter could be put in place for spreading out his work and allowing it to dry. When the counter was up and out of the way, there was a long boxlike structure that Brenton had deemed could be used for sleeping or sitting for those times when they were traveling in rain. He'd even managed to secure a goose-down tick for cushioning the top. Beneath this was storage for their clothing and personal goods, and overhead were hooks and nails for hanging a variety of goods. All in all, Brenton thought they'd made a marvelous use of the space.

He drew out his camera equipment, then went to work preparing the collodion glass plate. With meticulous care he arranged everything so that the moment the picture was taken, he could quickly return to the task of processing. He thought about how he wanted to set the scene as he prepared the glass negative. He could see it even now in his mind's eye—a steep embankment that overlooked the river. Framed by trees and distant meadowlands, Brenton believed it would make a most captivating photograph.

Caitlan stood ready to assist him, taking on the job of toting whatever needed toting, and running back to the wagon for any forgotten article. When they reached the specified spot, they were some distance from the wagon, and the real trick would be to make sure no dust particles or bits of dirt could work their way into the camera to attach themselves to the wet glass plate. Brenton didn't fret about such things, however. He was becoming quite competent at his work, and it pleased him immensely to have Caitlan take such an active interest.

No sooner had he finished taking the picture and begun to gather the equipment together than the unmistakable sound of horses could be heard. Exchanging a worried look with Caitlan, he hurried back to the wagon and put the equipment on the tailgate.

"Jordana!" he called, glancing around them for any sign of the riders.

Jordana appeared from out of the wooded brush. "I just staked the horses at the stream. What's the matter?"

"Riders," Brenton said, still trying to figure out from which direction the sound was coming.

He didn't have long to wait because, without warning, a group of seven or eight men crashed upon the camp from the trail to the south.

"Whoa!" one of the men yelled and slid his horse to a stop in the muddy path. He pulled a gun at the same time and pointed it directly at Brenton. "Well, well . . . what have we here?" he asked with a menacing scowl.

Brenton pulled Caitlan protectively behind him. "We're making our way to St. Joseph."

"Well, ain't that nice," the rough-looking man declared. His companions laughed heartily at this as he pushed back a filthy brown felt hat. "I do hate to be interruptin' your little trip, but I'd like to relieve you of your money."

"We don't have any money!" declared Jordana, stomping across the camp to join her brother. "Do you think we'd be sleeping out under a wagon and camping in the woods if we had money?"

"You just might. . . ." The fellow threw his leg over the horse and jumped to the ground.

Brenton took a step forward as the man approached Jordana. Not for the first time in his life, he wished his sister had been more a cowering wallflower. Silently he prayed she'd keep her mouth shut. This man hardly looked much older than she was, but it was apparent he was years beyond her in experience, and, Brenton guessed, the fellow certainly didn't hold the same values.

"She's right." Brenton thought of the rifle tucked snugly, and uselessly, in the back of the wagon. "We don't have anything of value," Brenton added rather lamely.

The other men were dismounting and handing their reins over to a boy who appeared to be the youngest in their group. Brenton guessed him to be no more than twelve or thirteen. In fact, none of the group looked old enough to be making war on passing strangers. Brenton figured the ring leader to be the oldest with the others looking more like fifteen or sixteen years of age.

"You got these purdy women," one of the ruffians called out as he approached. "I'd say they would be mighty valuable to some of us."

The leader reached out to take hold of Jordana, while Brenton, torn between protecting Caitlan and his sister, knew he was doubtless at a loss to help either. All of the men, if they could be called that, had guns, and none seemed adverse to using them.

"Where are your horses, little lady?" the leader asked Jordana, grabbing her arm and yanking her around to face him. She fought against his hold, which only irritated the ruffian.

"They're down that way," Brenton answered, pointing in the proper direction. "There's a stream that leads down the ravine to the river."

"We know this territory like the back of our hands," one boy said, sidling up to Brenton with his gun drawn. "Don't rightly think we need someone givin' us directions. Do we need a direction giver, Newt?" he asked their leader.

The gang laughed at this and Brenton knew he was rapidly losing ground. Caitlan let out a scream as one of the bushwhackers took hold of her. Brenton whirled around, but the kid who'd been taunting him quickly stuck his gun in Brenton's face.

"I wouldn't be interferin', mister. Jake don't hardly cotton to anyone comin' between him and his good times."

"Say, what's this stuff?" another of the boys asked.

He indicated the photographic equipment and Brenton grasped at this opportunity, hoping it would take their attention off the girls. "I'm a photographer—that's my camera."

"A photographer! Hey, Newt, wouldn't it be just the funniest thing to have this here pho-tog-rapher take our picture?"

The boys all laughed and offered their own comments on this.

"We've outrun them blue-bellies. I say we let this city dude take our picture before he dies."

"You can't kill him!" Jordana screamed, biting and kicking at her captor with renewed venom. "He's done you no harm."

The man called Newt tightened his hold on Jordana and jerked her head back by pulling on her hair. "Shut up, woman. I didn't ask for your opinion."

"Come on, Newt. Let's have us a picture. Your ma would be right proud to see us all a-workin' for the cause."

Newt laughed. "Guess a picture would be nice." He tossed Jordana to the ground, causing Brenton to once again start forward. "Stay where ya are, picture-man. She ain't goin' nowhere and she ain't hurt—not yet."

Brenton was seething inside. Behind him Caitlan was fighting and protesting her treatment. He could see Jordana sizing up Newt as if she were about to take him on. Somehow, he had to put an end to this without getting them all killed.

"All right. I'll take your picture." Brenton glanced upward, then looked across camp. "The lighting would be better over there," he said and pointed.

"Sam, you tie off those horses to this here wagon and come stand by me," Newt directed. "Jake, let the girl go—you can have her later." The bushwhackers moved into position, all the while keeping their weapons trained on their captives.

Brenton took his time in getting his "subjects" arranged just so, stalling for time, hoping some way of escape would materialize. If he ever did get the photograph taken, it would make for an interesting story, especially explaining the fact that the guns pointed toward the camera were all cocked and aimed at his head as well as Jordana's and Caitlan's.

"I'll have to get my supplies from inside," Brenton said when Newt began complaining about how much time he was taking. "I'll only be a minute."

Newt eyed him suspiciously. "Bear, you go with him," he instructed a burly young man—the meanest looking of the bunch.

Brenton tried not to appear disturbed by this. "I have some special paper I have to use for the photograph and a different camera. Why don't I hand these things down to you?" Bear just looked at him with a fierce expression that suggested the time for talking had passed.

Brenton felt the sweat trickle down his back. The weak, spongy feeling in his legs left him to wonder if he'd recovered from his sickness enough to do whatever battle was necessary to protect Jordana and Caitlan. He knew getting to the rifle would be impossible, and his fleeting notion of using his chemicals to create an explosion was also out of the question because the girls were too near the wagon.

"Hurry up, picture-man," Newt called. "And don't even think of doing something to irritate me. I'll kill this little gal as sure as I'll kill you. Won't much matter what order we go in."

Brenton froze in place. The feeling of helplessness washed over him. Please, God, he prayed, deliver us from this nightmare. Save us, Lord.

He found what he needed for the photograph and handed it down to Bear. Not wishing to waste expensive glass negatives on these criminals, he planned to use the calotype process. Taking the photograph would take longer, but it might buy them some precious time. He would also be careful not to mention that developing the photograph would take hours, not minutes. He didn't want to discourage them or—heaven forbid!—anger them. Without giving any more thought to what he would do, he walked across the clearing.

"You girls get over here at the end of the wagon so I can see you real clear-like," Newt ordered. "And if I so much as see you move, I'll kill him where he stands."

Caitlan hurried to where Jordana was just now getting to her feet. She brushed off her dress and opened her mouth as if to retort, but Brenton shook his head.

"Do what he says, Jordana."

"Jordana?" Newt repeated the name. "Now, that's a right unusual name for a girl. I kinda like the sound of it."

Jordana gave him a fierce look before crossing her arms defiantly. Brenton had seen that look before, and he feared that Jordana would try something stupid in order to save the day.

"All right," he said, forcing his voice to sound calm. "I'll need all of you to stand in close." He positioned the camera and motioned them to squeeze together.

The men moved together as instructed. Besides the three guns aimed at their victims, all the other men also held up their weapons to make sure they were captured in the photograph. They all arranged their faces in their most stern expressions.

"You'll have to hold very still. This type of photography requires that you remain absolutely still for several minutes or the picture will blur."

"We'll do our part," Newt called back. "You just remember what I said. One of you moves more than to scratch an itch and I'll shoot him—or her."

"They'll stay put," Brenton replied. "You hear me, girls? Do what he says."

Jordana wasn't about to stand by and let these smelly, mean-tempered ruffians have their way. The leader, for all his youth, looked as if he'd kill them all just as sure as look at them, and Brenton was ten kinds of fool to think otherwise. Spying a rifle strapped to the side of one horse, Jordana gently nudged Caitlan, getting her to carefully shift her gaze in the direction of the horse.

"Gun," she muttered under her breath only loud enough for Caitlan to hear.

"No" came the clench-jawed reply of her conspirator.

Jordana didn't have time to argue with Caitlan. Without a weapon it was hopeless to think they would get out of this alive. She moved the slightest bit toward the horse. If Caitlan didn't follow, it would soon be evident that she was moving from her original position.

"Please," Jordana mouthed silently, praying that Caitlan would finally realize the sense in her plan.

Caitlan moved an inch closer and Jordana breathed a sigh of relief. Good, she thought. Now they would have a chance.

"Just stay still a few more minutes," Brenton instructed. He had ducked his head under the camera drape. He continued to talk to fill in the long minutes of the exposure time, telling his subjects about the photography process. If his intent was to bore the ruffians to distraction, he was succeeding excellently. They were hardly paying any attention at all to Jordana and Caitlan.

Jordana moved another inch toward the horse. She could almost reach out and touch the rifle, but when she did, she would have to be fast. There would be no room for error.

"Hold it!" one of the men yelled out.

Jordana felt her heart clench. She'd been caught.

"Riders!"

"Blue bellies!" another yelled.

They rushed past Brenton and the camera, knocking over the tripod and nearly doing the same to Brenton.

"Get your horses!" ordered Newt, though it hardly seemed necessary, since the men were already scrambling toward their mounts.

 30

Jordana screamed out in pain as Newt grabbed her by her long, thick braid and dragged her to his horse. She pulled away from him, wincing at the pain of her hair being twisted at the roots, but she was determined to keep him from taking her away.

"Let me go, you animal!" she yelled and kicked.

Oblivious to her struggles, Newt jumped up on his horse and, still holding Jordana by the hair, reached down and pulled her up by the waistband of her skirt. Leaning his bearded face close to hers—and smelling so foul that Jordana thought she might throw up—Newt seemed to take pleasure in torturing her.

"We'll have us a real good time once this is all over, sweety," he leered.

Jordana threw herself forward, trying desperately to force him to let her go. Surely he wasn't strong enough to stay atop the horse and fight her at the same time.

Brenton raced toward them, calling out, "You don't need her! She'll just slow you down!"

Newt ignored him. "Jake, you take the other one." As he wrestled Jordana into place, he looked back down at Brenton and added, "You tell them blue bellies that we've got your women. If they don't want to see us kill 'em, they won't follow after us."

"I won't let you take them!" Brenton frantically reached for the man's reins.

At this, Newt's boot slammed full into Brenton's face, knocking him to the ground. Jordana screamed at the sight as blood spurted from Brenton's nose. Struggling to get back up, Brenton put one hand to his nose to staunch the flow, while his other hand worked to reposition his now bent eyeglasses.

Livid at this uncalled-for treatment of her brother, Jordana wildly swung herself sideways, an awkward procedure from her position slung across her captor's lap. But Newt hadn't expected her retaliation, and she managed a stunning blow to the side of his head.

"How dare you! He didn't hurt you!" she screamed.

"Ow! Why, you little—" Newt must have realized there was no time for verbal haranguing. Instead, he yanked back on her hair and raised his gun. "Just remember what I said about killing them!" he told Brenton, then put his heels into the horse's side. "Haw!" he yelled, and the others followed suit.

Jordana felt him tighten his hold on her, but she didn't care. Already she looked for ways to escape this seedy gang. Glancing around Newt's back, she could see that Caitlan was similarly imprisoned, and she, too, was fighting the man named Jake, even as his horse gained ground on Newt's.

"Where to, Newt?" Jake called out.

"There's a good place to turn and fight up here!" Newt yelled. "We'll get there at least five, maybe ten minutes ahead of them Union boys. Just follow me!"

For the first time in her life, Jordana was truly afraid. This was no lark. The fear that trembled through her body was nothing like what she had experienced that day she had climbed the building at Deighton. This time the fear was not only for herself but for others as well. For Brenton who might foolishly attempt to chase after them, and for the soldiers who would surely mount a rescue. There seemed no doubt now there would be gunplay, and people could well get killed.

And Jordana knew, with a terrible ache inside, that it was all because of her. She had dragged Brenton and Caitlan on this foolish journey. If anything happened to them, or any other innocent people because of her misjudgment, she didn't know what she would do.

But perhaps Brenton, ever the practical one, would convince the soldiers to give up pursuit for fear it would only jeopardize herself and Caitlan even more. However, the thought that no rescue might be made was as fearsome as anything.

The bushwhackers and their prisoners crossed through thick undergrowth beneath forested canopies before coming out on the other side into a small clearing. Newt urged his mount forward to jump a fallen log. Jordana nearly slipped off the side of the horse and gasped aloud, actually reaching out for Newt in order to keep from falling from the flying animal. In her utter fright over the possibility of falling to her death, Jordana actually ceased fighting Newt for a moment. He pulled her back into place, his unshaven face breaking into a grin as he looked down to see Jordana staring up at him. She quickly let go of him and gave him what she hoped was her most menacing look. She thought him the ugliest man she'd ever seen and considered telling him so, but he reined back on the horse, once again causing her to reach out to steady herself against him.

"Over there!" he called to his men. "In those trees."

Jordana craned her neck around to see what area her captor believed to be their sanctuary. Newt dismounted and pulled Jordana after him, grasping her braid once again when her feet touched the ground. She lost her footing and stumbled to the hard ground on her backside before Newt even realized what was happening. Laughing, he yanked her upward by her hair and squared her on her feet, then pushed her forward. "Get to those trees."

Jordana did what he told her. There seemed to be no benefit at the moment in fighting him. These men were desperate, and already they were calling back and forth to each other as to how best they could save their own skins.

"The river is smack behind those trees," Newt instructed. "Ain't gonna have 'em sneakin' in behind us. Bear, you take the right! Sammy, you get those horses and get over here with me. Everybody else, spread out and take cover." Just then Caitlan let out a bansheelike scream. "Keep her quiet, Jake!" Newt growled, throwing Jordana a threatening look. "If you want to live, you'd best keep your mouth shut."

Jordana felt the urge to spit in the man's face, but she restrained herself. She supposed it would be senseless to irritate him further. After all, if he thought her too cowering and afraid, maybe he'd ignore her long enough to let her escape.

They hit the brush running and Jordana felt the branches tear at her muslin blouse. By the time they took cover it would be ripped to shreds; then she laughed at herself for even thinking about such a thing at a time when her very life, and that of her good friend, was on the line.

With sobering realization, Jordana began to wonder if they would manage to get out of this alive. *Even if I get away,* she reasoned, *how will I be able to help Caitlan? And what if my escape actually causes them to kill her?* These thoughts haunted Jordana, filling her with confusion as Newt continued to drag her into the cover of the trees.

Catching her off guard, Newt threw Jordana down on the ground behind a huge oak. He put his booted foot on her braid and laughed as she struggled against his hold.

"I got you just where I want you. Now settle down and maybe I won't have to kill you," he demanded.

Jordana opened her mouth to protest, then once again got the feeling she should just relax and pretend to be afraid and to cooperate. Not that she had to *pretend* anything. Jordana looked up fearfully and nodded her acquiescence.

"Good. I like my females smart," he said, then checked his revolver to make certain it was loaded.

Jordana waited on the damp ground for what seemed an eternity. Suddenly it was as if the entire forest had gone silent. She could hear

JUDITH PELLA / TRACIE PETERSON

her own breathing—Newt's too. She could hear the Missouri River coursing and churning from somewhere behind her, and she tried to raise her head enough to see where everyone else had taken cover. She could barely move an inch, but her slight head movement immediately captured Newt's attention.

"I told you to stay still," he growled in a whisper.

Jordana went limp.

The anticipation of what was sure to come drove Jordana half mad. She had never been a patient person, and waiting for what would surely be her own execution hardly seemed the time to begin practicing such a virtue.

A shot rang out and Newt's head twisted halfway around to see where it had come from.

"Barnes, ya might as well give up. We've got ya surrounded out here!" This came from somewhere across the clearing.

Newt growled again and raised his gun. "Never! You blue bellies are askin' to die."

"You're signing your own death warrants if you hurt those women!" came the voice from across the clearing.

"If anything happens to these girls, it'll be your fault, blue belly!" Newt yelled.

Several shots were fired from Newt's men with a couple of returning volleys from the other side.

The obvious danger of the moment became quite clear to Jordana as a bullet ricocheted off a nearby tree and whizzed past her head to play itself out in the dirt. Panic stirred her to action, and spying the hilt of a knife in Newt's boot, Jordana decided to fight for her freedom.

With Newt preoccupied firing off his revolver, he didn't even notice as Jordana slipped the mammoth blade from his boot. Facedown on her stomach, her braid still firmly fixed to the ground by Newt's foot, Jordana wondered what her best course of action would be. She could stab Newt, but then he'd probably shoot her before she could

268

do any real damage. She drew the knife up to her face and found her braid was in the way.

Her braid! That was it. Cutting it would free her! Without a second thought, Jordana gingerly, so as not to alert Newt, reached around and sliced at the braid with Newt's knife. The blade was razor sharp and easily parted the waist-length brown hair.

She was free!

But what next? Run, she thought. I need to run. But to where? She couldn't very well run into the middle of the gunfight. She'd have to take her chances with the river.

With Newt fixed on his attackers, she started inching backward, still lying on her stomach, across the ground. Bullets flew by her, striking objects to her left and right, but they didn't find their way to harming her. It reminded her of a verse in the Psalms where God had promised David something about a thousand falling at his side and ten thousand at his right hand, but harm wouldn't come to him. The memory made her stronger, braver.

Just then one of the soldiers' voices rose above the gunfire. "Release the women, and we'll let you go free."

Newt responded by firing several rounds at the rescuers. Jordana took the opportunity while he was thus distracted to ease to her feet; then in a sprint, literally for her life, she raced toward the river.

She cleared a patch of sapling elm, and had there not been a rather sturdy parent tree right beside these, she might have plunged headlong down a steep ravine. The river was nearly twenty, maybe thirty feet below her, and it was clear that the water was quite shallow at this place along the bank.

"I can't go this way," she muttered, jumping as yet another bullet buzzed like an insect past her ear. "Well, I have to get out of here someway."

She glanced back from where she'd just come. Maybe if she gave them a wide berth and moved around the main clearing, she could get to the other side to where the soldiers were. That seemed logical.

But she couldn't run off and leave Caitlan. Now that the soldiers were attacking, the bushwhackers could easily kill her in retaliation.

She had a general idea of the direction Caitlan had gone. Perhaps if Jordana circled around she could approach the area without being seen. Holding the knife tight, she moved out in a low, crouching position until she felt certain she had passed the point where Newt was fighting. As brush thinned out she could see the clearing with its thick, overgrown grass waving like wheat just beyond. Jordana felt a surge of hope. She was going to make it!

Rushing out from the clearing, she focused on her steps as the battle raged from somewhere to her left. Keep moving forward, she told herself. Don't look around. Don't look back. She moved steadily, her heart pounding, her body tense with fear. She was nearly to the other side of the clearing when she heard another bullet zing past her. She heard it hit the tree directly in front of her almost at the same moment a white-hot pain coursed up her left arm and into her shoulder. She'd been hit!

The thought so stunned her that Jordana stopped in her tracks and looked at the white muslin of her blouse as it turned crimson. Blood. Her blood. It didn't seem possible. Reaching up with her right hand, forgetting about the knife still grasped tightly at the hilt, Jordana was about to grasp her wound when suddenly, before she could so much as figure out what to do with the knife, a solid body slammed into her, knocking her to the ground.

Sure that Newt had caught up with her, Jordana struggled to raise the knife.

"Get off of me!" she screamed. "I'll kill you!"

She was nearly hysterical, caught up in the horror of realizing she'd been captured once again and knowing that this fight might well be to the death of herself or her captor.

"Stop it, you little wildcat!" the man yelled as he struggled to pin her down.

Jordana wielded the knife with her eyes closed. If she hit the man, she wasn't entirely sure she could stand the sight of it. "I have a knife!" she yelled at the top of her lungs, all the while flailing it at the man.

"I can see that for myself," her attacker countered. He finally managed to grab her right wrist, twisting it painfully backward.

Jordana's whole arm went numb as the pain of his hold on her shot all the way up to her shoulder. Her fingers instantly lost their grip on the hilt. "Aghhh!" she sputtered, angry and frustrated and afraid all at once.

"Now stop fighting me," he commanded. "I'm here to help you."

The words barely registered in her brain. Help me? He's here to help me? Forcing her eyes open, Jordana finally saw for herself that the man was not the ugly, smelly Newt, but instead, a rather stern-faced soldier with a dark moustache over thin, taut lips and steely blue eyes beneath a mess of windblown hair, the color of a raven's wing.

"Oh," Jordana barely managed to utter as the unmistakable sound of bullets whizzing by them filled the air.

The soldier fell across her with such a thud that Jordana instantly felt the wind knocked out of her. It was a terrifying sensation, and between struggling to breathe and trying not to scream in pain, Jordana couldn't help but wonder if the man who had so bravely risked his life for her—was dead.

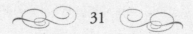

31

"We have 'em, Captain!" a voice called out from somewhere to their left.

Jordana struggled to draw a deep breath. Were the bushwhackers captured? She prayed it was so. Pushing at the body on top of her, she was both surprised and relieved when the man rose up on his own accord.

"Secure the area," he called, then looked down at Jordana. "Are you still alive?"

She nodded. "And you, sir?"

He smiled for the first time and the steel in his eyes softened, looking more like a pond in summer. "I'm feeling fit as a fiddle." Despite the smile, there was an edge to his voice that Jordana couldn't quite place.

Before she could figure it out, she noticed the blood on his shirt. "You're bleeding," she gasped.

He looked down and shook his head. "Nah, that would be your blood, miss."

"What?" Jordana stared in disbelief, then saw that her entire left side was now drenched in red. "Oh my!" She suddenly felt light-headed.

"We'd better see just how bad it is," he told her, ripping away the torn pieces of her left sleeve. "I'm going to get some gear from the horse. You best stay put right here," he told her, then got to his feet.

Jordana eased herself up into a sitting position. She could barely see over the tall grass. The soldier, clad in the dark blue of the Union, was leading his horse back to where she sat and seemed to be shaking his head.

"You shouldn't be too quick to get up," he remonstrated.

"I'm fine," Jordana replied. "I'm strong."

"That's good, because I'm in no mood to be dealing with silly females."

Jordana frowned. "I assure you I'm nothing of the sort." She bit her lip to keep from crying out at the pain when she unconsciously moved her arm. Her left arm throbbed from the open wound, while her right arm still felt a bit achy from the twist he'd given it to disarm her.

The soldier took a pack and a canteen from his horse and knelt back down beside her. "This is going to hurt a bit."

"It already hurts—a bit," Jordana replied from between clenched teeth.

"What were you thinking walking out in the middle of a battle-field?" he questioned, laying out some bandages and a knife.

"I was escaping. What did you think?"

He shook his head and his expression remained serious. "I wasn't sure what to think. Hardly seemed that anyone with brains in his, or her, head would walk into the crossfire."

"I planned to circle around—unless, of course, I wanted to jump twenty feet down the ravine, in which case I'd probably have a broken leg instead of a broken arm."

"You don't have a broken arm," he told her. Putting his hands on her shoulders, he added, "You best lie back."

"I don't want to." She met his commanding presence with new resolve. "Just do what you have to do." He actually laughed at her, and this only served to make her more determined. "Do it!"

Picking up the canteen, he opened the cap. His blue eyes, steely once again, never left her face as he began to pour water over the wound. To Jordana, it felt more like a knife raking over the wound rather than liquid.

She gritted her teeth, determined not to let him see how much it hurt. Her head began to spin, however, and fighting to stay conscious, Jordana blinked hard several times.

"Why did you want to circle around?" he asked as he worked. "You could have found a way to avoid the battle completely."

"I was . . . going to help my friend. . . ." She had begun to feel faint, but the thought of Caitlan revived her a little.

"That was a fool thing to do."

"Is Caitlan all right?" Jordana asked.

"Sure she is."

Jordana wondered how he could know, since he had been with her. She was deciding whether to trust him when he continued.

"So who are you and how'd you end up out here?"

She guessed he was trying to distract her and help her remain alert. Thinking it a good idea, she tried to keep up her end of the conversation, though at times her voice sounded far away in her ears. "My name is Jordana Baldwin," she said, her voice raspy. "I'm here with my brother. He's a photographer." She was breathing in shallow, rapid breaths. "We're taking pictures of the area."

"In the middle of a war?" he asked in disbelief.

She moaned in spite of her attempt to mask her pain. "It's a job."

"Stupid job, if you ask me."

"Well, I didn't." She gasped for breath as he swabbed her arm with a cloth.

"Try to relax. I know this isn't comfortable, but the wound's really not all that bad."

"According to you," she muttered.

"Captain!" a man called.

"Over here," answered Jordana's rescuer.

Jordana looked at the man and fought to keep her vision from blurring. "You're a captain?"

"That's right." He reached into his pack and took out a blue bottle.

"Captain!" A young man with a freckled face and red hair halted a foot away. Jordana watched as he gave a quick salute. "Two of them are dead, sir. We have the rest. The other woman is unharmed."

"What about Newt Barnes?"

"Wounded, sir."

"Get them secured and on their horses. We'll deposit the women with the young man we met on the other side of the bend."

"Yes, sir!" The soldier did a quick about-face and hurried to do as ordered.

Jordana screamed out in pain as the captain poured part of the contents of the blue bottle onto her arm. "That—hurts!" she declared, trying to pull away from his grip.

"I—know," he replied with the same kind of stilted emphasis on his words that she'd used with hers.

She thought she detected a certain amount of amusement in his tone.

"Just get me back to my brother and he'll take care of me," Jordana said.

"I have to stop the bleeding," he replied very calmly. "It isn't all that bad of a wound, but it's bleeding a great deal. We have to stop that or you'll bleed to death."

The idea of dying now, after she'd managed to escape Newt and live through the battle, stilled Jordana. She tried to think about anything but the ministerings of the captain, but it wasn't working very well.

"So how'd you give Barnes the slip?" the man questioned her as he applied pressure to her arm.

Jordana felt her head grow hot. It suddenly seemed as if there were no air. She let her head fall back so that she could open her mouth and draw a breath. It didn't help and she feared she might faint at any given moment. "I cut . . . my hair," she finally murmured and lowered her gaze to meet his amused expression.

"You cut your hair?"

"He had a knife and I took it out of his boot."

"Ah yes. The knife you tried to kill me with," the captain replied. "You know, you'd have a whole lot better time of knife fighting if you'd keep your eyes open during the actual fight."

She gave him what she hoped was a look of contempt. "I thought you were going to kill me. I'm still not sure that isn't your intent."

He chuckled dryly. "You sure have a temper and a mouth to match." He checked the wound, seemed satisfied with the results of his work, then started to bandage her arm. "So you cut your hair off? How does that figure in for an escape?"

"He was holding me down on the ground by standing on my hair. I had it braided and it was pretty long. When I pulled his knife, I cut the braid and ran." She shook her now shoulder-length brown hair back and forth and marveled at the lightness. The movement did nothing whatsoever for her dizziness. Reaching her right hand up to steady her head, she murmured, "I think I'm going to like it short."

"You look silly," he told her, then tore the end of the bandage and tied it tightly around her arm. "I know this is tight, but it needs to be. Leave it that way until tomorrow."

"Yes, sir!" she said, saluting as the young soldier had done. "Any other orders?"

He studied her for a moment, then began putting his things away. "Yes, give me your hand and I'll help you up—unless you want me to carry you."

"I'm not an invalid, nor a silly female, as you put it earlier." Jordana scrambled to her feet. "I can . . . I . . ." But the instant she was in a vertical position, the field spun before her eyes. Helpless, she looked down at the captain, who still knelt beside his pack. Her knees wobbled and gave way just before her world went black. From somewhere in her mind she heard the captain growl something about "aggravating females who never listen" and then she knew no more.

———

Jordana awoke to feel strong arms around her and a warm chest behind her. Momentarily disoriented, she stiffened, thinking her nightmare with Newt was still going on. In a panic, she twisted around nearly shaking loose the blanket that had been secured around her shoulders. Only then did she realize that though she was atop a horse, the rider behind her was a different man. They were being followed by a half dozen or so other mounted soldiers. She did not see Caitlan with them but remembered one of the soldiers saying she was all right.

"Sit still," he demanded.

"Where are we?"

"Making our way back to your brother. Now stop squirming around."

"I am not squirming," Jordana protested. "I merely woke up to find—"

"You passed out cold, making me nearly break my neck to catch you before you hit the dirt. Had you listened to me in the first place, you might never have taken a swoon."

"I did not swoon," Jordana retorted, her mind filled with distasteful visions of helpless young women. "I lost a lot of blood and it made me light-headed."

He said nothing, but Jordana heard him heave a sigh of disgust. He certainly was a difficult man to get along with. It hardly seemed to matter that she could be just as stubborn.

"Why is it taking so long to get to my brother?" she asked. It seemed they had been riding forever, even if she had been unconscious part of the way. Twisting back around in order to get her bearings, she was startled when the captain jerked her against him.

"Sit still, Miss Baldwin, or I'll be inclined to discipline you— something that I daresay should have been done long ago."

Jordana was quite taken aback. "Of all the nerve!" she exclaimed, crossing her arms against her chest. "I'm merely concerned about my brother and my friend. I'm anxious to see that they are well."

"Your companions are fine. Part of my unit headed back just before us and your friend was with them. We'll be at your wagon in a few minutes."

"Were all the bushwhackers captured?"

"That's right."

"Were any of your men hurt?"

"That's kind of you to ask." He seemed sincere. "As far as I know, they're all right."

"I would have felt terrible if any had been harmed trying to rescue me. I don't know what we would have done if you hadn't come along. However, I think I could have done some damage if I'd been forced to. I certainly thought long and hard about it once that knife was in my hands."

"Good thing you ran instead," the captain murmured. "You're not much of a knife fighter."

"Perhaps I shall learn," Jordana replied haughtily and turned back to face forward.

They picked their way along the barest hint of a trail, and Jordana prayed it wouldn't be much farther. The pain in her arm shot upward into her shoulder. She longed for a good long rest and maybe some of her mother's pain remedies. Smiling at this thought, she relaxed and eased back against the captain. She decided he wasn't such a bad sort of man. In some ways he reminded her of G.W. with his laughing blue eyes. He wore his gruff exterior much like his uniform, and Jordana wondered if he hoped the attitude would impress people as much as the cavalry garb. But he had tenderly cared for her wound and even wrapped her in a blanket.

She spied the wagon first. "There's our camp!" she exclaimed, leaning forward.

"And not a moment too soon," the captain said in sheer frustration.

Several soldiers were already at the campsite. Jordana could see no prisoners, a fact she was quite thankful for. She hoped never to lay eyes on Newt and his gang again. But she was extremely happy to see Brenton and Caitlan standing in the midst of the camp.

"Brenton! Caitlan!" Jordana cried as they approached the wagon in single file.

"Jordana! Thank God!" Brenton rushed forward and reached his arms up as the captain came to a stop. Jordana was shocked to see his face all black-and-blue and his nose swollen from the kick he had received earlier.

Jordana went eagerly into his arms, fussing about his appearance and forgetting her own pain. "Brenton, what have they done to you! Oh, you look terrible."

"Thanks," Brenton said with a lopsided grin. "Good to see you too." He then extended his hand to the captain, who was still mounted. "My name is Brenton Baldwin. I'm grateful for what you've done here today." They shook hands. "I'm sure we would all be dead now but for you and your men."

"We've been chasing this particular gang of bushwhackers all over the Kansas and Missouri border," the captain replied. "They're a deadly bunch. They kill pretty much at will and don't much need a reason. Your sister and her friend are lucky to be alive."

"I see your shirt is covered with blood. Are you wounded?" Brenton asked.

"No, but your sister is. She took a bullet in the left arm. I dressed it as best I could, but you need to be getting her to a doctor. It's not a bad wound; the bullet appears to have mostly grazed her, but it bled a lot."

Brenton paled at this news and turned to put his arm around Jordana. "Are you all right?"

She smiled. "I'm fine. Just a bit weak."

He frowned and for the first time took a closer appraisal of her, noticing the blanket wrapped snugly about her. "What happened to your hair?"

"It's a long story," Jordana replied. "I'll tell you later."

"I'd like to know your name, sir," Brenton said, looking up at the captain. "It's important to know who one has to thank for these kinds of things."

The soldier nodded. "Captain Richard O'Brian," he replied. "I've just been transferred to Fort Leavenworth from Larned. I'm heading up a unit of mounted volunteers in a campaign to quell the border wars."

"And would you be Irish, then?" Caitlan asked.

"On my father's side, but his people came to this country a few generations ago. I had a great-grandfather who fought in the Revolutionary War."

"On the side of the colonies or the British?" Jordana asked tartly.

A smile lightened O'Brian's stern features. "Actually, he was one of George Washington's officers."

"Well, you have done him proud, then," Brenton replied. "And I won't hesitate to write letters to the proper authorities and let them know of our gratitude for what you've done this day."

The captain touched the brim of his forage cap. "I'm glad we came in time." He turned in the saddle and motioned his men forward. "Now I must take my leave. I need to see our prisoners back to the fort."

"Certainly," Brenton replied.

"Oh, and not to be telling you your business," O'Brian said, locking his gaze with Jordana's, "but don't be letting your sister tell you she doesn't need to be seen by the doctor."

Brenton laughed. "I see you got to know my sister rather well out there."

O'Brian's expression never changed, but he nodded and replied, "I'm glad to be only dealing with the likes of outlaws."

"I resent that remark," Jordana said, pushing away from Brenton's steadying hold. "I didn't cause you any more grief than . . . than—" Her vision blurred again, but she was bound and determined not to pass out. "I wasn't any trouble . . ." she managed to say before she began to sway on her feet. Brenton quickly supported her from behind.

"Godspeed to you, Captain O'Brian," Brenton replied. "I'm sure we both have our work cut out for us."

The troopers rode on. Brenton turned Jordana in his arms. "So have you finally had enough of adventure?"

She smiled weakly and reached up to touch his battered face. "Have you?"

"I'm not the one who craved adventure. I merely wanted to explore the nation and take photographs."

"And that's not adventure?" Caitlan gave Brenton a coy grin.

"I suppose it is a form of adventure, but you know my sister. She seems to thrive on putting herself in danger. Now let's get you inside the wagon and then I'll hitch up the horses."

"No, you tend to Jordana and I'll hitch the horses," Caitlan said softly. "After all, I've not had anything but my pride injured today."

"Your pride?" Jordana and Brenton said at the same time.

"Aye," Caitlan replied, smiling. "That outlaw Jake said he liked a woman with a good broad backside." She shrugged. "Never really saw meself from behind, so I was always supposin' it wasn't that bad."

Jordana laughed. "It's not, Caitlan. I certainly wouldn't be worrying about the opinions of those mangy outlaws. Would you say her backside is too broad, Brenton?"

Brenton flushed crimson at this. "I hardly think . . . well, that is to say . . ."

Both Jordana and Caitlan burst out laughing at his discomfiture. "Men," Jordana said, weakly leaning against Brenton's hold. "Sometimes they can be so peculiar."

 32

"I've tried to be very frank with Mr. Thorndike," Victoria confided in Anna, "but I'm afraid things are a bit out of hand."

"He knows you're a married woman?" Anna replied, pouring Victoria a second glass of lemonade.

It was an especially warm July day. Victoria had come to visit her friend in part to escape the oppressive heat in her tiny apartment. But she knew she had also come because she could no longer bear the burden of her crumbling marriage. She desperately needed to talk to someone before things grew any worse.

"Yes, but I fear I've led him astray." Victoria's voice betrayed her guilt.

Anna smiled sympathetically. "Why don't you tell me about it?"

Victoria nodded. "I've longed to tell someone. You were away with Ted in San Francisco, and then Kiernan was leaving for Donner Pass, and there never seemed to be any time to come and have a long talk about the situation." She paused for a moment to consider her words, then added, "Christopher Thorndike is simply a most persistent man." She took a long sip of the cool drink and waited for Anna to say something.

"Persistent in what way?"

"He sends me flowers and notes. He pleads with me to meet him for luncheons and dinners. I've made it quite clear that such things are unacceptable and that my husband would never approve, even based on the innocent friendship that Mr. Thorndike swears he is offering." She hurried on to continue explaining. "He tells me I stand on eastern ceremony and that out here in California, things are much more relaxed."

"Well, that much is true," Anna admitted. "But a married woman is still a married woman."

"That's what I told him, but he insisted that even a married woman is entitled to friendship with other men, and that this was all he was asking of me."

Anna frowned. "I really don't know much about the man. Ted says he's contributed heavily to the Central Pacific, but that his main interest is in importing oriental treasures and oddities."

Victoria wished she could tell Anna everything, but she couldn't come to terms with her own feelings, much less try to explain them to Anna. She enjoyed Thorndike's attention. She tried not to, but the truth was the truth. Thorndike recognized her neediness and took advantage of it. And Victoria was not so very naïve that she didn't realize there would one day be a full reckoning for all of his attentions and gifts.

"I wish I knew what to do," Victoria murmured. "But short of joining Kiernan at Dutch Flat, I don't know how to avoid the man. And frankly . . ." She paused, considering what she was about to say.

"Yes?"

Victoria swallowed her guilt and replied, "Frankly, I'm not always sure I *want* to avoid his attention." There! She had said it.

Anna smiled. "Attention is something we seem to thrive on as a matter of human nature. Kiernan's not around to give it, and I've been preoccupied with other things. You naturally longed for a friend, and Thorndike presented himself as one. There's nothing wrong with that."

Victoria knew that if her feelings stopped at accepting friendship from Thorndike, then there would be nothing wrong. But she was dreadfully fearful that if she looked deep inside, she might well be thinking of Thorndike in some way other than that of a friend.

"I'm a Christian woman," she told Anna miserably. "I shouldn't have to struggle with this. I must be doing something wrong."

Anna laughed. "Just because you're attracted to the packaging doesn't mean you'll necessarily like the contents. We're made with an appreciation of beauty, be it the glorious colors of a fall morning in New England, or a handsome man who seems to hold great interest in our needs. Are you desiring to leave your husband and set up housekeeping with Mr. Thorndike?"

"Anna!" Victoria gasped, nearly dropping her glass. "I would never consider such a thing."

"Then why are you so upset?"

Although she was no more than ten years her senior, Anna Judah was as close a mother figure as Victoria had managed to find for herself since leaving Baltimore. She sighed, finding Anna's uncanny knack for uncovering her feelings to be almost equally matched with her mother's.

"I sometimes wonder what it might be like to be Mrs. Thorndike instead of Mrs. O'Connor." She looked up guiltily. "Does that shock you?"

Anna laughed. "Not at all."

"Truly?" There was a note of desperation in Victoria's voice that pleaded with Anna to show her the way back to normalcy.

"My dear Victoria, we all wonder how we might have lived our lives differently. However, you have to put aside such silly nonsense before it gets out of control. You once found life with your husband to be most satisfying. You told me that despite being poor and traveling from place to place, you felt nothing but an overwhelming thanks to God for having given you Kiernan."

"That's true," Victoria replied. "But then the issue of having a child came up."

"And it's that issue once again, and not your distaste or lack of interest in Kiernan, that is at the root of your trouble here." She reached out and took hold of Victoria's hand. "I believe God is trying to warn you, Victoria. He's giving you all manner of discomfort in your actions and thoughts because, while you may not yet have crossed any improper line, the time may be near when you won't have much say about what happens. Thorndike strikes me as one of those men who is used to taking what he wants, regardless of the consequences. I don't want to see you hurt, Victoria."

"Neither do I," Victoria said seriously. "It haunts me day and night."

"Give it over to God and put it away from you before it's too late."

Victoria nodded. "I know you're right, but what should I do?"

"The next time Thorndike appears with his gifts, reject him firmly. Tell him you will no longer have anything to do with him. Better yet, write him a letter. Tell him that he should in no way ever approach you again. That you are a married woman who is deeply in love with her husband." Anna's expression softened. "Then you must, for your sake and Kiernan's, accept that you may never have a child of your own. Pray about it, turn it over to God, and trust Him for the outcome, but realize that the answer may be no. You have to accept this and learn to move forward. Otherwise, I fear you'll take it out on Kiernan and he on you until . . . well, then your marriage will struggle to survive."

The front door opened and slammed shut with such a resounding echo that both women jumped.

"Ted?" Anna called. "Is that you?"

"Yes" came the exasperated voice. "Who else would threaten to bring down the walls?"

"Perhaps I should go," Victoria said.

"Let's just see what has happened with Mr. Judah's railroad," Anna replied and motioned for Victoria to remain seated. "Now I'm sure I can use *your* moral support." Then she added to her husband, "We're in the sitting room, dear. Why don't you come join us for lemonade and pastries."

Ted appeared in the arched doorway and forced a smile. "Good day, ladies. I'm sure I'll find you infinitely better company than Collis Huntington."

"Collis again, dear?" Victoria remained silent and watched as Anna sought to comfort her husband.

"He's changing everything, Anna. He doesn't care about a transcontinental road as I do. He wants prosperity for Sacramento—even California—but he doesn't seem overly concerned with how we connect to the nation and the profit to be made from making the course easier for travel."

"What is he doing now?" Anna asked softly, handing her husband a glass of lemonade.

"He's changing the route. Instead of allowing the track to pass by the north levee, he has determined that the cost will be too high. This route requires a $200,000 work of riprap to protect the line from the flooding of the river. Huntington has decided that the route will be moved from the present site and positioned up 'I' Street."

"And the governor agrees with this, I suppose?"

"Don't even get me started in regard to Stanford. I swear, Collis has the man eating from his hand. He and Stanford talk of the line as though I have no part in it. They discuss matters openly in front of me but not with me. I might as well not exist as far as they are concerned." Instead of the conversation mollifying Ted's anger, it only seemed to inflame it. With a suddenness that startled both women, he slammed the glass down on the side table and got to his feet to pace.

"I've told them over and over that we must work together. That we must act as one body, but they never listen. Now Collis is all up in arms because I dared to say that he was wrong to reroute the line without consulting me first. I am the engineer here. I surveyed the line and told *them* where to build. Not only that, but they are hoodwinking the president and Congress to believe that the Sierras begin just seven miles outside of town, and they all believe this to be a perfectly acceptable business practice. How those men can show their faces in church on Sunday is beyond me."

Anna smiled at Victoria before speaking. "Perhaps they live by different rules than we do."

Ted finally stopped pacing and came to lean on the back of his chair. "I'm tired, Anna. Tired of trying to help them see what this project means to this state. Tired of fighting one battle, only to have it open up the field for ten more. I'm seriously thinking of leaving it all and going home."

Anna got to her feet, and Victoria marveled that she remained so calm in light of Ted's declaration. She didn't seem in the slightest way concerned for their future.

"My darling, if that is what you want, then you know I am behind you. I hate to see you give up on your dream after working so hard, but as you've shown me many times, often we have to let go of a thing in order to see it more clearly in the light of truth. Maybe this project will never be what you foresee it to be, but then again, maybe it will be something even better. Just know that I will support whatever decision you make."

He took hold of her hand and patted it lovingly. "You are a good wife, Anna. Standing by me these many years of traveling and being unsettled has certainly not been easy for you."

"No, but loving you has made it tolerable," she said, smiling sweetly.

Without warning, Ted's entire countenance changed. He dropped hold of Anna and exclaimed, "James Bailey!"

"What?" Anna questioned, somewhat taken aback.

"James Bailey. The new secretary for the Central Pacific. He feels much the same as I do in regard to the line. I will solicit his help and see if we can't forge a scheme together and eliminate Collis Huntington's interference."

"Do you suppose that's possible?"

Ted rebuttoned his coat and headed for the door. "I supposed a transcontinental railroad possible when no one else would even

287

consider it! Bailey may well be the answer to all my problems. Don't wait up for me!"

Anna shook her head as Ted fairly flew from the room and slammed the front door on his way out. She looked at Victoria, but instead of smiling, she was quite grave. "I fear this railroad will be the death of him, Victoria."

Victoria nodded sympathetically. "I've feared the same for Kiernan, especially now with him off at the Donner Pass site."

"I suppose we must be strong." Anna sat back down in the chair she'd earlier vacated. "But I love Ted so, and without him, my life would not be complete. I can't even bear to imagine it."

"Then don't," Victoria replied, reaching across to comfort Anna with a gentle pat. "We needn't seek out trouble."

"No, I'm sure trouble will be more than happy to seek us out in time."

Her grim expression left Victoria fearful inside. She longed with all of her heart that Kiernan might be at the apartment when she returned, but she knew that wouldn't happen. Their separation was weighing her down, and in light of Anna's obvious concern, it only made matters worse. It was then and there Victoria decided that should Kiernan return home safe and sound, she would insist on being allowed to follow him on the line. Living without him was driving her to places of temptation and bitter anguish. She would do as Anna suggested and find a way to accept her lot in life, but she would do it with Kiernan at her side.

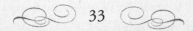

33

The heat of the August sun bore down on Kiernan's neck as he rode to the Central Pacific supply office in Sacramento. Having traveled the better part of a week on horseback, Kiernan was on his way to find out what the problems were with the CP building schedule and secure supplies for the Donner Pass road.

Crocker had wanted to send someone else, but Kiernan felt a desperation to see Victoria. He couldn't stop thinking of her, and with each passing day it became more and more apparent that he would be of little good to anyone if he didn't get back home and sort through their differences.

It still grieved him to know that they'd parted on less than the best of terms. There had been a sort of amicable separation as Kiernan went north with Crocker, but the issues between them were still hovering ominously over them. Kiernan realized he'd allowed things to get completely out of hand. He should never have gone with Crocker without first making certain Victoria knew of his deep, abiding love. He should have dealt with his own guilt and grief long before leaving Sacramento, and he should have talked things over with Victoria.

It was funny how it all seemed so clear now. Maybe it took getting away for several weeks in order to see the truth of their circumstances. The fact of the matter was that long ago they had stopped talking to each other. Oh, they still maintained a surface appearance of discussion, but usually they talked only of mining or the railroad. Now that their separation had allowed him time to think about things, Kiernan realized he'd stopped seeking intimate discussions with Victoria about the same time he'd lost her fortune. This was hard to accept and take responsibility for, especially in light of the six years that had passed in the meanwhile. Kiernan could easily see every point where their refusal to speak on important issues of the heart had further driven a wedge in their marriage.

Lord, I've been a fool, he prayed. I'm hopin' it's not too late. I'm askin' ya to help me make things right again.

"Kiernan?" the voice of Ted Judah called from up ahead.

Kiernan waved and reined back on his mount. "Ted, it's good to be seein' ya."

"I must say the same," Ted replied. "We've nothing but a nightmare on our hands."

Kiernan smiled and dismounted. "So the elephant refuses to be harnessed?"

Ted shook his head. "The elephant refuses to be an elephant."

Laughing, Kiernan questioned his friend. "So what is this all about? A message came sayin' to discontinue work. What's happened?"

"Huntington," Ted fairly growled. "That man will be the death of me yet. He has taken up refusing to listen to any advice I try to give him. Thinks he knows it all. I went to him with James Bailey and suggested he rethink his plans for moving the line from the river to 'I' Street, but he wouldn't listen to me."

"And when did he go decidin' to make this move?" Kiernan asked, pulling his horse over to the hitching post.

"Several weeks ago. I tried to reason with him, but he was concerned about the cost of putting in the flood barriers. Said it wasn't prudent and moved the line."

"Did he, now?"

"He did, and when James Bailey and I complained, he simply told us it was for the best. The next thing we know, we're each presented with our share of the bill for the cost of moving the line."

"How's that?" Kiernan was surprised about this sharing of the bill. It seemed odd indeed. "I was thinkin' ya had a central fund for these things."

"Oh, we do, but money is tight. The board members all agreed to equally share the additional costs. James flatly refused, however. He said he'd not been given a voice in the matter and he wouldn't pay. Huntington proposed Bailey either sell out or pay up, and still James refused. With that, Huntington decided to halt production on the line. James and I have spent these last weeks trying desperately to find someone to buy out Huntington. I believe with him gone we'd be able to finally accomplish something positive with the line."

"And did ya go findin' someone to buy him out?"

"No," Ted replied, shaking his head in total dejection. "I thought we had Charles McLaughlin from Boston. But once Mr. McLaughlin found out that it was Huntington's stocks he'd been buying, he backed out. He wired to say that whatever would send Huntington out from the project would also keep him out."

Kiernan considered suggesting his father-in-law as a prospective buyer, but with James not long in the country, a business transaction of this size might be difficult at best. Moreover, Kiernan feared that in discussing such a business arrangement, the loss of Victoria's money might come to light. He knew he was going to have to confess what had happened to James and Carolina. He just wished that when he did so, he might be a prosperous man in his own right.

"So now what?" Kiernan said.

"James is going to resign his position as secretary and sell off his stock."

"For sure that's too bad. What about yarself?" Kiernan studied his friend. Ted was a man of determination and purpose. It seemed a shame that such misfortune should have to come to him in the midst of his dream.

Ted shook his head again. "I don't know. I'm beginning to think it may well be the only way."

"Quittin'?"

"I've never been one to back away from a challenge, but this time is different. I'm tired of fighting a war nobody else seems to want to win."

"Just doesn't seem like somethin' ya would be doin'."

"I know it doesn't," Ted replied. "And that's what makes it particularly hard. I'll probably sell out just as Bailey will do. Then Anna and I will return east, where things are more civilized and people understand the value of listening to those who have knowledge of a thing."

"Oh, and they do that back east, do they? I never saw it when I was there."

Kiernan laughed, but Ted would not be cheered or humored. "I should go talk to Anna. This will affect her too."

Kiernan suddenly realized that Ted was quite determined about quitting the Central Pacific. "Wait, Ted. Don't be actin' in haste! Remember there's still a war going on back east!"

But it was too late. Ted Judah was no longer interested in discussing the matter further. He made his way down the street, shoulders hunched in his misery, his head bent as if in prayer.

Kiernan felt a deep sorrow for his friend, and even as he conducted business in the supply office, his mind was on Ted. After handing over the orders and paper work Crocker had sent with him and making provision for his mount, Kiernan dusted off his pants and headed up the road toward his apartment.

He quickly forgot about Ted and the issue of their possible move east. Now his mind was fixed on Victoria. He had to talk to her. Had to help her see that his heart had changed. He knew the problem and wanted to help bring about a resolution.

Pushing up the bill of his cap, Kiernan entered the apartment and took the stairs two at a time. He silently wished he could have stopped and cleaned himself up a bit more, maybe purchased Victoria some little trinket as a surprise, but there'd been neither the time nor money to waste.

Reaching the top step, Kiernan could see that the door to his apartment was wide open. That didn't make sense. What was Victoria thinking leaving it open like that? He approached without further consideration and stopped in stunned surprise at the sight before him.

Victoria was in the arms of another man—the very man she had danced with so long ago at the party. And Thorndike was taking a very obvious liberty by kissing her full on the mouth. Kiernan felt as though he were frozen in place. He saw the situation much like a dream, where he could only watch and do nothing.

"I told you to leave me alone!" Victoria demanded, struggling against the man's arms.

"But you don't mean it," Thorndike said, trying to kiss her again.

Only when Kiernan saw that Victoria was fighting the man off was he able to shake away his stunned surprised and spring into action.

"And what would ya be doin' with me wife?" Kiernan yelled in a roaring voice that caused the man to instantly let go of Victoria.

Christopher Thorndike turned in surprise at the very moment Kiernan's fist connected with his nose. Thorndike gasped and cursed, his hand flying to his face only to encounter a trickle of blood oozing from his bashed nose.

Victoria backed away from the fight, but Kiernan caught the distinct expression of relief in her face as he went after Thorndike to finish the job.

Thorndike, however, was no fool. He was now ready for Kiernan and managed to get a glancing blow off to the side of Kiernan's head before Kiernan fisted the man again, this time bloodying his lip.

"Get out of me house and leave off with botherin' me wife." His brogue was heavy, his tone deadly.

"You don't deserve her," Thorndike said, pulling a handkerchief from his pocket. He obviously believed this would signal an end to the physical portion of their fight.

But Kiernan was panting, thirsting for more, rage flaming in his green eyes. "Neither does the likes of yarself," Kiernan retorted.

Kiernan, never one to stand on ceremony where a fight was concerned, grabbed the man and threw him out the door. Thorndike nearly fell over the banister, and Kiernan secretly wished the flimsy rail would give way and plunge the man to the floor below.

"If I ever see ya makin' after me wife again, I won't be responsible for what happens," Kiernan shouted after him and slammed the door.

Turning back to face Victoria, Kiernan forced himself to calm down. It was one thing to see a man take obvious advantage of his wife, but it was another to wonder if she had encouraged such actions. Yes, she had been fighting him off, but Kiernan could only wonder and fear what might have led the man to take such liberties in the first place. Seeing her expression so totally stunned and filled with trepidation, Kiernan doubted the situation was her fault—praying, at least, that was the case. However, he was still hurt and angry, and the memory of Victoria in Thorndike's arms—not only here, but at the dance—was more than he could stand.

"So, wife, what do ya have to say for yarself?" His voice trembled over the words. He hated the accusation in his tone but could not help it.

Victoria shook her head in miserable despair. "I didn't ask him here, if that's what you think."

Kiernan wrestled with his temper. He had to remain calm. "So what happened?"

"He came here of his own accord," she replied, tears spilling from her eyes. "I was leaving to see Anna, and when I opened the door, he was there. He said he had to talk to me and he pushed his way in and . . . well . . . you saw the rest."

"Aye, I did." Kiernan pulled out a chair from the table. "I still don't understand why the likes of that man would show his face here." He sat down and looked up at his wife. The expression on Victoria's face and the words that followed could not have stunned Kiernan more than had she slapped him.

"I suppose it was my fault," Victoria confessed in a shamed whisper.

"Yar fault?"

She nodded and a sob broke through her lips. "I don't know where to begin—how to tell you."

"Just tell me this, Victoria . . ." He could hardly force the words out, but he had to know. "Have ya been . . . were ya an' . . . ?"

She rushed to the table and dropped to her knees before him. "Please believe me, Kiernan! I was never unfaithful to you!" Tears flooded from her eyes, dampening his trousers as she bowed her head before him.

"Maybe ya better be tellin' me about it, then." His voice was surprisingly even. But he feared he might start weeping with her if he gave in to the emotions raging inside him.

"Yes, I suppose I must."

She looked up at him with such woebegone eyes, glistening with tears, that Kiernan thought his heart might break. Was she going to tell him their marriage was over? Had she given up on him and sought out Thorndike to rescue her from her fate? He waited in agony for her to continue.

"I didn't want you to leave me here," Victoria began. "You know that." Kiernan nodded and she continued. "I felt so alone. I've felt that way for a long, long time. I know it's because I can't give you a child. You made it clear to me when we discussed this on the night of the dance that you felt less love for me because of it."

"I never said that. Those were yar own words, not mine."

"Yes, I know they were, but they held an element of truth that you could not deny. If you could, you would have done it that night." She held up her hand as he started to speak. "No, please hear me out. We've been silent for much too long."

She took a seat on the opposite side of the table and folded her trembling hands in front of her. "Mr. Thorndike apparently realized how lonely I felt. He preyed on that, but in truth, I did nothing to stop him. I enjoyed the attention. I enjoyed that someone cared about me and wanted to know my feelings and thoughts."

"Ya know very well I care for ya, but that wasn't enough for ya, was it?" Kiernan asked sarcastically. He still wasn't certain that she was not about to admit some form of infidelity, and the thought both enraged him and broke his heart at the same time.

Victoria sighed. "Just saying the words isn't enough, Kiernan. You cannot deny there were walls, thick walls separating us. I wanted attention from you, but you refused to give it."

"I was never allowed to give it. Ya can't deny that ya started pushin' me away a long time back."

"You took yourself away more than I pushed," Victoria countered, her voice now edged with anger. "I suppose you see all of this as my fault. You become absorbed in feelings of guilt and inadequacy and then run off and leave me for weeks on end while trying to find the elusive golden dream. Then you come back, and without more than a handful of words between us, take me to your bed, being sure to leave before first light. I felt like a mistress more than a wife."

"Is that the role you took with Thorndike as well?"

"How dare you!" Victoria declared. "I might have encouraged his attention at one time, but just as a friend. When he began pushing for more, I dealt with that and told him to stay away from me. I reminded him that I was a married woman, and even if my husband was absent most of the time, I would still honor my marriage vows. But I suppose you don't believe me."

"Apparently *he* didn't believe you."

"That's not fair!"

Victoria crossed her arms and stared at Kiernan in silence. Her face betrayed her misery, but Kiernan also saw something else. Regret.

"I did not allow Thorndike to take liberties with me, if that is what you are worried about. His attempt to kiss me today was as far as he ever overstepped the lines. He sent me gifts and flowers, most of which I returned, and he sought out my company whenever he found me in town alone. That is all. We talked, we shared a luncheon, and I penned him a letter telling him that I desired for him to leave me alone. He came here today to convince me otherwise."

Kiernan watched as she closed her eyes and the tears began again. They streamed from beneath dark, sooty lashes and trailed down her cheeks. His heart grew tender toward her, and he knew he'd be an utter fool if he didn't believe her. And in that moment God gave him a kind of peace. She had done nothing to compromise their marriage. He was certain of this.

"I'm sorry, Kiernan," she whispered. "Please forgive me for my indiscretion. I know it was wrong to be flattered by Thorndike's attention. I know it was wrong to share conversations with him that should have been shared with you. I'm so sorry." She buried her face in her hands and wept again in earnest.

Kiernan slowly got up from the table and went around it to take hold of her, praying with each move that she would not reject him as he so rightly deserved. As he wrapped his arms around her he nearly sagged with relief that she stood up and returned the gesture.

"Oh, my darlin'," he said softly.

"I know it isn't right," she sobbed. "I can't give you a child and you deserve to have a wife who can. It hurts so much to see other women and their children and know that what should be such a simple thing for me to accomplish is beyond my means."

"I'll admit," he said, hoping it was the right thing to do, "that I'm disappointed we have no children. But if God is the one to be givin' them, then I can't see ya blamin' yarself for somethin' ya have no control over. I know I don't blame ya."

Victoria shook her head against him. "Perhaps God is punishing us."

"And why would He be punishin' us?"

"I don't know. There must be something we've done—something I've done."

"Now, don't be takin' on so," Kiernan said firmly. He urged her to look at him by lifting her chin ever so gently with his fingers. "I went through such ideas meself, and they do no good. I can't see God workin' that way. Perhaps we need to be patient and realize that it simply isn't our time."

"But it may never be our time," Victoria replied. "Maybe I should just go back east when Anna and Ted leave. Maybe I should seek out a solicitor to make arrangements so that you . . . so that we—" She burst into tears anew.

"Is that what ya want?" Kiernan asked, his heart breaking at the thought that she would actually divorce him.

"No," she cried and buried her face against his neck.

He tightened his arms around her. "And neither do I, so don't be talkin' such nonsense again."

She raised her head, sniffing back tears. "Then you'll forgive me?"

"Victoria," he said her name like a sigh, "I will always be forgivin' ya whatever ya ask. Will ya do the same for me? Will ya forgive me for puttin' ya off and leavin' ya to fend for yarself?"

She nodded. "Oh yes! I love you. It's always been only you."

He smiled, his own eyes filling with moisture. " 'Tis a good thing, then, for I'm feelin' the same." He lowered his mouth to hers and kissed her with all of the longing he felt deep inside. Her lips were soft and warm, eager for his kiss. She melted against him, her hands reaching up to play with the hair at the nape of his neck. He tightened his hold on her, desperate at the thought that he could have lost her.

Without warning, Victoria pulled away, pushing at his chest. Kiernan stared at her in surprised disappointment. "What now?"

"Why are you here?" she suddenly questioned. "I mean, when did you get back in town?"

Kiernan laughed so hard at this that he dropped his hold on her. "The railroad is at a standstill. Didn't the Judahs tell ya that?"

"I remember something about it, but I didn't expect it to include you."

He reached out to take her in his arms again. "Well, it does. I don't have to be back to work until the matter is settled." He reached up and pulled out the combs that held her hair in place. "And what about yarself? Do ya have to be goin' to see Anna just now?"

Victoria's eyes widened in surprise. "Kiernan O'Connor! I'm shocked at your behavior."

In one fluid motion he lifted her in his arms and grinned. "I've missed ya, Mrs. O'Connor. I'm hopin' ya feel the same."

Victoria wrapped her arms around his neck. "Anna can wait," she murmured simply. It was all the encouragement Kiernan needed.

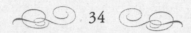 34

Victoria was excited and pleased at the prospect of spending an evening with Anna and Ted. Kiernan had come home with the invitation earlier in the week, and the anticipation of having some affair to attend completely delighted Victoria.

She had taken great care to dress for the occasion, hoping—even praying—that Kiernan would be especially pleased. Her feelings for him were stronger than ever in light of their recent reconciliation. She felt confident again, as if there was nothing she could not face with Kiernan at her side.

They walked arm in arm to the Judahs' that night, a slight chill to the September air causing Victoria to lean closer to her husband for warmth.

"Ya look quite lovely," Kiernan told her as he bent his head to her ear. "I do believe ya favor that shade of blue."

Victoria felt a tingling sensation of pleasure run down her spine. "Why, thank you for saying so, Mr. O'Connor."

He laughed and started to say something else but realized they had already come to Anna and Ted's house. He knocked on the door while Victoria reached up to make certain her bonnet was straight.

A rather sedate Ted Judah met them at the door. "Come in," he said in welcome. "We've been looking forward to this evening."

"So have we," Kiernan replied.

Victoria followed the men into the front sitting room, where Ted took charge of Kiernan's hat and Victoria's bonnet. It was only a moment before Anna appeared, embraced Victoria, and bid Kiernan welcome.

"Please have a seat. There's something we wish to tell you," Anna said in a rather subdued tone.

Victoria glanced at Kiernan, then nodded. Kiernan had already mentioned that there was a strong possibility of Ted resigning from the Central Pacific board, and Victoria wondered if that was what they wished to announce.

Ted returned and stood beside the chair where Anna was sitting. "We thought to wait on our announcement until after dinner," he began, "but then we decided perhaps it would be kinder to put aside unpleasantness first."

"Unpleasantness?" Victoria questioned.

"I'm afraid it is unpleasant for us," Anna replied.

"I have resigned my position with the CP," Ted stated without further ado. "I have sold my stock and am even now making the final arrangements for Anna and me to return to Greenfield."

"Massachusetts?" Victoria asked in stunned disbelief.

"Yes," Anna replied, nodding. "My old home."

"But for how long?"

"For good." Anna's voice was resigned and marked with sorrow.

"But why would ya be handin' it all over to the others?" Kiernan asked.

"Because they've lost sight of the dream," Ted replied. "Or they never had sight of the same dream I did. Huntington, Stanford, Hopkins, and Crocker have gone forward with establishing the Dutch Flat and Donner Lake Wagon Road Company."

"Aye. I know."

"They are focused on what can be accomplished on a small scale, while I am dreaming of that feat which can be accomplished on a much grander one."

"But is that reason enough to give up the dream?" Kiernan asked.

Ted sighed and Anna reached up to pat his hand. "It's no longer Ted's dream."

Li came to announce dinner and Victoria fought to keep back her tears. "It won't be the same without you here," she told Anna as they stood to go into dinner.

"Perhaps not, but maybe something even better will come your way. Maybe someone will come to take my place."

For the first time in months, Victoria remembered her mother's letter announcing the arrival of Kiernan's younger sibling. She now thought of Caitlan's arrival in California along with Victoria's own brother and sister. It panicked her for a moment. She had become so self-absorbed in her own problems that she'd entirely forgotten the letter she'd hidden away in her baby quilt.

The evening was clearly spoiled by the sorrowful news of the Judahs' departure. And added to this was Victoria's guilt over having kept from Kiernan the news of his sister's coming. She had hoped to keep him from worrying about their whereabouts, especially in light of the fact that her mother had sent no further word of their plans. Now she knew she must tell Kiernan at the first opportunity. There could be no more secrets, well-intentioned or not, between them.

———

Walking home that night, Victoria broached the subject with Kiernan. "I'm afraid," she began, "that my selfishness has caused me to forget something."

"I'm sure I don't understand," he replied. The golden moonlight illuminated his face when he glanced down to meet Victoria's pained expression. "What is it?"

"Several months ago I received a letter from my mother. It was actually the first letter I'd had in some time. Do you remember?"

"Aye. Ya told me all about it."

"No, I didn't tell you everything," she replied. "I thought part of it might upset you, and so I decided to keep it from you until things were calmer with the railroad and with us. Then I forgot about it."

Kiernan stopped her. "And what was it ya thought I needed savin' from?"

Victoria's expression seemed to plead with him. "Please don't be mad at me. I've had no further word about it, and so I couldn't have helped to ease your worries, even if I'd told you then."

Kiernan's eyes narrowed. "Victoria, tell me what it is. Don't be keepin' any more secrets from me."

"Your sister Caitlan arrived in America. I don't know when!" she declared, seeing the dark expression on her husband's face. "Mother said that she met up with Brenton and Jordana and that the three decided to come west."

"To California?"

"Yes. Brenton and Jordana thought they would bring Caitlan here to us. But Mother said they went about it the hard way as usual. Apparently they are under the employ of someone, and Brenton is taking photographs on the way. There's no telling where they are or when they'll actually make it here. And Mother said because they were only inclined to send the briefest telegrams to our solicitor, who in the interim has passed away, she has no address in which to contact them now that she and Father are back in the country."

"Ya should have told me." His tone betrayed the hurt he felt.

"It was during that very bad time of ours," she replied. "I'm sorry. I didn't do it to be mean. I thought I would keep you from worrying. And then as I said, I forgot. I honestly got caught up in my own problems with you and Thorndike and . . . well . . . it just didn't seem important. Please don't be angry with me."

Kiernan's expression softened. "I'm not angry. But where could they be?"

"I don't know. I'll write to Mother tomorrow and see what I can find out."

"Better yet, let's send her a wire. We need to know where they are and when to expect them."

"I know," Victoria said, looping her arm with his. "I'm sure everything is all right. Mother would have written if there was any word to the contrary."

Kiernan nodded, but Victoria could tell that he didn't seem all that convinced. They both knew how unreliable communication was. She knew she'd done the right thing by finally telling him about the letter, but now she would have to deal with his worry over where Caitlan was. It hardly seemed a fair trade.

———

October brought rain and the departure of Anna and Ted Judah from Sacramento. Victoria allowed herself a time of tears over missing her friend. Her sadness became even more acute when Kiernan returned to the railroad work, which was progressively demanding more and more of his time. As the weeks moved on into November, he hadn't yet returned to Crocker at Dutch Flat, instead sending another worker with a load of supplies and men. Huntington had needed him there in Sacramento, at least for a few weeks while they made serious decisions about expanding the work along the proposed line.

Victoria had secretly rejoiced over this arrangement. She couldn't have endured losing Anna and Kiernan at the same time. She also still worried that Thorndike might try something once word got out that Kiernan had returned to the mountains. It seemed a silly fear, especially in light of having agreed with Kiernan to turn the matter over to prayer. But she couldn't deny it existed. She knew what it was to be lonely for Kiernan's companionship and felt that somehow she would have to convince him to let her come to Dutch Flat when he returned.

Sitting and stitching together pieces of her baby quilt, Victoria tried not to worry about the days to come. The quilt seemed a good way to focus her attention, even if there was no baby to plan for. Perhaps one day there would be, and if not, then perhaps her sisters or Kiernan's would have a child and she would give them the quilt. Either way, it kept her busy.

A knock at the door sounded and a quick glance at the clock left Victoria with a feeling of dread anticipation. It was too early for Kiernan. Thorndike's face immediately flooded her memory. Had he dared to show himself here?

Hesitating, Victoria put aside her sewing and got to her feet. She stood silently for a moment, wondering if she should call out and inquire as to whom the visitor might be, or simply go open the door and take her chances. Her nerves got the better of her.

"Who is it?"

"Letter for Mrs. O'Connor" came the voice.

Victoria thought of her mother and prayed it might be some wonderful news of Caitlan. Hurrying to the door, Victoria smiled, recognizing the landlord's boy. "Thank you," she said as he handed her the telegram. Victoria dug in her apron pocket and produced a penny. "Here's a penny for candy."

The boy smiled. "Thanks, ma'am!"

She closed the door and hurried to open the letter, hardly even noticing the handwriting on the outside. Surprised by the script, she glanced to the end of the letter to see that it wasn't from her mother but rather from Anna Judah.

Sitting down in a lovely oak rocker, which Kiernan had made for her during his time away from the railroad, Victoria felt as if she'd been given the most glorious of gifts.

My dearest Victoria,
I can hardly believe I am writing these words to you. My heart is so heavy with sorrow that words seem impossible.

Victoria frowned and felt the joy leave her. Something was wrong! She continued reading, only now she was more wary of the news.

> *Our journey by sea from California was uneventful until we reached Panama. Crossing the isthmus through the mosquito-infested swamps has always held risks, even after the railroad was built there. My dear Ted contracted yellow fever in a blinding rainstorm while helping a group of women and children get from the railcars to the steamer. I feared he was doing too much as he shielded them with his umbrella, but he cared nothing for himself. That night he fell ill with a terrible headache and from that point grew steadily worse.*
>
> *Our arrival in New York should have heralded better care, but of course by then it was too late. My beloved was gone. He passed from this earth in a delirium on November the second.*

Victoria felt as though a huge band constricted her chest. She could scarcely draw breath for the shock of it all. Ted Judah was dead. It was impossible to believe. Why, only a few weeks ago she had sat beside him at dinner.

> *Victoria, I don't know how I can go on without him. He was so young, only thirty-seven. So full of life and so much a part of my heart and soul. I turn even now when I hear someone upon the step, certain that when the door opens it will be him. But of course it isn't him. It will never be him again. What am I to do?*

Tears poured from Victoria's eyes as she finished reading the words of her brokenhearted friend.

> *Word came yesterday that the Central Pacific had laid its first rail only a week before Ted's passing. I think he would have been glad to have known it, even if he doubted the final outcome for the line.*
>
> *So now I sit here in Greenfield, thinking back over the events of the past week, knowing that life shall never be the same for me. We buried Ted in a quiet little cemetery just outside of town. I shall walk*

*there often and see to his grave. It seems wrong that this should be all
that is left to us. Please write to me or I might go mad in this anguish.*

Ever your friend,

Anna Judah

Victoria let the letter fall to her lap. She could hardly fathom the
truth of this situation. Anna had feared the railroad would one day
kill her husband, and in a sense, Victoria supposed that it had. If Ted
would not have been so discouraged by the attitudes of Huntington,
Hopkins, Stanford, and Crocker, he might have stayed in Sacramento
and would never have contracted yellow fever.

Victoria hugged her arms to her body and rocked and cried. She
remembered her mother talking of losing younger sisters to yellow
fever. What a hideous and awful disease. It seemed wrong that such a
thing should be allowed to snuff out life at will. Why did no one find
the cause of such an illness and give them a way to defeat it?

She lost track of the time, and when her tears were played out, she
simply sat rocking and contemplating the letter in her lap. Kiernan
arrived home to a darkened room and no supper on the stove. He
called out in greeting, then saw her sitting in the chair.

"Did ya run out of oil for the lamp?" he asked good-naturedly.

"No," she managed to say. She got to her feet and crossed the
room even as her husband was striking a match. "We've had bad news."

His hand began to shake and he was just barely able to light the
wick of the lamp. "Bad news?"

"Yes. Anna wrote me a letter."

"Anna Judah?" He took the letter she held out to him.

"It's very, very bad, Kiernan."

He scanned the sheets, then met her sorrowful expression. "Oh
no," he murmured, tears coming to his own eyes. "Ted is gone? It
can't be true."

Victoria took the letter back. "But we both know it is. Oh, Kiernan, how her heart must be breaking. How can she even bear to live without him?" Then she realized her own fears and threw herself into her husband's arms. "How could I ever live without you?"

They clung to each other, as though letting go might well allow the other to slip away from reach. It was impossible to know what to say or do. One friend was dead and another suffered a loss far more painful than they had ever known.

35

Jordana stared over the railing of their steamer and wondered at the muddy, churning water below. The Missouri River seemed to be a focal point for the eastern railroaders, and as with them, it represented an exciting challenge in the life of Jordana. To cross it meant going deeper into the heart of America, to brave unseen forces, to experience what most had never dared to try.

The thought of it thrilled her to the core of her being. After so many delays, waiting for photographic supplies and for the border skirmishes to settle down, they were finally on their way. It didn't matter that the West had already wounded her. She proudly bore the scar of her confrontation on the way to St. Joseph. The fact that the wound had become infected and had taken longer than normal to heal did not daunt her in the least. It only confirmed once again that Jordana's life seemed guarded by more than mere mortals.

Jordana smiled when she thought of how Brenton had fussed over her during her convalescence. His overwhelming fear that she might die had caused him to be a sullen and difficult companion. Even now, with them safely on their way to Omaha via the tiny riverport cities in between, Brenton still eyed her with the look of a worried parent. It was at his insistence for the safety of the girls that they were now aboard a riverboat, having spent a good portion of the money that should have taken them along for several months. Jordana wished she could ease his mind but knew it was impossible.

"Afternoon, miss."

Jordana turned to find a dashing stranger paying her homage with a deep bow. Hat in hand, he reached up to smooth back the lines of his thin moustache. Jordana contemplated him for a moment, then decided there was no harm in returning his greeting.

"Good afternoon," she replied.

"I felt some concern at seeing you out here alone. It hardly seemed fitting for a lady of quality to be unaccompanied."

"Oh?" Jordana gave a quick look past the man for the ever-present figure of her brother. "You must have been listening to my brother, for he feels exactly as you do."

The man smiled, only to Jordana it came across as something of a leer. "No, I've not yet made the acquaintance of your brother, Miss—"

"Baldwin," Jordana answered.

"Well, Miss Baldwin, I'm Charles Cunningham. I must say, I've been taking this paddlewheeler from Kansas City to Omaha for many months now, and never before have I seen a more lovely woman grace the decks."

Jordana would have laughed out loud had the man not appeared so serious. He was such a dandy with his brocaded satin vest and his new black wool suit. The suit barely showed a crease or wrinkle, and Jordana had no doubt that should one appear, the man would simply hire someone to eliminate the problem. Even his outer coat appeared new, as if he had stepped from the clothing emporium with the new goods on his back.

Of course, her own navy wool cloak was new—a purchase insisted upon by Brenton for both her and Caitlan. He had told her he was tired of the way men looked at them both. He believed the cloak would hide most of their more feminine features from view, but rather than causing disinterest among male observers, it seemed the coverings only added to the intrigue.

"I suppose you think me rather ill-mannered to approach you in such a fashion," Cunningham stated. "Here in the West it's often thought that protocol is unnecessary, but I like to preserve the old customs."

"If that is true, Mr. Cunningham, then why are you speaking to me now?" Jordana asked unabashedly.

His smiled broadened. "Ah, a lady with a quick wit as well as a beautiful face." He toyed with his top hat for a moment, then replaced it on his head. "You might say that while I stand on protocol, I would not be so foolish as to allow a beautiful young woman to slip away unnoticed. Nor would I find it appropriate to see her left unattended."

"Well, she is hardly that, my good sir," Brenton said, coming up from behind the man.

Jordana lowered her head, a grin on her own face. She'd hardly gone unnoticed; in fact, Mr. Cunningham was probably the fourth or fifth to make certain she was not left unattended. Brenton was no doubt becoming weary of asserting his position.

"I'm Miss Baldwin's brother. I suggest you make your way elsewhere while I escort my sister to her cabin."

The man touched the brim of his hat. "It isn't wise to leave a young woman alone to fend for herself—especially one so beautiful."

Brenton stared at the man without blinking. "For your information, she has never been out of my sight. Good day to you, sir." Brenton encircled Jordana's waist with his arm and nudged her forward, away from the river dandy. "What did I tell you about talking to strange men?"

"He didn't look all that strange," Jordana replied with a taunting giggle. "Besides, I think you worry too much. You have been positively impossible ever since my mishap."

"It was hardly a mishap," Brenton said, leading her to their cabin. "You were shot by border ruffians and nearly died."

Jordana laughed softly. "I came nowhere near death, so stop being so dramatic. It's over and there's no reason to continue dwelling on it."

"There's plenty of reason," Brenton replied. "Now that Omaha has finally been chosen as the eastern terminus for the Union Pacific, I'm of a mind that your part in this little affair is over. I believe it would be wise to send you back east to New York."

"Unchaperoned? Why, Mr. Baldwin, it simply isn't done," Jordana drawled.

"Stop mocking me; I'm serious." Brenton's growing frustration was evident in his tone. "You know that I sent a wire to Mrs. Vanderbilt to tell her that we'd be in Omaha, and by now Mother and Father should have returned to America. I advised her to inform them of our whereabouts, should she have the opportunity."

"Why did you do that?"

"Because I've lived with the guilt of dragging you out here for these many months. Mother said they would return by summer, and I can only trust that they have done so. Since communications are so poor with the war wreaking havoc on the telegraph system and the post, they probably couldn't have caught up with us had they wanted to. I had hoped they would send a letter to St. Joseph, but perhaps they never received our address there. Then again, maybe they've not returned from Russia. But either way, I'm responsible for you."

"I want you to stop worrying about me. I'll be eighteen in another few months," she declared.

"That makes you even more of a concern."

"But why? I intend to make my own way in this world and do as I please—to break with tradition and travel at will, living in the wilds if I choose. I intend to do everything Mother always dreamed of doing. Her stories were so vivid—so stimulating—and now I shall be able to make the journey and write and tell her every detail."

"But in the meanwhile, I am responsible for you. Father gave you over to my care, and I take that very seriously."

They maneuvered down the stairs to the next level of the steamer, and Brenton quickly brought her to their cabin. Unlocking the door, Brenton half pushed, half pulled Jordana inside.

"Caitlan!" Jordana declared upon seeing her friend sitting in a straight-backed chair, hands folded in her lap. "So you are to be a prisoner as well?"

"Yar brother—"

Jordana held up her hand. "Please, you needn't say more. I know very well how my brother can be."

Brenton had closed the door by this time, and as Jordana removed her cloak and went to hang it up, he began his speech. "Look here, I'm only thinking of your safety. You neither one realize the way men look at you. As we've moved west, there have been fewer and fewer women. Past the Missouri there are even fewer. You will quickly become a commodity in and of yourselves."

"Are you suggesting that we will be no better than slaves to be auctioned off to the highest bidder?" Jordana asked with a hint of sarcasm.

"I suppose in a sense that is exactly what I'm fearful of," Brenton replied. "I only desire your safety. I had no idea that things would be like this. I'm certain now that I've made a poor choice and should take you both back to New York. And were I not so worried about getting there without the interference of war, I might never have left for Omaha."

"You are being a goose about this," Jordana replied. "Caitlan and I are quite capable of taking care of ourselves. I know society stands on the formality of having unmarried females escorted at all times, but I certainly do not hold with such nonsense. Perhaps I should don trousers and a frock coat and pass myself off as a man. Would you worry less then?"

"I might," Brenton answered in a clearly agitated manner. "You could cut your hair even shorter."

"I like my hair," Jordana said, reaching up to strip away the netting she wore on the back of her head.

"It's just one more thing to draw attention to yourself."

"When I wear the net, no one can tell that it isn't as long as Caitlan's," Jordana countered. "You, Brenton Baldwin, are a worrywart."

"Jordana, he only cares about yar safety. I tried to warn ya some time back that men were eyein' ya with a different look."

"Yes, I know, but my brother would have me sit in this cabin and do nothing more."

"Exactly!" Brenton declared. "That is what I want from both of you. I want you to remain here for the duration of the trip so that no one is ogling you or trying to entice you to join in whatever games they might have in mind."

"That isn't fair!" Jordana cried. "That's nearly three days! I will die of boredom." Jordana was thinking of the several stops on the way that might be interesting and all the new sights along the river she would surely miss.

"It may not be fair," Caitlan interjected, "but it might keep Brenton from harm."

This sobered Jordana. "What do you mean?"

"I'm meanin', if he has to defend our honor by settin' himself up for the possibility of a fight every time we step out of the room, then what good is that? He could end up hurt or worse."

Jordana sat down on the edge of the bed. "I hadn't thought of it that way. I suppose sitting here and waiting out the trip is better than having to deal with that. I'll be glad when I'm of age and can make my own way into the world. Then I won't worry about whether or not someone is getting hurt. I'll only have to concern myself with me."

"Fine, but until then," Brenton said, his expression softening, "please do as I ask. Just stay here unless I am escorting you. I'll see to it that you have whatever you need, but stay out of the sight of the other male passengers."

Reluctantly Jordana nodded.

"Good. Now, you wait here and I'll go see about having your meals brought in," Brenton said, walking to the door. "I'm counting on you, Jordana, to behave yourself."

"What about Caitlan?" Jordana said with a pout.

Brenton smiled. "Caitlan has never given me half the grief you have. I know she sees the importance of this matter." With that, he left them.

"Oh, but he can be so irritating," Jordana said, slapping her hands against the bed.

"He only cares," Caitlan replied, still staring at the door. "He's a fine man and his heart is in the right place." Her dreamy-eyed stare made her feelings evident.

Jordana stopped and studied her for a moment. "I wish you two would just be honest with each other."

Caitlan looked at her in surprise. "And what would ya be talkin' about now?"

Jordana shook her head. "You're in love with him and he's in love with you."

"What!"

"You know it's true. Don't try to deny it. I haven't seen Brenton this moonfaced since he was in fifth grade and Elsie Smith let him kiss her on the cheek."

Caitlan's face grew red. "I'm thinkin' yar imagination is carryin' ya away."

"Oh, Caitlan, really. You needn't try to hide your feelings from me. I love him with all my heart, and if I have to lose him to someone, I'd just as soon it be someone like you."

"But I'm Irish—nothing more than a poor peasant."

"Ha! Not in my brother's eyes. And so what if you are Irish? Your brother is already married into the family, or have you forgotten? My family hardly worries about such matters, as they are usually too busy building railroads."

They were silent for several minutes before Caitlan finally said, "I don't want to go to California."

"What?" Jordana asked. She looked hard at Caitlan and found the barest hint of a smile on the young woman's face.

"I *have* grown an attachment, but it includes yarself as well. I'm enjoyin' the adventure as much as yarself. I'd just as soon stay on and help Brenton with his pictures. He's been teachin' me, ya know."

"Yes, I do know. He said a good assistant is critical. But are you serious? You'd give up going to California and seeing your brother?"

"I don't even know the man. He left when I was just a babe, remember? It's hard to consider goin' to him if it means leavin'—"

"Brenton?" Jordana filled the word in with a twinkle in her eye. Caitlan sighed. "Aye."

————

Brenton returned to the top deck and felt the cold November air hit him. He was twenty years old and headed to Omaha on behalf of a man who was now across the Atlantic and quite unconcerned with his progress. Brenton had already decided that Omaha would be the limit of his duties for Vanderbilt. He would break the association and move out on his own. Considering Vanderbilt's new circumstances, Brenton was positive such a move on his part could not offend the man.

It wasn't that the association hadn't been a good one, but Brenton realized with a heavy heart that he'd spent nearly a year trying to get Caitlan west to her brother. It didn't matter that because communication was so poor he hadn't a clue as to where Victoria and Kiernan had taken themselves. The point was, he had selfishly kept busy with his photography and Vanderbilt's land schemes. Why, Caitlan had even taken an interest in his work, and she was becoming a very adequate assistant. Not two days before embarking on this trip to Omaha, she had taken her first pictures, and he had been thrilled to see the results. They weren't in fact the best quality, but Brenton thought them perfect, even if one was a photograph of himself.

He remembered fondly the way Caitlan had treasured the thing. She had refused to allow him to put it with his other pictures, insisting that this one belonged only to her. He recalled feeling possessive in that same way about his first photograph.

He leaned on the rail and sighed. The light was fading from the skies as the sun sank lower and lower onto the western horizon. The thick forests of trees were now mostly void of their leaves, and the black outlines of their branches cast shadows upon the water. They looked rather like bony fingers reaching out to touch the paddlewheeler.

"Oh, Caitlan," he murmured, watching the landscape slip by. "If you only knew my heart."

He knew he had crossed a line where she was concerned. His heart was totally hers, and now the thought of taking her west to her brother caused Brenton not fear but grief. How could he leave her once they finally arrived at Kiernan's door? He couldn't imagine life without her, and yet he could hardly expect her to jump at the opportunity to become his wife. He was only twenty, and his chosen occupation held no real promise of fortune or fame. He longed for life lived from the back of a wagon, with the smell of chemicals all around him and his eyes ever fixed for that perfect picture. He could hardly expect a woman like Caitlan to desire such a life. She had come from poverty and sorrows. She deserved more from life than he might be able to offer her. He certainly did not want to depend on his parents' money his whole life. He wanted to make his own way. But it might be a difficult way, which Caitlan did not need.

He shook his head. "It wouldn't be fair to expect such a thing of her."

The paddlewheeler chugged on as twilight deepened. Brenton loved the colors in the sky and wondered if someday they might actually find a way to capture colors in photographs. It seemed an impossibility, but then, so too had the images he captured now on glass negatives. His mother and father had taught him that anything was possible. If one wanted it badly enough and worked hard enough at it, one could have most anything.

He wondered silently if that included Caitlan.

Guilt consumed him as he wrestled with the feelings of desire and longing. He'd been told of a stage line that ran out of Leavenworth,

Kansas, all the way to California. Perhaps he should have them get off at the next port and go back south to that small river town. He could put Caitlan on the stage, unaccompanied, but at least chaperoned by the driver and other passengers. She could be in California in little over a week.

But then what? She'd be alone and have no one to care for her once she arrived. Brenton considered the possibility of going with her, but that would hardly be appropriate. It wouldn't be fitting at all for two unmarried people to travel alone together. Especially when one was in love with the other. He could book passage for all three of them, but he had little desire to encourage Jordana's flare for adventure.

Of course, that wasn't the strongest reason for pushing on to Omaha rather than turning back for Leavenworth. The strongest reason was Brenton's desire to keep Caitlan at his side.

"But that hardly seems fair or right," he muttered with a sigh. There seemed to be no simple answers where the heart was concerned.

36

"Well, Omaha certainly isn't much to look at," Jordana said from the window of the unpleasant hotel where they'd managed to take refuge. The place had only one room available, so Brenton took it and slept on the floor, while Jordana and Caitlan shared a small bed together. It was hardly acceptable procedure or convenient for privacy's needs, but together they had worked to create an amicable existence.

"I've checked with the telegraph office four times, but there is still no word from Vanderbilt's associates," Brenton said, his voice betraying his concern. "Our funds have dwindled considerably, especially in light of shipping the wagon up here on the steamer. I suppose we should have just taken the roads and risked driving it ourselves, but with winter setting in, I was worried we'd get bogged down somewhere along the way."

"Ya made a good choice," Caitlan tried to encourage him.

Jordana nodded. She was coming to realize, by watching Caitlan's interaction with Brenton, that he was far more encouraged by positive words than negative ones. She had always chided him for his lack of self-confidence, but Caitlan chose another route. Caitlan helped him to see the strengths he had inside. It humbled Jordana to realize that, unlike Caitlan, she often made Brenton feel less of a man for the words and actions she carelessly aimed at him. It seemed in spite of her deep, abiding love for Brenton, hers were actions that did more to tear down than build up. Caitlan used her love to make Brenton strong, encouraged, hopeful. She was the best possible woman for Brenton, and already Jordana wondered how she might help her brother to see this for himself.

Of course, Jordana was certain Brenton felt the same way toward Caitlan. Yet ever since they'd steamed upriver to Omaha, he had distanced himself in a strange way. Even now, sharing a very cramped room, Brenton always seemed hesitant to comment much one way or another on things concerning Caitlan. Maybe he was worried about the issues of their faith. Caitlan might have softened a bit since their journey had begun, but she was still clearly negative toward religion and spiritual matters. Brenton hardly seemed likely to take a wife who didn't approve of his religious views, which were important to him.

"Since we plan to be here a spell," Caitlan said, getting up from where she sat on the edge of the bed, "I think gettin' a job would be in order. I can do laundry for those busy railroad men. After all, once they actually break ground in a few days, the work will probably be plentiful."

"I don't think it would be wise for you to take on such a position," Brenton said rather curtly.

"And why not?" Caitlan questioned, hands on hips. "I know how to wash clothes. Haven't I proven as much with yar own things?"

Jordana saw Brenton blush ever so slightly.

"I think I should be the one to get a job. If the Vanderbilts aren't available to keep us supplied, I believe I should cease to be under their employ and seek out something else."

"Ya needn't suggest that yar the only one to be responsible for such a plan," Caitlan said, putting on her bonnet. "I won't be takin' charity. So long as we've been on this journey for Vanderbilt, I've tried to earn my keep. I won't be sittin' back and doin' nothin' while ya take on all the burden for yarself. Besides, washin' clothes might be hard work, but it's somethin' I know well."

"You don't understand the connotation that accompanies the women who wash for the likes of railroad men and soldiers," Brenton stated.

"Oh, so yar a-fearin' for me reputation?" Caitlan asked defensively. "Don't ya believe me capable of dealin' with such a thing? After all, I had it worse in Ireland than I'll ever have here."

"But it might well become every bit as bad," Brenton countered.

Jordana watched with amusement as the couple had their first real battle of wills. How funny they both were.

"Washerwomen have the reputation for being . . . well . . . being—"

"Yes?" Caitlan challenged.

"Well, you know what they have the reputation for being."

Caitlan laughed. "I can hardly help what their reputation is. I can only vouch for meself. Now, stop yar frettin'. The sooner we get jobs, the sooner we'll have a bit o' money and can move from this place." She took up her wool cloak and headed to the door.

"I'm coming too," Brenton muttered. "Maybe there will be someone interested in hiring me on for the purpose of taking pictures for the ground-breaking ceremony. Jordana, you stay here."

Jordana thought to protest, but he was already at the door before she could speak. As soon as he'd closed it, however, she went for her own cloak. "You don't know me at all, Brenton Baldwin, if you think I'm going to let an opportunity like this pass me by."

Out on the muddy, windblown street, Jordana wrinkled her nose in a perplexed manner. There didn't seem to be much of interest going on in the small town. She strode away from the hotel and wondered exactly what it was she could do to help them earn money. She had a brilliant mind, or so she'd been told often enough. Maybe there would be a newspaper or business that could use her skills at writing.

The wind picked up and a light snow began to fall. Jordana couldn't imagine anyone calling this town pretty, but maybe it would look better buried in snow. She tried to picture such a winter scene as she walked past two saloons and a butcher shop. Wrinkling her nose again, this time from the smell, she crossed the street, and as she did so, she spied a red brick bank with the sign "Position Within" staring back at her from the window.

Opening the door, Jordana was greeted by a wash of warm air. Apparently the banker liked to keep the place heated for the comfort of himself and his customers.

"Good day, miss," a black-suited man greeted her as she crossed to the tiny bank window. "What can I do for you today?"

"I'd like to inquire about the position," Jordana stated matter-of-factly.

"I beg your pardon?" The man, an older, balding fellow with a stocky midsection and beady blue eyes, raised a quizzical brow as he studied her in return.

"I saw your sign in the window," Jordana explained. "I've come to inquire about the job you have available."

"Oh, I see. Is this for your father or perhaps your husband?"

Jordana smiled. "No, it's for me."

The man let out a bit of a chuckle. "Well, we can hardly consider that, now, can we?"

"And why not?"

"Well, because you are a woman."

"Yes, I've noticed," Jordana replied snidely. "And you are a man. Now that we have that established, perhaps you could tell me what the job is."

"The position is that of bank teller and that requires a man."

"And why would this be?" she pressed.

The man put his thumbs in his pockets and threw his shoulders back in a stance that appeared to Jordana to be some sort of authoritarian position.

"Because, my dear woman, the job requires an ability to deal with columns of figures, and to understand the workings of bank transactions."

"My grandfather owned a bank in Washington," Jordana said without taking her gaze from his face. "It was, of course, much larger than this one and held a great deal more money. Actually, the bank provided service to the federal government. The workings of bank transactions are something I've grown up with all of my life. The men in my family did not limit the women in learning, nor did they relegate them to the hearth. Banking is in my background," she said, letting it be implied without having to give an outright lie that she had been a part of such a background.

"I see," the man replied, clearly intimidated by her ability to stand her ground. "Perhaps then I could at least administer the test."

"A test?" Jordana cocked an interested brow. "Why, that would be wonderful."

What had she gotten herself into? What would a banking test consist of? Would there be questions about current investments and philosophies of government regulations? Well, she wasn't about to reveal any insecurity to the banker.

The man went to a desk and pulled out two pieces of paper. He held one out to Jordana and kept the other for himself. "Take these columns of figures and sit here to work them. There is a pencil for you to use. I have the answers and will verify whether you have an aptitude for mathematics when you have completed the problems."

Jordana looked down at the columns. Math had always been an easy subject for her. "The answer to the first column is three hundred sixty-five," she replied without bothering to use the provided pencil. The man gasped lightly. "The second column is four thousand, six hundred fifty-three. The third column," she paused for only a few moments, "ten thousand, two hundred and one." She looked up and smiled before glancing back at the fourth column. "The last one is . . . two hundred sixteen thousand and thirty-four. And if you add all four together, you get—"

"Never mind," the bank man replied with a loud "harrumph." "You've proved yourself to be more than capable. How did you learn to do that?"

Jordana handed him the paper and shrugged. "Mother says it is a gift from God. Father says it's because numbers have always been in our blood. So do I get the job?"

The man looked down at the papers, shook his head, then replaced them in the desk drawer. "I suppose I could try you out for a short time. However, if and when a male applicant applies for the job, I will have to let you go."

"Even if I'm better at the job?"

"Well, you have to understand," the stocky man continued, "a man would be likely to have a family to support, and jobs are scarce out here. I couldn't very well allow a young woman, who probably has a father or husband to care for her, to steal food from the mouths of a man and his family."

"Well, I suppose I understand your reasoning, even if your assumptions are false. I am here in Omaha with my brother and sister-in-law. I am responsible for myself, and earning a living is something I shall take very seriously."

"That may well be, but I will stand by my statement. You may take it or leave it."

"I should like to accept the position, Mr.—?"

"Chittenden. I own this bank, and my son Damon works with me. I'm afraid he's out of town on banking business, however, and you will have to wait to meet him another time."

"I am Jordana Baldwin," she replied with a smile. "When shall I report to work?"

The man shook his head as if still stunned that he was actually giving the job to a woman. "Well, tomorrow is Saturday and the bank is closed for the weekend. Be here at nine o'clock Monday morning and I shall begin your training."

"Very well. Now I have a request," Jordana said, deciding to brave yet another sticky situation. "I'd like to request an advance against my salary. My family and I need to find a place to live, and our funds are running precariously low."

"I couldn't even consider such a thing, Miss Baldwin. Why, we haven't even discussed salaries."

"No, that's true. We haven't. So what, then, shall you pay me?"

"Well, you are a woman—"

"Yes, we've established that," Jordana said impatiently.

"Fifty cents a day should be more than enough," Chittenden replied.

"More than enough for what?" she ventured boldly. "Would you pay that poor unemployed man with his needy family fifty cents a day?"

"No," the man replied, clearly flustered by Jordana's ability to twist his words into something useful for herself. "No, I wouldn't."

"Then I shall expect you to pay me more reasonably," Jordana replied. "I would think a dollar a day would be acceptable."

"A dollar a day would be entirely too much." Chittenden took a handkerchief from his pocket and mopped his forehead.

"Sir, as I've stated, we must find a place to live. I certainly cannot see us managing on less than a dollar a day. What if my brother and sister-in-law are unable to find employment?"

"Send your brother here and let him have this position," the banker suggested.

"No, that would never do. He's a photographer and very poor with numbers," Jordana countered.

Then just when she feared she would have to take on a stronger approach, the man's expression changed. "I have an idea. Perhaps it would be acceptable to you."

"I'm listening, sir."

"There's a small house at the edge of town. It's certainly not much to look at, but the bank now owns it. I could make you a deal whereby that house would be available to you and your family, in lieu of pay."

Jordana considered this for a moment. It was a very generous offer, but of course, she'd not yet seen the house. "What about winter fuel? We can hardly set out to find our own and afford to purchase it without money."

"I'll give you a six-month supply of fuel and a lease for the same amount of time," Chittenden replied.

He looked at her eagerly, and Jordana felt just a little sorry for him. "Very well. I will accept your offer. A six-month pledge to allow us use of the house and fuel for the same amount of time." Reasoning to herself that surely they wouldn't need to remain in Omaha for much longer than six months, she shook the flustered banker's hand with great flair. "You draw up the proper papers, and I shall look them over and see that they are acceptable. How soon may we take possession of the house?"

"Immediately," the man replied with a smile. "I have the key right here. I'll send someone over with the fuel this afternoon." He went to the desk and pulled out the key. "You take the street just to the side of the bank and follow it to where it heads out of town. There you will find a small, unpainted clapboard house. That is the place."

Jordana smiled. "Mr. Chittenden, thank you very much. I shall see you on Monday."

She left the bank feeling quite smug. Even if the house was a hovel, it was still something. She made her way back to the hotel, not at all surprised to find Brenton pacing and fuming in their room upon her return.

"Just where have you been?" he demanded angrily. "I told you to stay here."

"Yes, I know, but hear me out before you go losing your temper." Jordana held up the key and smiled at Brenton and then at Caitlan. "I have secured a house for us."

"What?"

"I have taken a job at the bank, and my salary is to consist of this house for six months and fuel for the same amount of time."

"I don't believe it." Brenton shook his head in bewilderment.

Caitlan laughed. "Well, I can be believin' it. Yar sister has a way of takin' the world by storm. If she'd come back with jobs for all of us, it wouldn't have surprised me in the least."

Jordana grinned. "Well, I didn't do that, but I figured first things first. Come on. We can go see the place right away."

Brenton shrugged and took up his outer coat. "Very well. Let us see this mansion you have secured for us."

Ten minutes later, they stood at the front of the simple dwelling. It was small—very small—and the unpainted boards made it look old and unstable. The structure sat completely by itself except for one rather twisted and gnarled cottonwood tree. The barrenness of the landscape made the proposition of living here seem even more dismal.

"Come on," Jordana encouraged. "Let's go inside."

"I'm afraid it might fall down upon us," Brenton said, looking doubtful.

"Oh, so it needs some fixin'," Caitlan replied. "I've seen worse in me life." She laughed then and added, "I've *lived* in worse."

"It reminds me of the stories Mother tells about when we first moved to Greigsville." Jordana could just barely remember the run-down dwelling her family had once called home. This house seemed nicer than that one by far.

"Yes, I remember that place as well," Brenton said, still not encouraged. "I also remember the work it took to put it in order."

"Do you remember, too, what Mother said about fixing it up?" Jordana asked. "She said she claimed the promise of being able to do all things through Christ. That shall be my hope as well. Now, stop being a goose and come see my new house."

37

The day before the ground-breaking ceremony for the Union Pacific, Jordana and Caitlan finally felt satisfied in what they'd managed to accomplish with the small two-bedroom house. Despite the way it looked on the outside, the frame proved to be sturdy, and this allowed Brenton to feel confident in taking on the project.

For a week, they had scrubbed and cleaned every corner and cranny of the house, until Caitlan had pronounced it acceptable. There was no furniture to speak of, but that didn't deter the trio from moving in with great gusto and hope for their future.

Caitlan had secured a job, not washing clothes, but rather taking in sewing, much to Brenton's relief and approval. And Brenton, though not formally commissioned to take pictures of the ground breaking, had decided to approach the persons in charge during the celebration and see if he couldn't convince them to hire him on. It seemed that everything was working together in proper order, and with the last of their money, Brenton purchased food, a few pots and dishes, two lanterns, and several other items to better equip their new house.

Though Caitlan had proved to be a wonderful cook thus far in their journey, Jordana now began to take more of an interest in the task. She reasoned that she would need to know basic cooking skills for the time when she actually decided to go her own way and explore out across the country.

They were just sitting down to Caitlan's mouthwatering stew when a knock sounded at the front door.

"Oh, I'll get it," Jordana told the others. She got up from her packing-crate chair and rolled her eyes. "It's probably Mr. Chittenden. Do you know that man is positively lost without me? I don't know how he managed to get this far in banking without my help."

Caitlan and Brenton laughed at her melodramatic performance while Jordana went to the door.

"Yes?" she said without waiting to see who it was on the other side. She opened the door wide and was stunned at the appearance of two rather weary-looking travelers.

"Mother! Father!" she exclaimed and threw herself into their arms. "I can't believe you're here."

James Baldwin hugged his daughter, then held her at arm's length. "Neither can we believe you are here. Last I knew, you were supposed to be getting your education at the Deighton School for Young Women. Young women of exceptional intelligence, I might add."

Jordana laughed, completely undaunted by her father's serious expression. "I graduated and now I'm getting my education elsewhere, Father. It's just not in those stuffy, hallowed halls."

"Well, are you going to have us in?" Carolina Baldwin asked her daughter.

"Absolutely," Jordana said, taking a step back. "Look here, Brenton. Look who has come to see us in our new house."

The color suddenly drained from Brenton's face, and his stunned look made Jordana laugh. "I haven't seen him look like that since I got shot in Missouri."

"What!" Carolina and James exclaimed at the same time.

"Oh, it's a funny story," Jordana quipped, pulling her mother into the house. "I'll tell you everything over supper, but first you must come meet Kiernan's sister Caitlan. She came to America while you were in Russia."

Carolina smiled at the redheaded young woman and nodded. "We heard all about it from Mrs. Vanderbilt. When we went to the Deighton School to locate you, we were led to the Vanderbilts. As soon as Mrs. Vanderbilt learned you were to be in Omaha for the ground breaking of the Union Pacific she notified us. And since your father wanted to check into investing in this whole transcontinental scheme—"

"I beg your pardon, Mrs. Baldwin," James interrupted. "Who wanted to check into investing?"

Carolina grinned rather mischievously. "All right, so we both were interested. Anyway, knowing you were here, it made taking the journey to Omaha seem quite logical."

"As you can see, we don't have much in the way of furniture," Jordana apologized as she motioned her parents to the last two crates. She was now glad Caitlan had thought to take the extra crates for guests. "We've been bartering for what we could get our hands on. My employer, Mr. Chittenden, gave us a few things on loan. The table, a bed, and, of course, our lovely bench where Caitlan and Brenton are sitting."

Brenton had been so shocked at the presence of his parents that he'd forgotten all about getting to his feet. Now he jumped up. "Mother, please take the bench."

"Well, we don't want to interrupt your dinner," Carolina said, taking it all in. "Why don't you go ahead and eat and—"

"But you must eat with us. I know things don't look very nice," Brenton said rather apologetically. "And we might have to share the plates and silver, but"—and for the first time, Brenton took on an expression of pure pride—"Caitlan is a great cook and there's plenty of stew and biscuits."

Carolina smiled at her son and reached up her gloved hand to touch his cheek. "It looks just fine," she said, seeming to understand that her approval meant the world to Brenton.

An hour later, when the last of the stew had been eaten, Caitlan asked Jordana and Brenton to allow her to clean up while they walked their parents back to the hotel.

"I'm surprised you found a room," Brenton told his father as they strolled ahead of the women.

Jordana heard her father murmur something about receiving help in that area due to the possibility of his investment in the Union Pacific.

"I can't tell you how worried we were when we couldn't find you," Carolina told her daughter.

"I'm sorry for that. It just seemed too good an opportunity to pass up." Jordana looped her arm in Carolina's. "Oh, Mother, I'm so happy. I'm living the life you always dreamed of. I wake up every morning and picture the things that might come my way, and I can't imagine living any other life."

Carolina patted her daughter's arm with understanding. "I can't believe I'm actually going to say this, but what about the dangers? You are a single woman, and if you choose to take off on your own, as you've mentioned numerous times, you must realize the problems you could find yourself up against."

Jordana tried to look serious, but the attempt failed in her unabashed delight. "I know. I've thought about all of that and . . . well . . . when I weigh it against the thought of settling for a simple, sweet life with a boring little house and a boring little husband, it seems to tip the scales. Taking a chance doesn't worry me," she added more earnestly. "But losing your approval does."

"Oh, my dearest, you would hardly lose that. I'd admire your fearlessness and, in fact, I rather envy your youth and abilities. I know I can't hold you back—and still sleep in good conscience. I can't become a worrisome mother who chides her daughter for the very choices she herself would have made had opportunities been different."

"I knew you would feel this way!" Jordana smiled in assurance.

"I can't tell you how I envied Victoria when she and Kiernan went to California. I used to have to pray every day that God might forgive my envy." She looked up ahead to where Brenton and her father spoke in hushed tones. Brenton held the lantern to guide their way, but the light was minimal, and Jordana thought they actually might have seen better without it. Still, it allowed her to catch the shadowy outline of her father's face as he glanced over his shoulder to confirm that his wife and daughter were still following safely behind.

"He won't understand," Jordana told her mother. "He will worry about me."

"Your father worries for all of us. It is the way of men. Even when they aren't responsible for the circumstances, they worry. Your father once told me it was rather like the army. A general is still responsible, even when the lowliest private makes an error in judgment."

"But the private still suffers the consequences of his actions," Jordana replied.

"Perhaps to some extent, but he does not bear it alone," Carolina countered. "A private can make a choice that will in turn threaten the lives of those around him. Then they, too, suffer from his poor choice, and the one in charge of all suffers most because the crisis came upon his watch."

Jordana nodded, understanding what her mother was saying. "Men think so differently from women."

They rounded the corner to the main street and walked on toward the hotel. The saloons were doing a lively business on this mild winter night, and thus the men held back a pace or two and allowed the women to come up even with them.

"Brenton's been telling me of your adventures," James said, putting an arm around his daughter. "It's a wonder you're still alive. Did you really scale the Deighton School?"

"What's this?" Carolina looked first to her son and then to Jordana. "Why, those buildings are all at least four stories tall."

Jordana grinned. "I was much younger then."

They all laughed at this as they reached the hotel.

"I'll be taking pictures at the ground-breaking ceremony," Brenton told his parents.

"How long will you be here in Omaha?" Jordana asked her parents.

"We had only planned to stay long enough to retrieve you two and return home after the matters of the railroad were better understood," James replied. "But now I see that neither of you are of a mind to return to New York, or even Baltimore."

Jordana thought she denoted a tone of sorrow in her father's voice. "Someone should stay out here to keep you apprised of the progress of the railroad," she said with a winning smile she knew would disarm him.

James looked at Carolina and nodded. "I suppose so. It's just hard to let you go."

"But you aren't letting me go, Papa," Jordana said, placing her head upon his shoulder. "You are merely lending me out for a time." She wrapped her arms around him and hugged him tightly. "I'll be back, and then I shall have even more wonderful stories to share."

"You're awfully young," James whispered, his voice catching in his throat.

Jordana worried that soon they'd both be in tears if she didn't say or do something to lighten the mood. But for the life of her, there didn't seem to be anything left to say. Her parents were struggling to make a decision about allowing her to go her own way. It was tough enough that they had given her up to boarding school in the North, then journeyed to Europe. And, as her father pointed out, she was very young.

Lifting her head, Jordana said nothing but kissed her father on the cheek. Their eyes met and she knew in that instant that, while he didn't like the idea of leaving her in the West, he understood. And understanding was enough to set her on her course.

———

The bare branches of cottonwoods swayed gently in the mild, wintry breeze as James and Carolina Baldwin stood on the Omaha docks with their children and Caitlan O'Connor. Jordana could not believe the time had come for her parents to leave. She was assailed with a perplexing mixture of sadness and anticipation. She would miss her parents as she had so often during their previous separation. Yet the departure of James and Carolina held a deeper meaning for Jordana because it showed what deep faith they had in their children. No doubt, it showed even more just how deep their faith was in God to protect their children. Nevertheless, it meant a certain acknowledgment that Jordana and Brenton were indeed worthy to be allowed such great independence. Jordana prayed mightily that she would not disappoint them.

Tears rose in Carolina's eyes as she embraced and kissed her daughter. But Jordana sensed something other than sadness in her mother's eyes. "You must tell me about all your adventures," she murmured in Jordana's ear, the eagerness in her voice obvious.

"I will, Mama. You will feel as if you were there yourself!"

The steamer arrived in due course and the passengers boarded. More tears were shed and hands grew tired with waving. The three young people stood on the dock and watched until the vessel was nearly out of sight; then they headed back to their little house.

While Brenton and Caitlan busied themselves with developing some of the photographs from the railroad celebration, Jordana tried to distract herself with a book. But her mind was racing far too much even for Sir Walter Scott. There were so many things to think about. So many plans to be made with this new gift of independence her parents had bestowed upon her. Somewhere out there lay her future, and Jordana wasn't about to let it slip away without making the most of it.

"Westward the railroad!" had been the battle cry of the crowds at the recent celebration. Westward the dream was the vision Jordana held for herself.